Good Night,
Mr. Holmes

Good Night, Mr. Holmes

Carole Nelson Douglas

FORGE

A Tom Doherty Associates Book
New York

GOOD NIGHT, MR. HOLMES

Copyright © 1990 by Carole Nelson Douglas

Readers' guide © 2005 by Carole Nelson Douglas

Map and Adler silhouette by Carole Nelson Douglas

Map illustrations by Darla Malone Tagrin

A Forge Book
Published by Tom Doherty Associates, LLC
175 Fifth Avenue
New York, NY 10010

www.tor-forge.com

Forge® is a registered trademark of Tom Doherty Associates, LLC.

Library of Congress Cataloging-in-Publication Data

Douglas, Carole Nelson.
    Good night, Mr. Holmes : an Irene Adler novel / Carole Nelson
Douglas.—1st Forge trade paperback ed.
        p. cm.
    ISBN 978-0-7653-0373-8
    1. Adler, Irene (Fictitious character)—Fiction.   2. Holmes, Sherlock
(Fictitious character)—Fiction.   3. Private investigators—England—
Fiction.   4. Women detectives—England—Fiction.   I. Title.
    PS3554.O8237G6 2009
    813'.54—dc22

                                                            2009028188

First Trade Paperback Edition: November 2009

Printed in the United States of America

0   9   8   7   6   5   4   3   2   1

For S. H.
and the many hours of delight
and mystification he brought:
a heroine worthy of him.

Cast of Continuing Characters

Irene Adler Norton: an American abroad and a diva/detective introduced in the first of Sir Arthur Conan Doyle's sixty Sherlock Holmes stories, "A Scandal in Bohemia"; now the protagonist of her own adventures, beginning with *Good Night, Mr. Holmes*

Sherlock Holmes: the London consulting detective with a global reputation for feats of deduction

Penelope "Nell" Huxleigh: an orphaned British parson's daughter on her own in a hostile London environment

John H. Watson, M.D.: British medical man and Sherlock Holmes's sometimes roommate and frequent companion in crime-solving

Wilhelm Gottsreich Sigismond von Ormstein: the handsome, recently crowned King of Bohemia, whose capital city is Prague

Godfrey Norton: a British barrister

Oscar Wilde: friend of Irene Adler; a wit and man of fashion about London

Bram Stoker: theatrical manager of London's finest actor, Henry Irving, and burgeoning writer, who will later pen the classic *Dracula*

Quentin Stanhope: the uncle of Nell's former charges when she worked as a London governess

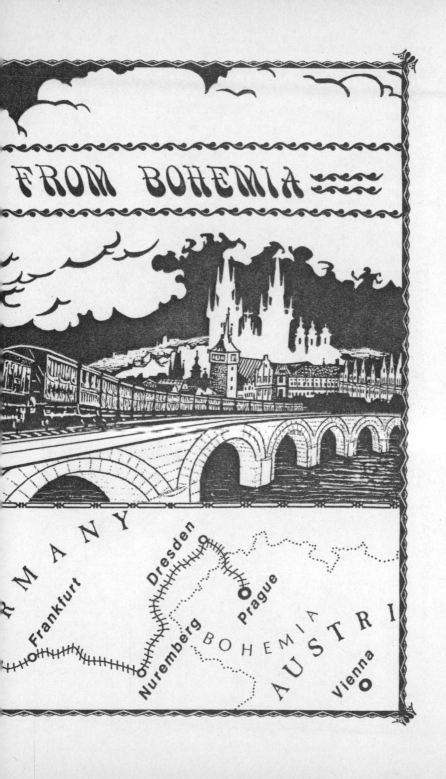

FROM BOHEMIA

Frankfurt

Dresden

Nuremberg

Prague

BOHEMIA

GERMANY

AUSTRIA

Vienna

A Baker Street Reminiscence

❧❧❧

"I see, Watson, by an old issue of the *Strand* magazine, which was lying about for some reason, that yet another narrative of one of my little problems—the Irene Adler affair—has reached the public," my friend Sherlock Holmes remarked over the remains of Mrs. Hudson's ample dinner one warm summer evening.

I hid my smile of pleasure in a sip of burgundy. It invariably struck me as ironic that my companion, the most observant man alive, could so successfully ignore the stack of *Strand* magazines I imported to our lodgings whenever a fresh story of mine was among its monthly offerings. Such accounts had appeared for the past three years, commencing only after Holmes had been presumed dead in 1891.

It was my fond hope that Holmes, now resurrected, should acquaint himself with my past efforts to memorialize his astounding deductive abilities. Yet his public stance of belittling his own achievements reflected on my literary offerings. Thus any admission that the great detective actually read his own adventures as penned by myself was a singular and rewarding occasion.

"These little stories seem quite popular," I remarked mildly.

"Popular, hmm." Holmes's angular features grew momentarily

unfocused as he groped for his postprandial pipe. "No doubt the lurid title accounts for it."

"I deemed 'A Scandal in Bohemia' quite an accurate description of the case." My tone harbored some asperity, as no amateur author writes but for praise.

"Did you?"

Holmes's reticence only spurred me on. "And what would you have titled the affair, may I ask?"

His eyes sharpened through the blue mists of tobacco smoke. " 'A Superior Woman.' "

"The King of Bohemia did not find Irene Adler a superior woman, Holmes, or he would have married her."

"If lineage outweighed suitability as the criterion for investigative work, Watson, I should be hard put to acquire the few genuinely intriguing problems that come my way. Besides, you forget"—the relish of Holmes's smile promised a rare mood of reminiscence—"His Majesty himself exclaimed, 'Would she not have made an admirable queen?' It was his only sensible remark in the entire affair. But you mistake me, Watson. I quite understand the need for exaggeration in the press. What I object to in your account is the key fact you have got wrong."

"Key fact? Wrong?"

"Indeed."

"Surely not. The case is replicated from my notes, and I am used to recording details accurately in my profession. Admittedly, the events occurred six years ago, but—"

"It is not your *relation* of the case's particulars I contest, Watson. It is your acceptance of later, unascertained facts on face value."

"Which facts?" I demanded, setting aside Mrs. Hudson's excellent lemon tart half eaten.

"The facts of Irene Adler's—now Norton's—untimely demise. You quite unforgivably refer to her as 'the late Irene Adler.' "

"The report of her death was in the *Times*. A terrible train wreck in the Italian Alps. Both her husband, Godfrey Norton, and herself were listed among the fatalities."

"Much is in the *Times,* my dear Watson, that is not true." Holmes had assumed the professorial tone that I often found myself contesting for the pure sake of it. "And many deaths are prematurely reported. Consider my own."

Holmes alluded to the matter of the Reichenbach Falls, recalling my own cruel delusions as to my friend's disappearance and death. These had only been banished by his startling "return from the dead" the previous April. Authorial vanity absconded as I followed the path Holmes had paved for my less nimble mind.

"You actually believe, Holmes, that Irene Adler, too, is still alive?" said I with some astonishment.

Holmes's gaze moved to the framed photograph of the woman in question, which occupied an honored place among his memorabilia.

"She is one of only four individuals—and the sole woman—to outwit me, Watson. Why should she not cheat death as well?"

At times I found Holmes's colossal but unpremeditated vanity as annoying as I found amazing his ability to deduce volumes of testimony from the smallest shred of evidence.

"You believe she is alive?" I demanded again.

"I suspect it, Watson," he answered crisply after a long pause. "I have not investigated, hence it is pure supposition. But you know on what methods my supposition is based."

There was no quarreling with Holmes's phenomenal reasoning powers, which honed instinct on some inflexible inner logic until it attained a lethal edge.

I again studied the photograph of the woman in the case. Although she had married Godfrey Norton before fleeing London and a confrontation with Holmes—signing a letter she had left for the detective 'Irene Norton, née Adler'—it was as Irene Adler, operatic *prima donna* and adventuress, that I invariably thought of her.

Like many actresses, she had been a markedly handsome woman. I had only glimpsed her once from a tantalizing distance during the course of the case, but the photograph conveyed all her regal bearing, crowned as she was by richly arranged masses of dark hair. She wore formal attire in the photograph, bare about the bosom—and a magnificent bosom it was, even I was unbiased enough to concede—but the gown and jewels only set off her graceful form and beautifully composed face.

According to Holmes's index, Irene Adler had been a full-blown beauty of thirty when we had encountered her six years before in 1888. Holmes himself had been only four-and-thirty. I confess that his open admiration then had nursed my hopes that the world's most dedicated deductive machine harbored some hint of manly susceptibility among the admirably efficient gears of his mind, heart and soul.

"And then there's that twaddle you wrote about my lack of regard for the fair sex in general," Holmes murmured, breaking into my reverie.

"Twaddle? I fancy I explained it rather scientifically."

"Love in my life would be 'grit in a sensitive instrument,' " he mocked good-naturedly. "What a way to describe the emotions that drive nine-tenths of the human race, Watson! You are becoming quite a romantic in your middle years."

"And what is wrong with a bit of sentiment in this harsh and often rude world?"

"Nothing, so long as it does not conflict with the facts."

"But it invariably does! Facts have nothing to do with the emotions. Witness those who love against all likelihood, even love vicious murderers."

"Exactly my point. And you are right in that, Watson, I cannot go against reason. I cannot allow the glamour of a fair face to obscure the facts my being is dedicated to laying bare. Besides, why must you be compelled to explain my solitary way of life? I am not the first man to eschew the company of women for the pursuit of an intellectual aim."

"You have, as usual, put your very finger upon it, Holmes! Why must you equate the company of women with diminution of your intellectual powers?"

"Because most women are impediments."

"Impediments? That is cold, Holmes. Even you are not so inhuman as to dismiss half the human race as a nuisance!"

Holmes produced the tight, tolerant smile that meant an opponent had fallen into a verbal trap of his setting.

"I know you are somewhat prejudiced in the matter, given your close association with the former Mary Morstan, unfortunately and truly the late Mary Watson," he murmured sympathetically, "and an excellent woman she was. But regard the whole, not the worthy exception, Watson. Think! How would an ordinary female accompany me through the night streets unhailed and unhampered? How would she navigate the suburban outlands we have trod together, upholstered in thirty yards of train and a veiled bonnet? Could she pick up a revolver and leave upon a midnight moment's notice, as you often have? How would one reared to faint upon the slightest pretext remain conscious in the face of violent death?"

"We have met some brave women in the course of your cases," I put in.

"Exactly. We have encountered some admirable women, particularly those independent creatures thrown by fate upon their own resources. Your own Mary Morstan showed herself possessed of great nobility of character in deeming her inheritance of so little consequence compared to her regard for a modest doctor of my acquaintance. Yet did not even she swoon as the case reached its climax? It is written in your own account of the affair, which you call 'The Sign of the Four.' "

I colored to find my more tender premarital moments exhumed by my friend's relentless memory. "Irene Adler did not swoon," I muttered in confusion.

"Exactly my point, Watson! Irene Adler did not swoon. Nor is she the kind to perish in a train wreck, any more than I am likely to fall off a cliff, even in Professor Moriarty's lethal embrace. Not so passive an end is permitted the likes of Irene Adler."

"That is hardly a logical reaction."

"It is the result of the most impeccable logic. Review the facts.

Has not Irene Adler demonstrated time and again an indisputable control over people and events around her? She was perceptive enough to foresee the King of Bohemia's forthcoming royal marriage and wise enough to flee when she saw herself supplanted in his plans, if not his affections.

"She also anticipated a need for future protection and brought with her the compromising photograph of herself and the King. She evaded his best agents on five separate occasions. When his Majesty allowed my humble self to partake in the problem, she not only detected the net closing around her, but had the audacity—the audacity, Watson!—to follow my disguised self, and you as well, to the very doorstep of two-twenty-one-B Baker Street. There, dressed as a young man, she boldly bid me, 'Good night, Mr. Sherlock Holmes.'"

Holmes sat back against the chair, smoke rising from his fevered face like steam from an overtaxed locomotive. "I bother to quote the King of Bohemia on only one subject: 'What a woman!' "

"Forward hussy, if you ask me," I put in, still defensive about my fine-natured Mary.

Holmes smiled ruefully. "How unfair it is that enterprise is called a harlot when it wears a female face. How did you put it in your account, Watson—'the late Irene Adler, of dubious and questionable memory.'? You call her an 'adventuress' as well. Two centuries ago the word designated a woman who lived by her wits; today it has been debased to describe a woman who lives by her willingness—especially in regard to men of influence and wealth. I believe you misjudge Madam Irene there, but you may speculate upon her character as your authorial right. Her death, however, is mere rumor until proven. No, Watson, I fear we have all played our roles in *L'Affaire Adler* as mere supporting actors to the woman's wit and will. Had she been a man, I should have immediately penetrated the charade of her greeting—and farewell—that night here in Baker Street. Being hampered by the strictures of her sex, she uses our arrogant male underestimation of her to camouflage a daring nature. *The* woman is without equal."

"You do especially admire her, then!" pounced I, for to him she is always *the* woman.

"And to much better purpose than romantically, Watson, although it would please those monthly readers of your little tales and your conventional heart if my admiration were merely amorous.

"You see, I suspect that she fled England not only because the King of Bohemia was on her trail—and not simply because I myself was about to close the net on her. I suspect she had other reasons, some of them involving the mysterious Mr. Godfrey Norton."

Holmes's eyes narrowed fiercely. "But Irene Adler is not dead—oh, no, Watson, no more than Moriarty did not exist. I would stake my life upon it!"

I sat silent in the face of such wholesale conviction. I had never known Holmes to be wrong when he expressed himself so strongly. As much as logic directed his remarkable detective powers, so, too, did a knowledge of human behavior, sifted through his inhuman isolation from the softer sensibilities.

"Yet, Holmes," said I finally, "so many of our cases require delving the deepest emotions in their solving. Perhaps you encounter enough misdirected passions and misunderstood family matters, sudden disgrace and death in your work; you need not import such heartache into your personal affairs."

"Quite right. Many cases depend upon reasoning back to events of years ago—family secrets, vengeance visited even onto the second generation. In a sense, the past shapes those who become victims or villains in the melodramas of my cases.

"It is my role to act as playwright to the whole, to draw the curtain open and then reveal the scenes in one logical series. Every event must be cobbled into place in the long train of previous events, as rungs make a ladder of logic. I would give a great deal to know what inevitable stages of incident produced the likes of Irene Adler. Show me a method of forming more women so, and I would show more interest in women!"

My eyes wandered to the photograph again. I confess myself

stirred by a new admiration for something more intangible in that familiar form than mere surface attractions.

"There is one thing I regret deeply about the Adler case," Holmes confessed in a lazy drawl.

I held my breath. Had the unthinkable moment finally come when "*the* woman" would claim her final victory over the great detective's infallible intellect?

Holmes sighed, his face assuming that state of dreamy concentration I had only observed at the concert hall. There, lost in the swelling orchestral chorus or the soulful aria of the solo instrument, Holmes permitted me to glimpse the stern mathematics of music erecting a bridge of glorious sound between his rigidly separated intellect and emotions.

"I regret," the great detective mused gloomily, "that I have never heard her sing."

Disappointed, I watched Holmes raise his glass to the photograph.

"Good night, Miss Irene Adler," he toasted with a smile that even I could not quite decipher. "Wherever you are."

Chapter One

Tea and Sympathy

❧

By night, when gaslights glitter through the fog and the cobblestones gleam like bootblack, London seems a landscape
glimpsed in some *Arabian Nights* tale. By day the effect is more commonplace, as the city streets throng with omnibuses, hansom cabs and
pedestrians.

Yet that daily, daylit London can intimidate even more than its
dark nocturnal side; at least a respectable young woman like myself
found it so in the spring of 1881. I walked the streets of London
town, wondering how I came to be adrift on this tide of strangers, my
few belongings tumbled into the carpetbag at my side. I was alone
and friendless, and—for the first time in my four-and-twenty years—
homeless and hungry.

My story was a common one. The only child of a Shropshire
parson, himself widowed, I had been reared in spare comfort but utter
emotional and physical security. On my father's death, no relations
close enough to claim me came forward.

Marriage was an impossible dream for a woman with only genteel poverty and a mild case of myopia to bring a prospective suitor.
Indeed, I knew little of male company and—save for a visiting curate

who possessed a golden tenor if rather overgrown ears—had never noticed a man in a sentimental way. Needless to say, the omission was mutual.

Although from time to time I might ponder my lost curate—Jasper Higgenbottom by name—an unfortunate onslaught of consumption had compelled him to take a foreign mission in a warmer clime. Even now he might be saving savage souls with the liquid syllables of "Lead, Kindly Light."

As for myself, local parishioners soon found a local family in need of a respectable, well-read young woman to attend to their children—and, lo, I was a governess.

Inevitably, my need for continued employment drew me to the same magnet that has lured so many of my rural compatriots. My country family moved to London, that great hub at the center of the mammoth spinning wheel of the British Empire, on which the revolving sun truly never sets.

My subsequent position found me installed in Berkeley Square in the home of Colonel Codwell Turnpenny, tending three well-mannered daughters and, on occasion, a less-than-well-mannered Pekinese dog. Life was comfortable, secure and predictable, and I was quite content until an incident occurred that permitted my sole glimpse of life as it is depicted in romantic novels.

My charges' uncle, their mother's brother, Mr. Emerson Stanhope, was a well-favored young gentleman of four-and-twenty with a merry disposition. How merry I discovered whilst playing a game of blind man's bluff with my young ladies after some strenuous lessons in geometry. They gleefully blindfolded me, spun me like a top and set me loose in the schoolroom. I could find not a one of the minxes until a sudden hush came. I stumbled into an immovable barrier. My exploring fingers found an expanse of woolen frockcoat rather than the cotton pinafores of my charges. I hesitated, but their giggles goaded me on and upward: to a satin-faced lapel, a set of side-whiskers . . . really, I could not continue, nor could I imagine who stood silent and unrevealed before my tentative fingers. Then I realized that the girls' laughter flowed with a freedom seldom exhibited before adults, save myself and . . .

"Mr. Stanhope," I whispered.

"Free!" said he, undoing my blindfold. Even then I suffered from myopia. Mr. Stanhope hung in a haze before me, his features resolving into an expression I could not name.

"Why, Miss Huxleigh," he said, "you look like one of your charges." And his fingers brushed back a tendril of hair that had fallen onto my cheek. Then the girls were pulling me away by the hands and begging for another game; by the time I had smoothed my hair into a semblance of order again, Mr. Stanhope was at the door and bidding us good-bye with a wink.

After the Afghanistan trouble broke out in 1878, Col. Turnpenny's regiment was assigned to the war, and Mr. Stanhope joined another regiment soon after. His nieces giggled upon seeing him on parade in his fine uniform. Soon, however, Col. Turnpenny's wife and children returned to India, without me. The children were reaching that age of independence that they make quite plain to one and all around them, so my services were redundant. With the war, governesses were in oversupply, and my sterling references failed to secure me another position.

I studied the employment columns, with little success. Often my eyes strayed to the regimental reports, for which I admonished my foolish imagination, and turned my attention firmly to the news from Africa, where my first sentimental loyalties lay. Nothing could distract me from the seriousness of my present situation.

Even clerical employment seemed barred, for London offices had recently been invaded by a small black beast—a humped, clattering machine that spit words onto paper seemingly by itself. Although I write a fine and quite legible hand, the call now was for callused fingertips to punch the bewildering buttons—including a new-fangled shift key that made both upper and lower case letters possible—at a speed that defied human endurance, at least mine.

At length I found a position as a clerk in Whiteley's emporium in

Bayswater. My pay was low, but food and a room were provided. I found the fine-woven chintzes and silks that daily slid through my hands soothing, as was the murmur of shopping women's voices, the clean slice of the scissors and the neat lengths of goods measured out on the cutting tables.

So I might have continued into frugal old maidhood had I not, after three years' employment, swiftly and unfairly been cast onto the streets. In short, I was dismissed without warning, and without a reference. Numb with shock, I soon found the stipend of a weekly wage indispensable. The day came when my choice was food or lodging. My landlady ordered me to pack my few possessions into whatever would hold them and vacate the premises.

So I wandered London's teeming streets, hearing the iron-shod hooves of passing horses ring like the great black beast's keys clanging my doom in three-quarter time. My late father had always chastised me for an over-vivid imagination, but that day I had no idea of where I would go or what would become of me.

Set, indifferent faces swarmed by as I passed shopfronts where once I might have idled among the goods. Now I felt barred from all human intercourse and commerce. Penniless! I cannot tell of the horror that word conveys to a sensibility such as mine.

I began to notice the filthy boys who prowled even the better streets of this great metropolis, wondering how they fed and housed their scrawny bodies. I even began to conjure a tinge of horrified sympathy for the haggard, wretched women who resorted to selling themselves on the dingy byways of Whitechapel.

Thus brooding, I shouldered through passersby, my right arm leaden at my side, the carpetbag beating against my woolen skirts with every step. Hunger had passed into that happy state in which it is felt as weakness but forgotten as an urge. When night fell, I did not know where I would be.

An abrupt tug on my carpetbag, as if it were caught, roused me from stuporous despair. I glanced down. A street Arab crouched at my side, avid eyes bright as two pennies in his dirt-tarnished face.

"Yes?" I inquired, too dazed to be rude even to such an ill specimen of London life.

Before I could act or the awful child could answer, someone else
was in our midst. A lady had wheeled from the crowd to seize the
lad's arm. Had she not been so well dressed, my protective instincts
would have led me to defend even this wretched ragamuffin.

But the lady was magnificently attired—a sheared beaver muff
cuffed one entire forearm. The brown felt hat smartly tipped over her
brow was lavished with velvet ribbons and crowned with a peacock-
blue bird in full flight.

She descended upon us like some glorious goddess, her dark eyes
flashing fire, her pendant amber earrings swaying exuberantly. Then
that angelic face screwed into an unlovely snarl. A stream of Queen's
English translated through the scullery poured from her mouth.

" 'Ere now, you scabby little guttersnipe! Let loose that lyedy's
baggage or I'll 'ave you washed and folded into pieces your own mum
wouldn't know."

"Got no mum!" the boy snarled back in the same disgusting pat-
ois. Yet the pressure on my carpetbag was suddenly released. I realized with a start that the lad had intended to take it.

The lady's grip on his arm was not so slack. "Shouldn't wonder,"
she retorted in a softer snarl. "'Ere's a farthing. Keep your 'ands off
decent folks for a while. Get on wi' you."

The sly grin the lad bestowed on his benefactress would have
done credit to a ferret. But he pocketed the coin, had the temerity to
tip his greasy cap to us both and wriggled away into the crowd.

My fingers tried to tighten on the bag handle, but shock had
squeezed all the blood from them. With a gesture so quick I barely
saw it, my alley-tongued rescuer caught the handle as it slipped my
grasp.

"Th-thank you," I managed to stammer. "How did you know—?
How did you see—?"

Her features had assumed a serenity that imbues beautiful women's
faces, and that is oftentimes mistaken for smugness.

"I have a bizarre avocation," she confessed, smiling. "I watch people."

The oddity of her words barely struck me; I stood mesmerized by her voice alone. It came as rich and expressive as a cello—no trace of Cockney lingered, although her accent did not sound quite . . . proper, either.

"My name is Irene Adler," she continued in the face of my mute confusion. Her eyes—a gold-lit dark brown that reminded me of a rich amber velvet among my former shop's most costly fabric rolls—darted over me. "This incident has given me a turn. Won't you join me for tea in that shop there?"

I hesitated, aware of a weakness in my knees and a greater hollowness in my purse than in my stomach.

"I'm quite respectable, I assure you—in most instances," she added mockingly. "And a . . . lady doesn't care to enter a public place unaccompanied."

The irony in her tone warned me that she spoke more for my benefit than her own. Yet her eyes remained kind despite the slight, quick curl of her lip on the word "respectable."

"Please be my guest," Irene Adler urged. Her gloved hand paused gently on my elbow, as if it had never wrung the urchin's arm but moments before. "I would appreciate your company while I recover from my fright."

Irene Adler was no more a victim of fright than I was Empress of China, but I found myself reluctantly drawn through the tearoom door to a cozy seat by the window.

"Tea. Peppermint, I think," Irene commanded the aproned girl who appeared beside us. "And a pastry selection—your largest, please."

I observed her in silence, as an audience absorbs the actions of a player on stage. Her walking suit was of dark Havana brown faille, a sensible costume for a brisk March day. The polonaise that surmounted its trailing skirt was draped back into a bustle and secured by heavy silk cord knotted in the Dominican style. My years in the draper's department had attuned me to fashionable nuances, but nothing had prepared me for the intimidating dash of my tea partner.

Irene Adler set down the imposing muff and began peeling off her leather gloves with dainty efficiency, finger by finger. She had, as I had noted, a face that could sell soap, as Miss Lillie Langtry's did Pears'—deep-set brown eyes, that changed from black to pale gold with her emotions, like the semi-precious gemstone called tiger's-eye; a generously curved mouth and straight nose; great thick eyelashes and a complexion like camellia petals. Her hair was obscured by the bonnet, but was a burnished chestnut color.

Everything about her was smart, and brisk, and disturbingly sure.

I forgot my hostess when the first bracing whiff of tea invaded my nostrils. How good and hot it was! It washed the bad taste of the past few days from my palate. I gawked like a schoolgirl at the three-tiered tray ringed with cucumber sandwiches, cakes and biscuits, each one shaped into tempting bite-size. A hunger pang pierced me like a dagger, and then another.

"You haven't told me your name." Irene Adler swept a cucumber sandwich off the tray with such panache that I found myself reaching as naturally for my own tidbit.

"Penelope Huxleigh. I . . . was a governess." Neither hunger nor curiosity could be contained any longer. I consumed the tidbit in one unseemly bite, then asked, "How did you do it, Miss Adler? No one else around us noticed even after you snared the child. I never saw him."

"Call me Irene, please, dear Miss Huxleigh. We are, after all, partners in crime-solving. But I am hardly surprised you didn't spy the little wretch. I didn't see him either," my new-found friend admitted. "I saw you."

"I? You were *watching* me?"

Irene Adler laughed. "Not 'watching' you, but I did notice you, for the same reasons that our young thief did. You were walking slowly, lost in . . . thought, an ideal target for a purse snatcher."

I found myself reaching for yet another pastry and blushed.

"Eat everything," my hostess urged with the same energy that vibrated through all her speech. "What's left over will only be gobbled by the kitchen staff. From the girth of our server, I doubt they require so much sustenance."

I blushed further, darting my eyes about for the unfortunate woman in question.

"She can't hear. She's across the room, at the tea trolley," Irene said softly.

"You *do* watch people."

"Of course I do. It's my profession. I'm an actress."

"An actress?" My hand paused guiltily over a particularly plump *petit four*. Father would never have allowed me to break bread with a person of the theatrical sort, and especially not cake!

"Now *you* embarrass *me*," Irene said blithely. "Such a tone. You might as well have said 'streetsweeper.' Yes, an actress, but first and foremost an opera singer."

I sighed and seized my prey. "Oh, an opera singer. That's quite different."

"Is it?" Irene's smile tightened into catlike inscrutability.

"Opera is quite a respectable art."

"Kind of you to think so."

"Music ennobles," I groped, for the sudden influx of food had unaccountably given me a headache, "what would otherwise be purely posturing on the stage. Although, were operas sung in English, more people would realize they're lurid dramas about rather immoral people."

"How fortunate, then, that I must sing in French, Italian and German. No one in London need know what I'm really saying."

"You sound as if you mock me."

"To the contrary, I mock myself. It is my fate to be misunderstood, I sometimes think." Irene's vivid eyes warmed suddenly, like strong tea when honey sweetens it. "But you've had a tiring day traipsing the streets. Eat some more."

"I can't." It was true. My abused stomach, presented with a surfeit, had rebelled. "And how did you know that I have been walking all day?"

"Early morning rain." Her eyes flicked to where the furls of my stiff horsehair flounce brushed the floor. "Your hem dampened, swept up a border of street grit, then dried. One can see the meandering waterline all along the material."

"Oh." I belabored the dirt with my gloves. "I hadn't noticed."

"You had other things to think of, no doubt," Irene answered so dryly that I glanced into her eyes. They penetrated me with such keen intelligence that I felt she knew my whole sordid story.

I began to gather my belongings despite her urgings that I eat more. I wondered whether she knew how hungry I was, whether she had always known it. The tray was still half-full; I realized that although Irene had struck me as eating, she actually had consumed little of the bounty, leaving the majority to me.

She laid out some coins, then lifted her beaver muff atop the table and began fussing with her gloves even as she rose.

Embarrassed to accept a stranger's charity, I simply could not face watching her lay money on the table. I occupied myself by taking futile strikes at my dirtied hem with my gloves until I had mastered my distress and quelled a sudden lump in my throat caused by an odd sense of imminent abandonment.

"Ready?" Irene asked brightly, rising and keeping a gloved hand outside her muff to guide me to the door, as if I were Parson Huxleigh's feeble widowed mother instead of his able-bodied orphaned daughter.

The street's crisp air, pungently scented with charcoal and smoke, reminded me of my circumstances. A familiar bleak numbness descended, as if my teatime with Irene Adler had been a dream and this hazy, glazed world outside were my true reality.

"Here." Irene's cheeks bloomed pink with the fresh chill, or perhaps with excitement. She drew me toward a doorway niche. "For later."

To my amazement, she began drawing pastries from the recesses of her capacious muff.

"You carry only that carpetbag, Penelope? Wait." She left the booty heaped in my bare hands and darted to the curb. After a word with a wizened chestnut vendor, she returned flourishing an empty paper bag. "Put them in here. You can have them for supper later."

"I can*not!* Irene, this is stealing. This is as wrong as what that urchin attempted to do to me. How did you . . . *when* did you . . . ? Oh, I must object, in the strongest moral terms."

"Yes, I'm sure you must," Irene agreed, heaping delicacies into the bag as if deaf to indignation. "But think! Were you and I as glossy and plump as that tearoom staff, we could have easily gobbled the entire contents of the tray and would have been charged no more for it. Are we to be penalized because we are dainty of appetite? We will simply remove our consumption to another place and time."

"Not 'we'—I! *I* will be guilty of this . . . robbery."

"Nonsense. I took these things, not you. Be it on my head," she insisted, tossing it until her bonnet plumes nodded frivolous agreement. Her eyes fixed on me, luminous and yet strangely piercing. I felt as if under the truth-demanding scrutiny of my father once again. "And will you not in fact be hungry again soon? Would you not have eaten all your share of the tray, and mine, too, were you not too hungry to break your fast so suddenly?"

"I . . . I . . ." Words failed me. To have my sorry circumstances so intimately known to another—and to a stranger—was more than even my tattered pride could stand.

Irene rolled the parcel shut and thrust it at me. "You can eat these at home later." Something in my face must have collapsed further, for her remarkably expressive eyes narrowed. "Or," she said abruptly, an actress improvising a scene and sweeping her audience with her, "why not come home with *me?* Since I am the true culprit? If goodness hampers your appetite, you can at least watch me devour the lot, for I will if you won't, and the sin will be on someone's head anyway."

"Home? With you?"

"And let us hire a cab before another street Arab snatches our ill-gotten gains. They are even hungrier than you are, you know."

I cannot defend myself except to say that I was worn and worried beyond any state I had ever reached in my life. I was faint from hunger and my pride had ebbed to the very edge of my endurance.

Without quite knowing how it happened, God forgive me, I found myself in a hansom cab rattling over the London paving stones to wherever Irene Adler, actress, opera singer and petty thief, called home.

Chapter Two

A Tale of Horror and Hope

~✵~

I was unused to the luxury of cab rides, but Irene Adler tripped up into the hansom's shadowed interior like one born to such convenience.

"Eversholt Street," she instructed the driver. He was a sun-burnt, gaunt individual with a hollow-eyed stare I didn't much fancy.

The reins snapped and then the cab jolted forward. Street scenes that had seemed all too heartlessly actual only moments before jerked past, offering an unreal stereopticon review of lowly pedestrians to privileged passengers like ourselves.

The clattering horse hooves masked my stomach's happy growls of satisfaction and rude rumblings for more. I sat silent, trying to place the address Irene had given.

The hansom turned one corner, then several in succession. The way grew narrow, darkened by the artificial twilight of looming buildings and oncoming dusk. The feeble glow of the cab side lights brightened on either side of us as I smelled the mingled aromas of unwholesome stews cooked in crowded urban tenements. I recalled the driver's fierce face with another twinge of regret, even as Irene drew a reticule from her all-purpose muff and began probing for coins.

Suddenly, the conveyance jerked to a stop that all but threw me from my seat. Irene unfastened the half-door that enclosed our nether extremities and vaulted down onto the gloomy street. I followed, loath to remain alone and ignorant in a strange place.

At the vehicle's rear the driver slumped over on the cab roof. Reins loose as hair ribbons draped the horse's undernourished hindquarters—poor beast, city coursers are always harder used than their country cousins.

Irene's attention, however, was all for the slack-limbed driver. "Why, this man is ill! Can you climb down, fellow?"

Her rousing tone lifted his head. I looked about anxiously for help. It was that hour when respectable persons draw indoors before dinner. We were utterly alone with our driver, ill . . . or simply feigning it for some sinister purpose.

I caught Irene's faille sleeve, murmuring discreetly, "It may be a ruse to disarm and rob us."

She shook me off. "We've little to be robbed of. Help me support him—he's a brawny fellow."

A leaden arm swagged my shoulders as the driver swung down to the street. Irene guided him into the passenger seat we had vacated, where he slumped like one dead.

"Quickly, Penelope, have you a handkerchief?"

"I? A handkerchief? Certainly!"

"Give it over. I need it."

I fumbled through my carpetbag and extracted an Irish linen square embroidered by my cousin Hyacinth with violets, an appropriate choice of color but an odd dislocation of botany. "Will this do?"

Irene didn't answer, instead clamping my pristine square to the driver's hangdog face.

"Nosebleed," she diagnosed authoritatively.

"Gracious," I protested as my prized possession stemmed a spreading tide of dark blood.

Irene leaned over the unfortunate man. "Are you all right?"

He laughed then, too loud, too . . . bitterly for one supposedly so weak. I clutched my carpetbag closer.

"Not by half," he answered in a rough yet breathless voice. "But thanks, lady, for asking. I've got this condition—"

Irene leaned away as if to memorize his strained face. "You are seriously ill—high color does not normally accompany extreme weakness. Heart, is it not? An extremity of the condition we all face ultimately, I see."

The man pulled my ruined linen from his nose and stared at her. "By God, I believe you do, Miss. Are you a—a—physician?"

Irene laughed ruefully. "That is one profession I've not yet been accused of practicing. I am American, however; aren't you as well, sir? From the West by your twang. Your callused hands say you have led a hard life."

The fellow seemed more disabled by her intuitions than his apparent ill-health. Again he stared at her—such a strange, concentrated stare, as if he were weighing thoughts on a balance far beyond the here and now. He began speaking with a desperate compulsion.

"A hard life I've had, and I'll have a harder death, but a satisfied one, thanks to my work of days ago on the Brixton Road. Ah." He massaged his left side, then continued with the same impulsive resolution. "I'm bound to leave London soon, one way or another. It might as well be dead as not. My work is done."

"No one should seek death," I felt obligated to put in, "desirable as the thought of reclining in the Deity's bosom may be."

The man's fierce black eyes fixed on me until I thought I should swallow my tongue.

"The Deity won't much like the notion of drawing Jefferson Hope to His bosom, Miss," he said roughly. "But you're a delicate female, like my late Lucy, and entitled to your illusions, I guess."

Agony clenched his features; his fingers made white-knuckled fists. "I'd give anything to see her again, anything but give up my eternal damnation."

"Your wife?" Irene inquired softly.

"Lucy?" Jefferson Hope's eyes remained shut. "Nope, but she should have been, would have been, had I returned but a day sooner, before Stangerson and Drebber, the damned hypocrites, had done in old John Ferrier and forced my Lucy into Drebber's Mormon harem."

Irene sank onto the cab foot-hold as if it were a stool, not appalled as any woman of delicate sensibilities ought to have been, but fascinated. I subsided against the hansom's side, too numbed to protest.

Jefferson Hope continued in a husky, exhausted voice.

"Found my Lucy lost as a child in the Great Salt Desert out West years ago, old Ferrier did. Ferrier was a done-for scout, but little Lucy had survived a wagon-train attack. Then the Mormons found 'em both and sheltered 'em on the terms that they join their damned church. John raised Lucy like she was his own. He followed their strange ways—though he never took a wife, much less several; he'd never subject Lucy to that polygamy notion."

"Polygamy?" I repeated faintly, as Jefferson Hope spoke on.

"Lucy grew up an heiress, for John Ferrier was a shrewd fellow and those folk prize worldly success. I came into the cursed wilderness on business and stayed to love Lucy, as she loved me. But Stangerson and Drebber wanted Ferrier's wealth and Drebber wanted my Lucy and they took both while I was away. They killed old John and made my Lucy—I won't call it 'marry,' though there was some shameful ceremony—made her live with Drebber."

Jefferson Hope's blood-shot eyes narrowed to wolfish slits. "I tracked them for twenty-one years through the desert and the vast, paved wastes of the great cities of North America and Europe. They knew it, too, and ran like sheep. And then—"

I quailed, seeing in that relentless face a likeness to the very hound of heaven itself. Irene leaned toward the sick man, her breath agitating the veil that swathed her face.

"Had they killed your Lucy, too?"

"Might as well have. With John dead, and me unable to rescue her—the whole enclave was tracking me—she . . . faded away; died a few months after undergoing God knows what." His face contorted, then relaxed abruptly. "Lucy was with me in spirit, every step of the way, just days ago when Enoch Drebber, whom I'd been tracking in my cab, hailed me. I drove him to an empty house in Brixton Road and confronted him with his sins. God knows it was for Lucy's sweet sake I did it. And would again."

"What exactly did you do, Mr. Hope?" Irene asked coolly.

His eyes opened to reassess her. He chuckled, the wretch actually chuckled. "You've a bit of what limeys call pluck yourself, Miss, don't you? Nervy, to minister to a murderer, and a dying one at that."

My gasp cracked on the foggy twilight air like a distant whip, but neither heeded it. They seemed to be in clandestine consultation, Jefferson Hope and Irene Adler, as sinner to confessor. It was a bizarre scene that unfolded in that still, smoky byway. Even I could not tear my eyes from the drama, for all its grisly implications.

"Might as well tell you," the big man said at last, regarding only Irene. "Might be my last opportunity to spill it. I want a sympathetic soul somewhere to know that John and Lucy Ferrier didn't die unavenged, no matter how tardily, not while Jefferson Hope lived." The man started, pressing a hand to his right side. "The ring, see if it's still there! Wouldn't want to lose it again clambering down from the dickey. Almost gave it up in Brixton Road."

Irene investigated the indicated pocket and drew out a plain gold band tucked in a doily of crumpled newsprint. "Is this what worries you?"

"Yes! Yes. . . . That ring was placed on Lucy's unwilling hand in a mockery of marriage, but it's clean now. Washed in the blood of the wolf, you might say, if you were a religious sort of person." Here, he cast me a sardonic look that quite sent shivers down my corset lacings.

"Now I can die in peace," he went on. "Not that I didn't give 'em a fair chance, more than they ever gave Lucy or her dad. Had two sets of two pills, one dosed with a nasty poison, you see. That's what I offered 'em. Choose a pill and let the Almighty decide who lives or dies. 'Course, I hadn't long to go anyway, not with the aneurysm eating up my heart. But I had to last long enough to make 'em pay and see their faces. And if I winked out, why at least I'd know I'd made 'em confront the death they brought to the ones I loved."

"But you didn't die, and they did." Irene sounded contemplative. "It was more of a chance than most would have offered such men."

"Died they did. Almost too quick. Drebber first and Stangerson at a holiday hotel later. But I lost the ring, that I'd taken off Lucy's dead hand just afore they buried her in that empty desert. Luckily, some gent advertised in the papers that he had it, so I sent a pal of mine along to fetch it, figuring the authorities might be laying a trap for me."

" 'In Brixton Road this morning,' " Irene slowly read from the torn newsprint by the hansom lamps' flickering light, " 'a plain gold wedding ring, found in the roadway between the White Hart Tavern and Holland Grove. Apply Dr. Watson, 221-B, Baker Street, between eight and nine this evening.' And was it a trap, Mr. Hope?"

"Don't know." He straightened as if revived by his grim confession. "My confederate played he was a little old lady and was out of this Dr. Watson's digs with the ring in a twinkle. He said some other gent was there, tall and lean with a damn sharp eye. Could have been a Scotland Yard 'tective. I'm a wanted man, Miss. You might get some reward for turning me in."

"Your story has been reward enough," Irene answered thoughtfully. "Until now I'd thought men like you only existed in Western dime novels written in Philadelphia. Lucy Ferrier must have been a memorable woman that you would track her wrongdoers to the ends of the earth."

"My only regret," he said, "is that my revenge will keep me from ever seeing her sweet face again, for I fear that your Deity, Miss"—here he regarded me again, to my dismay—"won't want commerce with a murderer."

"But Lucy *knows*, Mr. Hope!" Irene leaned inward to press his bony wrist as if she were consoling a relation. "She sees and knows and rests better for it. Perhaps she will prevail upon Him to pardon you. After all, the chances were fifty-fifty that *you* would choose the poisoned tablet, not them."

"Luck or God's own justice through my hand?" He nodded soberly. "I'll find out soon enough, I reckon." His paling features shifted as he glanced at me. "The fit is past, Miss. If you're not of a mind to call the coppers, I'll be going." In proof of his recovered health, he lumbered upright.

Irene rattled her reticule.

"No fare, Miss. I'll not need money where I'll be soon enough. You've made me feel a burden's lifted, just by telling another human soul my story. I don't want to go out in a cell, though, like a caged ferret, but on my feet like a man. So I thank you for what freedom's left to me."

Using the cab wheel as support, he stumbled toward the rear. Irene's hand stopped him. The precious, murder-tainted ring and scrap of newsprint lay on her gloved palm.

He reached for them, then his hand clenched. "You're a fine woman, not so sweet as my Lucy, but with a heart for all that. Keep the ring. I'd not want to wear it to the gallows, or have it thrown into some pile of police evidence."

"Is there nothing we can do for you, Mr. Hope?" Irene cried out as he climbed to his seat in slow stages.

Jefferson Hope picked up the flaccid reins. "You've done it— shown me kindness in a world where I've lived an unkind life too long." He lowered his shoulders and stared beyond the roofs' looming silhouettes to the darkling sky. A vast smudgepot of cloud and fog simmered in the last lurid light of the distant sunset. "I'd 'uv liked to meet my end in the open, but it's fit a foreign shore will serve as potter's field for a wanderer like me. Evening, Miss." Then he nodded to me, while I quailed beside Irene. "Miss."

With that polite farewell, he snapped the reins on the horse's weary flanks. The hansom lumbered into the murk that bottled Irene and myself in the nameless street.

"Astounding," Irene breathed. "What an incredible story! What a splendid, tragic man."

"A murderer," I cautioned, "and we have abetted him by permitting him to go. What will you do with the ring?"

"I couldn't have paid him anyway," she mused. "My purse is

almost as empty as yours after tea." I stood stunned at her matter-of-factness.

"As for the ring . . ." Irene's head tilted, dusk veiling her features more effectively than her hat's spider-silk netting.

"I believe I'll . . . keep it as a memento of lost love, loyalty and revenge large enough to furnish an Italian opera."

Her profile lifted against the muddy aura of light at alley's end to watch the bulk of Jefferson Hope's cab swell until it blotted out the gaslights beyond. Then the vehicle turned a corner and the street lamps were burning through the stinging mist like blurred stars. I could not read Irene's expression, but I believe she smiled.

"Or, if I ever have to—pawn it."

I gasped my shock again, most futilely.

Chapter Three

Perfidy Among the Draperies

~~~

"May I see it?" I finally could not refrain from asking Irene that evening.

She smiled in the mingled glow of gaslight, paraffin lamp and the cozy fire before which we sat, our stocking-clad feet toasting on the fender.

"Here." The object of my curiosity sailed into my lap. "An unremarkable ring, save for a certain grim sentimental value. It's the newspaper notice that intrigues *me*."

The wedding band lay in my hand, gleaming in the firelight, a perfect "O" of gold. I was tempted to slip it over my own finger. Perhaps I would sense some surviving spirit of the wronged and long-dead Lucy Ferrier who had worn it briefly in a blasphemous marriage. I felt a thrill of tempting horror at the idea.

"He loved her in his desperate, dogged way, that man," I commented. "Though revenge is an utterly empty emotion."

"Mr. Hope seemed far too satisfied to be considered empty," Irene answered.

I regarded her. Here we sat in humble yet comfortable circumstances with a ring that represented the violent deaths of four people, given to us by a man whose fingers virtually clutched the very knocker of death's door, and Irene was squinting over a small-print advertisement.

"The *Telegraph* item is useless now," I said definitely. "Mr. Hope regained the ring, even if he didn't keep it. We'll never know whether the finder meant to trap him or not."

"You would do well to read the agony columns more closely," Irene returned. "That is where the real stories are written in a metropolitan newspaper." Her alabaster forehead furrowed. "Two-twenty-one-B Baker Street . . . I have read this address before. But where?"

She rose and paced before the fire, her brocade wrap rustling around her like half-folded wings. I took advantage of her abstraction to survey our surroundings. On arriving at the top of four flights of stairs in an anonymous structure around the corner from where Mr. Hope had left us, I had been relieved to find Irene's rooms clean and cozy.

Yet she kept the ceiling gasolier and table lamp turned low, whether to obscure our modest surroundings or merely for effect I could not tell. Irene Adler seemed to be highly enamored of effect. The parlor thronged with an exotic geography of furniture, and shadowy artifacts crowded us like ill-seen but close friends.

Earlier, Irene had retired to her bedchamber to loosen her laces and trade her street ensemble for a crimson silk Oriental robe dramatic enough to clothe a Borgia, preferably Lucrezia.

"Baker Street." Irene stared toward the ceiling gaslight, oblivious to the exotic picture she presented. "I have seen that address printed before with peculiar requests for information."

"It is near Regent Street," I volunteered.

"I know *where* it is! I wonder *what* it is."

"Likely a doctor's consulting rooms."

"So far off Harley Street?"

"A beginning doctor, with a small, struggling practice."

"Brava, Nell. You show a talent, however small, for extrapolation."

"No one's ever called me 'Nell' before."

"They should have. You make a perfect Nell."

"I don't understand what you mean by that."

"There, you see! A perfect Nell would say that. Besides, you have nicknamed me as well."

"I have not! I call you by your formal first name."

"You call me 'Eye-*reen*-ie.' The American pronunciation is 'Eye-*reen*.'"

"Indeed, how primitive. I doubt that the proper *English* pronunciation could be considered a 'nickname.'"

"However, I take no offense. The French say '*Ear*-ren-ay' and the Russians 'Ih-*rain*-ah.' I will allow you to call me 'Eye-*reen*-ie.' A more Continental pronunciation may aid my performing career."

"This island England is not Continental!" I corrected, uncertain how I had been put on the defensive for having objected to a liberty taken with my name.

Irene smiled as if the matter were perfectly settled, then tapped the newspaper. "But back to our Dr. Watson. He may not practice at this address. He may live there."

"And why not? It is a perfectly respectable address, far more so than—"

"Than mine? Ah, you cannot help letting that tone of disapproval, that cat-swallowed-the-lemon-tart pucker, enter your voice. I *listen* to people as well as watch them."

"It's not that I'm not grateful . . . Irene." I pronounced the name as I always had. "Your lodgings are more than I have—" I paused at this bald admission.

"Why do you think I invited you to share them?"

"You knew?"

"I guessed, which often is as good as knowing. You looked so forlorn, with your shabby carpetbag and tattered pride. If I hadn't taken you in you would have been taken in by far worse, believe me, Nell."

"I've never said—"

Irene shook her head, lay the newsprint atop a cluttered end table and vanished into the bedroom with a crisp flounce.

She returned bearing a parcel I knew well, announcing, "Dinner will be warm." She began putting our stolen bounty on the fender to toast, a line of dainties that fairly made my mouth water.

"You must eat alone, Irene. I . . . cannot."

"You mean you will not."

"You said yourself that you were as poor as I."

"Not quite. *I* have lodgings yet. And dinner. And—" She flourished something from behind her back. "A bottle of *vin ordinaire*. I was saving it for a special occasion."

"I don't . . . drink alcoholic beverages."

Irene stabbed the cork with a lethal-looking steel buttonhook and expertly tussled the stopper out. "I think you ought to tonight, for medicinal purposes. We've had quite a day, you particularly. First you were nearly robbed, then you became the accomplice of a thief, and last but not least, you met a murderer."

"You mock me."

"Why should I not? Someone must. Oh, give it up, Nell. Events are completely out of hand. Forget what you would do if you could, and do what is sensible under the circumstances."

"Which is, in your opinion?"

"Eat, drink, and, if you cannot be merry, forget your difficulties until tomorrow."

"That is not a forward-thinking philosophy."

"Most philosophies are not forward-thinking, but instead hark drearily back to the past. There they dwell on former sins and lost opportunities until the fool's hope of a heaven is all there is to anticipate. I myself would prefer hell, which at least promises some interesting company in the hereafter. Have a scone, it's quite toasted now."

"I will not! Irene, only hours ago I heard you tell that miserable man that his dead angel, Lucy, watched him from heaven—"

"Bunk," Irene mumbled, chewing on the hard-toasted scone I had rejected.

"I beg your pardon?"

"And well you should, for spreading such bunkum. That's a good old American word for tommyrot. I told the poor fool what he wanted to hear, Nell. No point in disagreeing with the dying. They'll find out soon enough. Do have some wine."

I was so shocked—and my throat so parched by the nearby fire—that I raised the glass to my lips. "But you can't *not* believe in heaven . . . in God, Irene."

"Then let me put it another way. I believe in earth and in humanity, or some parts of it." She smiled suddenly. "You may be a parson's daughter and obliged to preach, my earnest sparrow, but I am only a professional nightingale. I cannot be expected to speak seriously on great issues. It matters nothing what *I* think, so long as you remain certain in what you think, is that not so?"

"Yes," I agreed, feeling my cheeks grow feverish in the firelight. Another swallow of sour, dry wine cooled my throat. I sampled a toasted cucumber sandwich from the fender.

"But I do think that you should room with me for the time being," Irene said, snatching another tidbit.

"I have no money."

"Nor have I," she retorted with cheery disregard. "You will find another position. I myself take our encounter with Mr. Hope as a sanguine sign. We theater folk are inclined to superstition, you know. There is an audition at the *Hope*-well Theatre the day after tomorrow. Perhaps I will get a role. You will find employment, too."

"I fear not." A great hiccough interrupted my thought.

"Of course you shall."

"I have no recent reference, save from families that formerly employed me as governess."

"Then I shall write one!" Irene swept back a crimson sleeve to flourish her pen hand.

I hiccoughed again, a sound disturbingly like a sob.

"Why, Nell . . . Penelope, I didn't mean to distress you. Of course I shan't forge a reference for you, although I could do a splendid job of it. I was jesting—"

"I don't have a current reference because I was . . . let go."

"Many have been let go—and lived."

"For . . . theft!" There, the horrid word was out of my mouth. I rinsed my tongue with more wine.

Irene leaned against the faded brocade armchair, looking so much like one of Mr. Burne-Jones's languishing painted ladies that I was quite surprised to hear her actually speak. Speak she did.

"Tell me."

I told her. It was a sordid enough yet simple tale. Whiteley's emporium in Westbourne Grove, Bayswater, offered its clientele, most of whom came by the public omnibus rather than private carriage, a staggering array of goods. The founder, William Whiteley, had begun as a draper but had expanded a series of neighboring shops into a depot of goods for every taste, until he dubbed himself a "Universal Provider," almost as if usurping the Deity, I felt.

"Shocking," Irene murmured insincerely.

"We female clerks were lodged two or three to a bedroom in Hatherly Grove near the emporium," I went on, determined to make a clean confession of it. "It was not a bad position in many ways. We were fed in communal dining rooms in the shop basement six days a week, excepting Sundays, when we were required to desert our rooms for wherever would have us. In my case, it was the park.

"The pay was not high, but we were housed and fed at least. Mr. Whiteley's one-hundred-and-seventy-six house rules addressed nearly every aspect of our lives within the twelve to fourteen hours a day we labored at the emporium and any hours we did not. Disregard of the rules would mean fines deducted from our wages. Worse, a list of offenders and their offenses was posted daily at the emporium.

"We had all signed a form stating that no notice was required either way—for dismissal or voluntary leaving, without reference, of course, at an instant's notice."

"The drapery clerks must have been on pins and needles," Irene interjected, sipping her wine. It precisely matched the shade of her blood-red gown.

"Indeed. Of course, *I* never broke any of Mr. Whiteley's rules—"

"Of course."

"Except—"

Irene sat forward. "Now, I fancy, we come to the interesting part. Your theft."

"It was *not* my theft! It was Lizzie's."

"Lizzie?"

"Liz Cheake, a dreadful, common girl. I don't know how she got taken on at Whiteley's, but she took a dislike to me, particularly as customers were partial to me and I could never be caught out breaking a rule. Lizzie broke all one-hundred-and-seventy-six, though no one caught her—or those who did had broken rules of their own and a bargain was arrived at."

"A politician, our Miss Liz."

"A liar," I retorted hotly. Irene raised an eyebrow, but I went on. "I had seen enough to know that if a customer too enthusiastically inspected a bolt of cloth and left her reticule aside for a moment—"

"Things vanished," Irene finished. "A pound note here, a sterling silver change purse . . ."

"Yes, exactly. Whiteley's employed private detectives to see that the customers did not rob us, but none were set to watch the clerks. I . . . seemed to be the only one who saw Lizzie. I didn't know what to do, and while I was debating my duty—"

"She accused you of *her* crime, a stolen item was found under the mattress of your bed and you were threatened with the police. Before you, in your astonished innocence, could object, you found yourself on the streets."

"Have you worked for Whiteley's?" I wondered.

Irene burst into laughter. "I have worked for Whiteley's in a hundred guises, most of them theaters. Oh, my poor country lambkin, debating duty will never arm you for an ugly world, nor did a childhood at Parson Huxleigh's holy knees! London is not Shropshire."

"I know." I hiccoughed again, drowning the affliction in more wine. *"Now,"* I added direly, "Have you ever heard of such perfidy?"

"I have acted and sung even greater."

"But I only did *right!* How could I have done differently?"

"You could not have. That is the tragedy." Irene rose, looking suddenly weary.

I stared up at her, struck by her commanding presence. "You know so much of the world," I admitted meekly. "May I ask how . . . old you are?"

She smiled. "Twenty-two, but I was born in New Jersey."

The reference escaped me. "I am four-and-twenty myself. Surely I should be the wiser."

"And will be by morning," Irene promised, bending to take the empty wine glass from my hand. "Come, I've a curtained alcove with a couch that can play a bed. I suggest rest. We have much to do tomorrow."

"But we are both unemployed," I protested, overcome by drowsiness for some reason.

"That doesn't mean we have to be idle—oh no, my dear Nell. We have scales to balance."

"I was very good at scales, at weighing ribbons and laces. I was really very good at everything at Whiteley's."

"Yes, of course you were—far too good for Whiteley's, don't you see? No, you don't. Never mind. Here's the alcove and I'll help you out of your things . . ."

✤ ✤ ✤

Morning came in a cymbal clash of sunshine through the open blinds of my alcove windows. I found myself ensconced in a bay, a great fern suspended over me like Mr. Poe's pendulum, and a line of drawn curtains separating me from the parlor.

"Up at last?" Irene's voice called from the room beyond.

The curtains whipped open. Irene, already dressed, wore a magnificent copper taffeta walking suit lavished with frills, like the pleated paper ruffs that house French chocolates.

"Come, Nell. I've a cup of hot milk and tea ready. You must dress quickly."

"But why?"

"No time for questions. We've an omnibus to catch."

Irene's entire manner bristled with a wicked energy. The tea scalded my throat, and she had me attired in a thrice.

"Such a plain ensemble will not do for where we are bound, Penelope."

No sooner had she spoken than an alien bonnet was settling on my head, nearly blinding me with a fall of veil and ribbons. Irene snatched up a reticule glittering with black jet, best suited for evening use. A hat nearly as overbearing descended upon the intricate arrangement of her hair and was promptly fixed with a hatpin long as a dagger.

I had found Irene Adler an intimidating figure the previous day; now she shone like some gaudy bronze sunset, far too grandly gowned for a daylight expedition.

"But," I began.

"Say nothing." Irene's gloved finger crossed her lips in a commanding gesture. "Do as I do. Watch, listen. And learn."

She would speak no more, but ushered me down the four flights to the street, where a wave of stale garlic and a rush of excited foreign speech washed over me. Swarthy young hooligans threaded the docile crowds, but Irene sailed with such confidence through the mob that a path cleared before us.

"*Buon giorno,*" a voice would call now and then as Irene waved a hand in greeting. The same Italian phrase rolled off her tongue with a gusto I had only heard previously from a street vendor.

She virtually herded me up the rear spiral stair of an omnibus, its patient horses as well reined as myself. She steadfastly refused to answer any questions as our vehicle bore us, with fitful stops and starts, through the morning bustle of London.

Irene's manner alone quelled me. She had donned an aura of intense concentration like a veil, her beautiful dark amber eyes smoldering with purpose and latent anger. Her lips were taut and her gloved hands lay folded upon her lap, but despite the outward composure of her figure, I sensed that some overwhelming emotion fired

her inner mood. I imagined she must look just so before moving on-
stage to perform—a creature of harnessed energy and leashed force
of personality, like a sleek thoroughbred straining at the gate before
its race-keen instincts are released to follow their natural bent.

I had never encountered a person of such volcanic temperament
before and admit it took me aback. I rode in silence beside Irene and
did as she had suggested—watched and listened and learned.

When we finally descended from the omnibus, I recognized the
neighborhood with a sinking feeling.

"Irene . . . not Whiteley's. I couldn't—"

She drew me before a shop window to meet our faint reflections
in the glass.

"You look nothing like yourself. See what a simple change of
headgear may do for a woman? That is all I require of you, Nell—
look nothing like yourself and accompany me into Whiteley's. Only
nod when you spy the enterprising Lizzie."

"I never want to see her again!"

"Once more into the breach, dear friend," she cajoled.

"Oh, Irene, I couldn't. I should be mortified."

Her hand clasped my wrist in a fixed grip. "Do you believe in
right and wrong?"

"Of course!"

"Do you believe in wrongs righted? In justice?"

"Naturally."

"Then follow me and say nothing."

No explorer has entered the darkest African jungle, no soldier has
faced the unknown foe with greater trepidation than I did on finding
my feet crossing the threshold of Whiteley's again.

My heels echoed on the wooden floor as smartly attired manikins
peered stiffly over the rails from the three floors above us. Human
heads turned as we passed, but I needn't have worried. They all regarded Irene, not myself.

The main floor held the yard goods. I could hardly bear to view
the familiar bolts, to pass the measuring stations. Then a tall, whip-
thin hateful figure riveted my gaze.

My fingers tugged Irene's coppery sleeve. "There," I whispered. She looked once in the right direction, then nodded. "Fade away among the trimmings, Nell; I have business elsewhere."

Obediently I ambled among the reels of lace and ribbons, while watching Irene through the glamorous fog of my veil.

She was marching toward the costliest bolts, her costume rustling noisily. Lizzie, always lazy unless there was sure money to be made, appeared with serpentine quickness at Irene's elbow. Irene addressed her without turning, sensing her presence.

"I'm looking for some really pretty stuff. Silk, with lots of shine, if you know what I mean. Something you can see from fifty feet away."

"Our more expensive fabrics are right here."

"I don't care what it costs, dearie," Irene continued in a loud, flat American twang. "My Homer runs the Velvet Swing mine in Deadeye, Nevada, sweetest little shaft to float a man to fame and fortune, and money ain't no object. What've you got in changeable silk taffeta, say peacock-blue and mauve?"

"Here, Madam, a selection of the best China silks," Lizzie simpered. "Liberty's couldn't do better by you."

Liar! I hissed to myself. Liberty silks were peerless.

"Hmm," Irene sighed, slinging her reticule atop one bolt as she unceremoniously thumped another to the floor. "I got to see it unfurled, you know? All that glitters ain't silver. Many a nice bolt is all glisten on the outside and frayed on the inside. I've been sold some dogs of so-called China silk in my time."

While Irene spoke, Lizzie dashed glances at the untended reticule, the same obvious behavior I had observed before, to which everyone around us appeared annoyingly oblivious.

Irene threw a length of changeable silk plaid over one shoulder and preened before a pier glass. Lizzie very nearly slavered over the abandoned reticule.

Take it, I found myself urging silently, to my horror. *Take it!*

She didn't. Irene whirled to ask a question, then wandered farther afield to a more distant and even more disreputable fabric. I held my breath.

"I'll have this," Irene decided, her fist clenching a cerise-and-emerald-striped satin that would have looked brash on a jockey.

Lizzie carted the heavy bolt to the measuring station while Irene dug in her reclaimed reticule. As soon as another clerk materialized to help with the cutting, Irene's face fell dramatically.

"Why . . . my favorite powdercase is missing! My antique German powdercase Uncle Horace gave me when the Velvet Swing came through. Solid sterling silver. With peridots. It was with me in the hansom on the way here!"

Everyone stood transfixed by Irene's air of outraged loss. Her whole rustling, glittering figure throbbed with wounded indignation. Then her eyes darted to Lizzie.

"You! You was hovering over my bag when I was rummaging with these here bolts. I demand you turn out your pockets, girlie."

Lizzie assumed her Queen of Siam pose. "I will not! Perhaps they do such things in America, Madam, but not here."

"I don't care where we are, missy. You was the only one around my bag and my powdercase is plumb gone—"

One of Whiteley's floorwalkers, a cold-eyed man the shopgirls called the "Maharajah's private guard," slipped alongside Lizzie.

"I'll have the supervisor of clerks take a look, Madam."

"Thank you," Irene sighed. "I knew a man would know how to handle this kind of matter. Search her good."

Lizzie disappeared in the custody of the floorwalker and a buxom female supervisor. The gentleman appeared moments later, a small silver object in his palm.

"With Whiteley's greatest apologies, Madam. It was in her sleeve cuff. The girl has been dismissed. Please accept a length of whatever fabric you wish at Whiteley's expense."

"Why that's mighty kind of you! 'Tain't your fault if you have a lying snip among your clerks. Say, I can't stand the sight of this here stuff since I almost lost my Uncle Horace's powdercase over it." Irene beamed at the returning woman supervisor. "But I will take, um, fifteen yards of *that* nice amber velvet by the wall."

Not a face cracked as the fabric was measured, cut, folded and bundled. Irene nodded thanks all around, promising to return, and flounced out of the establishment. At least I showed the presence of mind to follow discreetly and join her a street away from the emporium.

"The amber velvet is our—*was* our best fabric," I announced, breathless from the fear of being unmasked.

"Of course. Do you think I would have had that horrid silk taffeta on my life? And by the way, Nell, Americans do *not* speak in that ludicrous fashion you just witnessed, though Londoners like to believe it so."

"I don't care how Americans speak! That was wonderful, Irene, how you caught her red-handed."

We had arrived at the omnibus stop. Irene laid the fabric in my arms like an infant while she combed her reticule for the fare.

"Thank my Uncle Horace's silver powdercase." She waved the object. "*German* silver, Nell, nickel and a mere kiss of sterling. Not the real thing at all, just like the Velvet Swing mine."

"But you caught Lizzie! That almost makes my dismissal worth it." I hugged the parcel to my bosom. Irene would look magnificent in the velvet, but no more glorious than she looked to me at that moment.

"Trapped her is more like it. She refused to take the bait of my reticule, perverse girl. I was forced to . . . deposit . . . the powdercase on her person without her knowledge."

"You . . . ? I don't understand."

"Listen. Lizzie *would* have taken it, given world enough and time—which we did not have, especially with you in that ridiculous hat that wouldn't fool a child. So I . . . accelerated events. Mohammed wouldn't come to the mountain, so I brought the mountain to Mohammed."

"What have Moslems to do with it?"

"Not Moslems, powdercases. I slipped the case to Lizzie when she was too busy eyeing my reticule to notice."

"However did you learn such a . . . dishonest skill?"

"From a music hall magician in Philadelphia—a Napoleon of

the soft touch. I've never filched anything myself, but the skill proves useful now and again. Don't frown so pathetically, Nell; real thieves are far less visible than my humble self. Do you recall the woman who sat across from us on the omnibus?"

It took a moment to extricate that morning ride from a tangle of more recent memories and violent emotions.

"The dignified lady in the Persian lamb capelet with matching muff?" I recalled. "Oh, yes, the muff was almost as large as yours! I wondered why such a well-attired lady should have to ride a public omnibus."

"You are becoming quite a judge of fashion, my dear Nell, thanks to your sojourn in Whiteley's drapery department and my tender tutelage. Now I will tell you that your 'dignified lady' rides the omnibus because it is her profession."

"Her profession? However could that be?"

"You saw a literal false front—the lady's arms were not within her sleeves nor were her hands inside her muff."

"She was . . . missing them?"

"Not at all. Her hands were liberated behind the fashionable facade to rob her fellow passengers. Where but in the crush of an omnibus can one get close enough to fleece one's neighbor?"

"How awful! She looked quite respectable."

"It was a quite respectable roll of bills she lifted from the pocket of the commercial traveler beside her, the fellow in the checked suit."

"I tried not to look at him."

"Quite right. It *was* a rather dreadful check; yellow and brown look well together only on certain thrushes. At any rate, as we left I relieved the lady's muff of its recent acquisition and returned it to the gentleman without mussing so much as a wrinkle in either of their attires. I told you my gift came in *hand*-y." Irene wriggled gloved fingers in my face until I smiled at her dreadful pun. Her *insouciance* was indefatigable.

"Couldn't you have called a bobby?" I said.

"Such a fuss, and our light-fingered lady was likely to vanish in the confusion. Instead, she will pummel her muff in vain for its treasure. She may begin to believe her skills are slipping and take up honest work, such as clerking at Whiteley's."

I smiled despite myself. "Perhaps, though the means were somewhat . . . unconventional, the end was just."

"Exactly, my dear Nell. As in your own case."

"But in my case and that of your reticule—" The omnibus was coming with a dull clop of many horse hooves pounding a headache into the pavement. I could hardly think, but I knew Irene's logic had some flaw. "Lizzie *didn't* steal it."

"She would have, wouldn't she?"

"Yes . . . no! Perhaps—"

"If not *my* reticule, some less resourceful person's?"

"Possibly, but—"

"So Lizzie has been found out; you have been avenged, which we know from Mr. Hope is a most rewarding feeling, and I have fifteen yards of gorgeous amber velvet, which I well deserve for ridding Whiteley's of an unscrupulous clerk."

The omnibus was upon us. Irene tripped up the stairs. I lurched upward in her wake—numb, dumb, the ill-gotten goods clasped in my innocent arms. I could no more have unloosed the velvet than I could have resisted Irene's firm hold upon my imagination, my demoralized moral standards and my . . . my deliciously avenged dishonor!

"There, you see," my newfound friend crowed a few days later, handing me the day-late *Echo* our landlord, Mr. Minucci, gave her in return for voice lessons to his tone-deaf young daughter, Sofia. "Didn't I tell you so?"

Mystified at first, I found a familiar name catching my attention on the indicated page. "Ah, so he's dead, then."

"Quite. But that was not what interested me."

"Poor man," I went on, for the dead always are easier objects of sympathy. "Hear how these Grub Street hacks put it: 'The public have lost a sensational treat through the sudden death of the man I Iope, who was suspected of the murder of Mr. Enoch Drebber and of Mr. Joseph Stangerson.' As if murder were a 'treat' in any circumstances!"

"It might be when the victim is a Caligua," Irene said. "But read on."

"'. . . the crime was the result of an old-standing and romantic feud, in which love and Mormonism bore a part—'"

"We know all that," Irene interrupted.

"'. . . the efficiency of our police force will serve as a lesson to all foreigners to settle their feuds at home—'"

"Not likely! Keep reading. Look for the telling detail, my dear Nell, always and only the telling detail. The thing that is *not* said."

I read in silence, learning that "the credit for this smart capture" went to the Scotland Yard officials, Lestrade and Gregson. That Mr. Hope had been taken "in the rooms of a certain Mr. Sherlock Holmes," an amateur detective of sorts "who may learn a thing or two from the successful officers."

"I fancy he will learn to avoid such sensational circumstances in the future," I murmured.

"Who?"

"This Mr. Sherlock Holmes." I shuddered for effect. "How awful to have the police arrest a murderer in your very own rooms. I should never sleep there again."

"Perhaps they were not solely his rooms."

"Company would hardly be a comfort."

"No . . . unless it was the company of a medical man who could soothe one's frazzled nerves after the event," she said mysteriously.

"Irene!" I put down the paper with a smart crack. "What nonsense *are* you implying?"

She picked it up, smiling. "I have seen the name of Sherlock Holmes affixed to agony column items before, often enough that he might want to use a fellow lodger's name—say Dr. Watson's—instead. An 'amateur detective.' Hmm, I wonder where he lives, this aspiring sleuth?"

I snatched back the newspaper. "It doesn't say and what does it matter anyway? Such unhealthy inquiries into where a strange man may live are not the proper business of a lady."

Irene laughed until she braced her hands at aching corset sides. "I am not in the business of being a lady, proper or improper."

Naturally I assumed at the time that Irene referred to her theatrical profession. I was dreadfully wrong, as I was to be so many times in my assumptions about Irene Adler . . . and Mr. Sherlock Holmes . . . and, most oddly of all, about myself.

Irene patted my hand as she withdrew the newspaper to study it further. "Don't fret, Nell. You are far better off for assuming the best of a wicked world."

I was no longer so sure.

Chapter Four

A Sparking Commission

〜ᵔᵕᵔ〜

"I fancy, Watson, that we are about to be visited by an eminent American," my friend Sherlock Holmes remarked as he parted the curtains overlooking Baker Street.

"I didn't know that there *were* any eminent Americans," I huffed in reply. At times I found Holmes's habit of discerning the rank and occupations of visitors before they had set hand to bell tiresome, most especially when I was deep in the latest edition of the *Daily Telegraph*.

"A successful American, then!" Holmes corrected cheerily. "Once again you show a remarkable skill at the fine points of social observation, Watson. Come, take your nose out of the newsprint and have a look yourself! A second opinion would be welcome."

"But not necessarily right," I grumbled, rising to Holmes's bait. I had never yet outdone, or even matched him in reading people's histories on first glance.

"That robust-looking gentleman in black is bedeviled by where the 'B' of our address should be," Holmes indicated, "a sure sign of a visitor to our shores."

"I suppose you know he's coming here because he's hesitating while looking for the address."

"Ah, Watson, you do absorb my methods."

"But how do you know that he's an American?"

"I have an advantage over you, old fellow; I've been watching him for several minutes. He *walked* here, Watson!"

"Walked? How very extraordinary."

"Yet he is a fine-feathered fellow for all that. Poverty cannot have inspired his choice of shank's mare for transportation, ergo, walking must be the fashion where he hails from. There is no one like a rich American for walking to preserve the constitution when he may easily ride."

"He looks like a judge," I admitted, taking in the high silk hat and the stiff, gate's-ajar collar visible beneath the velvet lapels of his chesterfield.

"A judge of the marketplace, I fancy, Watson; a commercial man and self-made. Note the dignity of his bearing; it is something he was not born to, for he's not so tall as he makes himself look. The hat and collar raise him in the eyes of the world—and only in New York City does a hatter make a top hat that so resembles a crown, by the way. Yes, our gentleman caller is an aristocrat of free enterprise, Watson, as I am a mere pauper in that system. But he is adventuresome only in some respects; in others, he is as cautious as yourself, I daresay. See how short he wears his whiskers, as he doubtless did in his thirties' youth, when our Victoria was a girl."

In a moment the bell rang, once and firmly. In a few moments more Mrs. Hudson ushered the dignified gentleman into our parlor.

"Mr. Sherlock Holmes?" he inquired in unmistakably American tones, looking from Holmes to myself.

"At your service . . . Mr. Tiffany," Holmes said with a bow and a smile.

"Pinkerton's told you that I would be consulting you, then?" said the old gentleman, taken aback that his presence was apparently expected.

"Pinkerton's tells me nothing. I have never had any dealings with that firm."

"They recommended you."

"Ah, Watson, do you hear?" Holmes turned to me with real plea-sure. "Apparently word of my deductive efforts has crossed the At-lantic. But I must present my associate, Dr. Watson. This is Charles Lewis Tiffany, Watson, the gentleman who makes women the world over so ecstatic that even a Casanova would envy him."

"Of course," I murmured respectfully, for the name of Tiffany was a byword in London as well as New York.

Tiffany's vivid blue eyes were hardening to lapis lazuli. His Ro-man nose spoke of stubbornness and his florid complexion looked more so against the snowy whiskers that crisped around his jaw, yet he seemed in the peak of health for a man in his seventies.

"If Pinkerton's did not send word that I would be calling, how are you aware of my identity, Mr. Holmes?" he demanded.

Holmes pointed to my castaway *Telegraph*. "When that most . . . eminent . . . and successful American jeweler, Tiffany, visits London it is usually in search of old jewels for new clients. Such things are noted in the press, and it is *my* calling to note them."

"My portrait has not appeared recently in the London papers."

"My dear sir, when your hat is made by only one possible hatter in New York and the maker's mark is plain in every line, there is no need for identification as mundane as photographs. Also you have a diamond token in the shape of a cursive 'T' at your watch-fob.

"But do sit, Mr. Tiffany," Holmes urged with that charm of his for cajoling a story from a client. "I am thirsting for the tale that has brought you to my obscure door."

The old gentleman removed his hat, paused and extended it to Holmes, who peered inside the silk-lined rim and nodded with a sat-isfied smile.

"As I predicted," Holmes noted. "Have you considered, Mr. Tiffany, that the article of a man's dress most likely to be labeled is his hat? I made a small study of the subject once, which explains my fa-miliarity with the premier hatters of Europe—and the United States and Canada, of course."

"I see, Mr. Holmes, that you are as particular in your line of work as I am in mine," Tiffany said, setting his hat aside. "I, too, must keep abreast of a world market."

"Truth is like a diamond, Mr. Tiffany. It must have the proper clarity, color and weight to be worth anything—and must be searched for everywhere. I trade in truth."

"Odd you should mention diamonds—or did you deduce that, too, in that disconcerting manner of yours?"

Holmes spread his hands modestly. "Mere chance, my dear sir."

"Well, diamonds it is, Mr. Holmes, and a good many of them, that I seek," Tiffany said, settling into the easy chair Holmes offered clients. "A queen's ransom in diamonds."

Holmes raised an eyebrow and tented his long fingers to indicate his attentiveness as the world-famous jeweler went on.

"Europe is a rich source of stones for my firm. The crown jewels of various royal houses may come up for bid at any moment—not that we are not finding superior diamonds fresh from the mine. I confess myself partial to the semiprecious colored gemstones so often overlooked—but there is a romance to a splendid diamond's history that appeals to the adventurer in us all."

"Indeed," Holmes said, his eyes sparkling and fever spots of excitement blossoming on his lean cheeks.

"Have you ever heard of the Zone of Diamonds, sir?"

"Watson, my index!"

I produced the volume, Holmes's personal encyclopedia, which was filled with odd bits of information useful only to a chronicler of humanity's eternal dedication to crime.

Holmes paged through in silence. "No reference, but I seem to recall some connection with the unhappy Marie Antoinette."

"You amaze me, Mr. Holmes. Even in ignorance you are surprisingly knowledgeable. Yes, the Zone belonged to her. It is what its name indicates, a girdle—or belt, if you will—of diamonds. No single stone is superior, but together they make a very pretty chain. She clasped it around the waists of court gowns; it is said to have reached to the floor."

I whistled under my breath, for such a length of diamonds would be spectacular.

"My exact reaction, Dr. Watson, when I first learned of the piece," Mr. Tiffany said.

"How long has it been missing?" Holmes asked abruptly. "Since the French Revolution?"

"No, that is what is so . . . tempting, Mr. Holmes. The Zone of Diamonds survived the Revolution. Along with the remaining French crown jewels, it was kept in the Tuileries and not lost until the Paris mobs overran it while overthrowing King Louis Philippe in 1848."

"Thirty-three years ago," Holmes mused.

"Not much longer than you yourself have been on this planet, I'd imagine," Tiffany noted.

"It may take infinite time to make diamonds, Mr. Tiffany," Holmes said crisply, "but the human deductive faculty matures much earlier, I assure you. At least in my case."

"I believe you, Mr. Holmes," Tiffany said with a solemn nod. "I am leaving no, er, stone unturned in my search for this object. My best information Is that it came to England. I will put all my resources behind this enterprise. I have used private detectives before, notably Pinkerton's, but they do not have the contacts abroad that this task requires."

"Mr. Tiffany," said Holmes, "I am not commonly in the game of finding lost articles. Frankly, it is the singular nature of the cases I take on that intrigues me. Your assignment is a trifling matter of tracing the path of stolen goods; surely, other agents could do as much for you."

"I should be grateful, Mr. Holmes, if you would look into the matter. Pinkerton's spoke highly of you, especially your flair for following the unexpected clue. And are you not the world's only consulting detective?"

"At least the trail is cold and the cast of characters is unknown." Holmes's long, agile hands clapped his chair arms in concerted decision. "I am at an interval now, with little to occupy my mind. As Dr. Watson could no doubt tell you, Mr. Tiffany, I become annoyingly restless—even insufferable—at such times. And my family tree does extend a root or two into France, thus my interest in restoring a French queen's diamonds to history."

"As the Three Musketeers did once long ago," Tiffany suggested with a laugh.

Holmes looked at the man as if he had gone mad.

"The Three Musketeers, exactly," said I hastily, "and the famous incident of the Queen's diamonds." Few besides myself knew of Holmes's abysmal ignorance in matters outside his immediate interest, of which literature was only one. " 'One for all and all for one,' you know."

"A noble motto, Watson," Holmes said vaguely, rising. "Rest assured that I will bend my best efforts to locating your wandering cincture, Mr. Tiffany."

"And rest assured that your efforts will be rewarded, Mr. Holmes. I offer my cheque for your preliminary inquiries."

Holmes accepted it, bowed, handed back the gentleman's hat and saw him out.

"Think of it, Holmes," I speculated as he returned to the chamber, "a string of diamonds . . . why, it must be seven or eight feet long!"

"That's assuming that Marie Antoinette tied her belt into two tails like an ordinary woman, Watson. There could have been a single strand from waist to floor."

"Still, a spectacular find, Holmes."

"Ah, I see," said he, reaching for his black clay pipe and the Persian slipper fragrant with loose tobacco. "You grow impatient for a more dramatic subject for another of your accounts. My usual problems are too mundane for your literary ambitions—"

"Not at all, my dear fellow!" I protested. "I have learned from our association that no detail is too insignificant to be noticed and that no problem is small to the one it plagues. Aren't you the slightest bit eager to set out on the trail of this fabulous artifact?"

"Eager, Watson? To trail the glittering slick of a loathesome slug across this green garden of England? Whatever the beauty or worth of this girdle of diamonds, for men it has been nothing but a snare, its sheen dulled by the countless greedy hands through which it has doubtless passed. There is sorrow in its wake, and betrayal and destruction, count upon it."

"'A thing of beauty is a joy forever,'" I rashly quoted the poet. This literary reference was not lost on Holmes, unlike Dumas's *Three Musketeers*.

"'Rarely do great beauty and great virtue dwell together,'" Holmes responded, citing Petrarch. "I find it pathetic, Watson, that this 'thing of beauty,' this Zone of Diamonds that was once an accessory to a queen will remain as empty a symbol of worldly success to whomever possesses it. In our industrial age, merchant princes and celluloid czars buy such baubles for the vanity of themselves and the women upon whom they bestow their largess so publicly. Better that the Zone stay lost; then it will tempt fewer men to commit more ill deeds than the world needs."

"Might it not be displayed in some museum?"

Holmes laughed. "Mr. Tiffany is not a curator, but a merchant. He will likely sell the Zone stone by stone and reap a greater value from this subdivision than if he had honored its original form."

"Surely not, Holmes."

"Still keen for the treasure hunt, eh, Watson? There is a joy in finding that seldom extends to the having of the found object, I admit. And there is something of the boy in every Englishman in our day, a not undesirable trait. I'll have a go at it, Watson, but forgive me if I can't muster enthusiasm for the hunt. I may uncover human misery as well as lost jewels if I look for it; I will certainly do so if I find it."

"*When* you find it, Holmes."

"When," he amended calmly.

Chapter Five

Repast at Tiffany's

❧

I have never known anyone with so little regard for personal possessions as my friend, Irene Adler. It was not the case that she had no possessions; indeed, even when we first shared modest lodgings in Saffron Hill, the Italian district, her two rooms were crammed to the sconces with the excess of her accumulations.

Like a kitten too curious to be completely timid, I explored the crowded landscape of my new residence by relentless stages. My first discovery was Irene's utterly cavalier attitude toward her possessions. What was hers, was mine. If my eye strayed too long to an exotically figured shawl, she immediately noticed.

"Catch your fancy, does it, Nell? You may have it."

"No!" I would protest hastily. Those fevered shades of dye, that deep fringe of swaying silk were not to my taste or, more important, my station in life.

At that Irene would produce another shawl—say, an ivory slubbed silk with a modest eyelash of fringe—from the gaping trunk that spilled a dressmaker's treasure trove upon her bedchamber rug.

"Perhaps this is more to your liking," she would say with such amused certainty that I almost felt obliged to claim the gaudy one to prove her wrong.

Though I never did any such thing.

Once, frustrated by the profusion littering our two large rooms, I listed the contents. Of furniture there was little and that awash in a sea of accessories. Chief among it was the square piano, the only object kept free of effluvia, so that its lid might be raised. Two easy chairs, both moth-marked under their colorful throws, flanked the hearth. A sway-backed sofa held the opposite wall while a poster of Henry Irving's *Hamlet,* with Ellen Terry as Ophelia, played the role of a painting above it.

The mantelpiece was a shelf for assorted kitchen implements— all of them illicit, for cooking was forbidden in our chambers. The mantel's only decoration was the empty wine bottle Irene and I had shared during our first night together. Now it contained an inverted duster that spilled forth a bouquet of green-and-copper cock feathers in lieu of fresh flowers.

I might add that the feather duster had been seldom disturbed in its repose until I arrived and released it to do its duty.

Irene's bedchamber—into which she urged me welcome as if it were a noted salon—was even more eccentric. My first foray into this Byzantine retreat nearly gave me a fatal turn when I spied a dark silhouette lurking in an unlit corner.

"La, Nell, don't let *her* startle you," Irene advised. "A lady without her head is not only harmless but useless, although few gentlemen appear to have realized that."

I studied our silent lodger—a dressmaker's model with an hourglass torso upholstered in black jersey. Like most such devices, it ended in a metal-capped neck stem, upon which bloomed a large, lavishly pale silk lily. No wonder I had thought for a moment that a ghost with a mutilated face had been haunting us!

Irene assumed a pose beside the manikin, hand on its homely black shoulder, and grinned like a street Arab. "I call her my Jersey Lily," she said with sly fondness, jabbing a hatpin into the fabric.

"After Lillie Langtry!" I realized with a start. Irene's wit often took unconventional turns. I came closer to view the figure. "Do you suppose she really . . . well, you know . . . with the Prince of Wales, as they say?"

"If she didn't she's a fool—or he is a greater one," Irene retorted.

I had not expected so shocking an answer. "But she is a married woman!"

"The Prince is a married *man*."

"And she's a churchman's daughter."

"Churchman's daughters are often the first to fall. It's such a bore being good when there is so little reward in it."

"Irene! If I did not know you were jesting I should fear for your soul, or at the least your reputation."

"I have neither, remember? I am an 'actress,'" she returned.

"Surely you do not endorse Mrs. Langtry's immorality?"

"Of course not. Yet one cannot fault the cleverness of the woman. Have you seen her? No? I have."

"What did she look like?" I had not meant to sound so eager.

"I was about to tell you," Irene said with a smile. "An *overrated* woman, Nell, with a profile like a hacksaw—that chiseled, masculine silhouette that aesthetic painters like to call Greek."

"But the picture on Pears' soap—"

"Is a picture. A drawing. Really, any man of sensitivity would find her no more attractive than a hod-carrier. But she does have a certain *elan*. The evening she met the Prince of Wales she was wearing mourning—solid black with her hair in a discreet little bun. She stood out among the ladies in their gaudy plumage like a grackle among robin red-breasts."

"And this caught the Prince's eye?"

"Indeed. In a forest of autumn leaves it is better to be a trifle green than flame-colored and common. Then, too, the Jersey Lily has a habit of going corsetless—a great scoffer at social conventions, she, at least the trivial ones."

"Corsetless." Such behavior was incomprehensible to me. "But why . . . ?"

"Say no more. Lillie Langtry has had her day. Now that her liaison with the Prince is over, she has exhibited the bad manners to go upon the stage, thus pushing back into the wings those of us who have won our places by dint of talent and long study; meanwhile she absconds with the limelight."

Irene seemed genuinely irritated for a moment. "Ah, it is hard to succeed in an immoral profession, Nell, when immoral nonprofessional upstarts take to the boards."

"Your cynicism doesn't shock me, as you mean it to, Irene," I assured her insincerely. "*You* would never lead such a life as she, not even to advance your singing career."

"No," Irene agreed, her face sobering. The hatpin stabbed another pinch of taut black jersey. "I refuse to win my plaudits in a horizontal position, like a pincushion, and will likely see little success in life for it."

"Perhaps you will marry and retire from the stage."

"Never! Marriage is the same tawdry exchange of freedom for security, and that a false one, for the husband can command all that a wife may do. Marriage is merely a bargain sealed with civil and religious rites instead of unspoken social customs."

"I myself have always regarded marriage as sacred, a woman's highest calling. Circumstances may put the state beyond the reach of some women"—here my sad recollection of Jasper Higgenbottom's illness and absence clotted my voice before I recovered and went on—"but at least we treasure the mirage of it. Now you call even matrimony a snare and a delusion. You quite make me despair for a woman's lot."

"Oh, don't despair, Nell. No. Because the many choose to leave their fates unquestioned, like so many sheep herded through gates, does not mean a few nimble lambs can't leap the traces and go merrily down the lane."

She turned away from the rather gruesome Jersey Lily with a smile. "Speaking of leaping traces, you must help me decide what to wear. I have an important interview Tuesday morning next."

"Is it the new opera? The Gilbert and Sullivan?"

Irene shook her head. "Nothing so commonplace. I am to see Mr. Tiffany."

"Mr. Tiffany?"

"The famous New York jeweler! Do you live with your head in a barrel?"

"Usually in a bonnet," I retorted, more disturbed by the implications of the "Mr." than the "Tiffany." "But surely you are not going to New York?"

"Hardly. I am fleet, but I do not have wings. Mr. Tiffany will come to me, or rather, I will go to his hotel in Trafalgar Square."

"You cannot."

"Whyever not?"

"Go to his hotel? Alone? And in the morning? You might be taken for an—"

"An actress? Yes, I know. But do you not see, Nell, what an opportunity this is? Charles Lewis Tiffany is consulting *me* on a matter of confidential importance! The Pinkerton Detective Agency has directed him to me. Would you rather he came here?"

"Heavens, no! That would be even more improper."

"Besides, Morley's is a very fine hotel. I shall endure no more comment than Mrs. Langtry would if she did the same."

"That settles it. I shall accompany you."

"I have never heard you sound so determined, Nell. Shall you not be also subjected to unwelcome speculation?"

"That does not matter." I squared my shoulders. "Let them speak against two of us."

"Well said." Irene smiled. "Your presence might lend a certain weight to the occasion. I could say you were my secretary."

"That would be a lie," I began dubiously.

"Not if you take notes," she came back triumphantly.

"Well, no, not if I take notes."

"Then it is settled. We will see Mr. Tiffany at Morley's Tuesday next, where you will take notes. And now you will help me choose the proper costume for this important *rendezvous* of ours."

This I did, for I found it increasingly amusing to outfit Irene.

Despite its lavish appearance, her wardrobe consisted of surprisingly few ensembles. The jumble of hand-me-down trims she collected in street markets transformed this raw material to fit any occasion, station in life or mood that suited her.

Nor did Irene give a figleaf for how nicely she accomplished her transformations. Often of an evening I, who had been taught to sew spiderweb-fine stitches, would watch Irene driving her large-eyed needle in great galloping strides as she affixed a glittering swag of trim to a plain-Jane gown. The same long, loose stitches would be as roughly ripped free when the gown required another change of character.

For our meeting with the famed jeweler, we settled upon what Irene called "*bourgeois* dignity." I dressed with my usual quiet rectitude, though I admit that my gloves clung damply to my palms as we took the early omnibus to Trafalgar Square Tuesday.

Morley's presented a solidly reassuring facade overlooking the mounted statue of Charles I. I was more intrigued by the Time Signal Ball above the Electric Telegraph Office to our right, a device that gave a precise reading of Greenwich Mean Time in central London.

Such ingenious inventions greatly consoled me for the crowded city bustle. Pneumatic pressure raised a six-foot-diameter zinc ball that was dropped ten feet at precisely one o'clock daily, thus activating an electric current transmitted direct from the Greenwich Observatory. By the sphere's daily plummet, all London could set its watches and clocks accurately, and I took full advantage of this convenience.

On our left the fool's-capped steeple of St.-Martin-in-the-Fields church loomed over the hotel's lowlier bulk, which I thought reassuring for our enterprise.

Thus sandwiched, as it were, between God and modern science, Irene and I glided into Morley's Hotel. Heavy Turkish carpet discreetly hushed our footfalls within as we were ushered to a private dining room. The coffered double doors sprang open on a spry old gentleman with a stern but kindly face.

"Miss Irene Adler?" he inquired, looking from one to the other.

"At your service, Mr. Tiffany," Irene said, extracting one hand from her muff to shake hands with him. "This is my secretary, Miss Huxleigh."

Mr. Tiffany bristled a bit at her bold greeting, as I must admit did I. Yet Irene looked so charming in her blue brocade suit and bonnet with the cobalt ostrich feather dipping toward her dimpled cheek that we both forgave her at the same instant.

"I had not expected an American," Mr. Tiffany said next. "Pray be seated, ladies. The hotel has set out a repast, as I am a busy man and must meet over the meal hours."

"How delightful," Irene commented, seating herself before a tea table burdened with delicacies and a porcelain teapot in the likeness of a well-fed rabbit. "Perhaps you would do the honors, Nell, while Mr. Tiffany and I discuss business."

I accepted with alacrity. If I had mastered one duty of a parson's daughter—and beautifully, I might add—it was the preparing, pouring and serving of tea.

The old gentleman flipped aside the skirt of his black frockcoat and settled a trifle uneasily in a wing-back chair.

"I must confess, Miss Adler," he began with a frown, "that despite Pinkerton's highest recommendations I remain hesitant to consign my matter into your hands. You are so young—"

"As were you when you founded your firm. Five-and-twenty, was it not?"

The puckers at the bridge of Mr. Tiffany's imposing Roman nose faded momentarily. "And the nature of my business is confidential, extremely so."

"I keep confidences, extremely so. Miss Huxleigh is a parson's daughter and the soul of discretion."

"That may be. Yet there could be some . . . danger . . . involved."

"Capital!" Irene accepted the first cup of tea I extended and beamed over its dainty lip at Mr. Tiffany. "If danger is involved, then the object of the assignment must be worth a great deal. What jewel is it?"

"I did not say the matter involved jewels."

"You did not need to; your name alone makes that plain."

"But I could be seeking aid in a personal matter—"

"You would not allow yourself to be forced to use an untried agent like myself for a truly personal matter, no matter the circumstances."

"You are quick, Miss Adler, I'll say that for you."

"Then perhaps my wit will persuade you to reconsider hiring women clerks in your New York establishment, Mr. Tiffany."

The gentleman looked apoplectic for a moment, his color warming far more than my cup of milk-mild tea called for.

"My establishment presents an image of impeccable dignity, like a bank, Miss Adler. You also overlook the fact that Tiffany's, among city stores on either side of the Atlantic, was the first to provide retiring rooms for shopping women and their children. Women, no matter how charming in the parlor or the salon—"

"Or shop," Irene interjected.

"Women clerks would . . . disrupt the surroundings," Mr. Tiffany said in final tones.

"Yes, your gentlemen clerks do dress like a convening of undertakers," Irene murmured into her tea cup.

"You have visited my Union Square establishment?"

"When I lived in America." Irene smiled. "But only, like most passers-through, to gawk at its glories."

"You are a forward young woman! I half think you mock me. Perhaps these very qualities are required to do what I propose, though I admit myself still highly dubious of employing a woman for such a delicate task."

"Which is?" Irene asked pointedly.

He glanced at me as if reassured by my plain English demeanor in the face of Irene's full-blown confidence. His voice lowered.

"I seek not a single jewel, but a string of them."

"Pearls!" I couldn't help crying out. They both regarded me with pity and returned to their negotiations.

"Nothing so predictable," Irene murmured to me.

Mr. Tiffany nodded and went on. "These gems are large, matched diamonds, linked one after the other until they circle a dainty waist—and then fall to the floor. You frown, Miss Adler. Do you by some chance recognize my quarry?"

Irene shook her head. "Not at all, but the setting sounds quite . . . antique."

"If one considers the end of the last century antique—and at your tender age I imagine you do."

"And the piece is lost?"

"Indeed."

"Then if it were to be found, there would be none to claim it from the finder?"

"No."

Irene smiled suddenly. "No. Any of *her* relations are entangled in years, lost records and court battles beyond redeeming by now."

" *'Her,'* Miss Adler?"

"The original owner of your missing belt, Mr. Tiffany: the late Queen Marie Antoinette of the late, *antique* French monarchy."

"How—how did you know?" The old gentleman's high color drained from his cheeks and nose.

"I did not know, I guessed, for you could not resist giving me a hint. A piece as valuable as you describe could only have belonged to a royal house; it is now fair game, so with the French crown jewels rumored to come on the auction block some day not too distant, interest would naturally revive in such a missing piece."

"Egad, you are well informed for a humble avocational agent! I fear I underestimated you, young woman. Pinkerton's said you were quick and clever, but I begin to think you would seek to outdo me at my own game and take my prize for yourself."

"My knowledge springs from common sense, not secret information. I know nothing about your business, Mr. Tiffany, but I do know fashion. A belt of the type you describe could only belong to a queen, and a profligate one at that. As for the French crown jewels, I will never wear a stone from them, but cannot resist any rumor of them. Most women are highly intrigued by precious stones, but you long since have learned that from your business, no?"

"And should I trust such unnervingly precocious enterprise as you display?"

"Indubitably. Pinkerton's has recommended me. If I find your treasure while acting in your interests, wild stallions could not persuade me to retain it."

Like Jefferson Hope not many days past, Charles Lewis Tiffany leaned forward and stared into Irene Adler's magnificent dark gold eyes. She accepted his regard with regal indifference, as cat-calm in the certainty of her integrity as Marie Antoinette must have been in her queenship.

"Very well." Mr. Tiffany sounded winded, like a man who had just climbed a higher flight of stairs than he had anticipated. "The piece is called the Zone of Diamonds. It has not been seen since it vanished from the Paris Tuileries in 1848 as the Paris mobs overthrew Louis Philippe. Word is that it found its way to London. Later, in the upset of 1870, the Empress Eugenie fled with many of her jewels, and her confidant, Comte de Montglas, and took them to the Bank of England."

"Surely we are not to wrest this wonder from such a peerless institution?"

"The Empress's jewels are accounted for. I mention them merely to point out that imperiled French royalty have a historical habit of fleeing to England, and vice versa, which makes it even more likely that the Zone is in London. I've hired other inquiry agents to pursue it, but there is a subtler path that you may be ideally equipped to follow. A wealthy collector may have been keeping the Zone for his anonymous pleasure. Chances are high that he cannot resist showing his prize to an impressionable female now and then—"

"An impressionable female not his wife," Irene put in.

Mr. Tiffany nodded, relieved that she had spared him from outlining a sordid situation. "*Very* quick, Miss Adler. Since you are familiar with the theatrical world—"

"Where such impressionable females are most often to be found . . ."

"Indeed. It was felt you would be well placed to make discreet inquiries. I could offer such a gentleman an attractive profit. Perhaps the joys of private ownership have palled by now."

Irene considered, sipping tea. "I must tell you honestly, Mr. Tiffany, that this avenue of inquiry is unlikely to lead to your Zone of Diamonds. Hiring me may be a waste of your money and my time."

"I know it. But I am intent on leaving no possibility unexplored. It is true that a woman's delicacy could best elicit the information I seek, but I also hesitate to submit a woman to such an indelicate business."

"I perform indelicate businesses on the stage at every opportunity I am given, Mr. Tiffany, though I must admit my performing career wanes more than it waxes, which is why I undertake such assignments as yours."

"Still, to set you prowling about the unseemly underbelly of society—"

(I, taking frantic notes, nodded vigorous agreement.)

"Nonsense, Mr. Tiffany! One who has sung grand opera knows the artistic underside of seemliness intimately. I will do my utmost to uncover your diamonds; all it will take is a bit of persuasion. As you know, women are well supplied with that quality, for is it not their persuasive power that feeds your business? How else did Miss Lillian Russell persuade Mr. Diamond Jim Brady to bestow a pair of garters in the shape of spiders with emerald bodies and diamond and ruby legs upon her not insignificant . . . person . . . only last year?"

"Again you are exceedingly well informed," he conceded. "And you are yourself, if I may be so bold as to say so, Miss Adler, a terrifyingly persuasive example of your sex. How is it that you accept such assignments as mine when you could no doubt persuade some wealthy admirer to buy the Zone for yourself?"

"Because there is no satisfaction in buying anything, not even beauty, with other people's money," Irene said quickly. "Wealthy admirers are worth nothing if they are poor in honor—or seek that which is." Irene stood, extending her hand. "Thank you, Mr. Tiffany, for your commission. I will be able to reach you at Morley's until . . . ?"

"The twenty-eighth. There is not much time."

"I do not need time for such an endeavor; I need luck. Let us hope I have more of that quality than unhappy Marie Antoinette, who has lost not only her head, but apparently her best belt as well— a tragedy in the long history of attire."

Mr. Tiffany laughed at her parting shot, extended a cheque and bowed us both out. I consulted my lapel watch outside the door; it was not even eleven o'clock, yet I felt as if I had lived through an entire day, and a long one at that.

"How will you do it?" I demanded.

"Do what?" Irene was striding through the hotel lobby with the confidence of a long-time guest, though I could barely recognize where we had entered.

"Find this"—I lowered my voice—"missing object."

"I will inquire after it in elevated theatrical circles."

"You travel in no such circles."

"I soon will."

"How?"

She stopped beside the doors leading to the street. "How now, brown cow! We will resolve that as we go."

"We?"

Irene held Mr. Tiffany's cheque up to the daylight spilling through the leaded-glass panes. "Ah, generous. This will cover any expense and far beyond."

"How?" I repeated.

Irene whisked out the doors. In the square, Charles I sat on his horse in bronze splendor. A chill spring wind darted through the steed's frozen legs and straight for us. I mulled beheaded monarchs, fabulous jewels, the spoils of war and revolution, honor, danger and death.

Irene paused to draw something from the dark reaches of her muff.

"What is that?" I demanded, though I would not have been

surprised had she extracted Miss Lillian Russell's ghastly arachnid garters. The object was even worse. "Oh, Irene, you didn't? Not Mr. Tiffany's crumpets!"

"And his scones and muffins as well!"

"How?" I wailed.

"While you were busy taking notes and he was busy speaking. People seldom watch one when they speak, have you ever noticed that, only at the beginning and end? Mr. Tiffany spoke a great deal."

"Oh, Irene, what about your vaunted honor?"

"Honor is too grand to extend to such trivia as teacakes. Besides, we must eat until I accomplish Mr. Tiffany's commission and these are the tastiest pastries I've ever had. I couldn't bear to leave them and neither of us had time to consume much—"

"No, I was rather occupied with taking notes."

"So . . . I took muffins."

I looked at her. She looked at me. Morley's teacakes *were* sublime . . . I laughed first, but Irene laughed longest.

Chapter Six

A Walk on the Wilde Side

~~~

Part of the money advanced by Mr. Tiffany paid my tuition at a typing academy, at Irene's insistence. I had fastened on the notion of taking such instruction as a surer means of earning my living than the genteel occupation of governess.

I did not relish doing daily battle with the black beast whose stiff keys required me to acquire the dexterity of a pianist while converting spidery copperplate texts into neat, printed letters. However, as my skills improved I came to take satisfaction in making the contrary machine perform to my demands.

While I was occupied in the hard-fingered pursuit of knowledge, Irene disappeared from our lodgings for long hours and in varied garbs. One day she looked to be a charwoman, the next an exotic foreign noblewoman. I never knew when I glanced up from my "study" chair what figure should appear before me.

"Is it Carmen?" I asked one afternoon. Irene, her hair intermarried with rats and false pieces until an architecture of ebony obscured her natural chestnut shade, had paused to study herself in the cracked glass over the mantel.

I had meant to be sarcastic.

"Clever Nell," she said. "It *is* Carmen in contemporary street dress. Nothing like updating the classics, eh? Well, do I look the part of a disreputable actress past her first bloom?"

"Well into her petal-shedding phase, I should say." I took in rouged cheeks and soot-blackened lashes. "Is it safe to go out so attired?"

"Safe, yes. I have combed the theatres, taking care to disguise myself so that I am not recognized, and it has become clear that only among the *crème de la crème* will I have any opportunity of unearthing the Zone of Diamonds."

"And this is how you attire yourself to go among the *crème de la crème*? My good father was well advised when he urged me to shun the theatrical."

"This is how I dress to hear when the *crème* decide to meet and make clotted cream. No one knows better when the best social events are to take place than those never likely to be invited. I hobnob with the chorus and the supers these days."

"Supers?"

"Supernumeraries. Those poor souls paid a sixpence to speak no lines and provide a background presence—spear-carriers and vestal virgins, the unsung legions upon whose mute service modern operas and plays depend to achieve their glorious voices . . . Well?"

"You look dreadful, Irene, if that is what you are asking."

She glowed as if gifted with high praise.

"One more foray, dear friend, and I shall be ready to mount my true attack. You must help me."

"I will do all I can—if it is not dishonorable."

"No more dishonorable than muffins, I promise," Irene said gaily. "And much more fun."

With that she slipped out the door.

In time, I would come to recognize this phase of Irene's investigations as the emotional peak from which she launched the dangerous execution of her schemes. Her mood invariably soared as she neared the moment of truth—would her plan prove itself or not? Perhaps, like a soldier, she welcomed the thought of action—however perilous—over the dull daily minutiae of preparation. Perhaps she simply enjoyed her charade of costumes and relished performing the final act of her self-written drama.

At any rate, she returned home flushed beyond the offices of her rouge and told me that evening what she required of me. Uncustomarily, her approach was circumspect.

"You pour tea divinely, good divine's daughter that you are," Irene began complimentarily.

"My father was a humble country parson, not a 'divine.' But I do pour well."

"Then that is all you need do. I have obtained you a position."

"A position? Typing?"

"No, pouring!"

"Pouring?"

"At Mrs. Abraham Stoker's Sunday salon in Cheyne Walk. Surely even the most blase pourer could not object to a debut at such a fashionable address, very near the street of Carlyle et cetera."

"I don't care if . . . if Oliver Cromwell had lived there! I cannot go anywhere under false pretenses. I am not a maid."

"But you do pour beautifully."

"That, yes. But—"

"If you do not go, I shall have to carry on alone."

"When have you not?"

"Oh," said Irene, leaving her chair to kneel beside mine and turn her most plaintive expression on me, "I admit I was foolish. I was . . . so counting on your part in my plan. Perhaps I have misjudged—"

"Yes, you have. I will not go among strangers pretending to be other than I am."

"But you need only be yourself, and pour beautifully. Everyone will be there—Ellen Terry, Henry Irving, Jimmie Whistler, Oscar Wilde."

"Oscar Wilde! He is . . . abominable."

"Yes, and he will be present, with long hair and a lily, I'm sure.

And"—Irene paused as an expression I can only describe as diabolical touched her angelic features—"and also, I believe, Mrs. Edward Langtry. Lillie Langtry."

"Why would I wish to see an immoral woman like that?"

"I have no idea, dear Nell, but I do believe you do." She sat back on her heels and waited, Cheshire Cat-complacent.

"Oh, very well. My head is aching from studying the keyboard positions, at any rate." I set the textbook aside. "In what role will you be?"

"Darling Nell, I knew you would do it!" Irene was not demonstrative, but she actually embraced me. I began to regret my rash commitment, but I knew not how to retract it. "It will be a rare evening, believe me," she promised.

I had no doubt on that score at all.

After that, Irene closeted herself in her room, sewing. I wondered what costume should emerge.

"Lillie Langtry has already used black," I reminded her, "and black is your best color, although that may seem a contradiction in terms."

"Never mind," her voice would sing out.

I could have intruded into her bedchamber during the days that followed and satisfied my curiosity, but was too proud to display it. On Friday she produced her plainest black bombazine gown, now accoutered with fresh white collar and cuffs, and held it against me.

"Most fetching in a sober-sided, Puritan sort of way," she pronounced, and vanished again.

Sunday afternoon came round. I donned her adulterated gown along with a martyred air that came more readily and waited for Irene to reveal herself.

A rustle from her bedchamber made me turn. She emerged, clad from head to toe in white silk, but not the opposite of black, not pure and simple white. No, this gown had been festooned like a wedding cake in layers of tulle, lace and paste stones until Irene's figure glimmered like an opal.

"I believe," she said modestly as she accepted my gawking tribute, "that we must hire a hansom. I will let you off early. Remember,

27 Cheyne Walk. Do not be surprised by anything I might do, and when you see me, you must not recognize me."

"I will not—and do not," I commented rather acidly, and thus began my brief employment as a domestic servant.

⚜   ⚜   ⚜

Cheyne Walk was a fashionable street extending behind the Thames Embankment, valued for the river view it offered residents.

I walked to No. 27, having been duly put afoot several doors away, and went to the tradesmen's entrance, as behooved a servant. Here, much to my surprise, I was greeted as if a guest and a welcome one at that.

"I've come to pour," I announced to the harried cook garnishing platters of tidbits.

"You must be Huxleigh, the parson's daughter!" she hallooed as though hailing the Second Coming. "Saints be praised! Mrs. Stoker will be relieved to see you."

"I don't know how my arrival can relieve our distinguished host-ess," I began modestly.

"Tut, tut," the buxom cook hushed me. "Amy!" she called to a maid. "Tell the Missus that Miss Huxleigh's here, and in good time, too. What a jewel," she concluded, pinching my cheeks until they burned.

A pretty, rather cool-mannered woman rustled in shortly after, her taffeta train sweeping the kitchen stones.

"You've come to pour—Miss Huxleigh, isn't it?"

"Yes."

"Oh, thank God! Is there anything you require?" she asked, her pale hands wringing prettily with all their rings awinking.

"Only a seat and the proper equipment."

The lady laughed. "You must think us mad. But the maid who poured last Sunday cast a cupful of hot tea over Mr. Whistler's hand. Such an uproar! Think what symphonies in pigment have not been fashioned this week because of it. Come, I'll show you the table."

She pivoted sharply so her train would properly follow and led me upstairs into a handsome drawing room where an even handsomer silver service stood guard over snowy linen and a regiment of empty cups and saucers.

"Irene—Miss Adler, that is—explained that you have the steadiest hand in London, having poured for a Shropshire parson, and we do know how clumsy country gentry can be." Mrs. Stoker beamed happily while I ensconced myself behind the white linen and assumed my most competent demeanor. "Is there anything you require, my dear?"

"Nothing at all, save that the samovar be kept filled and hot."

"Oh, the maid can manage *that*. It's the handling of the china and its contents that are needed."

She pivoted again and fluttered off as a towering, red-bearded gentleman paused in the archway, leaving me to regard an empty room.

It was not to remain so. As the clock struck three guests began to arrive. I had never seen such an assortment in my life. Each seemed to have stepped from some garish theatrical poster. I sat among these milling strangers, dispensing tea as I had been taught, my only words a dulcet "Milk?" . . . a tart "Lemon?" . . . and a simpering "Sugar?"

Ladies in languishing Aesthetic dress, their polonaises edged in Greek key embroidery and their hair banded by golden fillets, slouched past, redolent of the glories that were Greece. Sunflowers and lilies, the favored flowers of the Aesthetic movement, decorated the gowns. I even spied a green carnation in one gentleman's lapel and began to regard the towering Redbeard, in conventional dress for all his larger-than-life size, as a bulwark of conventionality.

It became a game to pick out famous figures from their cartoon versions in *Punch:* the dapper little man in cutaway coat and monocle, a lightning strike of white streaking his thick black hair—the very Mr. James McNeill Whistler whose hand had suffered from the ministrations of my predecessor.

I trembled inwardly as he approached my post. "Tea, sir?" I inquired.

The small hands, so delicate for a man's, twitched. "If you can pour it into a cup instead of a cupped hand, my good woman," he shrilled in an American accent.

This I managed, even while searching the crowd for the one familiar figure I had expected—Irene's. Where was she? Surely she was not asking our cabman to drive endlessly along the river?

"My earnest congratulations," Mr. Whistler remarked in Prussic acid tones as he gazed into the limpidity of his unadorned tea. He eyed the cup. "Blue china. Florence has improved her taste since last week—in both receptacle and tea mistress."

With that terse praise he moved on. A flurry near the archway caused a universal pause. A woman had arrived, but it was not Irene. I could only see thick, flowing hair and languid hands. Gentlemen buzzed around her like bees at a honey hive. I stared beyond them, wondering what awful eventuality had occasioned Irene's absence.

"You pour with the liquid rhythm of a villanelle," said a deep, musical voice at my elbow. My elbow! I looked down to find a large young man half-reclining on the carpet, gazing up at me like a spaniel through wings of long brown hair.

"I beg your pardon?" said I.

"And well you should for wasting the poetry of your pouring on this callow mob. You should pour only for a chosen, appreciative few."

"Indeed." As a parson's daughter I had found that word an adequate response to almost any situation.

"Quite right to keep your own counsel, prim nymph of the afternoon libation, as utterly, utterly cool as a marble chessboard, mute as concealed pain."

"Would you like a cup of tea, is that it?"

Long pale hands fanned into ten eloquently separate fingers— an overblown flower losing its petals. Everything about my admirer drooped—his shoulder-length hair, his soft velvet tie, the green carnation in his lapel and most of all, his expression.

"I seek ambrosia," he whispered.

"I am very sorry. I'm not serving any of that. Perhaps the punch table—"

"Cruel sprite of ancient rites. I withdraw, but my admiration remains."

With that the odd young man rose—which took some time as he, like Redbeard, towered over six feet when standing—and ebbed into the murmuring clusters.

Another hush. This time the woman who entered the room was she whom I expected—Irene, calla-lilly grand in her white gown. She was accompanied by a man I had never seen. I blinked and almost spilled a drop of tea.

"So sorry, Mr."—I looked up and suddenly knew Redbeard's identity—Abraham Stoker, the great actor Henry Irving's manager, properly known as "Bram." "Mr. Stoker."

Our host was watching Irene with as much puzzlement as myself and ambled off to survey her at close hand. Soon she had commanded her own swarm of humming gentlemen—Mr. Whistler, whose shrill voice made up for his short stature in asserting his presence, Mr. Stoker, the melancholy young poet and a half-dozen others.

Her escort, an unremarkable man who apparently did not mind being supplanted, presented himself at my station. "All is well?" he hissed as I served him weak tea with two slices of lemon, as requested.

"Of course."

"She said I was to keep an eye on you."

"Who are you?" I asked. I knew who "she" was.

"Pinkerton," he whispered, then winked and withdrew with his teacup.

I don't know why I was to have an eye kept on me, for all eyes were on Irene. Her ringing voice announced her progress as she sailed from group to group around the long room.

"Oh, this fashion for Aesthetics has its attractions, chiefly in its practitioners," she would say with a nod to all the oddly attired gentlemen. "And Mr. Tiffany was telling me only the other day of his preference for the ingeniously set semi-precious stone over the too-flagrant appeal of emeralds, sapphires, rubies and diamonds."

"So true," said he who had admired the perfection of my pouring. "Precious gems offer only four colors, but semi-precious stones rainbow the world. Art is not to be found in crude cost, but in effect and emotion."

"We know *your* too-too opinions, Oscar! What of the lady's?" someone gibed.

I sat appalled. Every word that Irene had uttered was truth— seen through a wavy glass. Heads had inclined wisely around her while she quoted Mr. Tiffany as if he were a favored friend, as if she were intimate with the wearing of jewels.

"I myself remain hopelessly partial to the gaudy appeal of fine stones, like diamonds," she spoke again, no doubt as honestly.

"Why not?" a gentleman quipped. "They bring out the fire of your eyes."

"Her eyes are crystals of seared topaz whose fire is to be most found in the hearts of her ardent admirers," another wit riposted.

Irene dodged these fulsome compliments and surfaced in the center of another group, always probing for news of diamonds. Her weapon was our scant half-hour with the American king of jewels.

"Mr. Tiffany was telling me of a magnificent corsage his artisans are readying for a future Paris Exposition," she whispered to the ladies. One in particular bowed her head to better hear the news, and in that cut-steel profile I recognized at last the infamous Lillie Langtry.

"Oh!" complained the young woman beside me whose white gloves had been baptized by a few tea drops as my eye fixed upon the Jersey Lily. So does idle curiosity lead to a downfall.

I mopped the mess up with a napkin and listened for more news of this mythical diamond corsage, for Mr. Tiffany had not breathed a word of it to either of us.

"A corsage?" Lillie Langtry repeated in her clear voice. "That does not sound a worthy centerpiece for a major exhibition."

"Not a simple shoulder corsage, my dear, but a lacework of two thousand diamonds swagged from shoulder to bosom to the opposite hip, thus," Irene explained, gesturing appropriately to her figure and thus drawing the gentlemen again.

The women sighed and gasped.

"There will be diamond roses at shoulder, center bosom and hip," Irene added. "Of course such a piece will be years in the making. A pity that the fashion for diamonds is spent. Mr. Tiffany wastes his time."

"Perhaps not," put in a portly gentleman who drank a cerise punch that echoed his choleric features. "There was talk years ago of a singular diamond belt, all matched stones falling to the floor in several strings, like a waterfall."

"Now that would be an Aesthetic application of a *bourgeois* stone," the young poet declared, "tied into a belt to secure a lady's Grecian draperies or a snood to hold her flowing hair."

"A thing of myth, no doubt, Oscar," jeered Mr. Whistler, "as is Tiffany's corsage. I'll believe such fabulous artifacts when I see them—and when I do, I'll grind them to powder and use them in my paints. The cool simplicity of Japanese blue-ware outshines the brightest French-cut stones."

"Was it French, do you think, Mr. Whistler? That belt?" Irene put in quickly.

"I don't know what the deuce it was, Miss Adler, or even *that* it was. Nor do I care."

"Norton did," the florid-faced man put in. "Great fancier of diamonds. Said there was a fortune in them. Now the Dutch own them all and half of South Africa as well, and we pay a pretty price for such vices as diamonds."

"Norton?" Irene inquired brightly.

"Must be dead by now," the gentleman rambled. "Old Norton. Wife had all the money, you know. One of Sheridan's granddaughters—three dazzlers with flashing dark eyes and wit to go with. Wrote verse and novels, you know. Left her husband, too—litigious barrister, no damn good, rotter through and through, but that's another story. She didn't have much for diamonds, but her novels made a pretty penny to buy paste with—until old Norton took it all in a lawsuit."

"Tell us more of Mr. Tiffany's fabulous corsage," a woman begged.

"I must not," Irene said quickly. "It is a secret. I have said too much already."

"Why is it that tales of rare jewels are always secrets?" drawled a pallid young man with lank flaxen hair.

"That is what makes them so rare," put in the poet.

Everyone laughed and the conversation turned. Irene remained abstracted, perhaps wondering how to divert the talk to her purpose again. But the stream of chitchat babbled on, interrupted only by the rougher rapids of witty venom from Mr. Whistler or the languid poet.

One by one and two by two the guests departed. I knew Irene had capitulated when she collected the quiet gentleman and withdrew despite all pleadings that she stay. Lillie Langtry left only then, drawing the remaining lone gentlemen after her in a train.

Mrs. Stoker finally revisited my table. "Nicely done, Miss Huxleigh. May we count on you for Sunday next?"

"No! That is, I will not be able to come here again."

"Oh?"

"It is not possible. I am sorry."

"Another position? But this is for a few hours only. Perhaps you can manage it."

"I cannot," I said firmly, trying to excuse myself with the truth. "I am not comfortable in such a role."

"Ah, you disapprove of our set. That is understandable, given your clerical background. Well, I cannot argue with philosophical differences. Cook will pay you on your way out. Good day."

My pay was a half-sovereign, nearly enough to make me reconsider. I waited where Irene had left me, and a hansom soon rattled up. Her escort leaped out to aid me inside, then tipped his hat and walked down the road.

"You were not planning to go alone at all," I reproached Irene. "You did not tell me about Mr. Pinkerton."

"A lady needs an escort, however perfunctory, but I required a more sensitive observer than he. We will have a tea party post-mortem by the hearth tonight. Did you manage to acquire any delicacies for dinner? You had motive and opportunity. Oh, do not bestir yourself so; I already feared as much. We shall have Mrs. Minucci's lasagna— again. By the bye, it is not Mr. Pinkerton. The gentleman is *a* Pinkerton, a fellow London agent, only one of several."

"Hmm. And what have you achieved by making a spectacle of yourself and a pourer of me?"

"A great deal. Someone mentioned the Zone. I shall have to look into the matter of 'old Norton' further."

"But he's dead!"

"The dead, my dear Nell, are often the surest source of knowledge. After the agony columns, you would do well to study the obituaries. Whole novels by Thackery and Hardy, scores of Wagnerian operas and dozens of Webster's 'White Devils' and 'Duchesses of Malfi' lie hidden among those succinct little threnodies to perished greengrocers and consumptive debutantes.

"Survivors and heirs, old family wounds and fresh new wills, marriage and remarriage, greed and sorrow. Sometimes I even suspect that they contain the traces of murder never found out—murder by hand and more frequently murder by word. The latter is not a criminal act but can be equally lethal."

This thrilling monologue, rendered with affecting drama, held me rapt but dubious. "You read all this into the daily obituaries, Irene?"

She simply smiled. "The dead speak volumes. And why not? Who—at last—is to contradict them?"

Chapter Seven

Unexpected Visitors

~~~

The jaunt to Cheyne Walk might not have uncovered the Zone of Diamonds, but it showed me Irene Adler playing a role in which I had never seen her: *femme fatale*.

I had always assumed that Irene's worldliness far exceeded mine and usually avoided speculating as to what extent. Certainly she rivaled the Sphinx in keeping silent on her past. As for the present, while she associated professionally with men, I saw no signs that the connections were anything other than that. I could never have stomached living with a courtesan, no matter how discreet.

Yet it puzzled me that a woman of Irene's beauty should ignore the giddy temptations presented to unattached women in her position. The only explanation was the pride she took in her many talents; she would not spend them cheaply—and most women cede their own pursuits when they wed (or even when they stoop to being some man's mistress), becoming more fabled for their role than their reality.

Then, too, possibly Irene had been wounded in an early romantic attachment and henceforward escaped the blandishments of hearts, flowers and other less sentimental realities that lurk beneath the

Valentine lacework. Even in my limited experience, romantic stir-rings brought painful confusion rather than joy.

Whatever my speculations, though Irene violated every minor convention governing a woman of good reputation during our asso-ciation, I never saw her bow in the least to behavior that hinted at the sordid scandal so beloved of the newspapers.

The spring of 1882—and of Irene's dazzling debut into Chelsea society as a personality, if not a gainfully employed artiste—brought sweeping changes to our chambers high above the operatic warbles of Saffron Hill street peddlers.

First, if I may edge my own small achievement to the fore, I re-ceived certification as a qualified "typewriter girl," as an operator of the new typewriting instrument was now called. The document, en-graved in a spidery longhand, struck me as incongruous given the me-chanical skill it celebrated.

I soon found myself in modest demand as a "temporary" em-ployee called into offices throughout the City and surrounding vil-lages to spin copperplate into cold type, so to speak. Other than needing spectacles—a tasteful if inhalation-inhibiting pince-nez that perched upon the bridge of my nose—to decipher these often illegi-ble scribblings, I found the work congenial. Unraveling the mysteries of various hands to produce readable type gave me a strange satisfac-tion. In grander moments, I saw myself as revealing Rosetta Stones of lost meaning to a waiting world.

Surprisingly, my nomadic employment suited me. Perhaps I had acquired Irene's taste for the ebb and flow of sudden assignments. More likely, my humiliating experience at Whiteley's had converted me to the benefits of will-'o-the-wispery: since I seldom stayed long at any establishment there was small opportunity to make enemies or edge into office intrigues.

I became a fearless patron of the ubiquitous omnibus and soon knew the major streets of London as if they were limned upon my palm. I had money in my handbag and feathers on my new workaday bonnet. In other words, I felt myself an independent woman.

If Parson Huxleigh's orphan daughter was surviving, Irene Adler was thriving. Her jaunt to Bram Stoker's tea had earned her an audition for the latest Gilbert & Sullivan light opera at the newly built Savoy Theatre on the Embankment. Her soon-won role did not suit her voice, she said dismissively, but she relished immersion in the theatrical life again and rigorously pursued the Zone of Diamonds among the Chelsea set.

I fretted that she must travel about town so late at night, but as usual was dismissed.

"You worry about me, Nell? You who so nearly donated all your worldly goods to a Whitechapel waif when we met? My profession requires the freedom of the city. I must go about alone at night; how else would I rehearse and perform?"

"I would feel better if you had escort home."

"Oh, that could be arranged," Irene said with flashing eyes. "A good many gentlemen of the town stand ready to escort even a bit player like myself home after the performance—with a detour to a private restaurant, a carriage ride through Hyde Park . . . No doubt you should sleep easier if I obtained such shepherding."

"Heavens, no! It's simply that I worry for your safety."

"Worry not. I have my devices."

"Wit will not talk you out of every corner," I warned.

"This will." Irene produced a sinister little revolver from her all-purpose muff.

"Gracious! I've never seen such a fierce mechanism. It's somehow more intimidating than a typewriter was to me at first."

"It's meant to be intimidating, darling Nell."

"You could actually discharge it at someone?"

"If it meant my life."

"Put it away! Its very existence proves that you take my point. London streets at night are dangerous for a woman alone."

"It is dangerous for a woman alone anywhere at any time," Irene retorted. "Such is the nature of the society and century in which we live. It is up to women to reverse the situation."

"You fancy yourself as dangerous?" I had never thought of a woman as a weapon, only as a bulwark and that of the home, not the larger society.

"Oh, I am very dangerous, Nell. You have no idea what a Bohemian you reside with. If I had my way, we would live in a very different world." She smiled and tucked the gleaming black revolver into a pocket inside her muff. "And I doubt you'd like it all."

"Hmph," I sniffed, knowing better than to pursue such a conversation. Irene would have her anarchist moods. I refused to let my own sensible opinions serve as a lucifer to light her incendiary ideas.

So Irene came and went at her late hours, and I came and went at my more conventional times. Often our paths would not cross for days. It was mere chance that I happened to be at home one windy and wet April afternoon when a note was delivered to Irene, who had risen late and was sipping chocolate in her Oriental wrap.

A sudden rustle of stiff silk jolted me from the latest novel of Mrs. Oliphant, which I had obtained at a circulating library.

"We must neaten up at once, Nell! We are to have an eminent guest."

"A guest?" I leapt up guiltily, straightening the antimacassars covering my easy chair's worn arms. Our only guests hitherto had been Mr. and Mrs. Minucci or their singularly untalented daughter, Sofia.

I began sweeping the scattered newsprint into the fireplace to both warm our environs and eliminate clutter.

"Not the Agony Column!" Irene shrieked, rushing to rescue the lurid pages from the blaze. "And it is ourselves we must first make presentable—very presentable. Mr. Oscar Wilde is to arrive at three."

"Oh. Him." I dropped the armful of ribbons I had swept from the seat of Irene's sewing chair back to the cushion. "A most nonsensical person. I don't doubt that disarray 'inspires' him."

Irene paced, fanning the note before her face. "However you judge him, he is a man of the moment in London's artistic circles. Notorious, yes, but with notoriety comes . . . notice. This is exactly what my poor stalled career needs. And"—she turned triumphantly to me, her eyes shining—"he mentions a private matter I might help with. I believe he is a client."

"Truly, Irene, I prefer you walking out at all hours to rehearse an opera over continuing in this tawdry investigative sideline of yours. Better Mr. Wilde be a sponsor than a client."

"Why not both?" Irene said lightly. "Besides, I am so put out at my failure with the Zone of Diamonds. All my inquiries have led no further than this 'old Norton,' whom I begin to swear does not and never did exist. If I successfully assist Oscar Wilde, who knows what doors shall open to me?"

"Unsavory ones, I've no doubt," I murmured.

"But I am a ruin!" she suddenly cried, shaking out her wrap. "I must make myself respectable."

I held my tongue as Irene dashed into her chamber, leaving me to tidy the main room and conceal my daybed niche behind the threadbare curtains that masked it. With our best efforts at our separate talents—mine domestic and Irene's cosmetic—our rooms and persons were ordered if not ordinary by three o'clock.

A knock did not come at our door until three-twenty. Irene opened it to the same tall, pale young man who had praised my pouring abilities at the Stokers' reception. Of course I did not expect him to remember me.

"Miss Adler." He bore a bouquet wrapped in tissue, which he changed from hand to hand as I unobtrusively removed his damp greatcoat and arranged it on the unnamed (and unclothed) dressmaker's dummy that Irene used in the front room as a coat rack.

Mr. Wilde noted the bizarre stratagem with an approving nod and began unpeeling wet tissue from the wind-chilled flowers. I thought of onion skins.

"I confess myself at a loss, Miss Adler, in selecting a floral offering to adequately pay you tribute. I rejected the lily for obvious reasons: another, although equal, beauty has claimed it. The sunflower, although greatly favored, is too full-blown for your refined loveliness. I considered the regal iris, but it is a touch common. Thus I have—"

Oh, get on with it, I thought uncharitably while subsiding into the background. Irene smiled politely at this flowery discourse as if she cared what blossoms he would produce. They would be wilted within a week in any case.

"—decided upon the rare Holland tulip!" With this he whisked away the last of the tissue, revealing a cluster of blood-purple blooms ruffled to cerise along their extravagant edges. Even I gasped at their glory.

"They are called Borgia Tears, but, alas, have no scent."

Irene laughed, delighted, as she took the glamorous bouquet. "You are not only a wit and poet, Mr. Wilde, but a sublime diplomat. You have chosen perfectly—give me the royal color and velvet sheen of the opera house curtain, give me mystery and drama over mere odor any day."

"And for your charming companion . . ." Here, to my horror, Mr. Wilde turned to me. "I see you were as taken with her pouring at the Stokers' as I and have stolen her away to preside at your hearth. I anticipated no other lady, but could not resist lily of the valley at the florist's for my rooms. Accept this nosegay, dear Miss . . . ?"

Aghast, I stood silent.

"Huxleigh," Irene trilled loudly as she settled the tulips in a white pitcher. "Miss Penelope Huxleigh, late of Shropshire."

"Penelope!" The poet seized upon my ungainly classical name as a rat terrier upon a bone. "Wise and loyal wife, clever and faithful spirit of hearth and home. These small blossoms swoon with scent and are said to attract nightingales to warble by one's bed. Alas, this humble human nightingale will have to suffice for you."

Picturing Mr. Oscar Wilde warbling by my bed was ludicrous enough to make me pale as I seized the nosegay and installed it in a tumbler on the table.

"Penelope was a fool," I muttered ungraciously. "I certainly should have never taken that bounder Ulysses back after he'd wandered all around the Wrekin."

"Wrekin?" The poet blinked, silenced.

"A Shropshire expression, Mr. Wilde. The Wrekin is a small mountain, which is what you are making of my poor molehill of

virtues. But pray excuse me; I have 'domestic duties' to attend to."
Here I withdrew to my daybed niche and took up some darning.

My exit, although I was still within earshot and had left the
draperies agape, seemed to wilt the poet's demeanor until it drooped
like the soft cravat of yellow silk at his throat. Irene led him to the
shawl-draped sofa, where he sat languidly. She, being corseted, could
affect no such easy posture.

"Your note mentioned a private matter, Mr. Wilde."

He glanced in my direction.

"Miss Huxleigh is more than discreet, as I'm sure you discern.
My dear Nell would no more reveal a secret not her own than a mar-
tyr would deny her God."

"Of course. But the matter is extremely . . . delicate and of the
most personal nature."

"I see," said Irene, her tone unencouraging. "I have occasionally
shed light on mysterious events, but not on the shadows of the heart,
I fear. I am no go-between."

"Certainly not! Though the difficulty began as a matter of the
heart, I fear it comes down to the rightful return of property now."

"As do so many so-called matters of the heart, ultimately. What
is the property in question, Mr. Wilde?"

"A gold cross—not of any great worth, I suppose, but valuable to
me as a memento. You may not be aware that in the late seventies I
was an admirer of that peerless beauty, Florence Balcombe. In that
capacity I gave her the cross, as well as assorted poems and even a
pencil portrait from my own hand." The poet's long melancholy face
lifted in a smile. "I secretly sent a floral crown this past January when
she made her Lyceum debut as one of a hundred vestal virgins in *The
Cup*. Ellen Terry herself gave Florrie the offering, though she never
revealed the sender."

"Of course, Florence Balcombe is no vestal virgin now," Irene
pointed out. "She is Mrs. Bram Stoker, is she not, and the mother of
a son, Noel?"

"Yes. And has been for a few years. Quite frankly, I would have
married her, but she preferred another Irishman, and who am I to

quarrel with so excellent a choice? Bram is such a hearty, straightforward fellow that I cannot be too bitter. But I would like my cross of gold back."

"Then ask for it."

"Ah, so direct, Miss Adler. After much hinting, that is exactly what I did. Florrie refused."

"Refused? I suppose by rights it is hers, but the value was trifling?" He nodded and Irene controlled her expression. "Have you considered that the lovely Florence still harbors a *tendresse* for you that prevents her from relinquishing your gift?"

"My first assumption," he admitted, "and I should respect her understandable sentiment, but she has shown an evasion in discussing the subject that is quite inexplicable. The cross is precious to my past; since Florrie is no longer mine in the present, I should like it back and she should be more than willing to return it. Her refusal is most . . . odd."

"What do you expect me to do?"

"Speak to Florence. Find out at least why she so unreasonably refuses to give it up. Knowing her motives would compensate for the possession of the cross."

"You are an easily satisfied creditor, Mr. Wilde. I shall inquire into the matter, but it is her business, at bottom."

"Of course." The poet stood and took Irene's hand, bowing low over it. "I shall be most grateful."

"Why come to me for such a service?"

"You are a woman of wit. You would have made a poetess, I think, except that when you see into the human soul you keep it to yourself and to your own ends. You are also possessed of a ceaseless curiosity. Witness your questions about this man Norton. You strike me as one bold enough to broach any subject with anyone. But then, you are American."

"Indeed I am," Irene said as she retrieved his greatcoat and showed him out. "I will look into the matter and let you know the result."

"A popinjay," I sang from my corner as soon as the door had

closed. "Shan't it be embarrassing to quiz Florence Stoker? And what will he pay you, after all, but compliments and posies?"

"Wilde's good will is worth a hundred pounds. What he declares to be fashionable, is. Look at his devotion to Lillie Langtry; it accounts in good part for her notoriety."

Irene had thrown herself on the sofa in that peculiar stiff, supine attitude seen in photographs of Sarah Bernhardt or the painted ladies of the pre-Raphaelites. Corseted "flowers" do not bend well; no wonder the Jersey Lily eschewed whalebone. Still, Irene managed to look comfortable despite her position.

"Ah, that Wilde Irish vanity!" she reflected. "I wager that Florence Stoker has utterly unsentimental reasons for keeping Oscar Wilde's cross. They should be interesting to discover. I am tired of Mr. Tiffany's foolish Zone, at any rate!" she burst out, putting a hand to her forehead as if an ache throbbed there. "A cul-de-sac, as I feared. I dread reporting my failure," she added morosely, "but he leaves shortly and I must."

A knock at the door interrupted her. I answered it to find thin-faced little Sofia—she looked like a shriveled rabbit—in the passage.

"A genelmun below said to give you this."

I took a card and moved into the pale light of our dying fire. "That's . . . odd."

"Another visitor? I can't! One poet is wearing enough. Send whoever it is away. How rude to call without notice."

"I suppose I could scrawl a dismissal on his card and send it back with Sofia, but Mr. Norton might not call again—"

"Good! Let him go to blazes—Mr. *Norton!*" Irene sat bolt upright in defiance of the laws of corsetry. "My Lord. Yes, Sofia child, tell Mr. Norton he may come up. Nell, what does the card say?"

She rushed over to pry it from my hand.

"Only his name and address," I explained.

"The Temple. He is a barrister—the very one!"

"A note on the back requests to see you, if you'd care to turn it over."

"Such hasty, bold strokes. No sign of feebleness here. Old Norton is spry. Why did no one know of him? Why come to me? Quick, Nell, I need an impartial witness. Behind the arras, my love. You must take notes; my wits are too addled to be at their usual pitch. Hide yourself! Be quiet, like the dead; be my ears. Perhaps I will have good news for Mr. Tiffany after all. Oh, what a coup!"

"I am not an eavesdropper!" I protested through the muffling curtains just as a knock thundered on the door.

It clapped again, that external thunder, before Irene could answer. I heard the knob turn and the hinges squeak. Then silence. I considered that Old Norton must be vigorous to muster so commanding a knock at his age.

"Miss Adler?" a deep male voice barked.

He was testy, I concluded, despite his apparent robust health.

Irene's voice sounded strangled with surprise as she replied. "I am Irene Adler. Do . . . come in, Mr. Norton."

Her invitation was uttered just as a pair of boots thumped over our sadly thin rugs. I envisioned a stout old gent, his ruddy face bristling with white muttonchop whiskers, his stomach bowed out like a punch bowl. Father William of the poem, if you will.

This Dickensian worthy stalked only in my imagination, but being restricted to sound alone made for fascinating speculations. I leaned my ear against the draperies.

"You seem surprised to see me," the gentleman observed.

"I am indeed. Won't you sit down?"

"That will not be necessary. What I have to say to you, Miss Adler, does not require civilities. You may sit if you wish. I fancy you will need to before I'm done."

"Indeed," Irene murmured faintly, sounding not at all like herself. I heard her clothing rustle as she followed his suggestion. His boots began pacing before the fire, which must have paled to ashes by now.

"To what do I owe your visit?" she inquired.

"To your damn impertinent questions into my family life!"

"*Your* family life?"

"Don't deny that you haven't been making inquiries about a certain Norton to every man jack around! I won't have you stirring up the family scandal just when tongues have stopped wagging at last. I warn you—I'm a barrister and I know how to deal with people of your sort."

"And just what is 'my sort,' Mr. Norton?" Irene asked, much too calmly.

The voice dismissed the matter even as it replied. "Some kind of performer, I understand. That's irrelevant. I don't care if you're a ragpicker; your vicious inquiries into my family history must stop!"

"My profession is not irrelevant to me, Mr. Norton. And it happens that I am a vocalist and an actress."

He snorted. "So claims Lillie Langtry these days."

"She is an upstart. I am a long-time student of my art. And I do not sell soap."

"I don't give a fig for what you do—so long as it does not include snooping into my family matters. You may ride a horse bareback and whistle 'Yankee Doodle Dandy,' for all I care."

"I also," Irene went on, serenely ignoring him, "act as a private inquiry agent on occasion. Perhaps it is in this professional capacity that my actions have so troubled you."

The boots' restless pacing stopped. "Someone *hired* you to rake up my family background? I don't believe it!"

"Why else should anyone want to delve into such an unpleasant clan?" Irene retorted. "Of course they must be *paid* to do it!"

I could imagine the fury pinking her cheeks and felt very sorry for old Mr. Norton.

"This is more perfidious than I had imagined," he retorted. "If you think that being a hireling of some gossip entitles you to assume the airs of a profession, you are sadly mistaken. In the eyes of the law you are an irresponsible and malicious slanderer—a mere tale-bearer. If I learn that you continue in your despicable inquiries, I will take whatever action—legal or otherwise—to ensure that you stop. Do I make myself clear, Miss Adler?"

A serpentine rasp of silk; she stood to confront him. I dared to part the curtain seam and press my eyelashes against the tiny split. Irene's profile looked carved in alabaster. Her cheeks were flaming. Of old Norton I could see nothing but a pair of wet black boot-toes pressing into the hem of Irene's skirt.

"I thought we were beyond courtesies, Mr. Norton," she pointed out in cold, silken tones.

"You will see how far beyond courtesy I am if you force me to it. Stop this inquiry now, while you can."

"And is that the mark of *your* profession—threats?"

"If you threaten me and mine, you shall be answered in kind."

The boots rushed to the door, which screamed open on its hinges, then banged shut on the man's exit. Boots thumped down the stairs until they dwindled into only the patter of rain on our roof. I launched myself at the bowed window, leaning over the daybed to press my nose against the rainstained pane of glass.

A hansom waited below, its shiny black paint greasy under the gathering raindrops. A figure in a plush velvet top hat burst from our building, pausing only to turn and stare up at our window. I flattened myself out of sight against the wall, but not before he spied me, I fear.

When I peered out again, the man was bounding spryly inside the cab. Mr. Norton must have been in a tearing rage indeed to have taken so fine a hat out into the rain.

The reins danced on the horse's slick flanks and then the hansom was rattling away. Something crackled like distant thunder beside me—Irene's taffeta gown crushing as she crowded into the bay with me.

She leaned her hot cheek on the icy glass as the hansom disappeared. I had never seen her so agitated, whether from rage or triumph it was difficult to tell.

"What an insufferable, odious man, Nell! But he told me the one thing he would never have wished me to know."

"What is that?"

"That there is something to Mr. Tiffany's Zone of Diamonds story. If I don't get to the bottom of it in Mr. Tiffany's employ I shall pursue it on my own. 'My sort,' indeed! Mr. Norton has no idea what my sort is if he thinks to discourage Irene Adler so cheaply."

Chapter Eight

In Dutch with Diamonds

⟿⟿

The violin reclined on the velvet half-shell of its open case. The pipe lay careened in a vacant gravy boat. Scattered *Daily Telegraph* pages erected tents around the chamber, like an occupying army.

Finding the Baker Street rooms in such disarray stirred my suspicions. I opened drawers and moved papers in search of the telltale syringe, but found no trace of my friend Sherlock Holmes's usual retreat to a seven percent solution in the face of ennui or idleness.

I had settled down to reading the newspaper I had reassembled when the door opened and an odor of onions and charcoal invaded the air.

A figure occupied the threshold, a stooped, white-bearded prophetic figure whose eyes were sunken in tubercular circles of garnet-shaded skin.

"I say, sir," I began indignantly at this unheralded intrusion. The apparition rambled toward me, its rusty black garb rustling. I thought momentarily of Poe's grim raven, then caught a sudden sly glimmer about the eyes.

"Holmes? Where on earth have you been now?"

My friend's laughter pealed from the stranger's lips as he straightened, doffed his shapeless black hat and collapsed on a chair.

"Whitechapel, my dear Watson. It's clear that my little disguises no longer deceive you. Luckily, they do better among the subjects of my inquiries."

"Whitechapel! What can draw you to such a slum?"

"Diamonds, my friend, a trail of gemstones long enough to gird a queen."

"You have discovered the Tiffany diamonds? Where?"

"Oho, already you deem them found and in our client's possession. I fear the case will not end so neatly. Yet I have traced them from Paris to London, and they have not reappeared on the market, so their first purchaser has them still."

"You know who has them?"

"Of course, Watson. It was a simple matter."

"That answers Mr. Tiffany's quest, then."

"Not quite, Watson, and that is where the greater mystery begins. The apparent owner vanished five years ago. Utterly. And with him, the diamonds."

"Perhaps you could report the events in sequence," I suggested, "instead of getting a fellow's expectations up only to dash them down again."

"Still hoping for grist for another tale, eh? This will be an unfinished symphony of yours, I venture to predict. You wonder at my garb; it explains itself if I tell you that there are no persons more expert in the disposition of fine stones than the Jewish diamond merchants of Holland."

"Now I recognize your role—an aged rabbi."

"An aged, learned rabbi, Watson. In such guise I can go among the merchants and glean rare nuggets of information. Who would believe that the narrow, rat-and-river-fog-ridden byways of Whitechapel would hold dealers in peerless gems as well as ragpickers, strumpets and thieves? The world's Christian nations did themselves a great disservice centuries ago when they forbade Jews all trades but the managing of money. As Rothschild and Disraeli demonstrate in our century, greatness will not be denied no matter the creed."

"But only the most impoverished Jews live in Whitechapel, Holmes. What can you learn from so low a layer of society?"

"The movements of the Zone of Diamonds, Watson, if an inanimate object can be said to progress." Holmes began peeling the spirit gum from his hollow cheeks, tearing away the patriarch's beard as if it were a soap wrapper.

"And?"

"All business today, eh, Watson? No time for social digressions. And you accuse *me* of indifference to the major political issues of our time? The facts are these. The Zone's timetable is as well ordered as the Great Western Railway.

"We know that the Zone vanished in 1848 when the Parisian mob overthrew Louis Philippe and managed to make off with some rarities from the royal vaults, as even the most righteously maddened mobs generally do. The first individual known to possess the Zone was Jean Claude Renard, a foxy fellow in more than name only, who brought it immediately to London. Here he found a Dutch diamond dealer, Zellerstein, who recognized that the Zone was as much a liability as a treasure in its present form.

"Renard insisted that Zellerstein find an immediate buyer, no matter how much such haste lowered the price." Holmes interrupted his narrative to nod my way. "Hand me my pipe, will you, Watson? A day spent stooping requires a relaxing ritual."

I fretted while Holmes primed the pipe to his satisfaction and lit it. When smoke was haloing his half-altered features he resumed the tale.

"This was a bit of luck for my inquiries. Had Renard broken the belt into separate stones, it would be as lost to history as chicken feed in a henyard. However, enough of the patriot was left in Renard that he disliked destroying such a spectacular jewel of French manufacture; he insisted the piece be sold whole, which complicated Zellerstein's mission and extenuated it. The younger Zellerstein—my informant, by the way—was but a child when this transpired, as were we all, but he well recalls seeing the Zone. 'A string of rainbows,' his young imagination named it.

"At any rate, Zellerstein let the Zone's availability be known amongst those of the nobility and certain wealthy tradesmen who would not stick at an object's provenance. By 1849, it was rumored to be everywhere, like the Scarlet Pimpernel. The notable would-be owners include Alfred Krupp, Alexander II of Russia, our own late Prince Albert, Jenny Lind and Sir Walter Scott. Among them was an odd pretender to the diamonds: one John Chapple Norton, known as 'Black Jack' Norton. Not a pretty piece of work, Watson, a scavenger on the rim of polite society. He had married beyond his expectations: one of Sheridan the playwright's granddaughters. She had left him, for reasons no one knows—"

"Left him? Only actresses and adventuresses live apart from their husbands, even nowadays. Back in the fifties it must have caused a roaring scandal."

"Oh, it was quietly done, Watson. She was a woman of artistic breeding. And she took three young sons with her."

"Then the man must have been a monster!"

Holmes shrugged. Domestic irregularities only concerned him when they were pertinent to a case.

"Whatever the man was, he soon became mad to possess the Zone of Diamonds. I suspect a mistress; unprincipled women and illegally obtained jewels often go together, along with greedy men. Black Jack was cunning rather than clever. He had no means, but his wife's connections from her grandfather had sustained her to the point that she had become a successful writer of romantic novels."

I must have frowned my puzzlement, for Holmes gave a quick aside. "No, you wouldn't know the titles; with authors, one decade's favorite is shortly a later decade's obscurity. Suffice it to say that Mrs. Norton was soon earning a tidy sum to support her boys and a separate household. So Black Jack sued her for it."

"He went to court and demanded her money?"

"She was his wife still. All that she had was his. So the court ruled, at any rate."

"Outrageous! And the blackguard then used the money to buy the Zone?"

"Why outrageous, Watson? Only 'actresses and adventuresses live apart from their husbands,' as you point out. The court concurred."

"Yes, but in this instance . . . And the three sons, what became of them?"

"They vanished into the history of the ordinary, as did their mother. She died in the seventies in the same shabby poverty she had once shared with Black Jack, her novels out of fashion and all her profits out of pocket."

"And what of Norton?"

"Hmm." Holmes drew deeply on the pipe, then let the smoke puff out in staccato punctuation between his words. "A good question. Norton went about a bit in society afterwards, very smug, as if the possession—although clandestine—of the Zone had elevated his self-regard. He gambled, raced, entered into numerous shabby schemes and enjoyed the meager fruits of his wife's labors, even after her death, for copyrights do not expire with the author."

"Shockingly sordid, Holmes. It fairly makes my blood boil to think of that bounder getting away with it—with the aid of the law in fact!"

"I will make a suffragist of you yet, Watson," Holmes said sardonically, a grim smile playing about his lips. "But the law's injustice is not our concern."

I leaned forward, realizing that the crux of the matter was about to be revealed.

"To make a sorry story short, Norton little troubled the world in a significant sense until five years ago—when he vanished. Utterly. The house in Brompton was sold, the proceeds handled by a lawyer, now dead. His old friends in dissolution never saw him further. The Zone never surfaced. He was in his seventies by then, but no headstone in London or its surrounds marks his resting place. It is as if he had been plucked from the earth by the scruff of his neck, along with the Queen's diamonds. And so I shall have to tell Mr. Tiffany."

Silence held while I contemplated the news. I confess that during Holmes's recital my mind had been forming a story that played very dramatically in my imagination: the wronged woman, forced to remove herself and her children from the home of that miserable man; her unexpected literary success turned to wormwood when the cad took her hard-won earnings. Her poverty-stricken death and then . . . justice in the person of my friend Mr. Sherlock Holmes catching up with the criminal after all these years and presenting him and the lost Zone of Diamonds to a wondering world . . . It was not to be, I could read in my detective friend's tone of finality. No one knew better than Holmes when a cause was lost.

I sometimes feared that I had for a friend not a man, but a brain without a heart, as lacking in fellow-feeling as he was preeminent in deduction. His aversion to women was but a symptom of a deeper alienation, it struck me. He had never even spoken of relations. I began to suspect that Holmes—of all beings on this earth—was the sole exception to John Donne's poetic assertion that "no man is an island."

Therefore I must set aside forever my naive hopes of injecting a tincture of romance into the ascetic formula of my friend's life. It should have been obvious to me by now that—however much Holmes might astound myself and others in the areas of logic and crime—in the personal arena no surprises were in store from a man who lived his life as a machine, without intimate connection or emotional quirks.

"Cheer up, Watson! You know that I find bloodhounding for gems tediously unrewarding. I warned our client that I would likely uncover villainy but not the diamonds. Such unholy stones often bury themselves in history's missing pages, as if tainted beyond our ability to redeem them. I myself am relieved to wash my hands of the matter. When our eminent American, Mr. Tiffany, arrives at four, as arranged, I will tell him so."

"Still, it would have been a coup."

"Greater coups await. It is a fine summer evening. I propose a stroll at six or thereabouts to the Diogenes Club, which is the queerest place in London, where we are sure to find my brother Mycroft and an interesting problem or two."

"Brother? Diogenes Club? I have heard of neither. How is that possible? Holmes . . . ?"

Chapter Nine

Unwanted Gifts

◦⊱◦

"It is hideous! Misshapen. Ghastly."

"Unusual," Irene admitted, pressing the object in question to her shoulder and studying the effect in the mirror.

It was a large brooch of enamel and opals formed into a sort of starfish-squid with writhing pearl-studded tentacles.

"This is a grateful parting gift from Mr. Tiffany?" I marveled. "I shudder to think what he would give one if he felt *un*grateful."

"His son, Louis, designed it," Irene informed me.

"I see. The father's blind eye overlooks the son's lack of talent."

"Not so blind." Irene jabbed the pin through her jacket lapel, having decided to wear the monstrosity. She turned with a thin, cynical smile. "Tiffany's in New York stocks all such creations of Louis Comfort Tiffany, but they do not sell, not even with the salesmen given a special ten percent commission for peddling them. So the elder Tiffany kills two birds with one opal by giving me this."

"Still, he didn't have to do more than pay you. He must be grateful."

Irene sighed. "I regret that I had nothing concrete to tell him."

"Mr. Tiffany himself said that better men than you had failed."

She laughed. "Yes. I would suspect him of a sense of humor except that he speaks in the universal male so unthinkingly he never noticed the incongruity. He hinted that even Sherlock Holmes had attempted to trace the Zone."

"Holmes? The name is familiar."

"So it should be; you've read it in the papers. The consulting detective, remember? The one who assisted in the capture of poor Mr. Hope."

"Ah, yes. Well, the case is closed now and you can forget about diamond girdles and concentrate on your career."

"As you must concentrate on yours, dear Nell," Irene said with a charming smile. "I fear that my little investigative matters have distracted you from the great business of typewriting."

"Not in the least. I have an assignment this very afternoon in the Strand."

"And I," said Irene, donning a fur-trimmed bonnet to foil the November wind and fixing it with a lethally long pin, "have an appointment with Mrs. Bram Stoker on Cheyne Walk regarding the whereabouts of Oscar Wilde's cross of gold."

So we parted, each to our errands, mine as usual more pedestrian than hers.

The chemist in the Strand wished me to transfer a roster of his various potions into a fresh listing. I spent the afternoon converting alien terms half-obscured by spilled chemical blots into legible type. Such words as "hydrochloric" and "sodium alginate" and the names of herbs like arsenic and jewelweed did not come trippingly to my typewriter.

I returned home cross, with a stiff neck and a headache, to find Irene still gone and a strange man quite at home in our rooms.

"I suppose you're a Pinkerton in search of Irene," said I rather brusquely from the threshold. "And I suppose Mrs. Minucci misguidedly let you in."

The young man nodded and shrugged, drawing my attention to his singularly dull plaid suit.

"Still, and however legitimate your business, there is no excuse

for your settling into our chambers with your bowler still planted on
your head and dried mud caked upon your boots."

"Sorry," he muttered indifferently, pulling a case from his breast
pocket, a lucifer from another and lighting an Egyptian cigarette.

I pointedly waved the emerging smoke away from me, suddenly
realizing that the young man might be an intruder rather than a visitor.

"I must ask you to leave, sir. These are my rooms and I demand
to know your reason for camping here so cavalierly! Otherwise, I
shall have to call Mr. Minucci, our landlord, to eject you."

He rose, forced at last into reaction.

"I wouldn't," he suggested in a silkily husky voice.

"I most certainly will." I recognized a veiled threat when I heard
it, and retreated into the passage, wishing that I had withdrawn as
soon as I had perceived our rooms to be invaded.

"Please don't go, Miss Huxleigh," he cajoled, perhaps alarmed
at my likely escape. "My close friend, Irene Adler, has spoken most
highly of you, and you certainly would not be one to panic."

"I am not panicked!" I paused in my flight to answer the charge
of cowardice. Too late I realized my mistake.

The man laughed softly, having already crossed most of the distance between us with the long, easy swagger of a lion. In the dim
light of the single gasolier I realized that I should be hard put to describe him beyond the rusty sideburns and mustache, nondescript plaid
suit and oddly innocent features.

"The least you can do, sir, is remove your hat, as is proper in a
lady's presence," I said with some asperity, attempting to restore the illusion of ordinary social intercourse.

Secretly, I feared that his next act would be to lift the ebony cane
at his side and strike me down, though why anyone should want to
rob Irene and myself I could not imagine.

I envisaged myself tumbling down the four flights of twisting
stairs, my poor aching head bobbing from riser to dusty riser . . . a
discreet mention in the papers headed "A Saffron Hill Mishap: Mysterious Man Vanishes in Wake of Tragedy to Parson's Daughter" . . .

Irene pacing and wringing her hands like Lady Macbeth at my untimely end and vowing to track the intruder to the ends of the earth . . .

"Oh, very well, Miss," the young man conceded a trifle rudely, taking the swarthy little cigarette from his mouth and the hat from his head at the same moment.

Masses of cinnamon-colored curls tumbled to his manly shoulders.

"Irene! You monster; what a fright you gave me!" Now that we stood toe to toe, the cigarette smoke swirled around my face like fog. "What is the meaning of this mummery? Surely you have not got a part in male guise?"

"Indeed no," she assured me in a normal tone, turning to display her costume. "But I did deceive you?"

"You nearly were the end of me! How did you—*do* you manage to look so masculine?"

She paced before me. "Long strides, to begin with. Amazing how much more efficiently one gets on without pantaloons and petticoats and pounds of flounces." She paused to tap her shoulders. "Shoulder pads and gloves, as you can see. Hands are the tricky part. A bit of spirit gum and some ginger crepe hair—do you fancy me with a redder tint? No? The bowler rides right over the ears and the muffler almost meets it, implying a thicker neck.

"And"—she expertly flourished the slim cigarette clamped between her fore and middle fingers—"the little cigar is the *pièce de résistance*. Only men smoke in public."

"Only men smoke at all!" I retorted.

"Do you think so?" Irene smiled mysteriously and inhaled delicately on the vile weed between her fingers. After my long afternoon among the chemist shop's mingled odors it nearly made me ill.

"But why?" I asked, edging over the threshold as she returned to her chair.

"I have business in town tonight. My interview with Mrs. Stoker was most productive; the next stage of my investigation awaits."

"You actually discussed the Wilde matter with her, and she did not toss you out for impertinence?"

"Why should she? I was not impertinent."

"Well, since my head aches and my nerves are aflutter, you had better tell me what happened. Nothing could put me more out of sorts than what has happened today."

"Sit then and hear an amazingly simple tale." Irene rolled her eyes toward the gasolier above. "Mr. Oscar Wilde would not like it, but there is no mysterious or melodramatic reason for Florence Stoker clinging to his silly cross."

"What then? Why would she possibly refuse to return it?"

"Because she does not have it to return! It was mislaid—or, as I think, stolen. She is too embarrassed to admit that the treasured keepsake of the Divine Oscar was cavalierly let go. Imagine his chagrin to find a gesture of his so ephemeral! It would quite slay the man. He might not speak in aphorisms for an entire week or two."

"Why do you think the cross was stolen?"

"Florence Stoker keeps a rigorously ordered household. It is her husband who leads the unmannerly theatrical life. I doubt she would mislay a fallen hair, much less an object of value. And this little cross is the kind of thing a servant might take, expecting no one to miss it."

"You have a suspect."

"Indeed. Your predecessor."

"My predecessor!? What on earth do you mean?"

"The previous pourer at Florence Stoker's Sunday afternoons at home—I suspect her of splashing Jimmie Whistler with hot tea as a ploy to get herself hastily dismissed. Numerous other small household objects are missing also. Bram Stoker lays it to pixies."

"Of course he would; he's Irish."

"So am I," Irene returned. "Half."

"I didn't mean to slander your origins, Irene. The Irish are actually quite, quite—"

"Misunderstood," Irene finished for me. "I know how fond you are of the breed, especially with Mr. Wilde among it."

Irene, whatever her antecedents, was American-born and on that basis alone did not share my British dislike of those spawned across the Irish sea. I could have called the Irish many things, but "misunderstood" would have been the kindest. There the matter lay, although I tucked away this rare fact about Irene's background as I would a fresh handkerchief—for use when needed.

"Surely you didn't visit Mrs. Stoker in your present guise," I said.

"Naturally not. I approached her woman-to-woman, doing a service for a mutual friend too tongue-tied to speak for himself." Irene gave a little shudder. "Mr. Wilde is well off to have lost her. A chill woman, Nell—quite lovely, but chill. I would think living with her could predispose one to despair."

"Perhaps she is misunderstood, and you mistake English reserve for something worse. We do not all share your *joie de vivre.*"

"*Joie de nécessité,*" Irene shot back, rising with a flourish of the cigarette. "As is my disguise now. I go to track down the clumsy Sarah Jane in her new lair."

"Which is?"

"A position in Berkeley Square. Mrs. Stoker seemed much surprised, but I am not. There are better pickings there than in Chelsea, no matter how fashionable. No doubt Sarah Jane made connections with the Stokers' wealthier guests at the Sunday affairs."

"But why do you go at night, and Friday night at that?"

"Because the master will be out and I can deal with Miss Sarah privately. I will tell her I'm a Pinkerton, I think. You inspire me as usual, Nell." Irene twisted her hair and pinned it up, then settled the bowler at a rakish angle. "Don't worry; I've never yet been accosted in such garb."

"You've done this before?" I said faintly.

"Frequently," Irene confessed from the threshold, leaning back with a conspiratorial wink like a music hall songster about to exit the stage. "I heartily recommend it."

Her advice not to worry fell on deaf ears. It was hard to stare into the black mirrors of our nighttime windows and see only the faint reflection of myself. I pictured Irene jostled on the street below with

the crowds of men, given no more courtesy than a hod-carrier. I
wondered if the wicked little revolver weighed down her pocket. I
even imagined the devious Sarah Jane with a burly henchman who
would attack Irene as if she were the man she pretended to be.

Thus my evening passed, with tincture of belladonna in my eyes
to ease redness and a medicinal rag around my throat to ward off la
grippe after my hard day at the apothecary shop. The cloth had been
pressed on me by the grateful chemist, along with sundry other remedies, all of an evil-smelling nature.

The gaslight seemed to dim as the hours passed, though perhaps it
was my sleep-hungry eyes that faded. At last I heard light steps running up our stairs and rushed to the door to admit Irene.

"Well!?"

She tore off the bowler. "No wonder men are so often rude on the
street; these headache-giving hats must sour their dispositions." She
threw the cane on the sofa and wrenched open the wing collar that
must have aided in making her voice husky by sheer compression.

"Well? What happened?"

"I found Miss Sarah Jane 'to home,' as we say in the States, in the
kitchen of a most elegant house. She has elevated herself to ladies
maid, the better to purloin, but came down from her attic retreat soon
enough when she heard 'a gentleman' was inquiring for her.

"We two closeted ourselves in the pantry, where I put the fear of
the Pinkertons in her, with the result that . . ."

Here Irene reached into the various pockets about her person and
began extracting trinkets—a gold watch-chain, a silver brooch, amber earrings and garnet rings.

"Miss Sarah Jane's entire collection. She rushed back to her room
and showered me with her ill-gotten gains. I made her swear to replace the items she had lifted from her current employers. As for the
rest, she could not remember where she had taken it all, so . . . I con-
fiscated it."

"But what of Mr. Wilde's cross?"

Irene's smile broadened as she lifted one last item from her vest
pocket. The chain was eyelash-fine and the slender Celtic cross that

anchored it was beautifully engraved, although thin enough to be of no immense value.

"He shall have it as soon as I can get it to him."

"And the rest?" I studied the array glittering on the faded Oriental turkey carpet atop our dining table.

Irene eyed me hopefully. "A . . . lucky commission? Since the owners can't be found and Mr. Wilde is paying me in nothing but flowery terms?"

"Stolen goods, Irene? There's no doubt about that."

"I did fancy the garnets," she said, her fingers reaching toward the gleam of tumbled jewelry.

"Stolen," I intoned.

"Oh, very well. We will donate them to St. Sepulchre Without Newgate. It is known as 'The Musicians' Church' and will likely use the proceeds to succor some poor, starving, unknown singer living only on her wits and the mercy of such moral guardians as she may find."

"I am not in the least sorry for you, though I am glad that Mr. Wilde shall have his cross back and never darken our door again."

"Charity, my dear Nell. Charity is the greatest of virtues. I have extended it to the unknown poor; now you must offer it to the known but unappreciated Mr. Wilde. Who knows, he may even make something of that Irish wit someday."

Irene paused to regard me sharply, and indeed, I must have made a sight with my makeshift medicinal muffler.

"Where do you labor tomorrow, good Nell?" she asked. "The chemist's again?"

"Yes. More verbena and foxglove, all transcribed in the crabbed hand of a medieval alchemist."

"You really should seek more congenial work now that your expertise is established. Have you considered advertising your services in some professional arena where the work is likely to be steadier and the pay more rewarding?"

"Where is there such a working girl's paradise?"

"I was thinking of the Temple."

"The Temple? That's just a lot of barristers' chambers. They all have clerks."

"Do clerks type-write?"

"The whole point is that legal clerks hand-write, and quite uppity about it they are, too. Most of the barristers' offices would not even have type-writing machines, I imagine."

"You could bring your own in a case, like a violin."

"Bring my own?" I took the cup of hot chocolate Irene lifted to me from the fender. It was thick and foamy. "I suppose I could."

"Why don't you put a notice up on the grounds—surely they must have some central message board—and see what comes of it?"

"That is an excellent idea, Irene, very businesslike."

She smiled with her lips still pursed on her cup rim. Then I realized who resided at the Temple.

"What makes you think I can worm my way into Mr. Norton's chambers, Irene?"

"Talent, Nell. Cream rises, like foam on chocolate. I have no doubt that if you put yourself in the way of work at the Temple, you shall soon be in high demand."

Chapter Ten

The Mysterious Mr. Norton Unmasked

~~❧~~

Irene had never been more wrong.

I duly pinned a neat notice—typed, of course—to the crowded Middle Temple message board. "Have typewriter, will work at your convenience."

The board commanded one of many narrow passages within the warren of buildings. This sequestered area of London comprised two of the Medieval Four Inns of Court, the Middle and Inner Temples.

Mr. Norton, I ascertained easily enough, kept chambers in the Inner Temple, an area deeply removed from the hurly-burly of nearby Fleet Street.

Irene's blindspot—optimism—had never glared forth with greater dazzle. My notice produced nothing for more than a fortnight. My visits in hopes of finding a reply found only my humble self-advertisement lost in a blizzard of other communications.

Irene had miscalculated. Though barristers generated a great quantity of foolscap and would seem in need of mechanization, the Temple was a rigorously masculine environment, save for its char-women. The new breed of type-writer girls, of which I had now become one, would not be routinely welcome on these hallowed grounds for many decades, I perceived, if even then.

My visits to the Temple became infrequent: I went in only if employed in the neighborhood, as I was occasionally. One such day I paused before the message board, stunned to see that another's *billet-doux* had usurped mine to the point of being pinned directly over it.

I was about to remove the intruding scrap of paper in proprietary indignation when I saw that it was a card. The name on it transfixed me as if I were one of the Temple Church's knightly stone effigies. I fixed on only that significant surname—Norton. The message scrawled across the card's face was even more paralyzing: "Miss Huxleigh, please see me about your services. No. 17, Inner Temple."

I looked about the deserted byways, needing Irene at my side, wanting to shout my amazement to whoever would listen. That *he,* of all persons, should be the first—the only—to rise to my bait! I couldn't credit my good fortune.

But suppose this were not mere coincidence? Suppose that, somehow, Mr. Norton knew of Irene's and my association, of my meddling in his affairs also? I remembered the angry voice that had thundered beyond my drawn curtains so many weeks ago, the furious heavy-footed retreat down the stairs and into the hansom cab.

I remembered also my intense curiosity to view this fire-breather in the flesh. Surely the miserable old Norton would be an ugly specimen of humanity himself. Certainly he had offended Irene beyond forgiveness, a rare reaction in her to any human being.

Pulling the card from the board, I marched smartly through the narrow passages, past the stately Temple Church (muttering a hasty prayer for my safety) and to the door facing the quadrangle that bore the number 17.

My knock brought a baritone "Come in."

The chamber beyond was as small as a scullery and crammed with papers. A raven-haired man hunched behind the book-laden desk. Behind him a coat rack held a chesterfield and—I recognized it with a thrill of remembrance—a velvet plush top hat. Many men wore such headgear, but only one such man had stormed Irene's Saffron Hill eyrie so forcefully.

"Yes?" The gentleman did not glance up from the desk.

"I—I understand you have need of a type-writer girl."

He looked at me then and I was struck quite mute. "Old Norton" was no more than five-and-twenty, young for a barrister, young even for a *child* of the senile monster I pictured the scoundrel to be. Numbly, I glanced at the card, finally seeing the "Godfrey" that preceded the surname. So it had been *Godfrey,* not John, all along. This then, must be a son of the villain in question! Why had not Irene told me? After all, I had never *seen* the man, as she had. In addition, Godfrey Norton was the most strikingly handsome man I had ever seen, save upon the stage, when I went to see Irene perform.

I am normally resistant to male beauty—many a skin-perfect apple has a rotten core. Indeed, the smoother the skin the fouler the rot, in my experience—Jasper Higgenbottom's selfless soul lay hidden beneath a bushel of freckles and ears of regrettably elephantine prominence—but this man Norton was as exceptionally handsome as Irene was beautiful. I was astounded that she had also forgotten to mention that inescapable fact.

"Please sit," he urged pleasantly, jumping up to sweep a pile of documents from the single oaken sidechair.

"You have not room for a type-writer girl or even her machine," I blurted, appalled by the mounded papers.

"I will have if you transcribe all this foolscap into type," said he with a winning smile. "A table lurks somewhere under the deeds there, and a spare chair as well."

The piled deeds that he had mentioned seized the opportunity of my attention being directed upon them to sigh, crackle and slowly . . . inevitably, slide toward the floor.

Mr. Norton leaped up again, as did I. We hurled ourselves at the glacial tide and stemmed it, then laughed in mutual embarrassment and self-congratulation.

"You see, Miss Huxleigh, I need help desperately!"

"Why are you so inundated with papers?"

"Because I am inundated with work. I am new to the law and must undertake the petty paperwork suits that my senior barristers have outgrown. A clever type-writer girl would perfectly answer my needs."

"How could you pay me if your practice is so fresh?"

He cleared his throat and looked away, revealing an aquiline profile a Caesar would have coveted for his coins.

"I have certain . . . obligations that I suspect will soon end. I have never been in a better position to pay anyone. But"—he eyed the cluttered room—"let us take a turn in the gardens to discuss the work. It is more pleasant there."

So I ended by strolling in the Temple gardens with Godfrey Norton. Irene, I thought, would be . . . what? Even I could not imagine how she would greet this news.

"You must realize, Mr. Norton, that the idea of a type-writer girl in the Temple is rather radical. No one besides yourself has answered my advertisement."

"Why do you think that I did?"

"You are perverse?"

He laughed easily. "No. I simply realize that no one like yourself solicits such work except out of economic necessity."

"That is true. I was a governess first."

"And before that?"

"A parson's daughter."

"Ah. He died, of course."

"Yes." A sudden vision of my kindly father passed before my eyes. Though I seldom thought of him, I missed him. Godfrey Norton had never known that bittersweet emotion in relation to his own sire, I feared, no matter how he defended his family.

"Died, leaving you penniless," he added a trifle bitterly.

"It was not Father's fault! The Church is not meant to be a profitable undertaking. The flock cared for me until I came to London and left their purview. That is my own error."

"Or good fortune," said he, taking my hand in a kindly way that I could not find the heart to object to, despite his handsome face.

"You will be the first type-writer girl in the Inner Temple; think of the honor! And you will save me from being buried alive by the scribblings of the law's delay."

His charm was as lethal as Irene's. Even if I had not known that the chance of just this employment with Godfrey Norton had inspired her to direct me to the Temple, I would have succumbed to his obvious need of an organizing hand. I had often come to my father's rescue just so with his sermons and correspondence.

"It is settled then," Mr. Norton prodded, shaking my hand on the bargain.

"When do I begin?"

"Tomorrow. With the deeds. When they are done we shall have a table cleared. I will demolish the pile on the chair myself tonight."

I laughed at the ludicrousness of it—that tiny room, the proximity of Irene's nemesis and possible rival for the Zone of Diamonds, my sudden installation in the heart of the female-free Temple.

Mr. Godfrey Norton took my laughter for the joy of employment.

Irene laughed even harder and longer that evening when I reported to her.

"Splendid! Only one fish bit, and that the one we sought. What will he pay you?"

"I . . . neglected to ask," I said, mortified. The shock of discovering that Godfrey was not the Norton I had assumed him to be had combined with the man's native charm to drive normal practicalities from my head, though I could hardly tell Irene that. Mr. Godfrey Norton had apparently had no effect on her whatsoever, else why had she omitted mention of his youth and good looks?

"Be certain to demand your best rate, Nell—above it, if you can."

"Mr. Norton expects to be freed of a financial obligation. I have the impression that his capacity for work is enormous. And I still do not understand why you did not warn me that I would be meeting the son, not the father."

Irene shrugged. "A Norton is a Norton as far as our quest is concerned; the son is cut from the same arrogant sailcloth as the sire. Besides, you make a better investigator if you form your own opinions."

"Indeed I have, and I do not feel that *this* Mr. Norton can have much in common with his father. For one thing, he is self-supporting and has evidently been so for some time, which means he has not benefited from the possession of the Zone of Diamonds. He is young to be a barrister—"

"Not so young," Irene corrected me. "Close to my age, no doubt, and I am becoming established in my work."

"Still, he must have begun his studies at a remarkably early age, with no or little monetary aid from his father, certainly."

"How admirable," Irene said icily. "We all face our obstacles. One of mine is being underestimated. See that you don't underestimate your new employer. He is a barrister and a Norton, untrustworthy breeds both."

With that she went off to the Lyceum Theatre and I prepared myself for my new position at the Temple.

Within days it was clear that Godfrey Norton refused to play the villainous character Irene had assigned him. His solicitude toward myself verged on chivalry—a pillow for my back, an eyeshade for my head, help in deciphering the clerk's abominable penmanship . . . His actions reminded me of the kindness the curate, Mr. Higgenbottom, dispensed to his flock; no doubt he would have lavished even more solicitude upon the woman he chose to wed—if only fate had permitted our paths to join as well as simply cross!

I would never confess it to Irene, but I found the position ideal. The Temple grounds, both Middle and Inner, formed an isle of tranquility amid London's fiercest urban uproars. Like a tide the stream of city life rushed past, only Fleet Street's faintest murmurs foaming through the narrow gates to both Temple yards. Across that thoroughfare bristled the Gothic towers of the Royal Courts of Justice, opened by Queen Victoria this very year of 1882.

Yet a stone's throw from such turmoil I could amble through courtyards reminiscent of my notion of Oxford and Cambridge, trod cobblestones unaltered since Queen Elizabeth's time, idle in the gardens along the tranquil river, even visit the lovely Temple Church with its twelfth-century round nave holding the stone effigies of knights naming the first families in the land. The *first* earls of Pembroke and Essex lay there with other noble knights, uncaring of the traffic upon Fleet Street.

To save me transporting it, Mr. Norton had bought a typewriter. Like Rapunzel I speedily spun the straw of longhand into the glitter of type—neat, efficient type that occupied so much less paper. Mr. Norton was often out, joining his fellow barristers—gowns flying and wigs askew—in racing between chambers and the Royal Courts across Fleet Street, daily breaching the flow of commerce with suicidal abandon.

The pay, it transpired, was generous and Twining's tea shop was just down Fleet Street, so Irene's illicit larder was soon stocked with exotic Orient brews.

To my surprise, employment with Mr. Norton led to invitations into other chambers at the same good pay. I came to learn the law's peculiar syntax and easily mastered the long, Latin phrases. Father had insisted I study the dead language, not because of any fondness for the Roman Church, but because Latin underlay English. Never had his foresight proved so useful. I flourished in the Temple, but I learned not a syllable of the Zone of Diamonds.

"What a wasted effort," Irene complained of my unrequited investigations after some weeks. "This Godfrey Norton is proving to be as dull as ditchwater. No irregular habits, no vices, not even a suspicious client or two, though the steady sums paid to that Hammersmith establishment called 'The Sycamores' are of mild interest. Perhaps you would deign to look into them. What a good thing that you are not a blackmailer, Nell; you would have slim success at it. To spend two months almost daily closeted with a man and know nothing more of him than the cut of his clothes strikes me as unlikely beyond belief." She yawned.

"I know a good deal about him! He is unfailingly courteous—"

"Ah, how incriminating!"

"Most conscientious in his work—"

"A saint among us!"

"Neat about his person if not his office, and not even vain about his appearance."

"A paragon, 'tis plain."

"You could benefit from his example," I added, "as far as the vanity is concerned."

"Vanity is an accessory of my profession."

"Which one?"

"You begin to interrogate me as if I were a witness; too many hours spent among the barristers, I fear. Vanity is of use to both the performer and the investigator. In both roles I wish to win applause; only in investigations, the audience is naturally smaller."

"I wonder which role is the more vital to you?"

"Why, my singing, of course! Playing detective is merely a necessity that underwrites the greater occupation. Once my singing future is secure, I shall let all these petty little puzzles go to their natural solvers—Scotland Yard, or Mr. Sherlock Holmes, the consulting detective."

"Would you really, Irene? Somehow I think the cart has come to pull the horse. You've shown no loss of interest in the Zone of Diamonds despite all this time and a cold trail."

"The Zone." Irene lifted an eyebrow. "No, I shall always want to solve that conundrum—but that is a major work of detective art, involving revolution and royalty and missing crown jewels. As for the rest, let it go. I shall be as indifferent to mysterious matters as a dog to milk once I am fully established as an opera singer."

Though this was said grandiosely, with Irene's offhand tone of conviction, I sniffed audibly before she swept out the door, which unspoken comment she pretended not to have heard.

✦　✦　✦

"You seem distracted today, Miss Huxleigh."

I tore my eyes from the window, where they had been staring at the treetops. "So sorry, Mr. Norton. I don't think I have fallen much behind." I began to admonish the keys sharply.

"I did not mean for you to attack the poor machine," he said, laughing. "Let me rephrase my comment. 'You seem pensive today, Miss Huxleigh.' Is there a difficulty?"

"No, of course not . . . I was merely thinking."

"Is thinking such a sad occupation?"

"No, only . . . I was thinking of my late father."

"Ah." His tone became abruptly noncommittal.

"And . . . guilt. I was meditating on the strange state of guilt."

"Perhaps natural in a parson's daughter," he said with a slight smile.

"Have you ever felt . . . guilty, Mr. Norton?"

His laugh was sharp and brief, like a bark. "What person who has passed through childhood has not? Have you not instilled guilt in your day, Miss Huxleigh, as a governess?"

"Yes. Guilt is quite a useful emotion. Now that I have experienced it more closely, I feel . . . wretched . . . for ever having induced it in another, even in the name of discipline."

"What have you to feel guilty about, for heaven's sake?"

I took my hands from the keys and folded them in my lap, staring steadily at Q-W-E-R-T. "I have not been fully frank about my situation with you, Mr. Norton."

"I sense a confession coming on. I should warn you that a barrister is not a man of the cloth."

"Perhaps you will have to do. I should tell you that, that I . . . share lodgings with another."

"You . . . share lodgings with another." A long silence, in which Mr. Norton cleared his throat. "Surely, you are not implying an unsanctioned alliance . . . ?"

I looked up, mortified. "Oh, no! I reside with another woman, of course."

"Of course." He sounded much relieved. "But that is becoming common as more countrywomen descend on London for work. There is nothing irregular in it—"

"My chambermate is . . . an actress."

"I see. No doubt an . . . unusual companion for a parson's daughter, but there are a good many actresses in London, and some of them even respectable, I am sure."

"She also . . . takes on clients—"

"Clients! I see."

"No! Clients of a quite respectable kind, although unusual."

"Respectable but unusual." His voice remained carefully neutral as his confusion grew.

By now he had no inkling of where I was headed and half-feared the direction. Yet he remained calm and not at all judgmental. I did not quite know how to conclude my awkwardly begun admission.

"What kind of clients?" Mr. Norton prodded gently. "For what services?"

"For . . . finding things."

"Finding things? Like those that are lost?"

"Or stolen."

"What you describe, Miss Huxleigh, is an inquiry agent. Many barristers employ such from time to time. Such men are of some use . . ." He paused to dissect his erroneous assumption. "But that is the point, is it not? Your chambermate is a woman, a female inquiry agent . . . and an actress as well—"

When the truth struck him, Mr. Norton drew himself up as if in court. "She is this Adler woman who has meddled into the history of my family, who is trying to locate my father!"

"I fear so."

"And you have been sent to spy upon me!"

I dared not even glance up to read his expression. Now the blind impression of "old Norton" I had received through the draperies and the man I knew merged as his indignation thundered above me.

"This is pernicious, Miss Huxleigh! I would not expect it of you."

"Nor would I. Truly, I have not 'spied'; there was naught to spy, and so I have told Irene. She was most annoyed with me."

"This is infernal!" He began pacing. "Intolerable. To corrupt a parson's daughter, to harry a man in the privacy of his own office—"

I wrung my hands. "Yes, it is dreadful. Irene has absolutely no compunction in the pursuit of a mystery. She is relentless."

"Mystery! What mystery is there about the Nortons but the usual measure of human misery in double dose?"

"Why, the Zone."

"Zone?"

"Of Diamonds." I swallowed. Godfrey Norton stared at me as if I were mad. "Queen Marie Antoinette's diamond belt, that your father reputedly bought in the fifties and that Mr. Tiffany wants to buy."

"Diamonds? Marie Antoinette? Tiffany?" Mr. Norton flipped up his frockcoat skirt and sat on the documents that cushioned the only other chair in the office. "You had better tell me more, Miss Huxleigh. Half-confessions are liable to lead to half-baked conclusions."

"That is what Mr. Tiffany had heard, that a fellow named Norton had purchased the Zone cheaply after it escaped Paris in the Revolution of 1848."

"I wasn't even born then."

"Nor was I. Or Irene. But that's why she was investigating the Norton family. It was her only line of inquiry. She was looking for your father; instead she apparently unearthed you."

"Diamonds"—he shook his head—"what . . . fairy tales! Oh, I don't doubt that some story is circulating. At least this tale is more glamorous than the sordid truth of my family's past. Perhaps I should be grateful to this fabulous 'Zone' for obscuring what is merely tawdry with its dazzle." He regarded me sharply. "You know, of course, then, of my call upon your chambermate."

I nodded, afraid that an unconsidered word would force me to confess to the miserably petty crime of eavesdropping as well.

Mr. Norton sighed, smoothing his dark mustache with a forefinger. He laughed suddenly. "Your Miss Adler must think me a greedy rival for the Zone, angered to have other hounds on the trail. Or does she think I have it?"

"She thinks no one has it, for no one shows signs of that kind of wealth, though, of course, we—she has not located your father."

"My father." An odd expression came over Mr. Norton's face. He tore a piece of paper from the corner of a deed and scrawled across it. "Here is my father's address. Perhaps she should speak directly to the supposed owner of this fabulous treasure. Take it! That is where he resides, at that address. You have my blessings, Miss Huxleigh. Let your indefatigable friend go directly to the source, and good luck to her!"

"Surely you are not serious!"

"You mean that I am not sincere. But I am!" He smiled again, bitterly. "I wish to forget my family, and particularly my father. I wish all others to forget him. Let Miss Adler find the cursed Zone and convey it to Mr. Tiffany and let them all forget the memory of Black Jack Norton. My mother is dead, at least. She can be hurt no longer."

"Please, Mr. Norton. It was quite unforgivable of Irene to go hunting over the ground of your family's history. She gets quite carried away in the pursuit of the unattainable—"

"So do we all. Do you want to know what is really unattainable about my sorry family, Miss Huxleigh? A happy memory. My mother had left my father when I was quite young. As I grew older, I began to see what a scandal it was that she and my brothers and I lived apart from him. I even began to see the price she had paid, despite the success of her novels. When my father sued her for the proceeds of her writing—and won—I certainly saw our lodgings, our food, our clothing decline in the face of his legal success. It quite broke my mother's heart to have the very law of England uphold such a scoundrel."

"I cannot say how sorry I am; really, you need not tell me more."

"I must tell someone the truth, since lies about my family are all that I have heard since my youth. Now your friend perpetuates more lies with this glittering tale of lost diamonds. Speak of lost honor, lost love, lost hope, lost livelihoods, rather than of diamonds. But such losses are too dull, too sordid in their everyday way to enchant the curious."

"Yet they are losses I can sympathize with more readily, Mr. Norton," I said quietly.

His thin-lipped smile grew rueful. "You find yourself quite in the middle, don't you, Miss Huxleigh? A parson's daughter must be used to firmer moral ground. Perhaps you think ill of my late mother, as so many did—"

"It sounds as if she were sorely wronged."

"Indeed she was, by the law of England that declares all of a wife's property is her husband's, even when she earns it and lives apart from him because he is the worst sort of brute. That's why I became a barrister, though my father before me had tainted the profession in my eyes, I wanted to right that law, and defend other women who are defenseless against the rapacity of their own husbands."

"Most admirable," I muttered, ashamed. "I quite understand why you cannot bear to have strangers probing into your family background. I shall tell Irene at once and insist that she abandon her inquiry."

"No!" He caught my wrist as I rose, releasing me as soon as he realized the strength of his gesture. "That, too, invades my privacy. This talk of ours is between us alone. As you sought discretion, so do I."

I unfolded my hand, in which lay the crumpled address of his demonic father. "What of this?"

He smiled with a mysterious relish. "Give it to her. Let her follow the trail to its natural conclusion. From what you say of Irene Adler, she will not rest until she is convinced every stone has been turned. Let her overturn her own stones, and deal with what . . . vermin . . . she finds under them."

I shivered a little at his tone, at the bitter blackness in his eyes. I knew and liked Godfrey Norton, but I realized that I had merely skimmed the unhappy surface of his family's past. I wondered now— with new guilt—whether I should let Irene pursue the path that Mr. Norton had so unexpectedly cleared for her.

Chapter Eleven

Black Jack Norton Unearthed

~ひ~

"You are certain that this address in Croydon is where God-frey Norton has sent so many of his funds?"

"Yes," I admitted, though I felt something of a betrayer for leading Irene blindly to it. I had not told her of Mr. Norton's revelations to me. It had taken me a full month to pass on the address. "Why ask now, Irene, when we are already embarked by rail and by hired coach, at great expense? If you have doubts about prying into this affair—"

"No." Irene lifted her chin as she did just before delivering the first note of a song. It was a gesture that both commanded attention and expressed Irene's deep commitment to her course. "This jaunt of ours may forever lay to rest an old mystery."

"Mr. Norton has been a most considerate and generous em-ployer," I mumbled. "Perhaps old mysteries should not be settled at his expense."

"Don't go sentimental on me, Nell, at this late date. 'Mr. Norton' was not most considerate and generous to me when we met. You say he is now aware that you and I share lodgings. No doubt he still thinks me a hired meddler with not the brains to solve who killed Cock Robin. I fancy I will change his opinion shortly."

"Then you know what to expect at The Sycamores in Croydon."

"Not what, Penelope. *Who*."

With the rare invocation of my full formal name and that clipped monosyllable, Irene lapsed into morose silence.

Late summer sunshine dappled through the roadside leaves and cast a lacy veil of light and shadow over her features. She would not heed any feeble objections I might care to make; for some reason, this journey tapped both her personal and professional wellsprings. No one knew better than I when Irene Adler would not be gain-said.

Our carriage slowed before an ornate wrought-iron gate. The fencing was fully as formidable as that surrounding the seventeenth-century Royal Hospital that Wren had built in Chelsea, but this establishment was buried deep in fragrant countryside. No sound came to us but the calling of thrushes and the occasional bleats of the black-feathered rooks perched atop the sycamore trees.

A sign on the right gatepost proclaimed the place to be that which we sought. A gateman's presence announced that our trek might have been in vain.

"Your business?" he demanded brusquely.

Irene leaned out the lowered window, expertly tilting her head so as not to dislodge her ecru straw bonnet trimmed in blue velvet and cream-colored plumes.

"We are here to visit one of the residents," she said in a tone equally alloyed of command and charm.

"You'll have to register with the main desk at the house."

"Of course. And you'll have to open the gate for my coachman." Soon I heard the squeak of hinges, oddly rusted for so well maintained an estate. "Many thanks and good day," Irene waved in farewell as we crunched over a gravel drive between an avenue of plane trees.

"In truth, Irene," I said, "I wonder that you don't simply use 'open sesame' in such instances and save yourself the trouble of chitchat."

She smiled at my tart tribute to her powers of persuasion but remained silent. I sensed a barely controlled excitement in her that our outing to bucolic Croydon hardly seemed to merit. The house hove to on our right, a massive Jacobean pile with immaculate grounds.

"I imagine some of Mr. Godfrey Norton's pounds have gone to clip these boxwood hedges, my dear Nell."

"Why? He is a pure city dweller. Why underwrite an estate in the country?"

Irene favored me with her most mysteriously knowing look. "When we arrive inside, allow me to set the scene."

"When have I not?" I retorted, following her out of our vehicle and up some shallow steps, then across a broad pavement to the doors of the house.

Irene yanked the bell. So large was the house that I heard only a far, faint ring. A peephole snapped open and a set of red-rimmed eyes regarded us.

"We are here to see Mr. Norton," Irene said boldly.

I tried not to start, but I believe that my hat plumes wavered a bit. How did Irene know what to expect without having been forewarned by the younger Norton, as I had been? My pulses began to flutter when I considered the depth of her perception and the guilt of my own secret.

The raffish eyes behind the peephole widened. "Then you don't know the news—I'll let you in."

"Thank you." Irene waited regally as bars, locks and various mechanisms grated free on the other side of the door.

When it swung wide the butler—for I assumed so grand a house would have one—admitted us to a hall paved in checkerboard marble after the Wren style.

"Mr. Edgewaithe is in the office, directly ahead," said he.

"*What* don't we know?" I whispered as I followed close on Irene's heels. "Why does a private residence require an 'office,' and isn't that butler's manner rather familiar?"

"He's not a butler, merely a doorman—and this 'residence' is both more public and more private than you suspect," was all that she would say.

Mr. Edgewaithe rose from behind a Queen Anne desk as we entered. "Ladies, please be seated. You are new to The Sycamores . . ."

"New, yes," Irene said, softly rustling into a chair. "I am

Clytemnestra Saunders and this is my cousin, Henrietta Rushwimple. We are distant cousins of Mr. Norton, and had not learned of his residence here until lately."

"Norton, is it?" Mr. Edgewaithe frowned. He was a lean, stooped man in a frockcoat. The thick swag of watch chain across his concave belly echoed the gilt spectacles on his worried face. "How tragic that you did not come yesterday, as his son did."

"Godfrey was here?" Irene inquired alertly. "Then I presume that our relation has—"

"—been called to quieter pastures," our host finished solemnly.

"Plainly speaking, he is dead? And only yesterday?"

Irene's businesslike tone brought a pained look to Mr. Edgewaithe's professionally furrowed features. "He was of an age for it. There was no irregularity, I assure you. His son would swear to that."

"Oh . . ." Irene blinked prettily, as if batting back tears, "we have come so far, after so long. It is possible to . . . see him?"

"See him? I'm afraid not. The Sycamores is accustomed to sudden death. The local doctor signed the death certificate and Mr. Norton was interred last night. You may visit the mausoleum, which is on a particularly lovely portion of our grounds . . ."

"Of course." Irene pulled a handkerchief from her reticule and waved it ostentatiously. "Cousin Henrietta and I must see the—the place of interment. But to make our journey and come away with no . . . feeling for the man. It is so sad. May we not at least see where he stayed?"

Mr. Edgewaithe's face took on a queer expression at her last words. Irene noticed it as quickly as I.

"Or perhaps I should say, where he was . . . kept? Pray do not think you shock us, sir. When we learned of our cousin's whereabouts, no secret was made of his condition. This is a private sanatorium for the mentally disturbed, is it not?"

"For the brain-feeble, yes. Your cousin suffered from the slings and arrows of old age. He had grown quite forgetful and confused. He even failed to recognize his own son; one can hardly blame the lad for visiting so seldom. But young Godfrey never failed in his financial duties to his father's caretakers, nor we, I trust, in our tending of the gentleman."

Irene buried her face in the linen. "To see where he spent his last days would do more to set our souls at rest than to see where he lies now."

"If you insist, ladies. The Sycamores has nothing to conceal in its accommodation, which is the best in the environs of London. If you will follow me."

We did, through waxed and dusted halls, up shining stairwells and down a corridor lined with doors equipped with small peep-holes.

This last touch overshadowed the place's beeswax-scented clean-liness, that grim line of barred doors with their spy-holes. Then, too, the odd chirps and moans that drifted from beyond all those doors did little to calm my fears.

There was apparently nothing wrong with their hearing—the mad—for as we passed nails scratched the far sides of the doors, and fists pounded and faint voices pleaded.

Then I realized that it was not our passing footsteps that so dis-turbed the unseen denizens behind the doors, but the cheerful jingle of the keys in their warder's hand. Mr. Edgewaithe made this word-less passage as if he heard nothing. Irene's face was composed as for a photograph, fiercely still.

Finally the keys made a last clash and our guide paused before a door. I noted a brass number on the panel: 12. The key turned; I fancied I heard wails all up and down the hall as those other locked doors stayed shut. This one swung ajar on silent, oiled hinges.

Irene stepped through. No carpet softened our footfalls. No cur-tains festooned the window, which was barred. How had I failed to notice those barred windows from the driveway? There was a bed, stripped to its ticked mattress. A bare table. A metal pitcher and bowl, even a brass chamberpot.

There was not a book, or a mirror, or a picture upon the wall. I had wondered at Godfrey Norton's paying so royally to keep his hated father here until I saw the emptiness of that room. It struck me that the son's mercy had literally killed his father with kindness—or what passed for it toward the feeble-minded.

Irene walked to the window. "Did . . . cousin John . . . have an opportunity to enjoy these lovely grounds?"

"Of course." Mr. Edgewaithe was eager to relate his institution's amenities. "Each resident is escorted outside on a regular schedule, as the weather allows. Your cousin particularly enjoyed sitting by the duck pond."

"By that great beech tree I see from here?"

"Why, yes. That was his special spot. How did you guess?"

"It's the only landmark visible from here. I imagine one would spend many hours staring out this window. No matter how shattered one's mind, it would still turn to the exceptional, else why do we all swoon at a sunset when they are so frequent?"

"Mr. Norton was not facing the west, unfortunately."

"Well, the sunrise then," Irene returned. "To Mr. Norton they must have been much the same."

Mr. Edgewaithe frowned, as if sniffing a criticism he couldn't name. "Is there anything else, then, ladies, before you visit the mausoleum, which is just the other side of the pond?"

"Via the little bridge. Ah, Henrietta, how charming. Our cousin found, at last, a lovely place to die."

We swept out, Irene sweeping as only she could, her layered skirts swishing, I merely swept up in her progress. Downstairs in the main hall another visitor awaited Mr. Edgewaithe's return, pacing on the black-and-white paving stones.

"Good day, then, ladies; many thanks for such humane concern for your cousin." Mr. Edgewaithe's words were a dismissal. He had already turned to his new visitor, an angular, hawk-nosed gentleman in a checked Inverness cloak and a deerstalker cap. Despite the dusty country clothes, the gentleman's clipped speech and impatient eyes bespoke a city dweller.

He glanced sharply at us as we passed, not with any impertinent interest, but as he would catalogue a new variety of tree, a sort of unthinking, ever-constant observation. Irene was burying her face in her handkerchief again, so affected by her own crocodile tears that she had to draw me against the paneling while she collected herself.

"Irene, why are you carrying on so?" I whispered. "Mr. Edgewaithe isn't paying us the least mind anymore—"

"Shh!" She seized my throat as if to strangle me.

"—Holmes," I heard the stranger's acerbic tones announce behind me. "I read the obituary in the *Telegraph* this morning and came down immediately."

"Norton's obituary?" Edgewaithe guessed.

"Yes. Norton. He had dropped from sight these last few years. Some of his old associates wanted to assure themselves of his well-being, such as it might have been."

"Come into my office, Mr. Holmes," Edgewaithe invited, with a cordiality alien to us. "I'd be happy to assist in any way I can. Never telling when a gentleman like yourself might require The Sycamores for a dear one. Tragedy can strike even a young man, perhaps a wife—"

"I am not married, Mr. Edgewaithe, nor do I expect to be. But I *am* interested in the particulars of Mr. Norton's life here and last illness—"

The broad doors closed, ending our eavesdropping.

"Yes, I imagine many an inconvenient wife languishes above," Irene said grimly. "Instead of a whited sepulcher we have a well-landscaped one. Only in England could greenery cover so much greed! But why Holmes? Here? Now? Ah, he has not forgotten the Zone, either."

"You talk of greed," I said quietly.

She gave me an incredulous look. "Greed does not motivate him, no more than it does myself. Or rather a higher form of greed; ambition to know all, that is our mutual flaw, Mr. Holmes's and mine. He is younger than I had imagined, and such a *busy,* interesting face. It's a pity he considers women beneath notice."

"But he noticed us!"

"As he would a garden variety of cucumber, Nell, with no real recognition. I fancy he will pay for the failing someday, though he does not strike me as a truly prejudiced man—only arrogant in his intelligence and self-sufficiency."

"As some might say of you."

"Penelope! You show signs of becoming a character reader. I shall have to set you up with a crystal ball in the King's Road and see how many fortune seekers you attract. It might pay better than type-writing."

"No, thank you. And may we go home now?"

"Certainly. But first we picnic."

"Picnic?" We had wandered onto the entry pavement. The bushes were alive with birds trilling like the emperor's nightingale. Honey-suckle and lilac bloomed along the lanes and fanned their fragrance to us on zephyrs of sun-steeped air. The day seemed the warm amber color of Earl Grey tea.

"Picnic," Irene reiterated, heading for the carriage. "I fancy a banquet by that towering beech tree. Coachman, could you fetch our hamper from the carriage—and have you a shovel aboard?"

His plain face froze in stupefaction.

"A crowbar, then?" she prompted him. "Surely you carry *something* in the nature of a tool for difficulties you may encounter along the road, man? I suspect our tins of sardines will prove somewhat stub-born to open," Irene finished with an air of helpless feminity as false as the rouge that pinked her lips.

Without a word, the coachman pulled a short-handled shovel from beneath his seat.

"Capital!" Irene said, seizing it eagerly. "We will bring you the leftovers." With that she slipped it under the lid of our hamper—the handle protruded quite visibly until she draped my best Chinese shawl over it—and we went together down the lilac-laden lane, the hamper swinging by its handles between us.

I was silent for some time, and then I could no longer contain myself.

"Tell me, Irene," I begged, "that you don't really intend to disin-ter the unfortunate Mr. Norton!"

She would not answer.

Chapter Twelve

Buried Treasure

~ঙ৷ৎ~

Mr. Beaverholt, our driver, munched the better part of our picnic on the box above us while our carriage rattled along the tree-shaded roadway.

Inside the coach, Irene and I lurched like loose sardines in a tin, our mud-stained hands clinging to the straps. In place of the picnic hamper that Irene had offered Mr. Beaverholt on condition he "drive like the wind" to the railway station was a small, leather-buckled chest as dirt-laden as our hands.

"Your best walking suit is ruined!" I wailed.

"It needed retrimming anyway," she answered.

"My Chinese shawl is in shreds!"

"We had to cover the chest with something."

"Your fingernails are worn to—to sawteeth!"

"That will make playing the piano easier."

Irene lifted the ivory handle of her parasol and tapped the coach ceiling. The horse quickened its already frantic trot as a discarded sardine tin flew past the open window.

"What a glorious day this is, Nell!" Irene shouted over the rush of the wind, the rattle of the conveyance and the screech of Surrey's prolific birdlife. "Just think! We have beaten Sherlock Holmes himself to the prize."

I regarded the battered box at our feet in silence . . . in silence until a particularly rough jolt lurched its metal-bound edge into my shin.

"What can be in this devil's chest that's worth all this deception and going behind poor young Mr. Norton's back and the ruination of our attire?" I shrieked, beside myself.

I confess to having been so unnerved at the notion of disturbing the late Mr. Norton's bones that our struggle to disinter something less than human at the foot of the sycamore tree had completely exhausted me.

"Treasure!" Irene replied, dimpling wickedly.

"I still can't fathom how you knew where to dig."

"I didn't until I thought like a madman. As Mr. Edgewaithe pointed out, his . . . cell, shall we call it? . . . and its sole window overlooked the sunrise. The tree was the only landmark for a mind as feeble as old Norton's to fix upon. During his outings, I'm sure the attendant's attention would wander while the old man drooled at the pondside—"

"Irene!"

"Then there was that peculiar pattern of roots fanning out into a sort of sunburst. That, too, would catch an unfocused eye. Old Norton was senile, not ordinarily mad. He must have had moments of clarity. In such a moment he secreted the things most important to him in this chest, then buried it."

"The Zone?" I eyed the bucking box between us with more respect. "You really think the Zone of Diamonds lies in this very receptacle?"

"And Mr. Sherlock Holmes does not have it!" Irene crowed. "Mr. Charles Tiffany does not have it. Mr. Godfrey Norton does not have it. But I do."

"Greed," said I, my heart pounding nevertheless at the notion of opening the box. So Pandora must have felt.

"Not greed," Irene teased me with a smile. "Glory."

How I survived that headlong return trip to London I shall never quite know. The chest was heavy, which very fact encouraged our dreams of booty. Irene and I were forced to cart it like some ungainly valise between us through the length of Victoria Station. The cabman we hailed outside offered to lift our "luggage" to the box. Irene refused so adamantly that I expected him, suspicions aroused, to whistle for the nearest bobby.

Our hansom rattled 'round the curve of Buckingham Palace along The Mall and across Trafalgar Square onto Charing Cross Road. I was so guilt-ridden by now that I anticipated the Royal Guard riding out and commanding us to "stand and deliver" our ill-gotten goods on the spot. Every nearing hansom seemed to conceal a Scotland Yard man. Every pause for traffic congestion to untangle seemed a plot to detain us.

"Amusing how convenient our rooms are to Baker Street," Irene mused as we turned onto New Oxford Road and away from the northwest section of the town. I said nothing, wondering if our efforts to smooth over The Sycamores' disturbed earth would escape the notice of Mr. Sherlock Holmes.

"He is sure to be suspicious," she said, as if anticipating my thoughts. "He may even find our 'dig.' But then what? The Misses Saunders and Rushwimple have naught to do with us."

"Our descriptions—"

"—could match a thousand women's in London—more, perhaps a half-million of these busy four-and-a-half million souls around us! Besides, even if he catches us eventually, we have the prize now."

My shoe-toe touched it gingerly.

"Yes, it's plain and ugly," Irene admitted. "Yet great beauty can dwell in a lowly exterior, do not Scriptures tell us, Penelope? As the earth accepted the remains of old Norton, so it gives up the better part of him, that prize which was bought, people say, and so does Godfrey Norton testify by inference, with the sacrifice of wife and sons."

"What will you do with it?"

Irene stared at me, her face uncharacteristically blank. "I have not considered! I thought only of obtaining it. I can hardly pawn it and I don't know . . . yet . . . how to sell it. Perhaps I'll wear it on the stage. I can do so more honorably than my sister singers who collect their stage jewels from rich admirers."

"You are still in the chorus."

"I will not always be."

"Oh, Irene." I found myself laughing wearily, fatigued by the day's surprises. "You are such an optimist. Why can you not aim lower—a supporting role instead of a starring one? A respectable marriage instead of such fevered independence? A modest suite of garnets instead of Marie Antoinette's diamonds? Such things are more naturally within your grasp."

"Such things are within any woman's grasp—which is why so few women make anything of themselves. I shall try at least."

She settled back in her seat, saying no more as the familiar streets rolled past, but I felt that I had offended her—even worse, had cast a shadow over her moment of triumph. I simply did not wish to see her fail, and she always reached so far beyond herself that ultimate failure seemed inevitable to me.

" 'A man's reach must exceed his grasp, 'else what's a heaven for?' " Irene declaimed suddenly from her quiet corner. "Why not a woman's reach?"

I need not describe the bruising progress of two women and one inexcusably heavy piece of baggage up four two-hundred year-old flights of stairs. Once our rooms had been reserved for hard-working eighteenth-century servants. We two were equally as prostrate as they after a day's labor when we finally dragged the accursed little trunk over the threshold. I panted in the doorway, loosened hairs trailing like witchweed around my face, as Irene rushed to light the gasolier and the lamps.

"Now, Nell, do you think we can swing it atop this table?"

"We can try," said I, preparing to heave up my end as she joined me.

We finally had the trunk posed like a homely centerpiece on the dining table, the gasolier's light directly above, glittering on the dull nailheads.

"It looks rather like a stage chest from 'The Merchant of Venice,'" Irene said.

"The one made of lead," I couldn't help adding pointedly.

Irene laughed as she seized a carving knife and ran it under the strapping. The buckles were rusted shut and the leather as stiff as whalebone. More fingernails snapped before we had pried the three leather tongues through their steel bits.

"Now." Irene paused to brush fallen hair from her brow with her forearm. The elegant lady of the morning was gone; she looked like a washerwoman after a long day's labor over the steaming tubs—save for the mud.

"Now," she repeated, pushing at the lid. It resisted. She snatched the knife again and ran it under the rim, ramming the handle with the heel of her hand.

There came a snap and a visible exhalation of earthy dust, then the lid sprang back.

"You show alarming signs of prophecy," Irene said, surveying the interior without a change of expression. She lifted out a score of small grey metal bars.

"Lead," said I.

An inventory revealed the remaining items to be lighter but no less puzzling than the lead bars: among them a box of starch, a huge ring of keys, and a piece of lambskin.

Irene scraped the knife over the lead bars as if peeling potatoes; no gold glimmered through.

"Perhaps this is the Zone of Diamonds in disguise." I lifted a long string of dusty amber beads.

Irene held them up to the light. "Hand-knotted Russian amber, not my favorite. Worth a few pounds, but—"

"But hardly the find of the century."

"You grow sarcastic, Penelope. It does not become you."

"Nor does chagrin become you."

"Still, old Norton went to considerable trouble to secrete these items. Think of a feeble old man toting and burying this monstrosity. He must have had a purpose."

"Yes, Irene! Purposelessness! He was muddled, don't you see? If ever he had the Zone, he'd forgotten where it is now. These few pathetic 'treasures' of his old age are only that."

"Mementos merely, you think, Nell? Lambskin and starch could signify the barrister's wig and stiffened collar bands."

"No doubt this necklace is some petty trinket that he extorted from his long-suffering wife!"

"And the lead bars—the keys?"

"Keys to the Kingdom of Afterlife, where he'd meet his Maker and receive justice when he died. He must have mused upon salvation in some disconnected way. And the lead bars signify . . . the weight of his sins against his family and fellow man—like the chains binding Marley's ghost!"

"Excellent, Nell! You find the makings for a sermon in this paltry array, but there is more order in your interpretation than Norton's disordered mind could muster. Though he did have the foresight to weight his casket with lead so it would stay hidden if the pond rose to engulf the tree roots someday . . .

"Hmm," Irene murmured, shutting the lid. "We'll think upon it. Certainly I'd rather have a trophy of our successful forestalling of Mr. Sherlock Holmes than nothing. Some happy find may help us interpret this jumble of objects."

"I'm going to bed," I announced, exasperated by her everlasting optimism. "Perhaps Rumplestiltskin will have made the amber into diamonds by morning."

The last I saw before I drew my curtains shut that evening was Irene standing bowed over the ugly chest, contemplating it as soulfully as Hamlet regarding the skull of Yorick. I fancied the box would yield as little to her, despite her hopes, as the skull had tended the melancholy Dane.

In the morning the chest had vanished, arduously buried, I suspected, under the effluvia in Irene's bedchamber. She never mentioned it again, but I knew that she had not forgotten it for a moment.

Chapter Thirteen

Astounding Propositions

❧

One of life's peculiarities is that necessity oft becomes preference and preference, necessity. This rule has governed some
of the more famous love affairs of history as well as the daily habits of
the least romantic among us.

My four-year association with Irene Adler had been fraught with
surprise, even shock, and the most unpredicted turnings in my own
life. We had lived the poor but unfettered life of Bohemians, which
is what the French call gypsies and the label modern social pundits
pin on followers of the convention-scoffing artistic life. Even as Irene
inexorably climbed the ladder of the London theatrical scene, singing
often and seldom resorting to acting, monetary security never dulled
the edge of her fierce independence.

Our Saffron Hill quarters suited us long after we could afford
lodgings elsewhere, and though the quality and quantity of Irene's
clothing increased as her theatrical presence grew, we remained content with our unlikely neighborhood. Even I had grown to like waking
to the street peddlers' Italian serenades and was as close to developing
a sense of pitch as ever in my unmusical life.

Irene still accepted—even sought—any puzzles that came her

way. I had steady work as a "typist," the word freshly minted that year to describe my skill. I confess to taking a pinch of pride in bearing a title reminiscent of the violinist and the ar*tist* (although similar words of far less noble connotation, such as atheist, swiftly humble one).

It must be borne in mind that Irene is the artist, the Bohemian, the free spirit. I have always been the mere chronicler. Yet over the course of our friendship I had altered many of the firmest prejudices of my sheltered upbringing, surprising myself at times—and even Irene.

Nothing, however, was to test my resolve and loyalty as did the long train of events that began in the wet and drear October of 1885.

The initial incident began innocuously enough. I shall never forget the transparent grey curtain of rain and fog buffeting our windows day after day. My shoes were seldom dry, though I faithfully deposited them by the fire each night. Typewriting assignments had been brisk. Irene's and my paths were in a state of what she called "Transatlantic crossing": we met only when each was bound in the opposite direction.

I was toasting my soggy stocking toes upon the fender late one Thursday afternoon when Irene came flying in the door, wearing the chill and damp like a cape. She could not doff her hat and gloves quickly enough, laying her indispensable muff so near the fire that the fur would have singed had I not rescued it.

"Let it burn! I've an opportunity that will permit me to buy a dozen muffs if I succeed." She began pacing in excitement, struggling to untie a bundle of oversize papers she carried.

"You must dry your shoes at least," I urged. "Sit down and have some Twinings—"

"Damn tea! Damn shoes. I shall wear glass slippers from now on, Nell."

Irene rushed to the piano stool and sat, pausing only to spin from side to side for a moment before facing the instrument and poising her hands over the keys.

"Are you mad, Irene?" I demanded, rising in consternation.

"No, merely wildly fortunate. Look at this! Music in the composer's own hand. Listen!"

She laid some sheets of music on the stand and began picking out the notes. The first hesitant rhythms soon smoothed into a lively and varied melody.

"Quite nice. A country piece, is it not?"

"Absolutely correct, my dear Nell. But what country?" Irene asked over the music.

"Not ours? Well, then . . . Germany, I should think."

"A very near guess. Read the lyrics."

I came over as she broke off playing, then I donned my pince-nez. "What an odd language—virtually nothing but consonants. I should go quite mad if I had to type this routinely. It can't be German, nor even Dutch."

"It is *Bohemian*." Irene beamed at me in smug triumph, though I couldn't fathom why.

"Bohemian? Who would write songs in Bohemian?"

"Mr. Antonin Dvořák, the noted Czech composer, that is who. And I shall sing them. Or one, at least."

"You don't speak Bohemian."

"It is not necessary to speak it, only to sing it."

"How will you . . . pronounce such unspeakable sounds?"

"I have transcribed a pronunciation guide with the aid of a visiting Czech violinist. By Sunday afternoon I must be letter-perfect. I perform at a concert honoring Mr. Dvořák at Henry Littleton's home. It is more than an honor for me, it is an unparalleled opportunity."

"Could they not have given you more notice? I would refuse such an imposition. How can you learn new music and a new language so quickly?"

"Practice," Irene intoned in the same stern way she instructed hopeless little Sofia, her fingers rippling over the keys. "I hope you have employment tomorrow and Saturday, for I must be a quicker study than I have ever been. I will eat and sleep at this poor piano until Sunday noon."

"I will not sleep at all then," said I. "Can I do nothing to help you?"

"Can you sew?"

"Certainly I can . . . oh!" I sank to the arm of an easy chair. "I see. You must not only learn Czech and a new song by Sunday, but must have something splendid to wear for the occasion. I will do my best. What else may I do?"

Irene sang a long, lovely phrase in gibberish so thick her mouth seemed full of potatoes. "Only tell me I sound Bohemian-born."

"My dear Irene, I would not know a Bohemian from a Fabian."

With that I fled the premises to pursue errands in a larger and infinitely more comprehensible world.

⚜ ⚜ ⚜

By Sunday morning I felt that I knew more Bohemian than I had ever wished. Irene's song was No. 4 in the Dvořák opuses, a peasant ditty titled *"Kydžmne stará matka."* I cannot transcribe here the bizarre diacritical marks that littered the lyrics like so many dead flies. Irene said the phrase translated to "Songs My Mother Taught Me." I would have accepted any translation as truth, including "Songs That Kept Me Awake."

Still, Antonín Dvořák was not one to ridicule. The Czech composer had become something of a sensation in London over the past few years. I remembered reading that his opera, *The Spectre Bride,* had been well received, so I understood Irene's enthusiasm for this Bohemian's music. Dvořák's favor could mean much to a young singer like herself, for the hidebound London operatic establishment forced an American abroad to pursue more out-of-the-way support.

Irene insisted that I accompany her to this private concert. I really would rather not have gone. I do not tolerate suspense well—and frankly feared that this time Irene had tackled a higher hurdle than even she could comfortably clear. I did not want to see her fail.

She had set me to stripping her best navy-blue moire gown of its trim: serpents of flounces, frills and braid coiled at my feet as the abominable syllables of songs my mother distinctly had *not* taught me

fell on my undefended ears. Small wonder that the vowel-ridden romance languages of French and Italian serve opera best; yet Irene
slowly and surely endowed the unfortunate assemblage of consonants
with dignity and even emotional appeal.

Despite her progress on the song, I despaired of finishing the
gown in time. Irene dismissed my anxiety about new trims.

"We must improvise, Nell. When there is no time, we must improvise."

On Sunday morning she ignored my eleventh-hour suggestions
for trimming and decorated the gown with only white lace collar and
cuffs. Despite the richness of the moire and the fineness of the lace,
she looked but one step above a well-dressed serving woman.

"Plain black suited Lillie Langtry quite well once, Nell," she consoled me. "Navy is black's first-cousin and Mr. Dvořák is a simple
man; these are peasant songs, after all."

So we went in a hansom cab as black as my expectations through
the grey day to Mr. Littleton's flat in Victoria Mansions. For once I
unwittingly outshone Irene in a tea gown of pale beige Sicilienne
trimmed in some of Whiteley's amber velvet, which Irene had insisted I have for special occasions. The gown had elbow-length sleeves
to which I was not accustomed and a narrow open neckline edged in
a froth of lace.

Thus I was the peacock and Irene the wren for a change, all of
which—taken with the hasty circumstances of her appearance—
made me exceedingly anxious.

Irene was expected and I was accepted as her friend. Mr. Littleton's
airy quarters were furnished with eighteenth-century antiques, including the piano. Many songs and singers made up the programme.
I waited impatiently for the chitchat to cease, for guests like myself
to be seated and the music to begin—or, in Irene's case, to be faced.

Each unpronounceable song title was introduced. Each song
was performed. All the other vocalists were men, and they preceded
Irene. I waited, wringing the cords of my reticule, as tenor or baritone delivered song after song. The music was enchanting enough—
quite different from our English country songs—but the tenors and

baritones all sang with a stiff operatic zeal that ill-suited the simple subject matter, even when conveyed in the incomprehensible Bohemian words.

Disaster. That was the one English word that rang in my skull. I had a headache and my neck and forearms were cold, not being used to such exposure, although the other ladies present were equally revealed.

As I recognized the title called, Irene rose from the front row and stood sheltered in the grand piano's inward curve. The accompanist awaited her nod. A silence from an audience bored to restlessness greeted her subdued appearance.

"At least we could have used the knotted fringe," I moaned softly to myself. But it was too late to trim her gown, the day, the opportunity. All was lost.

Irene nodded to the man at the piano, lifted her chin and began singing. She did not use full power, but her dark contralto ranged lightly through the melody. The restraint added a poignancy I felt even through the alien words.

As for the gown—Irene had chosen impeccably. The white collar and cuffs drew all eyes to her expressive face and hands; the navy blue moire gown acted as a dramatically dark curtain against which her pale hands pantomimed emotions that needed no translation.

Because she was the last to perform, daylight was receding. The room darkened around her while the candles' mellow glow waxed warmer, flickering on her face almost in time to the dusky, cello-sweet sounds swelling from her throat.

The song had ended for several seconds before the audience accepted that finality. Applause burst forth like thunder. I was on my feet for joy, laughing and clapping and crying—and so were those around me.

Irene nodded once, casting her eyes down, and slipped back to her seat. I rushed toward her but was anticipated by a short, stout gentleman.

"Beauty-ful, beauty-ful," he was murmuring, shaking her hand up and down like a pump handle, his eyes unabashedly bright with tears. "When I hear you at the Savoy I thought you might suit for this song. I prefer usually the tenor or the baritone. Nothing kills song so much as a wobbly contralto who must the Italians say how?—use too much *portomento,* you understand?"

"*Si,*" Irene answered quickly in Italian, with an unusually modest smile. "Too much gliding from note to note, rather than letting each syllable and tone speak for itself. Was my Bohemian passable, Mr. Dvořák?"

"Passable? This means . . . ?" The composer looked around.

"Acceptable," another gentleman supplied.

"Beauty-ful," the composer trilled, waving his hand to dismiss Irene's worries. "You will be only woman to sing my songs so long as Anton Dvořák has say in the matter. We must talk more later. Adler," he mused with narrowed eyes, "I know you are American. Adler is German, no?"

Irene retreated in a subtle way, as she did when anyone—including myself—inquired into her origins. "No," she said, and said no more.

Mr. Dvořák patted her hand. "Does not matter. Something in the soul is Slavic. We are easily touched people. But only by quality. Now go I to other peoples, but unhappily."

Waiting admirers quickly filled the gap the composer left. I toured the elegant rooms, contentedly eavesdropping on the praise being heaped on Irene's voice, phrasing, demeanor and dress.

How could I have doubted, after all this time? Irene was the ultimate mistress of molding the world to her will. Having witnessed and shared in her various adventures, from the seamy matter of the drowned sailor, which remains a mystery to this day, to the glorious subjugation of a concert audience, I of all people should have known by now that Irene needed none of my worry.

✤　✤　✤

Irene's Dvořák recital was the first blast of the horns of change in our harmoniously orchestrated domestic lives. Our ordered life in London was never to be quite the same although the great change itself was slow in coming.

The cold, wet weather of autumn had become the cold dry admonishment of winter before that day arrived. I had borrowed Irene's muff to make my long omnibus journey to the Temple. Godfrey Norton had called upon me again for a bit of typewriting, as he did from time to time.

Irene had not regarded her muff with the same respect since that October day when she had arrived home with news of her command performance before Dvořák. It often lay about our rooms, abandoned like a no-longer-favorite pet. I had finally claimed it that morning, both for the practical warmth it lent and because I couldn't bear to see an item once so necessary forgotten and tossed aside.

Mr. Norton had heard my step and was at the chamber door before I could knock.

"Come in, Miss Huxleigh, come in. A bitter wind blows through Fleet Street—why, what is the matter? Your face is rubbed raw from the cold!"

"The . . . wind, as you say. Quite bitter."

"Indeed. Have a chair and a dish of tea."

He had moved to larger chambers some months before, so I found myself installed in the sheltering arms of a leather wing chair in the inner sanctum with a piping cup presented to me shortly after.

The odor of peppermint tea wafting under my red nose undid me. I pulled a handkerchief from the recesses of the muff—Irene had long ago showed me its secret pockets—and buried my face in its unfurled folds.

"My dear Miss Huxleigh, what is the matter? You must tell me."

"It's the tea," I sniffled openly and not too logically. "The very kind Irene bought me when she saved me from the urchin on the pavement, don't you see? Peppermint." Off I went into a most humiliating wail.

"No, I don't see, but I think I'd better. Why don't you start at the beginning?"

I glanced with what I knew were very crimson eyes at Mr. Norton. I confess that his solicitude sat very pleasantly upon me, who was not used to gentlemen, handsome or otherwise, taking any no-

tice of me at all. Now I saw the sincerity behind it. I forgot completely that I had first met him in connection with a case of Irene's.
I was amazed to find myself regarding him as a friend.

"Irene has had another piece of great good fortune," said I. "I
learned of it just yesterday." He stiffened slightly, as he always did at
mention of Irene. "I must be weeping because I'm so happy for her."

"Oh? Has she found herself another prominent client?"

"A prominent mentor."

Mr. Norton's face tightened. I knew he still regarded Irene with
suspicion.

"Oh, no, nothing of that nature! It is her singing career. Mr. Antonín Dvořák, the composer, heard her sing in the autumn and was
so enamored—taken—with her talent that he recommended her to
the director of La Scala and Irene has been invited to become an understudy in Milan." I paused before I should hiccough. "They need
her immediately. She will study all the suitable major female roles; it
will give her formidable versatility and I have no doubt she will be a
prima donna one day."

"She seems to have mastered the role already," he hazarded.

"You have not seen Irene at her . . . warmest," said I. "Nor have
you heard her sing. She has a divine voice, difficult to cast at times,
because her range straddles dark soprano and contralto, so this latest
opportunity is what she has been waiting for, working for—"

"And she leaves for Milan . . . ?"

"Within the week. Oh, you should have seen her! She came home
so . . . vibrant. Even speaking she seemed to be singing. I had not realized how hard this life was for her, the struggle to train her voice and
obtain small singing roles, to pursue these 'cases', as you call them—
she was like a bird released from a cage, laughing and flitting about
the rooms. Very like a nightingale."

"Hmm." Mr. Norton lifted a dark eyebrow at the cup now cool-
ing in my hand, and I dutifully drank. "Yet she leaves you behind in
a cage of your own and never notices."

"Oh, no." I sat forward, sobered by his assumption of Irene's
dereliction. "She wanted—assumed that I would accompany her to

Milan. *Milano,* she calls it." I couldn't help smiling to recall her exuberance. "I pointed out that I do not translate Italian and there would be no employment for me there."

"She had not thought of that."

"No. Her face quite fell as it dawned on her. She had not considered the practicalities, you see." I sipped more tea, as braced by its mint flavor as I had been four years earlier when Irene had prescribed it for me on another occasion when I had felt lost and alone. How odd that Godfrey Norton of all people should be extending the same succor to me now on the loss of Irene.

He nodded stiffly. "I remember my mother on the sale of a novel, that same wild exhilaration."

"Irene said she would provide for me, but I pointed out that her understudy's pay was barely sufficient to keep her in respectable circumstances in a foreign land. Also, I reminded her that I had always paid my share of our expenses, my later earnings making up for the early days when I had depended on her. I am not about to abdicate my independence now."

"*Brava,* Miss Huxleigh. Miss Adler is not the only star in the firmament of women's independence. You have sterling qualities of your own, you know."

"I do?" I must confess that the depth of Mr. Norton's personal regard both startled and pleased me. His kind eyes rested on me, a hint of amusement in their slate-grey depths, like sun glancing off winter water.

"You do. I would go to court to defend the proposition. I wonder how Miss Adler will get on without you?"

"Splendidly, I know it. Our association was one of convenience, not likeness of temperament, surely. Still—" I felt a shower of tears gathering and quickly swallowed the last of the tea, now lukewarm.

"What will you do now?"

"Help Irene prepare. She intends to take very little; there isn't time."

"Will you move from Saffron Hill? The neighborhood is rough."

"Not to a native, and I am that now. I even speak the occasional Italian phrase and have grown used to the . . . the ease of the vicinity. I can afford to keep the rooms myself now, thanks to such generous payment as I get at the Temple."

"Nevertheless, it will be a great adjustment, my dear Miss Huxleigh. I wonder that you answered my call under the circumstances."

I set aside the tea to stroke the muff that lay, petlike, upon my lap. "To tell you the truth, I needed to escape our rooms for a bit, to get my mind off her leaving."

He took the cue briskly. "And so you shall." He swept a pile of documents off a corner of the desk. "These await and are guaranteed to divert you from all other matters."

"Exactly what I need." I set aside my wraps and extracted my pince-nez from the muff. "It is quite a relief to have expressed my feelings. I fear you are a captive recipient—"

"Not at all. I am honored by your confiding in me. I comprehend your position better than you think, even if I do not understand the inestimable Irene Adler."

"You would like her if you knew her," I put in mildly.

"Such certainty!" He smiled. "But I shall not have the chance now, shall I? She will be the toast of the Continent, and you and I shall stay behind on this dull little isle and write deeds."

The picture he painted was so ridiculous that I laughed, and once having done that, found it impossible to weep again.

I returned home before dark fell—Mr. Norton insisted that I leave early enough for that—to find the paraphernalia from Irene's bedroom flowing into the front room like effluvia of years past.

"What shall I take, darling Penelope!" she cried in distraction. "The climate will be quite different. The summer things, of course— but it is northern Italy. Alas, I feel like a character adrift in the wrong opera; I do not know my part and must improvise as I go."

"Here," I said, taking charge. "We must divide the things into seasons and then into categories—underthings, overthings, basques, jackets, skirts, bonnets, shoes."

"Yes, I see. Quite right." Irene looked up gratefully from under her disheveled forelocks—she had been unearthing clothing and dragging boxes and trunks around all day.

I sat on the floor with her and began sorting the explosion of items.

"I shall miss you dreadfully," she declaimed suddenly.

"And I you. But this relocation seems too opportune to miss."

"Will you not be . . . lonely?"

"Yes." I thought of peppermint tea and braced myself. "Perhaps I will buy a bird. A canary. I am used to music around the place."

There was a silence into which neither of us would leap.

"Poor little Sofia," I said with a half-laugh that edged into a sob. "Who will teach her to sing her scales now?"

"You can! God knows my perfect pitch stood the child no good at all. What harm can you do? Or—you can sell the piano, if you like."

"No . . . I can cover it and put the birdcage on it."

"I'm sorry to leave you with this mess." Irene fondly took in the eccentric array, her fingers absently moving across the melee as if saying farewell to old friends. I knew that every ribbon told a tale to her—of where she had bought it and where it might have originated and how she had transformed it into a key part of her chameleon wardrobe. "You can sell it on the Portobello Road."

"Or you may need it and send for it."

She nodded. "How will you do? Alone?"

"Quite nicely, especially now." I couldn't help looking smug. Irene wasn't the only one to come home with surprising news of her profession.

"You sly boots! What is it? You have news!"

"Only that I have a permanent position, so I shan't have to worry about an ebb and flow of income."

"A permanent position? Is it congenial?"

"Very much so. I find the work amenable and the vicinity soothing."

"At the Temple?" Suspicion embroidered her voice.

"Yes—"

"The *Inner* Temple? Oh, Nell, you are not going to rely on working only for *that man?*"

"As a matter of fact, I am. I find Mr. Norton a most considerate employer."

"He is using you," Irene said, her eyes flashing.

"How?" I challenged. "You will be gone. You are stymied at the moment in pursuing the Zone of Diamonds. There is nothing for him to learn from me."

"I mistrust him."

"Might he not want to engage me for my talents, my skills, rather than my association with you? I have worked for him from time to time for some years now. He has known most of that time that we share lodgings, and he has never sought to use that knowledge in any way."

"I'm sorry, Nell! Of course he would want a typist girl of your cleverness and skill—and your experience in my little investigations makes you an ideal assistant for a barrister. I meant to imply nothing except my . . . own fear of leaving you on your own."

"I am better fit to be on my own than before I met you," I said softly.

"Thank you," Irene said, an odd tightness in her voice. "Thank you, my dear Nell." We folded petticoats in silence. Then. "Perhaps I have misjudged Mr. Norton. His family tale is a sad one. I can even see why he might think himself entitled to the Zone."

"Oh?" I had never heard Irene concede another's right to the object of this treasure hunt before. "The odd thing is that he has never seemed to think that himself. I fear he doesn't believe in it as you do, Irene. You will take the chest with you, I imagine."

She stood, stiff from a day of delving into bureaus and wardrobes. "Take it with me? Yes, I should. Certainly it would not do to leave it here with you; it might attract some sinister interest."

"I doubt it; not after all this time. And even you cannot decipher the contents."

"No. They must hold some very specific meaning." Her voice

trailed into silent thought. Then Irene glanced down at me, her warmest smile lifting my spirits. She extended me a hand. "Come, Penelope! We will have teacakes toasted on the fender like old times— I bought three bags full today—and a bottle of champagne."

"Alcohol?" I said nervously, still not certain that ladies should consume such things.

"Ambrosia!" Irene insisted. "In this particular form it is ever so much more bracing than peppermint tea."

Even at the last Irene's prescience staggered me. How had she known what libation Mr. Norton had given me only that morning? Then I saw that she, as I, simply remembered our common past, which would have no role in our separate futures—save remembrance.

⚜   ⚜   ⚜

I saw Irene off at Waterloo Station. From there she would travel to Southampton and thence by boat to France and by rail to Milan.

She looked ever so handsome and brave under a bonnet of crimson feathers. She had taken the muff, after all. It guarded her arm like a talisman. Her other arm lifted to wave farewell.

Already the dusty carriage window had softened her image in my eyes; the engine chugged from the station, raising storm clouds of steam to obscure the passengers. And so Irene Adler vanished into the mist from which she had appeared. I turned and trudged through Waterloo Station's mausoleum-like immensity and made my way by foot to the Temple.

A long walk it was, but welcome. I arrived to find Godfrey Norton, his fists on his hips, studying an object whose weight was crushing the many papers on his desk.

I gasped when I saw it. He looked up, mystified, then handed me a letter. "It came by messenger—with this," he said. I recognized Irene's dashing hand in her signature green ink instantly.

"Dear Mr. Norton," the missive began. "I embark for a new country and a new chapter of my performing career. I doubt we shall ever meet again, but perhaps the possession of this chest, which belonged to your late and universally unlamented father, will be of some consolation in my absence." I looked up, almost hearing Irene's most acid tones sear the room in that last sentence.

Mr. Norton nodded, and I bent my head to read more.

"I know you have scant faith in the existence of such a prize, but it is my belief that the contents of this chest spell out a clue to Marie Antoinette's missing Zone of Diamonds. I have been unable to decipher them. With your knowledge of family history you may have better luck.

"As for pursuing the sort of distasteful inquiries for which you berated me, those days are behind me. I am happy to wash my hands of the last vestiges of such necessity and wish you good fortune in your quest.

"You cannot do better if you seek advice, support or a faithful friend than to rely upon Penelope Huxleigh. She is the true treasure I leave to you. Appreciate her well, as I always will."

It was signed: "Yours sincerely, Irene Adler."

I had shed all my tears, so looked up with only a smile when I had finished reading. Godfrey Norton seemed far less at peace. Irene's unexpected gesture had completely muddled his opinion of her. He looked so boyishly puzzled that I was tempted to ruffle his pretty dark hair, as I would have for a young charge who had bumped his head on an unsuspected obstacle, but of course I could do no such thing.

"Why the devil would she do it?" he demanded. "The Zone of Diamonds, if it exists to be found, would be worth thousands of pounds. What does she mean by this?"

And so he fretted on, suspecting more than the surface intent, but unable to uncover another motive. If Irene Adler had wished to discomfit Godfrey Norton, she could not have found a more fiendish means than this unexpected generosity of hers.

I concealed my smile, for it would not do for an employee to set herself above an employer, and interrupted his muttered stream of questions.

"Pardon me, Mr. Norton, but if you would be so kind as to

remove that chest—and I know it is dreadfully heavy—I could put some of those documents on your desk into type."

So he did, and so I did—and so Irene Adler and I had a last, long laugh together, after all.

Chapter Fourteen

Enter Casanova

∼⊙∼

The effect Irene Adler's absence had upon my life was most evident in my diaries during that period. I had recorded the minutiae of my days since receiving my first diary at the age of twelve. These sturdy volumes, bound in maroon cloth, were intended to be morally instructive on review.

Irene's absence meant many silent evenings sequestered in the Saffron Hill lodgings, so I dutifully reviewed. Whether my moral growth was apparent in those handwritten pages is debatable; indeed, my association with Irene Adler had led me down many bizarre offshoots of the straight and narrow path my upbringing had prepared for me.

The inescapable fact was that my diaries bristled with fascinating names, places and incidents during my five years with Irene. My pen crowded to the pages' gilt-edges in order to record fully the details: the case of the lost cross of Oscar Wilde, the indelicate matter of the birth control advocate, the mystery of the sinister Savoyard.

Before those halcyon days with Irene, my notations were scant and, I fear, dull beyond imagining. Now, her absence goaded me to fill my days with matters worth recording. I maintained connections with the more genteel members of the theatrical set—indeed, they made some effort to see that I not be ignored, whether on Irene's instructions or not, I do not know.

Such associations, however infrequent, led to such unlikely but amusing entries as my inadvertent role in the courtship of Oscar Wilde, the unpleasant encounter with the Mayfair hypnotist and other incidents that have no place in this narrative.

I found most rewarding, however, the renewed time to devote to good works. I began teaching English to Sofia and her friends; each Tuesday evening a troupe of these little larks enlivened the Saffron Hill quarters for two hours and depleted my hot chocolate reserves. Inspired by Irene's intrepid ways, I began working with the Salvation Army in Whitechapel, where I saw poverty, crime and despair enough to write several Dickensian novels, had I any gift for fiction.

Yet for all my expanded activities, Irene's frequent letters made the liveliest reading in my diaries nowadays. In a sense she remained a part of my life, however faint and distant her voice. From the first, I shared portions of her correspondence with Godfrey Norton, a natural consequence of our daily contact, my loneliness and his barrister's suspicion.

"Have you heard from your associate abroad?" he would ask. "Has she inquired about my progress with the chest?"

"No. She has not even asked in what kind of temper you received it. She has put it behind her."

"Not likely." He pushed his chair away from the desk as I brought his morning tea, his fingers drumming the mahogany. "She enjoys Italy, then?"

"The warmer climate is much kinder to her voice than London's eternal fog, damp and chill."

"True, true, but how does she get on there?"

"She has much to learn at La Scala, and is a newcomer. I believe she will win them over as she has everyone she met here."

"Everyone?"

"Do you consider yourself an exception?"

"I'll admit her parting gesture caught me off-guard, but then, gestures are stock-in-trade with her."

"Mr. Norton, I have sat in the Royal Courts of Justice to watch you argue a case. You are very grand in your robes and powdered wig—but you have a propensity for the grand gesture that is at least the equal of Irene's."

"Do you think so?" He leaned forward to stare at me. "Quite an unmercifully astute observer, aren't you, Miss Huxleigh?"

"Like most people, I am myopic about myself," I said modestly.

"And about her?"

"Oh, I may be partial, but never blind, Mr. Norton, never blind."

"I wonder," was all he would answer on that occasion.

Yet his queries cropped up again, and again. I began to take Irene's letters to chambers and read him the best bits. It soon became a weekly ritual to share a quiet morning tea over a fat letter from Irene.

"Do you think I shall ever solve the riddle of the cursed chest, Miss Huxleigh?" he would often ask with his hands clasped behind his neck, as he leaned back in his chair staring out the window at a lacework of bare branches.

Hearing of Irene always reminded him of the puzzling inheritance from his late father—and of the Zone of Diamonds.

"I don't know, Mr. Norton. Have you made any progress?"

He glanced at me sharply with those pale lucid eyes that missed so little. "I have been musing upon it, Miss Huxleigh."

He didn't trust me, of course, not completely. With matters of the chamber, utterly; with the link between his family, the missing jewels and Irene, not at all.

Thus I came in one spring morning chirping like a thrush to find Godfrey Norton frowning like a hungry vulture.

"Your heroine has not lost her taste for diamonds, after all."

He slapped the morning's edition of the *Daily Telegraph* atop a fat tower of documents tied with red tape. I lifted the paper, which had been folded to display the article that had caught his eye. A

sketch of Irene in evening dress—beautifully evoked by some anonymous fine Italian hand—topped the column.

Below it a headline trumpeted, "American Singer, Late of London,
Substitutes for La Calvetari in Rossini's 'La Cenerentola' Draped in
Fortune in Diamonds." A smaller headline noted that "Three Pinker-
ton Detectives Guard Diva."

"Oh, this is wonderful!" I sat to read the article. "What an opportunity! Listen to what they say: 'The dark tones of Miss Adler's
voice, which verge on the contralto, add a dimension and poignancy
to the mezzo-soprano role of Cinderella seldom heard on operatic
stages'—"

I read on, hungry for information, while Godfrey Norton pointedly rattled the tea things. I ignored my dereliction of duty in the
face of such delicious news. He finally brought me a cup and sat upon
the desk's burdened edge to coddle his own in his hands while I
blurted on.

"Apparently the opera is an Italian version of Cinderella, and Irene
has gone from the ashes of the understudy to diamonds at the ball
in true fairy tale fashion. Only listen: 'Miss Adler's brilliant col-
oratura singing enamours a new generation with the seductive charms
of Rossini's oft-forgotten masterwork. Even the spectacular diamonds
that bedeck her in the ball sequence cannot outshine her vocal glitter,
especially the fully faceted fire of Miss Adler's voice in the final, very
difficult rondo, *Nacqui all' affano* (Born to Sorrow).' Oh, Godfrey, she
is a triumph!"

"She certainly seems to have got herself center stage," he remarked.

"Is that not exactly what she went to Italy to do?"

"It is obvious why she lost interest in the Zone of Diamonds and
abandoned my father's chest." He sounded almost piqued. "How can
they compete with an admirer able to"—he lifted the newspaper to
read the headline through curled lips—"drape her in diamonds.' "

Mr. Norton rose and walked to the window, then went on much
like a prosecuting attorney with a hostile witness.

"I know, Miss Huxleigh, that you have made a heroine of your erstwhile chambermate. I am loath to invoke the counsel of your late father, but isn't it possible that you worship at feet of clay? Most actresses and opera singers affect real jewels on the stage to prove the regard of the many admirers who vie for their rather public favors. Evidently the redoubtable Irene Adler has succeeded once again in a less honorable arena. She has sold herself to evoke one day's wonder in the public press. The jewels are obviously the gift of a wealthy admirer who has obtained his own . . . gifts in return."

I could see only the edge of Mr. Norton's face as he stared out the window. His hands, clasped behind his back, worked with the same confidently impatient energy they often betrayed. I masked my indignation in a velvet-gloved counterattack that Irene would have delivered fairly purring. I merely managed to sound prim.

"These diamonds are more than ordinary baubles. They must be very costly—priceless," I breathed, quoting from the article: ". . . two thousand linked together lacelike from right shoulder to left hip and anchored at the *décolletage* by a magnificent diamond rose—"

"A fortune, obviously," he said curtly. "And you stomach the way it was obtained?"

"From an admirer," I admitted, as though reluctant.

"Wealthy admirers are like vultures: where there is one, others gather."

"No doubt you are more worldly than I, Mr. Norton. Yet the result has been a great piece of good fortune for Irene. No operatic debut has received such wide notice as this, I gather. And the reviews are excellent."

"Reviews!" He turned burning eyes on me, much as if I stood in the witness box. I should have been quite cowed, had I not known him in other moods, and had I not a courtroom surprise of my own to spring in Irene's behalf. "You consider *reviews* in circumstances like this? You shock me, Miss Huxleigh."

I smiled. I had never shocked anyone before. It was a rather pleasant feeling, as Irene once said. "I see nothing wrong in what Irene has done. It was most clever of her—in fact, quite worthy of a P.T. Barnum, to draw attention to her operatic debut this way. And she with so few resources—"

"Save for wealthy admirers!"

"Well . . . yes."

Godfrey Norton stood astounded at my complacent acceptance of the situation. I admired his air of fiery scorn, his pale eyes bright as lightning. He looked more handsome than ever when he was angry.

"You *know* the identity of the bestower of the diamonds!" he said abruptly, changing tactics. "You aren't surprised by this at all."

I bowed my head. "You have found me out, Mr. Norton. Irene's wealthy admirer is Mr. Charles Tiffany, the American jeweler."

"What?!" He seemed even more outraged to have his suspicions confirmed.

I felt like a cat toying with a rather cooperative mouse. It was most exhilarating.

Mr. Norton continued speaking, more quietly but in great disdain. "How can a woman of strong personal standards like yourself accept such an . . . adventuress as a friend?"

I answered in even lower tones. "How can a man whose own mother was so misjudged by the world turn the same wrong estimation on another woman?"

We regarded each other for some time, the anger and disbelief gradually fading from his face, a smile softening mine.

Godfrey Norton sat down suddenly. "I have taken events at face value; a grave mistake for one in my profession. Enlighten me, please, Miss Huxleigh."

I turned the paper to face me again. It was a wonderful sketch. Irene looked lovelier than Lillie Langtry. The swag of diamonds glittering on her bosom only underlined her own beauty. Yet this figure seemed beyond the two of us in this room, too—beyond the Inner Temple and London and the time we had each spent with her. Irene Adler looked as remote as Venus when it rises blue-white in the Eastern evening.

I smoothed the paper. "Appearances, Mr. Norton. You should know a thing or two of them. Irene is poor, as I am, as your mother was when she left your father's house with her three sons to rear. Irene cannot compete with divas who win their laurels in emeralds and rubies and sapphires—"

"Of course she can! She is as beautiful as any of them. I have never quibbled about that. She was born for the world's admiration."

"But she will not vie for it. Not in that way."

His eyes narrowed skeptically.

"Not in that way," I repeated firmly. "So, she finds another way. I am certain that she persuaded Mr. Tiffany to loan her this 'corsage' of diamonds, which his jewelers have been working on for some years. He does admire her—she investigated the Zone of Diamonds for him years ago—and he is wealthy. He is also canny enough to know that a debut attended by Pinkertons and publicity will whet the world's appetite for a priceless set of jewels like this. The diamonds are back in the Tiffany vaults by now, Mr. Norton. Irene has had the satisfaction of making her debut as a Cinderella on an equal footing, so to speak, with the other singers who *will* let themselves be bought, and who is hurt?"

"The world will think ill of her," he said softly. I saw his light eyes darken at the ever-rankling thought of his maligned mother.

"Irene does not care what anyone thinks of her but herself."

"A man may live by such a Bohemian code, but that is impossible for a woman."

"It would be for myself, but not for Irene. She is not an ordinary woman. You must not assume that of her, Mr. Norton, or you will be often wrong."

"My mother suffered greatly," he said suddenly. "Oh, she put a good public face on it—and a serene private one, too, before us boys. But I sensed it, her humiliation at being forced to leave that man; the worse humiliation of the court action, when all she had earned on her own became his . . ."

"I am sorry. There is nothing worse than watching one we love subjected to injustice, pinned into a false position in front of the whole world. That is why I cannot allow you to think ill of Irene; at least, not on this issue."

"Others will, who have no access to an advocate so eloquent as you, Miss Huxleigh."

I had the grace to blush at his praise, but would not be distracted from the main point. "In this case, I care not about others. I work for you, Mr. Norton. I cannot continue to do so if you believe that Irene is other than she is. I cannot defend her every act, but she would never sell herself, no matter the appearances."

"I hope your faith is never tried," he said, rising. "The truer the believer, the more bitter the disillusionment. Our tea has cooled; it was not well made, in any case. Perhaps you would like that, er, that article for a keepsake."

"Why, I am most grateful, unless you would wish to keep it to remind you of false conclusions . . . ?" I extended it, but he waved it away.

"No, no. I have learned my lesson without needing an eternal reminder of it."

So I went home that evening and pasted the portrait of Irene into my diary. It took up most of the page and saved me writing about the dull day. I was not certain that I had convinced Mr. Norton, for he was a young man and sure in his prejudices, although a clever one. And he did not know the power of faith. Though I only knew Jasper Higgenbottom for a short period, he never in that time behaved in a way that disappointed me; I was sure that wherever he was—still serving the Church in Africa or called to a Higher Service—he had not failed me yet. In the present instance, a letter from Irene soon arrived that described events exactly as I had anticipated them. I began to feel quite a competent detective, in my modest way.

Whether the incident elevated Godfrey Norton's opinion of Irene, it certainly altered his attitude toward myself. He began to consult me on the character of certain of his clients, recognizing that I was an impartial observer but not an insensitive one. He even began to ask me to "take notes," an invitation which invariably brought a smothered smile to my face.

The first such occasion was the oddest. An old woman garbed in the solid black of deep mourning surmounted by a Persian lamb pelisse equally as dark entered the chambers, some sort of clumsy green sack hanging at her side. It reminded me of my forlorn carpetbag. I summed her up at once: one of those half-mad old creatures who are convinced that the Fenians are about to assassinate Queen Victoria or that the ghost of their great-uncle Bloodgood still haunts the family manse.

Such eccentric clients did not often cross our threshold unannounced; solicitors who knew that Mr. Norton rarely declined a case involving an elderly lady's affairs would post documents on troubling cases to his attention or seek his advice in person.

"You're not a solicitor!" the old woman exclaimed, regarding me in my typewriting corner through spectacles as thick as quartz.

"Indeed not. Nor is Mr. Norton. He is a barrister. There is a significant difference."

"Oh, dear! I cannot cart myself to yet another doorway within this maze of bricks and passages and running men. Can't someone simply tell me what to do?"

I smiled to imagine this fragile personage caught amongst—not a parliament of crows—but a wig of barristers flocking to the Royal Courts of Justice across Fleet Street.

"My dear lady," I suggested, "I suspect you require a solicitor, someone to handle a family rather than a court matter. He will consult a barrister for you if warranted—"

"What is it, Miss Huxleigh?" Mr. Norton peered out from the inner sanctum his financial stability had afforded.

"A lady, who is seeking a solicitor—"

"I hardly know what I seek, only that it is help I need," said she, settling onto a chair so firmly her layers of garments rustled in a henlike manner.

"Help?" Mr. Norton crossed the threshold to regard the canvas sack beside her. "Please step in and explain your difficulty."

I sighed, seeing that Mr. Norton's native sympathy had snared him once again.

"Miss Huxleigh, perhaps you could fetch some tea."

I sighed more loudly. Now that I had weaned Mr. Norton from the routine brews of Lipton's tea chain and acquainted him with the rarities of Twinings, I was loath to lavish them on every indigent caller, for such the old lady clearly was.

Two steaming cups were shortly before them. I prepared to withdraw, when Mr. Norton addressed me again.

"Perhaps you could bring back a cup of this delicious tea for yourself, Miss Huxleigh, and some foolscap so that you may note down what Mrs. Mutterworth has to say."

"Oh, why, there would be nothing to it," I replied, my tone implying quite the opposite.

"Cut the cackle," the old lady murmured in a rough *sotto voce* only I could hear.

"Not merely muddled but rude," I complained beneath my breath as I collected my tea, paper and pencils and returned to Mr. Norton's office.

"You are a widow, ma'am?" Mr. Norton was inquiring.

"Widow!" she hooted. "I'm no Old Lady at Windsor. Never wed, not once. Not even twice."

"Well, then, *Miss* Mutterworth, what is your problem?"

"What is yours, young man, that you cannot see it plain before your eye? If I must have a solicitor, I should like one who can see *and* hear. You seem to have difficulties in both areas."

"Then please point out the obvious, Miss Mutterworth," Mr. Norton suggested with more patience than I could have mustered, forebearing to remind her again that he was not a solicitor and that he was in no way obliged to hear her woes; indeed, it violated professional protocol to do so.

The old lady gestured to the awkward parcel huddled at her skirts. "This. This is all my only brother has left me. Can you imagine such a turn of events? Not dead two days and his solicitor"—she fairly spat the word in a croak of contempt—"sits me down and says I'm to have nothing for my old age but *this!*"

Mr. Norton and I stared at the green canvas heaped on the floor, as though covering a beehive.

"Solicitor!" the beldame mumbled under her breath in an uncivil croak. "Solicitor!"

"Mr. Norton is a barrister," I reiterated in my employer's defense. The distinction meant nothing to Miss Mutterworth.

"The house will have to be sold," she went on. "I've not a penny now to keep it with, not with Cavendish gone. I shall have to sleep in the lanes . . . with *this* for company."

"What is . . . that?" Mr. Norton inquired delicately, not looking as if he cared to know.

"Nasty, foul thing!" The old lady shuddered until the jet beads on her bonnet rim chattered. Her gloved hand lifted the canvas at arm's length, like an oversize, tainted teapot cosy.

"Cut the cackle!" a voice screeched at us. "Cut the cackle!"

Behind the stained brass tines of a cage a lurid green parrot shuffled its clawed feet along a wooden perch.

"Quite a ferociously articulate bird," Mr. Norton said.

"Casanova," Miss Mutterworth named it, in tones of loathing. "I put up with it when the old fool bought it. Hours he spent with it Taught it to 'walk the plank' into a soup tureen for a bath. Taught it every foul phrase to be heard on the streets, things even a cart-house pins back its ears to blot out. Cavendish knew I couldn't tolerate the beast, and now he's left it to me."

"Tippecanoe and treasure, too. Tippecanoe and treasure, too," the parrot screamed amiably. "Cut the cackle."

I couldn't help smiling. Mr. Norton's face wore the bemused look of man who—for quite benevolent reasons—realizes he has invited the fates to play topsy-turvy with his sanity. He now not only had the eccentric Miss Mutterworth to placate, but the rough-tongued bird as well. It was clear that neither's voice had ever, like Cordelia's, been "soft, gentle and low," an excellent thing not only in a woman but a parrot. I'm sure the Bard would have concurred had he ever met Casanova.

"What was there for your brother to leave?" Mr. Norton inquired hopefully.

"A great deal! All our annuity from Father. Cavendish always got most of the income, but a portion was for my use. Now it has apparently vanished, and all I am left by law is this abomination!"

Apparently "abomination" was a favorite word of Miss Mutterworth's, for the parrot immediately cocked its gaudy head and cawed, "Abomination, abomination. The Fenians come, the Fenians come," or some such nonsense.

Mr. Norton frowned, though not at the bird's chatter. "So your brother had tangible assets which are missing?"

"Indeed. His solicitors say that Cavendish kept custody of it all, save for the miserable will. But where is it?"

"I don't know, Miss Mutterworth. Unless the solicitors are delinquent—"

"Brackenberry, Fettiplace and Mumbray, some such muddle that only a blasphemous parrot could pronounce."

I recognized the names of an eminent firm, and so did Mr. Norton. "No, I think not the solicitors," he said. "Then—" He stood, brisk and abstracted at once. "Perhaps you would not mind leaving your late brother's, er, legacy with me for a time. I'd like to see this house that you risk losing. May I meet you there tomorrow?"

"Hmph. Tomorrow's like as long as I'll be in it. As for keeping this ab—" She eyed the bird and it eyed her. Miss Mutterworth searched for a description of her nemesis that would not trigger a coarse monologue: "this absolutely useless creature."

The parrot shivered its feathers, shuffled its feet and gargled a razor-harsh sound. Mr. Norton seized the opportunity to drape the cage again.

"Here's the address on my late brother's card, Mr. Norton. Two tomorrow then; I need my nap before tea."

I saw her out and returned to find Mr. Norton squinting at the card. "Something of an eccentric, the late Cavendish Mutterworth. What do you make of this scribble?"

A drawing ran across the card's face, an address printed conventionally beneath it. I examined the sketch: a sort of cavern suspended over a china dish next to a pound of . . . butter and a pile of coins.

"A cavern, a dish . . ." I began.

"A *cave* in dish!"

"Butter next to money—money's worth?"

"Money . . . butter . . . Mutterworth." Mr. Norton smiled broadly. "I have seen my share of wills in my time, Miss Huxleigh, and have a notion that what we face here is an example of the vengeful will. Now that I see that the late Mr. Mutterworth was possessed of a bizarre sense of humor and a weakness for word games, I know how to precede."

" 'We' face here?" I repeated, dazed.

"Miss Huxleigh, I'm afraid I must prevail upon your good nature."

I heard echoes of Irene's most cajoling moments, when she urged me to actions diametrically opposed to my best instincts. Mr. Norton's eyes widened in boyish mischief as he waited and watched me, a nigh-irresistible expression in a man of his age and appearance.

He lifted the covered cage from the floor. "The vocabulary of this remarkable bird requires thorough study. Notes must be made. I will help convey, er, Casanova here, to your rooms if you will record all that he might reveal by, say, one o'clock tomorrow, when I collect you?" He smiled the smile of Lancelot to Elaine, the Lily Maid of Astolat, and every reader of Tennyson knows what became of *her*.

"That . . . beast," I answered weakly.

"I would be most grateful. It might help deflect an injustice—"

Like many barristers, Mr. Godfrey Norton knew not only where to start, but just when to stop. I was left to either turn my back on Dame Justice with her scales, blindfold and sword, or to embrace the company of the profane Casanova.

I shrugged and went to the outer office to collect my jacket. Mr. Norton followed with the oddly silent cage. A hansom speedily brought us to Saffron Hill. Because the neighborhood was so casual, no voice lifted to protest Casanova's installation in my quarters— save for several rude squawks from within while the cage swung pendulum-like from Mr. Norton's stiff arm as we climbed the four narrow flights of stairs.

"You have left things as they were," Mr. Norton marveled, surveying the room when we arrived.

It startled me to realize how much of Irene still occupied the lodgings; I had not noticed.

"She took very little with her," I explained. "Material objects are expendable to her, for all her love of beauty."

He lifted the cage and unveiled Casanova like a magician producing a rather rainbowed dove. "What would she say of this particular material object?"

"I have no idea. Put the croaking thing down on that table. He might as well have a window view, I suppose. The important thing is not what Irene would say to this new lodger of ours, but what the bird will say. You wish me to notate everything it articulates?"

"Everything."

"Then you had best withdraw and let me get on with it. I suspect this feathered Lothario has quite a roster of lines to deliver."

I put fresh water in the creature's cage when Mr. Norton had gone. One cannot expect even a parrot to sing without wetting his whistle. Then I sat down with paper and pencil, secretly intrigued by my assignment of evoking the bird's full range of phraseology. I decided to start with the basics, as I did with my children during my governess days.

"Polly want a cracker?" I chirped brightly.

"Cut the cackle," Casanova shrilled back, honing his intimidating beak on the bars. No wonder the brass was rubbed raw.

I dutifully transcribed "cut the cackle." One had to start somewhere.

Chapter Fifteen

Thus Spake Casanova

❦

Godfrey Norton read my list of the parrot's chatterings, which I had satirically titled "Casanova Contemplating the Dearth of Modern Expression," as our hired carriage made for an address in I Lᴀᴜᴜᴜᴜᴜ ᴄ ᴀᴜᴜᴜᴜ ᴌᴜ.

"Apparently you were obliged to transcribe some expressions not fit for the ears of a lady," he noted.

"As luck and my sequestered upbringing would have it, I am ignorant of the more vulgar connotations, Mr. Norton, so the bird could scream his worst and I was no worse for it."

"I imagine the cant would be lost on Miss Mutterworth also."

"Even more so," I hazarded. "I at least have had the benefit of an association with—"

"Irene Adler?" he interrupted.

"I was about to say, with a barrister's office where one often glimpses life's unseemlier side," I responded dryly.

"Yes, I suppose that most actions that require the law to untangle them are unseemly."

"You know quite well that it is unseemly for a barrister to meddle unsolicited in such a private matter at all, but like Irene, you will do what you will."

"No doubt that where there's a will, there's a way."

His roguish smile was wasted on me. "How do you propose to unravel this Mutterworth will?" I asked.

"I am relying on my infallible instincts about character."

I stared at him, having many times made clear my belief that he had utterly misjudged Irene. Mr. Norton smiled as if reading my thoughts.

"Here, Miss Huxleigh, I have *male* character to study; allow me some superiority on that score. The late Cavendish Mutterworth was a bitter man, a bachelor tied to an unmarried sister all his life until they became a kind of estranged couple sharing only the same house. I suggest that the parrot—the aptly named Casanova, for there was also a harem of lady parrots that Miss Mutterworth dispersed during her brother's fatal illness, say the solicitors—was bought purely to ruffle Miss Mutterworth's feathers, so to speak."

"What other reason could there be for acquiring such a beast?" said I grimly.

"Ah, you found him as ingratiating as Miss Mutterworth did, then?"

"Mr. Norton, I have spent half the night past cajoling the roster of verbal poul-troonery you have perused from that bird's lips—er, beak. No properly reared gentlewoman would tolerate an hour in his company."

"Nor pay any heed to his ravings?"

"Certainly not. Had I not been forced to endure them in the performance of my duty—"

"And most kind of you to accept this unpleasant task. Yet once you had begun listening to the creature, did not certain words and phrases recur?"

"Yes, and all of them foul."

"I perceive that you have marked the most common ones. When we see the Mutterworth house and grounds, we may gain a better sense of direction, I think."

At this juncture a strangled squawk of agreement issued from the shrouded cage at my feet, causing me to wonder whether stewed parrot would have any culinary appeal.

I recognized in my employer the same curious symptoms I had observed in Irene: impatience, the alert posture of a hound about to be slipped of its leash to follow the fox, a certain air of intellectual intoxication that has nothing to do with strong spirits.

It was with a mild stirring of these same emotions that I leaned toward the carriage window to watch Mr. Mutterworth's residence loom into view.

"An isolated, foreboding sort of place," Mr. Norton commented in the dramatic tones he employed to such fine effect before the bar.

"Quite a Wuthering Heights," I noted.

"*Withering*, Miss Huxleigh," he said sharply, glancing my way, "for Cavendish Mutterworth withered away here. Even the eminent Casanova had to watch his harem shrink to nothing under Miss Mutterworth's instructions."

"You seem bent on making the woman the villain of the piece," said I.

"Not I. Old Mutterworth. He put it into his will: 'To my sister, Jezebel—'"

"Jezebel?!"

"Not as aptly named as the parrot, I fear. At any rate, 'To my sister, Jezebel, I leave my prize possession, the parrot Casanova, that she may not have to hear herself talk.'"

The coach drew through the wrought-iron gate that stood ajar and along a driveway to the house. Chimneys bunched against the somber sky like huddled street Arabs. A rook cawed disconsolately from a leafless beech tree down the lane. I shivered.

"The house disturbs you?"

"A draft," I said smartly, and descended the carriage with the driver's aid.

Miss Mutterworth awaited us in the receiving room, to which a housekeeper showed us.

"The house looks Jacobean," Mr. Norton said.

"Looks are not everything," the elderly lady sniffed. "My brother had it built forty years ago to fool just such upstarts as you."

He glanced about in apparent innocent pleasure. "What a fine job he did, too. Is everything newly made, even the fence and gardens?"

"Forty years ago, all of it." Miss Mutterworth leaned toward the round table upon which Mr. Norton had set the parrot's cage. "They say these birds can live as long as that—even longer," she added with deep melancholy.

"How long did your brother have the bird?"

"Only the past few years, perhaps five."

"Yet he taught it a great many phrases."

"Dozens, though the tongue-waggling beast came with a whole litany of catchwords. Some say he'd been a sailor's pet. Certainly my brother made a bosom companion of him, feeding him seeds and whispering new abominations to his imitative ear as if they were partners in crime."

Mr. Norton raised an expressive dark eyebrow at me, a gesture he had mastered in the cradle, I warrant. "Might we explore the house and grounds?"

"All you wish, though it will not be mine to admit you to before long."

"We shall see," Mr. Norton said, lifting the parrot's cage from the table. He led me toward the entry hall where the stair forked into two flights before meeting on the landing and forking again.

"His own building," he whispered at me, and winked.

I followed him upstairs, resting my hand on the walnut railing until I discovered at each turn of the stairs that a grotesque carved face grimaced from every newel post. When I mentioned the gargoyles to Mr. Norton, he merely nodded and pointed to the plaster frieze beneath the hall ceiling.

The design was that odd pictograph of "Cave-n-dish Mutterworth," traced in the plaster over and over.

On the second floor a maid led us to the late master's quarters, where even the chamberpot wore a twisted ceramic face, and its handles were two uplifted hands. I hesitated to direct Mr. Norton's attention to it.

He was busy unveiling the parrot and installing its cage on the empty stand that stood ready for it.

"Awk!" Casanova cleared his throat, sidling down the perch until his seamed foot brushed the bars. "Awkward," he said, cocking a hidden ear my way.

"Most awkward," I agreed.

"Quick study," Mr. Norton approved, rubbing his palms together. "You used the word in the coach and it suits the bird's natural voice."

"It is awkward being here." I glanced around the bedchamber, struck by the recent presence of death, however naturally delivered.

The air held that sickroom tang of age and decay. I noted a cane leaning into a dark corner, the old man's nightshirt and cap folded at the foot of the testered bed.

"Let me have a look at your list again," Mr. Norton said.

The paper crackled as he unfolded it and Casanova edged nearer to absorb every snap.

"Tippecanoe and treasure, too," Mr. Norton mused.

"Go soak your head in it," the bird croaked. "Go soak your head in it."

"Tippecanoe," I mused in turn, feeling obliged to contribute something to this expedition. "Isn't that American?"

"Pertaining to an American political contest, I believe. A campaign slogan that became a popular song years ago, 'Tippecanoe and Tyler Too'. But the canoe is also an Indian boat of sorts, long and thin and made of birchbark."

"Tippecanoe and treasure, too. Nonsense then, just like Mr. Mutterworth."

"Mutterworth. I wonder if he was so enamored of making puns upon his own name—"

"Well, he had enough muttering around him, with all those parrots—"

"And one master mutterer." Mr. Norton extended an imprudent

finger into Casanova's cage. The bird shuffled over to the bars, then clamped its iron-grey beak shut on it.

This time Mr. Norton flapped and squawked. "Quite a grip."

"I got la grippe," the parrot shrieked back.

I went to the window and cast the casement wide, needing some fresh air, fresh thought and something other to regard than the odious and flesh-eating Casanova.

A row of grotesque green faces grinned up at me—topiary bushes cut into inhuman expressions, all marching away in a double row toward the formal gardens that clustered around a man-made pond and an airy wooden gazebo in the shape of a parrot's cage.

"What a bizarre garden!" I noted. "Those faces—'neither beast nor human,'" I quoted from Poe, a favorite of mine. "Ghouls."

Mr. Norton was at my side in seconds, which I found most gratifying. Chivalry toward the weaker sex is so lost to most modern men. However, it was not my possible peril that drew him, but my ungodly discovery.

"Faces . . . yes. And neither beast nor human, but—*bird*, Penelope!" he cried in his wonder, forgetting more formal means of address. "Not a . . . catwalk, but a *bird*walk. You've found it!" At that he clapped me on the shoulder in a most familiar—if unthinking—manner. "I was convinced the clue would be in the house. How did you come to think of the grounds, the garden?" he demanded.

How did I? Then I remembered Irene wondering where a half-demented old man might have hidden his greatest treasure and realized that I had duplicated her methods without knowing it. I had looked beyond the chamber that imprisoned him to the greater world and the fresh air. But I could hardly tell Godfrey Norton that, since his own late father's case had inspired my actions in this one.

"There seemed little of interest in the house," I said shortly but firmly.

Mr. Norton nodded and shook his head at the garden below us. Even as we watched, a pair of gardeners in baggy trousers with clay-stained knees advanced on the topiary bushes with hedge-clippers.

"Not a moment too soon," Mr. Norton said. "As the fair female parrots went, so shall the bushes. This is Casanova's late lamented harem, don't you see, Miss Huxleigh? And there, at the end, sits the cagey old bird himself."

I reexamined the faces with their curved proboscises and leaves upraised like feathers. Mr. Norton was right. At the end of the avenue, in perfect proportion to the distant cagelike gazebo, perched the hoariest, shaggiest shape of all—Casanova in green glory, one wing extended as he groomed his bedraggled chest feathers.

We hurried below and out to the gardens, Mr. Norton muttering from the list. " 'Cut the cackle; kill the grackle' . . . an aviary outdoors perhaps? 'Greenback'? The topiary bird backs? Bird bath?"

"The pond!" I exclaimed, stopping under a shower of clipped leaves. The gardeners on their ladders snipped away above me.

"Greenbacks! American money!" Mr. Norton responded.

We stared at each other in ecstatic agreement.

That is why, approximately half an hour later, the two gardeners drew from the pond waters, at Mr. Norton's direction, a birdcage wrapped in oilcloth.

From the bedchamber casement I had neglected to close, a raucous voice hailed our discovery: "Tippecanoe and treasure, too."

When the cage's contents were examined on Miss Mutterworth's parlor table, they proved to be a large amount of American dollars, or *greenbacks,* a rare stamp and coin collection, several packets of stock in our nation's most solid companies and various other documents of value. Miss Mutterworth fluttered and cooed as the treasure spread across the figured shawl that covered the table. Finally the cage was emptied. It was much rusted, although the oilcloth had preserved the papers, stamps and coins.

When it was empty, Mr. Norton on an impulse turned the cage upside down. "Another clue," he pronounced, "though I can't quite read it."

I lifted my trusty pince-nez to my nose and squinted through the rust at the word engraved in the metal, the maker's name. "Tyler."

"Tippecanoe and *Tyler*'s treasure, too!" Mr. Norton and I recited together.

From upstairs came a dim and awful echo.

Chapter Sixteen

Word from Abroad

❧

Our past words often come to haunt us, but rarely do so in such naked ringing tones as those emitted by a parrot.

Miss Mutterworth, naturally, had no desire to add Casanova to the tally of wealth left by her late brother.

"You've always fancied a canary, my dear Miss Huxleigh," Mr. Norton cajoled. We were back in chambers with work to do and the parrot's cage hanging from a makeshift hook too near my shoulder for comfort. "Casanova may possess unsuspected musical gifts."

"I doubt it," said I with a shudder, but the upshot was that the creature fell to me by default.

If I did not wish to hear its siren squawks while performing upon the typewriter at Mr. Norton's chambers, the lesser of two evils was to bring the bird home. At least the parrot had feathers and a voice, albeit rough, and—as it was prone to remind me from the amphitheater of the bay window, where I installed its cage, I had always "fan-cied a ca-nar-y, fan-cied a ca-nar-y—awk!"

I confess I found it company of a sort; I would not wish the beast to fall into uncharitable hands. What Irene would think of my aquisition, I often wondered; likely she would teach it to smoke those little cigars of hers. Casanova was soon the least of my concerns, however.

In examining my diaries for the year 1886, I find that no document can more tersely summarize the swift turns in Irene Adler's career abroad than her own remarkable letters informing me of the major events.

Thus I present her words unsullied, save that I have taken the liberty of repairing some lapses in spelling and punctuation. Irene Adler wrote as she spoke and lived: with flair and intelligence but not the tidiest of approaches. I have also interspersed annotations of my own, as needed.

Three pages of onion-skin parchment embellished in her distinctive green ink were needed to convey the drama of the first Great Event, dated twenty-first January, 1886:

My darling Nell!

You will find yourself most astounded by my latest great good news. Forgive the erratic path of my penwomanship—which is to a mistress of the typewriter like yourself shocking, I know; I am composing this missive while on a moving train. I confess that my heart is still beating a bit out of time as well. Between the rattle of the rails' snaredrums and the pounding of my own internal kettledrum my thoughts find small peace.

Where, you must be wondering, is your footloose friend bound now? Away, dear Nell, like a gypsy! To—well, you will hardly credit it. Let me begin by saying that I am no longer attached to La Scala in Milan. There was a certain unpleasantness among the resident sopranos after my recent debut. I may hint at ground glass in my rougepot, but will go no further. My sister sopranos, after all, were mostly Italian and cannot be expected to hold to standards of emotional civility; it impedes their art, they claim. *Mama mia,* say I.

Yet adversity has cast my cards of fate into an even more fortunate arrangement. I am crossing the Alps like Hannibal, only I ride a great, black, steam-propelled elephant. I soon will speed through Austria, Moravia and a tiny slice of Silesia to become *prima donna* of the Imperial Opera of Warsaw! Yes, your own friend and fellow-lodger—a diva at last! I am blissful to an excess. I am overjoyed! I am—running out of ink . . ."

(Here the words faded into a shower of green ink droplets as Irene shook her pen, as though abusing a thirsty writing instrument were ever a substitute for redipping it. —P.H.)

There. Fat with ink and free-running again. I feel rather like this pen, Penelope: brim-full of all I require, ready to work like a Trojan and let all the world's glorious words and music ripple from my throat. Not only roosters can crow!

My good fortune owes itself again to the recommendation of Mr. Dvořák, who has taken quite a fancy to my voice—also to my quick mastery of the languages for song. Warsaw is not, of course, Vienna. Ah, I sigh for the grandeur and glory of life in the imperial city of Franz Josef and the Empress Eugenie—but German is spoken in Warsaw, so I will be able to sing in a language I know rather than being required to master Polish, too, which would be rather too much acquaintanceship with consonants to my taste.

And *prima donna,* my dear, such a triumph for a voice such as mine, which is continually being labeled by one misnomer after another: "contralto," which would condemn me to singing faithful mothers and elderly gypsies for life, or "mezzo-soprano," which offers some delicious "trouser" roles of women masquerading as men—you *know* how adept I would be in such parts—but limited leading roles. At any rate, the director of the Imperial Opera witnessed my La Scala debut after hearing Dvořák sing my praises (so to speak), the deed is done and they shall have to settle upon a repertoire that suits my voice and style, that is all.

(Here the letter reverts to a travelogue of the Austro-Hungarian Empire's far-flung kingdoms, a paean that more expresses the writer's emotional

enthusiasm than the region's pastoral beauty requires. I next quote a subsequent letter, which conveys a flavor of Irene's life in Warsaw. —P.H.)

Well! Warsaw is so much more magnificent than I expected. Like many Americans, I pictured Europe as a mirror image of the United States—an Atlantic-edging confluence of states that represent the highest civilization with nothing but desert beyond it. I expected that delving so far East would be like going West in America—all sand and savages.

Indeed, there is a certain savage splendor to the Poles and their city that reaches back to a time when they had to repel the Tartars of Ghengis Khan. They are a gentle people who love peace almost as much as they love their land, but they love their land more—the symbol of Poland is a siren, half-fish and half-maiden, armed with shield and sword! Sirens are said to lure men to a watery death with their unearthly voices, so I suppose *this* fierce siren of Warsaw would be well equipped by both voice and weapon to sing at La Scala!

Warsaw has its river, as London has the Thames, and the faded yellow buildings seem cheery even on dark days. The Old City is most quaint, as is the traditional peasant garb. I undoubtedly shall have to appear in some bucolic opera or other in blouse, corselet and skirts as short as a circus bareback rider's. The Polish national anthem is no solemn processional, but a lively little mazurka like those composed by the great Chopin.

Chopin's genius is no accident, by the way; this land is infected with music. The simplest peasant tune plays tribute to the babble of a brook, the turn of the spinning wheel, the bleat of the sheep.

Yet for all the peasant roots (which seem very exotic to an American like myself) music is an ancient deity here and has many temples. Magnificent palaces and parks dot the landscape, but the Imperial Opera is housed in true rococo splendor, in this city where music is queen, and sits along the river so that

those Amazonian sirens may join the chorus, I imagine. I think
that I shall be very happy here.

*(I am no admirer of opera, despite my long association with Irene
Adler. Most of her letters detailed the hardships of rehearsing and mounting operas and the excitement of opening nights. I shall omit the technical
details and convey more of the Polish society itself. —P.H.)*

Poor Poland has had most of its reigning monarchs stripped
away, although several still rule over the streets in the form of
lofty public monuments. Yet, my dear Nell, I have actually met
a king!

You will no doubt raise silently skeptical eyebrows and I
shall be forced to be most precise so that I cannot be charged
with exaggerating. Very well. The man in question is not quite
a king, but he is a Crown Prince. And he is not Polish, but German. And his kingdom (when it becomes his kingdom on the
death of his father) is not Poland, or even Germany, but Bohemia!

Have I confused you enough, my literal Nell? His name is
Wilhelm Gottsreich Sigismond von Ormstein, Grand Duke of
Cassel-Felstein and one day King of Bohemia. (Lest this string
of Teutonic names overwhelm you, I must add that he is known
to intimates as "Willie.")

"Willie" is a needed familiarity: otherwise the prince's person would intimidate utterly. He stands nigh six-and-a-half feet
tall, with a physique to match this generous height. His eyes are
bluer than the Vistula River that ambles through Warsaw and
he has a great fancy for things operatic. Every Sunday he takes
me for drives in his open coach, its doors emblazoned with the
von Ormstein coat of arms (and very gaudy they are, too), along
Miodowa Street where all of Warsaw's fine folk gather, and we
are much commented upon. He has not much of a sense of humor, but perhaps that is a common failing of royalty.

I have also often seen Antonin Dvořák. While my operatic ambitions lie toward the West—Vienna, even Paris—Mr.
Dvořák had urged me in the past months to master more of his
Czech songs. I do have a facility for languages, no matter how
they maul consonants, so I am humoring the composer, who is,
after all, quite the musical lion in London these days. Still, I do
not intend to lavish my life and talent on the "provinces," no matter how princely the company!

*(I read hope of my friend's return into such sentiments. It soon died
as later letters chronicled Irene's title role in a mounting of Carmen;
told of her employing a German singing master to learn the Schumann
song cycle that so admirably suited her deep, dark voice; of dancing and
dining and driving out with "Willie" . . . So it came as small surprise
when 1886 had dwindled to a pair of leaves on the calendar, that there
arrived a landmark letter announcing a sudden turn in Irene's plans.
—P.H.)*

I go West again at last, dear Penelope, but not so far as I had
anticipated. Thanks to the persuasion of Mr. Dvořák, who is
quite commanding for such a plain and wholesome man, I will
become *prima donna* at Prague's new National Opera. (Yes, I
shall be singing exclusively in the Bohemian language, save
when I give concerts. How difficult that will be is clear when I
tell you that the name of my dresser is Petronilla Anckvicz—
only two vowels to her entire last name!)

Naturally, the Prince was most persuasive. He assures me that
Prague is an ancient, cosmopolitan city and that I shall not miss
Warsaw or even London. (Though I shall always miss you, my
dear; even *princes* are not persuasive enough to erase the memory
of my first and most loyal friend!)

I cannot say how divine it is, darling Nell, to be released at
last from the daily struggle for bread and to receive the roses of
recognition both at once. I am feted, praised, petted, paid very
well indeed and treated like a queen. I feel that I have found my

true place in the world, and though I find myself among strangers in a strange land, I feel very much at home.

If you have ever fretted about me in my exotic and distant travels, fear no more. I remain your devoted and ever-grateful friend (though I think it will be long e'er I see London again),

Irene

(Here, at the letter's close, the writing dissolved into a puddle of ink, though that was hardly the fault of the writer's pen, but rather of the reader's pensiveness . . . —P.H.)

Chapter Seventeen

A Summons

❧

Buds thickened on every bare branch, swathing the trees in a delicate veil of green. No rain fell, but the damp cobblestones gleamed like licorice in the clouded light. River fog drifted through the Temple's alleyways alongside me as I hurried to Mr. Norton's chambers.

The hour was early, but I found the office door unlatched, and Mr. Norton dressed, combed, brushed and alert at his desk, contemplating the open chest Irene and I had rescued from interment at The Sycamores. By that tender spring of 1887, it had been more than a year since Irene had departed Saffron Hill and left that homely object in Mr. Norton's keeping.

"My dear Miss Huxleigh, you are early! You have caught me puzzling over the old mystery. Take another look at the contents, perhaps you will discern a clue."

I guessed that he was chagrined that I had found him studying the mysterious chest; he had made no reference to it of late. Yet I was too distracted by my own news to wonder at his occupation with it.

"I am not good at puzzles," I began.

"Nonsense! It was your turning to the Mutterworth garden and its topiary messages that made me think of the chest again. Both the late Cavendish Mutterworth and my father were childish old gents; perhaps they thought in the same way. If we can apply the same illogicality to their surviving artifacts, we can—But you are quite pale, Miss Huxleigh! Have a seat, never mind the box. Are you ill?"

"Perplexed," I confessed. "Since this letter of Irene's arrived yesterday . . . letter! That is too grand a term for such a communication—"

"Let me see." He plucked the envelope from my hand. The instant he did he paused and said, "Forgive me, Miss Huxleigh. I have quite grown to feel that I share your concerns as a brother does. I have no right to interrogate you, no right to intrude."

"Oh, Mr. Norton, I'd welcome a calmer perspective. I am so . . . befuddled." I quite felt like a client, and indeed, I was in great need of advice.

"Letter you said," he noted a moment after, gingerly pulling several sheets of thick parchment from the envelope. "This is but a note—and barely that."

"That is what surprised me. Irene is an expansive correspondent. And these empty pages . . ."

He took the paper to the window, where light filtered through a veil of grey fog, then declaimed the scrawl that occupied the entire first page: " 'Nell—come at once to Prague! I need you. Irene.' "

Mr. Norton turned to me, the fog pressing against the window behind him like a ghost. I could not read any expression in the silhouette he presented me. "The message is brief enough to make a cablegram the speedier and more sensible method of communication, unless—"

"My thought exactly." I sat forward and clutched my reticule. "Irene has written to me almost weekly. Another letter would hardly be noticed, but a cablegram . . ."

"A cablegram would attract attention, but not another fat letter to you; hence the empty pages, to allay suspicion."

"But . . . who would be suspicious of her? And what circumstances would forestall her sending a simple cablegram? She wrote that Prague is a cosmopolitan city—"

"As compared to what?" said he. "All these little east European dukedoms are only fringe on the greater empires' petticoats—Russia, Austro-Hungary, even the Turks to the east. It is dangerous ground your friend treads, and she always had a taste for danger."

"No! Irene has never been so settled, so . . . conventional. She has been singing at the National Opera in Prague—"

"An Opera named 'National' only because Bohemia had to *force* Austria to permit its native language to exist side-by-side with the conquering German. She sits astride a political maelstrom at your bucolic opera house in quaint Bohemia."

"Irene is a friend to the King! The man soon-to-be-king, rather! Surely she would be protected?"

"Ah." Godfrey Norton folded the letter neatly before returning it to its envelope. I had a sudden sense of being abandoned.

"It is not what you think!" I returned, nearly crushing the letter as he handed it to me.

"Perhaps not," he said, a certain distance in his voice, "but the situation is certainly not what you assumed it to be."

He suddenly put a hand on my shoulder. "My dear . . . Miss Huxleigh. You have been seeing the world through your friend's bedazzled eyes, not reality. I do not wonder that she sends for you with such urgency; she has undoubtedly run afoul of some court intrigue or peasant rebellion. Or perhaps the would-be king has proved to be less than he should. Whatever the difficulty, as *your* friend, as your . . . barrister . . . I must advise you not to go."

"But I must! I must!"

"Alone? Into unknown lands, unknown situations? At least she could have explained—"

"Not if the letter risked interception!"

"And if it did—think, think what that implies! If her position is that delicate, you risk doubling the number of those endangered. You could send her a cable if you wish, to set your mind at ease—"

I stood. "Irene knows how to send a cable by telegraph. She knows that I could telegraph her. She did not ask me to telegraph; she asked me to come—at once!—and I shall."

He was quiet for a very long while. "I cannot approve," he said finally. "My mother was a headstrong woman and she paid dearly for it. I had not suspected you of such determination."

"Nor had I," I returned. "Something is very wrong, something that Irene cannot manage."

"And you can?"

I stiffened. "Perhaps. Irene would not waste her time asking for aid from one she did not rely upon."

That gave him pause. "No. No, I don't imagine she would. Very well."

His sigh was deep, and made my frown soften. It showed how much my welfare was on his mind. I have not known many people who cared for me in any capacity whatsoever—save for Jasper Higgenbottom—and another, upon whom I dare not think. That is why I had to answer Irene's summons, no matter how cryptic or hazardous.

Godfrey Norton rolled his gold watch-chain between his fingers, as if debating the nature of time. Then he, too, made up his mind.

"I will attend to the travel arrangements; they will be complex. And see that you do not forget how to send a cable, for I want to hear the instant you arrive—even sooner, should anything untoward happen."

"Yes! You are most kind, Mr. Norton."

"Godfrey," he said shortly. "Anyone capable of defying my best advice should call me by my Christian name."

I lowered my eyes before extending my hand. "Nell."

We shook hands, a gesture he ended by gazing at me fondly and shaking his head.

"I hope that you are up to Miss Irene Adler's high estimation,

for I fear that you are running right into the mouth of the maelstrom."

In that much Mr. Norton—Godfrey—would prove correct.

☩   ☩   ☩

With Godfrey's help, I paid some weeks in advance for the Saffron
Hill rooms, closed them and was soon leaving Charing Cross Station
en route to Dover, soon embarked by boat train for Ostend and, once
ashore, soon swallowed by a succession of trains that snaked their way
eastward to Brussels, Cologne, Frankfurt and Nuremberg.

I smiled at my reflection in the compartment windows as I recalled pointing out before my departure that someone must take custody of the formidable Casanova.

"What? Can't you . . . ?" he had begun.

"Sell a souvenir of a case? And at such short notice? Never."

"Surely some—"

"I have no suitable friends. Godfrey." He winced as I sweetly in-
voked his Christian name and then went on, "No, Casanova is in
your care now. No doubt he will liven the chambers in my absence."

Godfrey groaned.

"I have been teaching him the alphabet in an effort to distract
him from his less presentable vocalizations. Three letters at a time.
We are at j, k, l."

"No doubt as in 'Jekyll.' Have pity, Nell; I shall be transformed
into a raving Mr. Hyde by your return after the exclusive company
of the redoubtable Casanova."

"I must face my dangers abroad; you now have yours to attend to
at home."

On that firm note the matter was settled, yet even the image of
Godfrey merging Casanova into his set bachelor's existence couldn't
divert me for more than a few moments as I steamed across Europe
in answer to Irene's mysterious summons.

The Rhine was exceedingly picturesque, but any countryside I
gazed upon faded under the constant haze of my anxieties. I stopped

nowhere to rest, but slept on the trains, lulled by the rails' constant clatter as an infant is by a rattle. I imagined Irene writing me on the first leg of this centipede of a journey. I envisioned her viewing the same scenery—rolling forest and ruined castle towers beckoning like arthritic fingers from the hilltops and woodlands.

Nothing could seduce me from my purpose, not even the crowded common railway car that conveyed me and sixteen other souls from Nuremberg to Prague amid a cloud of all-too identifiable odors.

Prague was a tumble of gabled roofs, towers and Medieval buildings straddling a river—the Moldau, they called it. Reminiscent of Venice in the rungs of bridges that laced both sides of the river together, Prague boasted a castle perched upon a prominence like a plum atop a Christmas pudding. This great Baroque pile must surely be one of the principal palaces in Europe. I gaped to think that my friend knew the man who would one day rule from it, even if he would reign over only a small fairy tale kingdom.

I shook off my wonder and directed myself to practical concerns: finding Irene. To do so, I had begun to inquire about the National Theatre even while in the train. By the time it had arrived in Prague, I knew that the theatre stood near the Charles Bridge. Once disembarked, I instructed—or rather, gestured—to a man to hold my baggage at the station, then set out for the heart of town on foot.

Language was no barrier: I merely had to follow the river. The twisting Medieval streets often conspired to lead—or tempt—me astray, but I finally spied a grand building with a row of consonants keeping close company on its pediment. I entered with a show of boldness to find myself enveloped in a dark, empty lobby.

No one challenged me. I crossed the plush carpeting step by careful step and pushed through a gilded door. An opera house opened up to me, as if the shadowing lid had been lifted from a box of French chocolates. Gilt clung everywhere, like those foil wrappers that hide sweetmeats. I saw a sweep of red velvet seats and curtain, and—far away—a cluster of people in the seats nearest the stage.

And on the barely lit stage, I spied tiny figures as dainty as marionettes. I began walking down the slanted aisle, hearing unmusical voices lift and lower in turn. The language was mostly the guttural mutter of Bohemian that I had heard at such close quarters in the rail coach. Yet an English word would break into the round in a man's commanding voice. And, yes, a woman would answer in English . . . Irene!

I rushed toward the stage, forgetting myself in my joy at seeing her well and normally employed. One by one, the rehearsing singers turned to regard me.

Irene turned last, looking the same and not the same. Her hair was arranged in the kind of complicated interweaving of braids and curls that required a maid; her clothes spoke with a rich quietude far above the everyday sleights of scissors and thread. Yet her face broke into a familiar smile as she stepped to the unlit footlights and held out her hands to me even though the yawning orchestra pit separated us.

"My dear Nell, how kind of you to come," said Irene Adler, smiling as if I had just arrived from around the corner—instead of the far corner of the earth—to see her.

She did not sound in the least surprised.

Chapter Eighteen

A Prague of Poisons

◆◆◆

I gazed around the elegant apartment.

"Surely it is not quite proper—"

"Proper! That is a very English concept. I have not heard the word in over a year." Irene laughed and lifted her feet atop a chaise longue upholstered in gilt-embossed brocade. I stared at the slender satin slippers that encased her feet. They must have cost ten pounds.

"Six hundred and fifty kreutzers," she announced, having noticed me eyeing her dainty footwear.

The splendor of her surroundings made opera settings pale by comparison. My eye darted nervously from the nymphs and nude gentleman capering on the painted ceiling to the cherub-carved woodwork. A gaudy icing of gilt frosted it all.

On the wall opposite the windows, a lace-canopied dressing table was crowned with an array of crystal flagons holding multicolored liquids.

"I have never known you to use such a quantity of cosmetics," I murmured.

Irene joined me in regarding the array. "A whole chorus of potions—all cosmetics for the throat. The ancient peasant traditions underlying this land speak strongly still. Why do you think the word 'Bohemian' has become synonymous with 'gypsy'? Gypsy herbal remedies throng the marketplace and even the palace."

Irene pointed from bottle to bottle. "I give you calamus root, that gnarled mass in the decanter, for a clear voice and strong throat; carob seeds to chew for the selfsame reason; cinquefoil to gargle when my throat is sore; frankincense, which may be inhaled for the same purpose. Here stand heliotrope, honeysuckle, lavender and licorice water and purple loosestrife, five pretty, pale liquids also devoted to the humble art of gargling, which I can manage in three octaves. You have no idea what a singer must do to protect her voice."

"But you only drank hot tea with honey at home!"

"At home I was not a diva," Irene said with a self-mocking gleam in her eyes. "Here I must demonstrate that I take myself seriously. As a grenadier lines up his blunderbusses, so must I arrange *my* weapons in a row."

"I can quite understand your adopting the native cures, Irene, but you have evaded my main question. Is it proper for you to reside in the castle?" I persisted.

"A castle is a hotel, not a home, Nell. If you saw the numbers of guests that come—and stay for days and weeks and months—and then go, you'd know that! Besides, Willie insisted."

"It is a man's house, so to speak—"

"It is a man's *father's* house, so long as he shall live. The entire von Ormstein family resides here with enough servants to make up a Wagnerian chorus; surely all these people suffice to chaperone the most notorious courtesan, much less an innocent opera singer. No, propriety is not my problem. Would that it were."

"What is your difficulty, then? What has compelled you to call me all these thousands of kilometers . . . ?"

"The journey was wearing, I know, my dear Nell. You had better rest before I acquaint you with the . . . situation."

"I have not come all this way to rest!"

"Peace, peace, Penelope! Hush. This is a palace, after all. Even the arras has ears."

I looked quickly at the huge tapestries swagging the bed, the windows, the walls.

"He did say it was likely a palace intrigue," I murmured in sudden recollection.

"Who said this?" Irene asked sharply.

I hesitated. "Godfrey. Mr. Norton. My employer, the barrister."

"I know who he is, and what he is. I did not know that you were on such terms with him as to call him 'Godfrey.' Perhaps I should be questioning *your* working arrangements instead of allowing you to cross-examine me about my living ones."

"Oh, please, Irene. I have not come all this way to annoy you. I have been terribly worried."

She suddenly rose from her languid position and drove stiff fingers into the hair at her temples, as if easing an ever-present headache.

"Nell, I know only the most selfless motives brought you here, but lend me your patience as well as your loyalty. I must acquaint you with the *dramatis personae* of my unfolding little drama."

"You talk as though you were caught in the plot of a grand opera."

Irene laughed in a way I had never heard her express mirth before, a bit bitterly. She rose, the lace flounces of her robe curling behind her like seafoam as she stalked aimlessly around the chamber.

"Grand? No, the plot is not grand at all, nor is there any occasion for singing. I have mentioned you often as an old school friend of mine—don't lift your eyebrows at my fiction. These . . . noble . . . people know nothing of how working women in London must band together to survive; this explanation was simpler. Come, I will show you your room. Unpack, settle in, rest . . . then join me at dinner."

She took my hand to lead me down a broad hall flanked by gilt furniture to a set of rooms nearly as grand as hers.

"And there?" I asked on what would be my own threshold. "What should I do at dinner?"

"Watch and pray," Irene said cryptically, leaving me without another word.

I found my baggage within and a short, sturdy person who

identified herself as Ludmilla, my maid. I persuaded her to leave after she had loosened my laces and had seen me into a lavish dressing gown that no doubt was Irene's. Then I sat upon the testered bed—or rather, tried to sit; the feather quilt puffed so high that it nearly reached my waist.

Thus ensconced with my feet up so some blood should reach my head and aid concentration, I tried to puzzle out the situation. I had no mind to meet the overgrown "Willie" and his clan, nor to eat at a royal table where I should not know the fish fork from a pitchfork. I clasped my hands to clamp my rising dismay between them. The palms were damp. I tried to return my feet to the floor and found myself sinking even deeper into the down. It made the encompassing "situation" into which I had marched so confidently seem like the most luxurious sort of . . . quicksand.

Irene had apparently had no such qualms, for she was radiant at dinner. A servant stood behind each of us ready to assist in any way, so my table manners were handed to me upon a silver platter. It was impossible to go astray.

I bobbed with respectful independence on being presented to the Royal Family before the meal: the Crown Prince, so much of everything that Irene's letters had said that I was left quite speechless; his mother, an astoundingly tiny woman with Delft-blue eyes and hair the color of blonde lace; his sister-in-law, the Duchess Hortense, an unfortunate creature in whom every family feature had found its most ungainly expression, and his unmarried younger brother, Bertrand, who was not as tall as the Crown Prince, and was balding and stuttered.

The middle brother was away at the family estates in southern Bohemia; one look at the angular Hortense would explain why. The father, the King in this case, was ill in his chambers, which explained why all the women wore subdued colors, even Irene. I, of course, always dressed in sober shades, so was perfectly proper in my charcoal faille dress with wine-colored velvet trim, even among royalty.

For all the easy chitchat, it was a strained occasion. The desultory evening that followed was mostly lost on me when all relaxed and conversed in German. Indeed, there was nothing for me *to do*, save watch and pray as Irene had urged.

I was rescued from the tedium into which I had sunk by the un-heralded arrival of a small bristling grey dog, which flung itself at my skirts. Everyone laughed at this canine liberty, and I found it a relief to confront something that could communicate with me. I even began to cast my mind back to London, wondering how God-frey and Casanova were getting on.

"Spaetzl has found a new friend," Irene announced in English. "A Schnauser," she explained. "Pray let us give the dog a stroll in the portrait gallery while I lecture my friend on the von Ormstein ancestors."

"Excellent." The Queen's face was as pale and seamed as Antwerp linen under her age-silvered blonde hair. The Prince stood as if to escort us.

"No, no, your Highness," Irene said hastily. "You must not leave your family. It is my role to set my friend at ease."

She led me off so quickly that no one could gracefully follow. The little dog capered at our heels, snapping at the velvet bows trimming Irene's train.

She paid this attack upon her person no mind, but rushed me up marble stairs as wide as a Prague street (which were, on the whole, rather narrow) and into a long gallery. Trees of candelabra lit the length of the hall, flickering on the paintings that lined the walls and glinting from random curlicues of gilt frame.

"Look at this, Nell." Irene pulled me toward a dim oil painting.

I gaped at a puddle of female skin tones—an anonymous Renais-sance nude sprawling by a brook. Only a male painter would think so much billowing flesh artistic. "Must I?"

"It's Reubens, I'm sure of it! And this next one—no, not the ermine-collared gent with the harelip, that's some ancestor of Willie's—here, this one!"

I saw red—the painting's predominant color—and hazarded, "A Titian?"

"Yes!" Irene looked with narrowed eyes up and down the gallery. "And all labeled 'By an unknown artist'! It is a crime; this hall is lined with mislabeled masterworks. If I were queen I'd import a Louvre art expert instantly. These paintings are worth a fortune and they've been forgotten. I suspect the oversight occurred in the late seventeenth century when the Hapsburgs moved their capital from Prague to Vienna. They meant to take everything of value with them, but like all royal families in sudden transit, became careless in their packing."

I was possessed of an awful suspicion; Irene regarded unclaimed historical treasures like the Zone of Diamonds as fair game. "Irene. You don't mean to . . . rescue . . . these works yourself?"

"Abscond with the paintings? You have grown imaginative, Nell! I have become successful, not depraved. No, I merely point out that a firm hand is needed here."

"The King's business, surely."

"He is gravely ill and has been so since before I met Willie in Warsaw."

"The Queen, then."

"I said a firm hand."

"Ah . . . the Crown Prince."

She laced her arm through mine and led me down the portrait-strewn gallery. Behind us the little dog's nails clicked as it deserted us for the main chamber. "Willie . . . I have not yet told Willie what these paintings are."

"Whyever not?"

"Because Willie has not yet told me what I am to be."

"To be?"

Irene shrugged carelessly. "Or *not* to be."

"Oh, for heaven's sake, Irene, I have traveled relentlessly for five days, worried the whole while; I am in no mood to play cryptic games. As Casanova would say, 'cut the cackle!' "

She drew back, her topaz-colored eyes widening. Then she laughed until the marble echoed and the painted faces all along the walls seemed to smile with her.

"I had no idea, Nell, that Casanova numbered among your intimates."

The stamp of my foot ended the echoes. "Casanova is a nasty, ill-spoken parrot, but at least he makes his meaning plain."

"You are quite right. I have mystified you too long, only because I am mystified myself. Here, let us sit on this exceedingly uncomfortable marble bench. Thank God for bustles."

"Well."

Irene sighed. "Willie is madly in love with me."

"Of course."

She smiled at my partisanship. "He has showered me with gifts—most of which I have refused. He has escorted me about two ancient European cities as if permanently attached to my skirts. He was overjoyed when Dvořák proposed me for the Prague National Opera. He speaks as if we shall never part—"

"Then . . . ?"

Irene studied the paintings. "Then I may very well be in a position soon to 'rediscover' these lost glories. It would mean much to the kingdom's purse strings, and to the pride of the Czech people, of whom I have become very fond."

"Then why not do it now?"

"Because Willie has not spoken."

"Is it to be tit for tat?"

"No . . ." Irene turned back to me. "But I have struggled too long to turn over my high card without seeing what the other hand holds. Your Mr. Norton is right; court intrigues boil in these ancient cities. Warsaw, Prague . . . both are satraps of the greater Austro-Hungarian empire and spring from traditions of their own that resist the yoke of rule. It was only recently, after two hundred years, that the Czechs have been allowed officially to use their own language." She tapped her foot on the hard marble. "I will take no step until I am sure my ground is firm."

"So that is why I am here—to coax a proposal of marriage from Wilhelm Gottsreich Sigismond von Ormstein?"

She shook my arm admonishingly. "Nell, Nell, your memory is still inferior to none, but no, I need no aid with Willie. He gives all indication—"

She leaned nearer, her eyes bright. "It is no secret that most *prima donnas* wear genuine jewels, not paste, on stage, jewels bestowed by their wealthy admirers. It's even less secret that they are mistresses to many of those admirers. I refused Willie's offerings—even a suite of garnets, so gorgeous—but I could not compromise my independence. What one may accept from a client like Mr. Tiffany, who is after all a shopkeeper, one may not accept from a king, for a king—even a prince—has power and must not think he can use it in such a relationship as between man and woman.

"Willie was not used to being refused," Irene confided. "The novelty quite undid the poor man. One evening after dinner he took me to a room in this castle and showed me the crown jewels. He put them upon me with his own hands, then clapped those royal hands and a photographer emerged from the next chamber. We were photographed together, I with rubies and diamonds garlanding my wrists, my neck, my temples. He gave me the photograph, saying it was an offering I could keep until a day when I could accept his gifts in reality . . ."

"He does mean to marry you! But, Irene, you would be queen. That can't be!"

"And why not? Am I not queen on the stage, even when I sing the role of a Spanish cigarette girl?"

"You are sublime on stage, but . . . you are American, Irene. Surely a title holds no allure for you, with your native independence—"

"Independence! Independence is a step on the road to sovereignty. I will rise in this world as far as I can, and have you not seen the Prince? He is courtly, devoted, assured, a man of Continental upbringing, a lover of music—"

"Exactly. He is a European, a man of noble blood. However much he may admire you, he cannot, will not make you queen—"

She lashed upright like a whip, her silken gown crackling around her. "You know nothing of Willie, or the relationship between us.

He has extended me the greatest respect. Another man in his position would have expected my favors by now. Oh, how can I expect a
sheltered violet like yourself to understand these things, the . . .
unspoken promise that may exist between a man and a woman!?
That was not what I called you here to talk about!"

"Irene . . ." I had never seen her so agitated, so easy to offend.

It was I who should have taken umbrage. Irene blithely dismissed
my lack of sentimental education even as her words reminded me with
piercing clarity of my lone moment of romantic magic, when the scales
had fallen from my eyes with a blindfold, for just an instant—years
before in a children's playroom in Berkeley Square. Irene was too en-
meshed in her own difficulties to heed my involuntary gasp.

"My possible marital adventure is not the most pressing problem,
at any rate," she continued.

"What is, then?"

"The King."

"I have not met him, apparently he is ill."

Irene rose and took a tiny step away from me, paused, then
stepped back to press very close. Her face held the same brisk intelligence I had seen of old as she stared down at me. "The King is . . .
dying. That everyone knows."

"Oh. I'm very sorry, but I don't see how I can help—"

She leaned closer, her silks snapping like distant lightning, with
her voice the hushed contralto thunder that followed it.

"There is something that no one else knows—or, I should say,
that only one other knows. I am convinced that he is being slowly
poisoned!"

Chapter Nineteen

Romance in a Minor Key

~ஜ~

To see my friend, Irene Adler, and the Crown Prince of Bohemia together in early 1887 was to witness the idyllic enactment of a Viennese operetta or a Strauss waltz.

Even I, who was most skeptical of their future, found myself softening as I accompanied them through the baroque beauties of old Prague.

Yet I remained hopelessly tongue-tied in the Prince's company. Despite the fact that he, like Irene, was two years my junior, I found myself utterly intimidated by his foreign ways, his larger-than-life size, and even by his title. His heroic robust perfection awed me; Wilhelm von Ormstein made all romantic figures of fiction and fact shrink by comparison.

Certainly diffident Jasper Higgenbottom shriveled in my memory as if baked by an African sun to insignificance; even dashing young Mr. Stanhope's attractions blurred in the Prince's presence.

The Czech composer, Mr. Dvořák, was a man more to my taste, once one understood the two fierce vertical frown lines separating his dark brows—marks of intensity rather than irascibility.

As unprepossessing as the Prince was impressive, Mr. Dvořák's warmth radiated from his features despite his rough-cut beard and hair. He delighted in practicing his charmingly mangled English upon me, perhaps sensing the patience of a nanny in my demeanor. He endlessly sang Irene's praises—for her voice, her empathy in performance, her hard work in mastering both his music and his native tongue.

"Linguist born," he would say, a finger shaking in emphasis. "And a tone, a . . . sound . . . that would make a saint to cry." He never mentioned her beauty.

Seeing Irene with the Prince gave me a greater sense of removal from her than I had felt when all of western Europe separated us. She had never been a woman to be overwhelmed by men, but in relation to the physically imposing Prince she seemed a porcelain fashion doll, albeit one with a mind of her own.

They made a splendid couple; that no one could deny. His massive, mustachioed blond good looks and habit of wearing dress uniform and Irene's feminine dark beauty made them seem like a marzipan soldier paired with a milk chocolate ballerina. Even the Queen's eyes followed them fondly, though Hortense and Bertrand remained aloof. And the Prince doted upon Irene, his admiration shouted in every gesture, whispered in each word addressed to her.

Once that spring, when an unseasonable snowfall had whipped Prague's streets into froth, Irene hesitated to cross where carriage wheels had churned the melting snow into a grey mush. The Prince flung his silk-lined cloak over his shoulder and lifted her—cloak and muff and all. He carried her across the thoroughfare, vehicles jolting to a stop for their royal progress, his shiny black hessians spanning the puddles as if they were seven-league boots.

It was not a gesture I could fancy a country curate making—yet it thrilled me as melodrama moves an audience.

I began to see it—how Irene, having struggled so long on her own behalf, might relish success, might even relinquish somewhat her fierce independence to enjoy another's solicitude. Yet I saw danger in it, on every side . . . danger in the unseen King's decline, danger in the Duchess Hortense's sour, sidelong looks, in Bertrand's sulks, in the quick, fatherly frown Dvořák often cast at Irene when she was in the Prince's company.

"I know the English," he told me when I visited a rehearsal. "Have been many times in London. Five," he toted proudly. "They like my 'Spectre Bride' and 'Saint Ludmila.' Your friend, she is American. Not like English, or like Czech . . . not like German. I worry for her. She is too self-certain. These Americans know not the compromise we Europeans have make in our land, our language—for centuries. Old feelings stir. Politics. Pride. Not good for your friend to be here now."

"But you invited her—"

"Yes, yes. For voice. For artistry. Not for"—Mr. Dvořák glanced at the Prince, whose unmistakable silhouette had darkened the doorway— "not for . . . danger."

Mr. Dvořák's awkward English expressed my innermost worries. I had missed Irene's autumn performance in his *King and Collier*, a peasant opera, but that spring she sang *Saint Ludmila* in Prague, the part carried in Leeds the previous autumn by the contralto, Janet Patey.

I sat in the velvet-cushioned royal box on opening night, mother-of-pearl opera glasses, a gift from Irene, primed. The rest of the von Ormsteins were not present; the King's illness forbade a too-public presence. Willie sat beside me, his resplendent evening dress garnished with a scarlet sash from shoulder to hip and burdened by a glittering corsage of medals. I barely spoke to him, letting myself sink into the music, as eager as he to watch for and listen to Irene.

She was magnificent, as was the sweep and pull of Dvořák's melancholy music. It teased one like a tide, these notes from the heart of a landlocked composer. I found my own internal saltwater rising and glanced at the Prince. In the darkened opera house, his eye-whites glistened like wet pearls. His profile was rapt. I swallowed my own emotion and looked away. His tears made him human in my estimation, more than anything purposeful he could have done to win my favor. I vowed silently then to help Irene in any way I could, even if it led to an alliance I feared would invite tragedy.

"How was I?" Irene asked breathlessly after the opening night champagne had been consumed and we had returned to the castle and been divested of finery by our respective maids.

"Wonderful! They shall no longer speak of the 'Divine Sarah' but the 'Sublime Irene.' No, I am quite serious; I've never heard your voice so rich and resonant. It must be—"

"Yes?" Irene cocked her head wickedly.

"—Mr. Dvořák's music."

"A truly humble man for all his genius. These poor Czechs have been so downtrodden by their German masters that they return to their roots with incomparable zest. That is what you hear in Mr. Dvořák's music, the ecstasy of finding himself, and finding fellowship with other patriots like himself."

"Is it not difficult, Irene, to be part of the Czech national resurgence through your music, and yet live in the castle of their conquerors?"

"Oh, that . . . that is politics. Very old politics." Irene's dismissive gesture shook out the ringlets her dresser had spent an hour that afternoon impressing into her hair with a curling iron. "The last revolution here was in 1848—the same year France hiccoughed, politically speaking, and the Zone of Diamonds vanished. The Austrian Empire is wise now to restore some self-government to the people; it will avoid uprising."

I sighed and was silent. Irene reminded me of a Roman rider at the circus, each leg balanced on the back of a different steed, but she refused to see it. She had blithely permitted herself to bask in two irreconcilable seasons—the joyous spring of Czech cultural revival and the looming autumn of her Prince's hereditary rulership. I wondered how much longer there would be kings in Bohemia, even those who were mere figureheads for the Emperor, Franz Josef, in Vienna.

"It is true," Irene said after a moment, for she had been musing on matters quite different, "that this sojourn in Prague has deepened my musical experience quite unexpectedly. My ambitions, as you know, lie in the direction of grand opera and Vienna. Yet while here I have developed a fondness for the *lieder*, the simple love songs so beautifully done by Schumann, and Mr. Dvořák's lusty peasant melodies. Somehow they lie closer to the heart than the spectacular arias of grand opera. But—once certain matters are settled, I must direct my attention to my operatic career again."

"You do not expect to be Queen of Bohemia and still perform publicly?"

"Why not? Being a queen is one long engagement at performing publicly, save that it is in the service of duty. It should be quite a novelty and gain me a good deal of press. Besides, as you have pointed out, Bohemia is almost a storybook kingdom, like little Liechtenstein. Who will care what the Queen of it does or does not do? Royalty here is a mere formality. A charming . . . anachronism."

I lifted the photograph of Irene and the Prince from her bedside table. It was mounted in a small, velvet-upholstered cabinet so it could be closed or displayed ajar, like an open book. I undid the tiny gold latch to regard it. The crown jewels of Bohemia—the crown itself— seemed dull in the photograph's grey monotone, but Irene looked every inch a queen, every inch the match of the Crown Prince of Bohemia. I held the case out to her.

"If royalty were an anachronism, why did he give this to you in a case? Why do you keep it shut beside your bed so that the maid may not see it?"

She snatched the case from me and latched it. "Discretion. The Queen holds me in high regard, but the unlovely Hortense and the slovenly Bertrand do not. Willie asked me to keep it secret; only you know."

"So with one hand he appears to give, while with the other he takes away."

Irene shook her head and drew an Egyptian cigarette from a long, narrow tin box. She bent to a candle flame to light it, then straightened to exhale a veil of blue smoke.

"Time was when Bohemian royalty married into the greatest royal houses of Europe, but that was five hundred years ago. Willie is not under the same pressure. Even if he were, I could overcome it."

That ended the discussion for Irene, if not me.

Yet, the next day, as if to prove her power, Irene conducted me on visits to the royal family quarters. The Queen's suite was even more grandly gilded than Irene's. She served us tea in wan china, her worry-worn face morose. What in the Prince was handsome became slightly coarse in her older, feminine features. I wished I could see the King to compare him to his Herculean son.

"How is his Majesty?" Irene inquired.

"Still failing and still undiagnosed by the doctors," the Queen said.

"Have you . . . tried any folk remedies?" Irene asked so casually that I perked my ears like a spaniel to catch her true meaning.

The Queen sighed and pressed a handkerchief that was more lace than linen to her mouth. "So Hortense has been urging. And Bertrand swears that the tonics he takes for hair growth have had a wonderful effect."

"Indeed?" Irene arched an eyebrow at me while I searched for some significance in the fact.

From my observation, Bertrand's shedding pate needed far more aid than whatever mythical fuzz he believed the hair tonic had bestowed. So I told Irene as we left the Queen and her tepid tea and rustled into another wing of the castle.

"But is it not as I told you?" she interrupted me. "Even the palace resorts to these herbal remedies. I find that fascinating."

"Not so odd. You yourself have said that folkways linger here in Bohemia, as numerous as flowers in an alpine meadow, in fact. Even royalty is gullible."

"Or clever." Irene's face grew harsh with concentration. "Diabolically clever."

Our next call was paid upon the unhappy Hortense. Her suite of rooms faced south, so mullioned shadows criss-crossed thick Aubusson rugs that paled in the fierce sunlight. Despite the brightness, something soured in her chambers; an emanation from her soul, I fancied, which I envisioned as having a squint, for that was the sidelong, suspicious way she looked at us both and, apparently, life.

"The Queen, your mother, says your father continues to decline," Irene murmured sympathetically.

Hortense, who had been sitting by the window doing stitchery, kicked a ball of wool aside, nearly striking a fat, low-legged little dog that waddled off as if used to her sudden tempers.

"The doctors can do nothing," Hortense complained. "I have urged a return to a simple regime—herb teas and system-cleansing soups. Perhaps a stay at Marienbad."

"Ah, the spa the Czechs call Marianske Lazne, near the forest bordering Germany. Mud baths and mineral water, an excellent idea. The Prince of Wales has found it helpful."

Irene's approval lit a spark of life in Hortense's pallid cheeks. If she were an advertisement for the efficacy of her herbs, the cause was lost.

"Tell me, Miss Adler, do you find the lavender and licorice gargle I suggested useful?"

"Yes, thank you so much. I trill like a nightingale for hours after. Have you used it yourself?"

Hortense reached into a basket on the table to extract an apple, into whose red cheek she bit with yellowed protuberant teeth. The cores of the apple's consumed brethren littered a Meissen plate, pips piled in a neat anthill near one edge.

"My voice is not my livelihood, Miss Adler. With my husband gone at the southern estates so much, I need not even raise it."

Irene laughed far more than this feeble jest deserved as the Duchess dipped a handkerchief in a bottle of clear fluid and daubed her temples.

"For the headache," the Duchess Hortense said. "Lily of the Valley distilled in white wine."

"I should think the white wine would *give* one a headache," I couldn't help remarking.

The Duchess pinioned me with a disapproving stare. "It is Austrian wine," she answered, as if such a vintage was invariably free of flaws. She finished her apple and deposited the core on the plate, but not before idly picking the pips free and pushing them with a fingernail into the rough pile.

When we had taken our farewells and were again in a deserted hallway Irene kept silent beyond her habit.

"What are you thinking?" I unwisely asked.

"Of how I could get in brother Bertie's room to see his hair preparations."

"Now that is clearly improper! Even dangerous. I forbid it!"

"Of course I shall not, then," Irene said with mock meekness.

"Of course you will . . . oh, Irene, you cannot behave in Prague Castle as if you still lived in Saffron Hill. If you are caught doing anything out of character here, it will end your influence with the Prince. He is a stickler for appearances."

"You think so?"

"I know so. I also can guess what you're contemplating. If the Prince found you in male dress, even as an excuse to investigate Bertrand's room . . . !"

"Of course I shan't storm Bertie's room in pin-striped frock-coat," Irene said impatiently. "If I can't enter myself, I shall have to use another pair of legs. Perhaps his man."

There the discussion ended. Two days later I found Irene in the castle's huge and musty library. It was a fanciful chamber, a high-ceilinged tower with books and wrought-iron balconies strung around its perimeter like frills on the skirt of an evening gown.

Irene was seated under the curl of a wrought-iron spiral staircase, a small, much aged tome in her hands.

"Jaborandi," she greeted me triumphantly.

"I beg your pardon? Is that Czech?"

"Too many vowels. No, it is what brother Bertrand puts upon the billiard ball he calls his head, but perhaps a fiendishly clever head at that."

"Bertrand? Clever? Irene, tell me something I can credit."

"Jaborandi," she repeated. "An herb used to stimulate hair growth, so the loyal unsuspecting body servant, Kurt, tells me. This book in my hand—and, significantly, in the castle library—tells me that it is also deadly poisonous. The villain is a substance called pilocarpine. Isn't that a wonderful word? It sounds like something one could call a melodrama villain: 'Leave my house, you pilocarpine!' "

"Poisonous?" I ignored Irene's histrionics as I sat on a wrought-iron stair, my skirts cushioning me from its steely pattern. "How, if Bertrand is using it daily?"

"Externally." Irene patted the top of her luxuriant curls. "But Jaborandi is liquid and could easily be slipped into a sickroom broth. Especially since both Hortense and Bertrand have shown themselves aware of herbs."

"What of. . . . Willie?"

"Willie?"

"He is the heir. The others have nothing to gain."

"Willie would not stoop to poison; it is alien to his character—he who has always been bigger than life. When Willie wishes to speed a person on his way, he will tell that victim outright, expecting him to wither from sheer sorrow at the withdrawal of Willie's princely presence."

"Or her." I could not quarrel with Irene's knowledge of the Prince, but I could shiver a bit at this astute characterization. "You describe a ruthless person."

"He is royalty; they are all ruthless by birth. You harbor a bit of that attribute yourself, Nell."

"I?"

"You . . . when you think that you are right."

"Apparently *you* are right. This Jaborandi can be fatal and is at hand to palace intimates. Still, how will you accuse a princeling like Bertrand?"

"I will refrain from it, dear Nell. Not from fear, but because there is something in Hortense's behavior that disquiets me more—"

"There is a great deal in Hortense's behavior that is disquieting, but it need not be murderous."

"Still, did you notice her apples the other day? She had eaten half a basket—and it is her custom to consume a great many a day. I have inquired—discreetly—in the kitchen."

"Eating apples is not a suspicious act."

"It is if you save the seeds."

"Seeds? There are no seeds in apples—oh, you Americans call pips 'seeds' . . ."

"Whatever you call them, in quantity they are rife with poison, as are peach pits, which perhaps you British call 'pips.'"

I ignored Irene's linguistic baiting. "But how could one dose an invalid with a quantity of apple pips?"

"Ground in a mush, crushed in a tea. This volume states the interesting case of a gentleman who so loved the seeds that he ate the harvest of several apples a day—suffering no ills because a steady, small intake acclimates the person to the poison. Then, one day, in an orgy of apple seed indulgence, he saved up and consumed a cup's worth. Dead as a dodo by the next day, despite his previous tolerance.

"I wonder if Hortense could have been dosing the King with just enough to weaken him before administering the *coup de grace*. For a man of his age and weakness, a half cup should suffice and could easily be concealed in an apple cake or brewed into a heady concentrate of herbal tea."

"So the poisoner is Hortense then? But why?"

Irene frowned as she shut the book and slipped it in the pocket of her voluminous skirt. "I am unsure on both counts. As you point out so lucidly, the motive seems strained. Simply because I do not relish Bertrand or Hortense as an in-law is no reason to convict them of crime."

"You, like Willie, observe the proprieties," said I.

"Exactly, my dear Nell. So I shall muse upon the matter and ask the staff what and how they feed the old gentleman, the King—"

"Without exciting suspicions about yourself! Irene, if the King should die of poison, you would be a far likelier suspect than any member of the family."

"I?" The eventuality had not occurred to her, so much had the Crown Prince turned her normally practical head. "Why?"

"You aspire to be a member of the family and are not of noble blood. Your Prince may not care, but his family will. If well, the King might have enforced your separation."

Irene stood up. "Then I must solve this suspicion for my own sake. And yours."

"Mine?"

"Naturally, my astute Nell. Who has arrived only lately from afar but my friend and boon companion, Miss Penelope Huxleigh? Who is likely to be accused as accomplice?"

"Myself? Oh dear . . ."

"We never see the finger when it indicates ourselves." Irene shrugged her smile away. "At the rate my inquiries are progressing, I should see the bottom of the affair in a day or two. There is naught to worry about."

Chapter Twenty

A Pocketful of Why

~∽⌒∽~

We left the library possessed of its little book of secrets and a certain smugness at our own cleverness.

Within a day Irene was cursing her possession of it, but there was no way to disown it. The King had died. Rumors of poison ran rampant through the Castle, no doubt fueled by Irene's subtle but memorable inquiries among the servants.

Within hours of the death, distant relatives from the farthest wrinkles of the Austro-Hungarian Empire had been telegraphed and were wending their way across the picturesque frontiers of many lands en route to the state funeral. The Prince was virtually incommunicado, even to Irene.

We paced our respective chambers, as good as prisoners snared in a web of state ceremony. We could neither declare our suspicions nor defend our innocence. The castle was being methodically but secretly searched, for Hortense had swiftly revealed a book on herbs to be absent from the library.

"I'll take the book and conceal it somewhere," I offered.

"No, to move it invites greater danger. They have not dared search our rooms yet." Irene stood inspecting the spires of glass atop her lace-draped dressing table and their throat-soothing contents. "I wonder if any of these elixirs have a more malign use than I am aware of?"

"Or if something could be *put* into one of them to point the finger at you?"

"Bohemia has sharpened your fancy, Nell; that is a positively baroque idea. Hand me that candle and take another for yourself."

I caught my breath when Irene tilted the taper and let the wax drip down from the wick's liquid well. "You'll mar the lace!"

She ignored my worry, seizing a bottle and turning the seam where stopper met neck under the dripping wax. A waxen ring hardened around the container. She set it down before it was firm and lifted the next bottle to her improvised seal.

"They may want to break the seals to examine the contents," I warned, lifting a bottle to my own candle.

"At least we shall know if anyone has tampered with them from this point on."

"What of your throat?" came my afterthought.

Irene pressed a hand to her heart as she swore: "From this day forward, I shall tend it only with tea and honey; no foreign herbs. Now, I must discover the facts of the King's demise. Since even I cannot gain audience with the Prince while he is consumed with the formalities of a state funeral, I must use the occasion of dinner to find them out."

"Irene! Even you cannot question a bereaved family for signs of foul play over dinner."

"I must, Penelope, or the killer will go free and some innocent party will be tinged with suspicion. Like yourself."

Knowing Irene's propensity to strike while the iron was hot, I dressed for dinner that evening wishing that I wore chain mail, properly black, of course, instead of a sober bombazine gown suitable for mourning.

Irene's black velvet gown glittered with jet trimming, cut low over her shoulders; a mourning necklace of large faceted onyx beads was caught close around her throat. As usual, even the state of grief seem designed to display Irene to best advantage. The new-made King addressed her with melting looks from the head of the table while Hortense's disapproving fan switched like an angry black cat's tail.

"Have the arrangements been made, your Majesty?" Irene inquired of the King.

"It is nearly done," he said with a sigh.

Irene trailed her spoon through the clear oxtail broth. "It must be an intolerable strain for all of you—and especially the Duchess."

"Yes," he began, "but why especially Hortense? She was not particularly attached to our father."

"Willie!" Hortense said.

He shrugged at her outrage. To a man of his rank and size, others' objections were minute as gnats. "I do not mean that you failed to offer him filial affection, Tensy, only that Father did not encourage a show of emotion. The funeral will respect that tendency."

"I was, was . . ." Irene faltered prettily, then cast the confused Hortense a sidelong glance, ". . . referring to the Duchess's condition."

"Condition?" Hortense repeated the word in an indignant squeak. The Queen Mother trilled it. And Willie bellowed it.

"I merely thought," Irene stumbled on, "well, the quantity of apples her Grace has been consuming of late. Surely she is, that is—"

I had never known Irene to suffer from such delicate sensibilities. Her calculated silence forced Hortense to voice the thought Irene had planted in every head.

"I am not," the Duchess replied, her face scarlet, "in the condition which you so boldly imply, Miss Adler. I merely have an inordinate fondness for apples."

"Hmm, inordinate," Irene murmured. "Pardon my misapprehension."

"You seem to labor under a great many misapprehensions, Miss Adler," Hortense said coldly.

Everyone at table stared into the oxtail soup. The King's face slowly suffused with crimson. I reflected that Irene's presence at the family board—like my own—was due only to Willie's flouting of his family customs. We were commoners, interlopers and, of course, easy scapegoats.

For the first time I experienced a thrill of fear. How easy to charge Irene with the late King's murder as her way of making Willie the monarch beforetime! How well it would suit everyone's purpose, perhaps even Willie's, now that he was King.

He broke the silence with what rang out as a royal command.

"Miss Adler, you and Miss Huxleigh will take cognac with me in the library after dinner."

Irene bowed her head in acquiescence. Only I and the oxtail soup saw her minuscule smile. "That's one way to earn an audience; raise a row at dinner," she murmured without glancing my way.

I was never so happy to vacate a dining table as I was to leave that unhappy board. Soon after we stood like schoolgirls called to account as the King paced in the library's murky light, his elongated shadow casting ribbed reflections on the rows of book spines.

"My dear Irene," he began, flinging me a cautious glance.

"Penelope is utterly discreet, Willie; I would stake my life upon it."

The King favored me with a piercing look, then spoke to Irene as if I were not there.

"You may have to. Are you aware that the death of my father, the King, has stirred suspicions?"

"I am," Irene said coolly.

He stared at her composure. "Are you aware that certain speculations have placed *you* in the position of suspect?"

A rueful smile tilted Irene's lips upward. "Not until just recently, another reason why the reliable Penelope is also so valuable."

"Did you know"—and now the King began to thunder—"that a book on herbal potions is missing from this very library?"

"Yes . . . no," said Irene, bending to lift her skirt hem. The black velvet rose slowly as a stage curtain on ruffled black taffeta petticoats. The King remained transfixed by this theatrical display of flounce and black-stockinged ankle, but Irene merely pulled a small object from a pocket in her petticoat hem and handed it to the King.

"The book is not missing, as it is here."

"Then you *did* take it, as Hortense suspected!"

"Yes, and Hortense was consulting it frequently, as *I* suspected, or she would have never missed one musty little volume from among so many!"

They stared at each other, each one's words confounding the other. I sensed that Irene was as insulted by the King's accusations as he was by her ready answers.

"You say, Irene, that . . . Hortense . . . consulted the book. Surely you do not imply that a member of the Royal Family—"

"No more than you imply that I myself or a member of my loyal family—" Irene had mimicked his huffy tone to a nuance, but the King did not perceive it. "And," she continued, "the suspicions regarding your father's illness are nothing new to me. Why do you suppose I sent for Penelope? I needed an aide in my investigation."

"Your investigation!" The King sputtered silent, then spied the tray of French brandy the servant had left. "Sit," he commanded suddenly, as if remembering courtesy.

He handed two small glasses to us, then stalked to the spiral staircase to lean against its sinuous silhouette with his own oversize brandy snifter winking jewel-like in his huge hand. "Perhaps you had better state your case, Irene."

She sipped, and smiled. "I have had some small experience in investigating matters for certain individuals in London. Among my clients was Mr. Charles Tiffany—"

"The American who is crown jeweler to half the royal families of Europe!"

"Just so. He wished me to look into some missing crown jewels, as a matter of fact."

The King lifted a bushy blond eyebrow and waited.

"I suspected, your Majesty, that your father's illness was not natural long before the rumors began. I have not been privy to the doctors' reports, but I have concluded that the late King was being dosed with an herbal poison."

"Astounding! So the doctors concluded just yesterday."

Irene smiled tightly. "Which is why my reputation is under on-slaught today."

The King shifted against the railing. "There has been some talk in the family ranks," he conceded. "But it can*not* be Hortense—"

"No, it *could* be Prince Bertrand."

"What! My brother, now? You go too far! You forget yourself—"

"I do not, although you appear to have forgotten me!" Irene charged in return. "Oh, yes, how easy to point to the stranger in the family midst, but what motive would I have?"

"To see me King."

"Well, that is a very handsome sight, your Majesty," Irene said, suddenly lapsing into a teasing smile, "but you were equally com-manding as Crown Prince, Willie."

"True." He returned her smile.

"I did abstract the book. Penelope was with me and she knows I was investigating poisonous solutions that were already in the castle."

"And?" The King was frowning.

"Did you know that apple seeds are lethal in quantity? Or notice that Hortense has been eating an enormous number of apples—and saving the seeds?"

"Yes, but . . . it is a habit. Hortense has always been of a nervous nature. She . . . is compulsive, saves the seeds from oranges as well."

"Hmm. And did you know that Bertrand employs a hair tonic?"

The King laughed. "He is vain, my younger brother, so short and now so prematurely short of hair. What of it?"

"Jaborandi, which he uses, is immediately fatal if taken internally."

The King went to the table and poured himself more cognac. "So you are saying that two of my three siblings are suspects in the death of their own father. This is not possible. It will not be possible." He spoke very definitely, a warning in his tone. "It will not be possi-ble, not even to clear myself, should it be necessary. Not even to clear my dearest friend."

Irene sighed and sipped the cognac. The glass glowed like a huge topaz against her black velvet bodice. "Then, your Majesty, I shall have to produce another suspect."

I sat forward, my taffeta petticoats rustling like mice in a corner; my movements were as little regarded by the two of them.

The King's voice was husky. "Can you do it, my dear? And clear yourself?"

"I will try," Irene said, rising. She regarded the King as if addressing him on the same level, despite the disparity in their heights, their social positions. I would dare venture to say that she had attained an even loftier elevation in a moral sense. "But I will not accuse an innocent party, no matter how many royal skins it saves. Or hearts it breaks."

"Let us hope," the King said grimly, "that neither skins nor hearts shall suffer from this inquiry."

He left us there, listening to his heavy footsteps fade, as the shadows softened around us like an airy cloak descending.

"Irene, can you do it? Find another culprit? Prove it?"

"I can, as I told Willie, try. You see, of course, that his family wants to use this pretext to end our relationship. They did not expect me to have the wit to point out their own vulnerability."

"But the King will never allow a family member to be charged! You heard him."

Now Irene spoke in commanding tones as she trailed to the table and refilled her own glass.

"If a family member murdered the late King, Willie cannot stop me from saying so. But I pray that is *not* the case, no matter how much Hortense or Bertrand might wish to be rid of me. Accusing one's future in-laws of murder is no fitting end to a fairy tale romance in Bohemia, eh, Nell? Not good light opera at all."

Chapter Twenty-one

The Golden Seal

❧

"I go to town," Irene announced late the next morning. "Will you accompany me?"

"Of course? But why go to town when the crime was committed here?"

"I wish to see the doctors on neutral ground where they will be more frank. They, too, must fear royal retribution. After all, they failed to diagnose the ailment while the King was yet living. And then I will see Mr. Dvořák—"

"Irene, I enjoy visiting the National Theatre, but dare we take time from this problem?"

"We will not be taking time from this problem."

"To see Mr. Dvořák and talk music?"

"To see Mr. Dvořák and talk politics," Irene corrected me, drawing on pale lavender gloves that matched the rows of ruching on her walking suit.

"And then I want to consult a gypsy woman. Mr. Dvořák should guide me there; it is from such elderly ears that he has traced his native folk songs."

"A gypsy woman? Irene . . . whatever for?"

"Why, I wish my fortune told," she retorted with a sidelong glance through her heliotrope veil. "All brides-to-be are superstitious."

So off we went in a castle carriage down the steep hill and into the thick forest of gabled and tiled rooftops that was Prague.

The doctors resided in an impressively quaint house with window-boxes of pansies blooming on the first floor. Their long unpronounceable German names began with "S" and "D", so Irene instructed me to refer to them as "Sturm" and "Drang" in my notes, for what reason I cannot fathom. Their ground floor waiting rooms were crowded, but Irene merely scribbled a word or two on her visiting card and sent it in. Moments later, the housekeeper ushered us into a consulting room where both physicians awaited us.

"Jaborandi, Miss Adler?" Dr. Sturm asked. He was short and plump, with a Vandyke and mustache waxed to mouse-tail fineness at the ends.

"And apple seed?" put in Dr. Drang, who was tall, thin and beardless.

"Well, gentlemen, does either poison show in your tests?"

The doctors rubbed their hands together in tandem and exchanged glances. Dr. Sturm spoke first. "Detecting this type of poison is not an easy task when working backwards."

Dr. Drang nodded vigorously, then said, "Yes, we suspect poison. We even have ruled out the more common ones—arsenic, cyanide, belladonna."

Dr. Sturm spoke again. "Yet our tests of the stomach contents—excuse, ladies, my bluntness—show no trace of unacceptable elements."

"Not even of apple tea?" Irene coaxed.

"No apples at all," said Dr. Sturm.

"Not even Jaborandi?" she demanded.

"You are most familiar with the herbal apothecary," Dr. Drang added with a bow.

"No," Irene demurred, "only with what herbs are at hand in the castle. Then the late King was poisoned in some other manner than I have suspected and the substance may have been imported. What killed him?"

The doctors exchanged anxious glances. "Asphyxiation," they chorused.

Irene and I looked at each other. I was beginning to feel like an audience at a Punch and Judy show, thanks to the way the good doctors paired their wooden movements.

"Can poison asphyxiate one?" I inquired.

The doctors frowned in perfect harmony.

"The skin," said Dr. Drang, "appears to have been the medium. Then the lungs stopped functioning. Death would have appeared quite natural, even if witnessed."

Irene rose. "Believe me, a king's death is always witnessed; far too many people have a stake in it for him to slip away unnoticed. Thank you for your aid. Good day."

We soon stood in the square's sparkling sunshine, listening to swifts chirping under the gables.

"A different kind of poison, Nell," Irene said. "Perhaps Willie is right; the odious Hortense and hairless Bertrand are innocent—at least of patricide."

She eyed the young coachman, who sprang down to assist us into the heavily upholstered interior. "So attached to their comforts, these Germans," Irene murmured as we sank into the tufted-velvet seats. "So comfortable with themselves as well, so unsuspecting of the subtle."

I realized that she was digesting the new facts and remained silent while we rumbled over cobblestones to the National Theatre by the river, where Mr. Dvořák could usually be found when he was working on a production.

A theatre by day is a forsaken thing—like a puppet slumped with slack strings. Nothing drives the mechanism. It resembles a great stranded ship whose engines have silenced.

Into this grand lifeless expanse Irene and I moved down the carpeted aisle to the group of men clustered near the orchestra pit. A violinist tortured his instrument into tune. The conductor berated the bass player. Mr. Dvořák slumped in one of the gilded seats, scribbling on his score.

Irene's presence caught his attention slowly, like the latent scent
of lilacs on a May day. He looked up, then around and finally saw
her standing at a polite distance.

"Miss Adler, and Miss Huxleigh! Two maidens of spring. What
a pleasant surprise. My head is to ache for all the rearrangement I
do."

"Could we speak, Mr. Dvořák?"

"Of course, Miss Adler, speak. I like to exercise this English. Not
bad, eh?"

Irene perched on the arm of an unoccupied seat, bracing herself
with the shaft of her ivory-handled parasol. I could never master
such precariously casual poses and remained standing stiffly behind
her, but Mr. Dvořák's frequent glances kept me from being disre-
garded. Irene lowered her voice to a confidential level.

"I am on an errand for the King of Bohemia." (The assertion
was, I suppose, technically true.)

"Ah?"

"He is concerned about politics and the Czech national resurgence movement."

"So he should be," the composer said sternly.

"These Germanic families have long ruled other peoples in this
part of the world—Poles, Lithuanians, Rumanians. I know, Mr.
Dvořák, that even Bohemian . . . patriots . . . would not weep to see
that royalty wink out."

"My operas resurrect heroes of the old legends," Mr. Dvořák
said. "If these things inflame new heroes . . ." He shrugged, his dark
eyes expressively blank.

"The Prince—" Irene began, then corrected herself. "The King—"

"Is new man, new hero for people. He is safe—so long as he does
not become despot."

"But the old King . . . ?"

"Another story," Mr. Dvořák said gruffly. "Another score, another libretto. I do not write these modern dramas. I write operas of
the old days. Antique-ty, I think you say."

"Antiquity," Irene said, smiling. "So, it *is* possible, Mr. Dvořák?"

"In Bohemia, anything is possible. Even that a diva become a queen, who knows?"

"What of directing me to an authentic gypsy fortune teller, is that possible, Mr. Dvořák?"

"I thought you make your own fortune, Miss Adler?"

"Quite true, but even Macbeth had his witches. And I am innocent of his other sins."

Mr. Dvořák laughed and nodded. He and Irene had reached some understanding without putting their common thoughts into words, into plain English as I understood it. I must have allowed myself a gesture of impatience, for Mr. Dvořák suddenly leaped up and addressed me.

"My poor neglected Miss Huxleigh, she is like the mountain laurel, so sturdy and lovely that all take her for granted. Here, I sign this page I must rewrite anyway. For you, for 'Miss Huxleigh, who is remembered.' "

"Why, Mr. Dvořák, this is wonderful!"

"Now, you roll it like good music student, so it do not crack or the spring raindrops do not make the ink to run." The composer turned to Irene. "You know the Powder Tower near Wenceslas Square?"

Irene nodded. "The entrance to Old Town."

"Beyond that lies the University and the Joseph Quarter, where centuries ago Rabbi Jehuda Loew ben Bezalel is said to have made this monstrous thing called the 'Golem.' "

Irene nodded, but I asked, "What is this 'Golem'?"

Mr. Dvořák turned to me eagerly. "Good story. Very old story. Someday good Dvořák opera, perhaps? This rabbi, he make huge ceramic man controlled by holy words upon paper in his mouth. One day the rabbi forget to remove paper and the Golem thunders through Old Town, destroying all in his path. Your English lady author, Mary Shelley, use this old Prague legend to inspire famous story, I think. To this day, superstitious folk visit Rabbi Loew's tomb in the Joseph Quarter, leave papers with prayers and problems on them, for to be solved."

"And we must go there, where this . . . Golem . . . was born?" I said. "Are there no nearby gypsy fortune tellers?"

"None that know old ways," Mr. Dvořák said.

"We want none but those," Irene said firmly. "Thank you, Mr. Dvořák, for aid in matters both mundane and occult." He frowned at the words. "Politics and magic," Irene explained. "Both, I fear, are most overrated but bear investigation. Good day, then."

I was eager to leave the theatre's lifeless chill for the color and light of the riverbank. Irene told our driver to convey us to the Powder Tower. Once there, she instructed him to return in two hours.

I consulted the locket-watch on my lapel. "Two hours?"

Under the shadow of the huge Gothic tower lay a maze of narrow byways, crooked streets into which the sun could not stretch its golden fingers even at midday. I could picture the gigantic darker shadow of the Golem still stalking there.

"Two hours?" I repeated. "Irene . . . you know, what Mr. Dvořák said of the Golem's great size and relentless strength—it reminded me of the Prince."

She did not correct my use of the outmoded title. "Our quarry is not Willie, Nell, I am more certain of that than ever. You must not let your imagination run away with you. Simply pretend that you are exploring Portman market and tell me if you spy any occult signposts."

The quarter thronged with people and wagons. Many of the buildings that loomed above us dated to the Renaissance with crowded gables, leaded-glass arcades and steep tile roofs interrupted by mean garret windows.

Irene's comparison to a London street market was apt, for the old quarter exuded the smell—chicken noodle soup and poppy seed strudel—and sounds of a common folk's exchange. Peddlers' carts ground through the circuitous ways, wares ranging from glass beads to pots chiming to the motion.

"At least this area has a Biblical name," I said righteously, more to reassure myself than make conversation.

Irene flashed me an amused glance. "Alas, no. The name has nothing to do with the ancient owner of a gaudy cloak. The Joseph Quarter is named after the Emperor in Vienna, Franz Josef, who gave the

Jews full freedom of the city early in his reign. In a logic that escapes me, they then named the ghetto after him. Politics, Nell, is more mysterious than magic."

We strolled past a vast cemetery, its ancient headstones cluttered together like some monster's uneven teeth. One pictured generations of skeletons tumbled atop one another beneath the earth, their headstones above jousting for room as well.

"Rabbi Loew's tomb, I imagine." Irene nodded to a stately stone monument at which some figures clustered. "Perhaps we should leave a paper with our conundrum written upon it."

"Why not ask the location of the Zone of Diamonds while you are about it? No, Irene, I would not risk raising that awful Golem. I hope Mr. Dvořák never writes his opera. Besides, who would he find to play the mechanical monster?"

"Almost any romantic tenor," Irene riposted. "They are all large enough to play three people, although they tend to great girth rather than great height."

We moved deeper into the maze of cobblestoned streets, farther into a haunting shadow. I lost all notion of direction; my frantic scanning for signposts at last found exactly what Irene had ordered.

"There! That signboard of an outlined hand with numbers written all over it—or is it an inn?"

"The very thing." Irene made for the sign and darted under its shadow without a pause.

Meaning to urge caution, I followed. We plunged into a narrow, dark passage. Odd odors latticed the air, as commanding as if they had become physical. In the distance, chimes chattered their glassy teeth. Irene was as intent as a hound upon the trace. My whispered urgings, the tugs of my hand at her sleeve went unheeded.

She followed the scent and the sound; I followed her.

We entered a chamber—at least I took it for a chamber. The area was so draped with curtains, shawls and carpets that it could have been a cave, for all we knew. A paraffin lamp flickered eerie light over the fabrics, making their cursive Oriental designs squirm like maggots in overturned earth. I welcomed the light enough to study its

source—and gasped when I saw that the glass lampshade was formed
into a milky skull. The chimes we had heard came from red crystal
pendants dangling from its slack jaw.

"English ladies?" a voice as old as the Powder Tower inquired
from the dark side of the room.

"American *and* English," Irene caroled back, braving the clutter
to approach the ghastly lamp.

I saw then that the lamp sat upon a carpet-covered table and that
low stools surrounded this island of gloomy light.

"We'll cross your palm with kreutzers," Irene offered, "if you'll
grant our palms a reading." I jerked violently on her sleeve. "*My* palm
a reading," she amended.

A bundle of shawls detached itself from the background. Fringe
swayed as a bent figure neared the table. Some interior current stirred
the gaudy crimson glass to insistent chiming. It seemed the skull's
death-grin had broadened.

"Sit," the crone suggested.

I did, in haste. Irene settled more slowly, as theatrical in her impeccably groomed fashion as the gypsy woman was in her unkempt
way. I felt as if I witnessed a battle of illusion between two veterans
of the art from very different worlds.

The woman extended a time-seamed palm. Irene honored it with
a gold coin. The skull's eyes seemed to warm as the crone's clawlike
fingers closed on the money. Irene extended her palm in turn. It
looked smoother than plaster of Paris in the flickering lamp light. I
wondered how anyone could read such an unmarked palm.

The gypsy leaned her face into the macabre light. Time had
seamed her fragile skin into a lace mantilla of wrinkles, though coarse
black hair lanced past her shoulders. "I see," she began in the traditional
way, "a sudden, dangerous journey."

Irene glanced toward me and rolled her eyes.

"I see a tall, handsome nobleman, very rich. He is pursuing you
with all the energy at his command."

Irene winked at me.

"I see . . . death. Violent death. And great fortune, but it is hidden."

Irene yawned.

"I see many diamonds at your feet, lady, as well as a kingdom . . . and a small, dark case that is very precious."

Irene shifted on the stool to ease her back.

"I see much difficulty and heartache, but always I see a tall handsome man. His initial is . . . G."

Irene's free hand lifted the veil from her face. "Look again, fortune teller. Are you sure the initial is not W?"

"G," the old woman snapped. "I read what I see, not what you wish me to see."

"And you tell me what you think I wish to hear," Irene returned.

"No." The old woman was firm. "I read what I see."

I had been thinking and leaned over to pluck Irene's sleeve again. "Gottsreich," I whispered, "Willie's middle name."

Irene's eyebrows raised. "The reading was so direct otherwise. Why should she suddenly turn coy and use middle names?" She leaned across the table to eye the old woman. "I have come here for greater matters than my future."

"The future is all I sell. It is forbidden that we trade in things that unmake the baby or inflame the lover—"

"No, no," Irene said, laughing. "I need neither potion."

"Not you, but another . . . ?" The hag's berry-dark eyes feasted on mine.

"Certainly not!" I insisted.

"Then what do you ladies want?" She shrugged, ready to dismiss us. "I give you more in one meeting than many hear in ten years of readings."

Irene lifted her open hand and closed her fingers over the palm. "Perhaps you read the roles I have played on the stage. It doesn't matter, for I don't believe a word of it. I want facts, not fancy, for my gold coin."

"My fancies are my facts."

"What are these?" Irene drew a handkerchief from her reticule and laid it on the table.

The old woman's fragile claw peeled the linen back from the contents. "Apple pips, lady! Go make yourself a *kolache*."

"What if I were to brew them into a tea and serve it to a friend?"

"No! The pips of the apple are as deadly as the flesh is sweet. But you know that."

Irene nodded and tucked the handkerchief away. "I didn't know if you did."

"The lore that you laugh at when I read it in a hand governs the things that spring from earth as well."

"I have a puzzle," Irene said. "Someone has died of poison, yet it is not by the pips of the apple or the squeezings of the Jaborandi root."

"Very bad." The woman turned her head as if to escape hearing the last words. "You know much for English lady already; what can reader like myself offer?"

"News of another herb—one that sifts into the skin, clogs the pores, smothers the lungs in its powder, its scent, its very essence . . . yet cannot be eaten or drunk. It must be almost invisible and quite deadly."

The woman lurched up and retreated. I thought she would leave Irene's question unanswered. She reached the wall of carpets strung from a rope, then, by some exertion far beyond the power of her slight frame, flung a rug aside.

A dusty library of bottles and potions, elixirs and hanging roots lay before us. "Not eaten," the gypsy repeated. "Not drunk." She turned and gave Irene a narrow, bitter smile. "Not easy to find. But at least a . . . unique . . . herb." She lifted one of several dust-frosted glass jars, waiting for Irene to inspect it.

"Golden Seal," the old woman breathed. "Touch not the stopper or the vial's deadly golden fingers will touch you!"

Irene had gone to the tiny vial as if drawn by a magnet. "How much?" The skull's chimes chattered like frightened teeth.

"Not much, but often."

"It is undetectable?"

"Is the lady's face powder visible?"

Irene nodded thoughtfully, "I could have a sample? The merest vial, I assure you, not to be used, of course, only to be . . . compared."

The woman clutched the bottle to her flat bosom. Irene held thumb and forefinger two inches apart. "One vial."

"That would not kill a sparrow."

"But it might catch a killer."

The gypsy looked as dubious as Irene had when her fortune was being read. "More gold."

Irene frowned. The first coin had been princely. "One more coin, then."

The gypsy nodded and drew the carpet down behind her as she vanished into the dusky clutter. Moments later a hand thrust through a seam clutching a vial of bronze powder. Irene exchanged the vial for a brighter brand of gold.

We emerged from the drapery-hung chamber and the passage blinking in the spring sunlight, finding time had run on without us. Pigeons were already flocking to the rooftops to capture the sun's warmest rays. We walked the tangled streets, guided by the Powder Tower's Gothic peak. Had my life depended on retracing my steps to the doorway of the numbered hand, I could never have done it—nor I imagine could have Irene. Nevertheless, she seemed content.

Our carriage awaited in the Tower's shadow. We rode back up the winding road to Prague Castle with our souvenirs. I had the Dvořák signature cradled in my arm like a baby, and Irene had the vial of Golden Seal secreted in her reticule like a weapon.

✦   ✦   ✦

Irene held a command performance in the late King's bedchamber that evening. In attendance, besides myself, were the current King, the Queen Mother, his brother and sister-in-law—the absent brother apparently was not a factor in Irene's calculations—the pair of eager-to-please doctors and the late ruler's body servant and chambermaid.

Though it was the apartment of a king, the room seemed as eerie as the gypsy woman's skull-lit tent earlier that day. The candelabra's relentless flicker etched bizarre shadows into the furniture's gilded carvings and changed the ceiling cherubs' smiles into leers. Everyone present, even servants, wore black.

"Penelope, you will record events as they occur," Irene directed in stern tones.

I nodded, making a dutiful note by the palsied dance of a nearby candle. A fireplace log broke with the sound of a spine being snapped. I was not the only one who jumped.

"The question," Irene began, "is the precise cause of his late Majesty's death. The general cause is already known—some variety of poison, probably herbal, certainly lethal."

She bent to lift a candelabrum. The nervous flames cast unflattering shadows upon her features, drawing them down, making her seem illuminated by a hellish light. Irene stalked, bearing her branch of tapers, to the royal siblings.

"Herbal poison. It could have been something as simple as the crushed seeds—or pips—of several apples administered as food . . ." She paused while Hortense's haughty face blanched. "It could have been an exotic herbal hair restorer poured into a beverage, an innocuous tea, perhaps." Bertrand winced.

"It could have been other, more imaginative substances administered by other, less likely candidates." Irene passed before the King and his mother, her candelabrum briefly illuminating their stiff disbelief.

I feared she had ventured too boldly on this course: von Ormsteins were not likely to put up with playing possible suspects for long.

Irene paused before the doctors, silent, her gaze compelling. An awful suspicion dawned in my mind. No one had considered the royal physicians! Were they the "patriots" Irene suspected of poisoning the King?

"The doctors," she declaimed, pausing, "the doctors tell me that the poison was neither drunk nor eaten. If . . . they are to be believed."

Here, both began stuttering at once. "Y-y-es! Cer-certainly so!"

"If they are to be believed," she emphasized, "the poison was . . . inhaled . . . through the skin. Something that was present daily, like a baby's powder. Something that could gradually weaken the King's resistance and then—at the right moment—could be administered in a massive dose that would kill. Silently. Invisibly. Or . . . almost invisibly."

The Queen Mother began to sob quietly.

"Enough!" The King put a giant arm around his mother's doll-like shoulders.

Irene ignored him, stepping instead to the bedcurtains. She swept them back as if revealing a stage setting.

"Nothing here has been changed since the late King died. Nothing. Not even the one thing that would change every day, for the victim was a king and was given every luxury. The bedlinens!"

With a long fluid gesture, Irene threw back the coverlet and bedsheets, creating a wave of lace-frothed linen. Everyone gasped at the bald presentation of the bed bereft of its occupant. Irene lowered the candelabrum to the revealed yellow silk linen. A fine golden dust glimmered amidst the weave.

The Queen Mother tottered forward to look. "Gold . . . gold dust."

"Lethal gold, your Highness," Irene said. "The herb is called Golden Seal. It stifles its victims' breath and is nigh undetectable."

"The sheets," Dr. Sturm said with a start. "Yes . . . the victim was *wrapped* in his poison, his every move grinding it deeper into his pores."

"And such lethal wrappings could be changed daily!" Dr. Drang added. "Clever, oh, so very clever."

"Who," Irene asked, "would suspect a chambermaid?"

She turned her fistful of candlelight upon the silent young woman standing in the shadow of the huge wardrobe. The maid was of peasant stock, solid and plain. Under the melodramatic light of the candles, her stolid features crumbled into disbelief.

"It cannot be!" the accused maid cried. "I changed the sheets myself afterward, though the doctors ordered me not to! No trace should be left, nothing!"

Irene lowered the candelabrum and her voice at once. "Why?"

The maid's head had lolled onto her chest. When it lifted her voice was leaden, indifferent. "They felt, the others, that the eastern kingdoms could separate from the Empire, that we should take every opportunity to topple a king. I was already here in the castle."

"You did the deed because you were *convenient?*" The King's question clapped like thunder.

"We have always been here, waiting," the woman answered. "We are your subjects," she added bitterly, "your servants."

The Queen Mother spoke at last. "If the perpetrator had not been apprehended, she would have waited longer—until Willie was vulnerable . . . or myself, or any of us."

"Mein Gott!" Bertrand mumbled, realizing for the first time that he had risked losing more than his hair.

"I've taken the liberty, your Highness," Irene addressed the Queen Mother, "of having the captain of the castle guards standing by to take the wrongdoer into custody."

"Excellent," boomed the King. "Take her from this place she has dishonored. We wish to see her no more."

The old King's body servant left as the girl was removed.

"And he?" the King asked Irene.

She shook her head and set down the heavy candelabrum, shaking her strained wrist. "Only one was needed."

Hortense turned from her inspection of the sheets, her fingertips bronzed. "How could this powder remain in laundered sheets?"

Irene lifted the slender vial of Golden Seal, only half full. "No powder remained, but I needed to stimulate a confession. I suppose this subterfuge will be awkward to defend at the trial—"

"Trial?" The King was incredulous. "My dear"—he glanced to his family and plunged into the formal manner of address—"my dear Miss Adler, there will be no trial."

"No . . . trial? What *will* you do with her?"

"Question her for her confederates' names and whereabouts. Keep her where she can never do more harm."

"But—" Irene hoisted her candelabrum again to inspect the four royal faces regarding her stiffly.

"We are most grateful." The Queen Mother swept forward to usher us from the room. "You have solved a great misdeed and taken the weight of suspicion from our own shoulders. Now all must be forgotten."

"All," repeated Hortense, reaching to snatch the notes from my unsuspecting fingers.

"I will speak to you in the morning." The King bowed over Irene's hand to kiss it. "Until then."

"Yes," unprepossessing little Bertrand put in as if repulsing peddlers, "the family has much to discuss now that this business is behind us. The affairs of the kingdom have suffered of late. Good night, ladies."

Irene and I found ourselves in the corridor—unfeted and unsung. I joined Irene in her chambers, loath to retire until the evening's surprises had faded.

"Poor little fool!" Irene said bitterly as soon as we had crossed her threshold and found ourselves alone. For a moment I thought she referred to herself.

"Your performance was brilliant, Irene," I said to console her for the anticlimax of ingratitude that had ended the evening.

"I'd wager a toxic sheet dye was the long-term assassin, perhaps Chrome Yellow. Paris Green is a lethal arsenic-laden wallpaper pigment. The 'planted' gold herbal powder made the method 'visible' to our witnesses and, most dramatically, the perpetrator. A bit overdone, but the peasant mentality is still fresh enough to respond to melodrama." Irene laughed suddenly. "I thought Willie should have me carted away to a sanitarium when I began making my rounds with the candelabrum."

"No one could anticipate where you were leading us. I thought for certain you were about to accuse Hortense."

"If I had been forced to accuse a member of the Royal Family, I would have chosen a far more public arena. As it is, that poor would-be patriot will pay an ugly price for her crime, heinous as it is."

Irene cast herself onto the chaise lounge and lit a cigarette with a lucifer from the table. "Don't look so disapproving, Nell; I've had a frightful evening." She threw back her head as she inhaled the strong smoke, then let it drift out in lazy tendrils. "I never dreamed that the little fool would not face public justice."

I huddled forward on the ottoman. "Where do you suppose they will keep her?"

"Below," Irene intoned grimly. "There must be a dark, dank 'below' we never saw beneath all this candlelit gilt and frou-frou. Oh, it quite takes the frosting off my cake," she burst out, "this . . . high-handed royal trait of handling traitors in secret. I am responsible for that girl's admitting her crime; I will not live in ignorance of the price she pays for it!" Irene's foot began tapping the chaise frame, rapping like Mr. Poe's raven as smoke spiraled around her head.

"It is not the triumph you imagined, then?" I said.

"I expected more direct dealing. And more gratitude. The family von Ormstein seem more obsessed with hiding the crime than wringing justice from it."

" 'Court intrigue and peasant revolt,' " I murmured.

"What?" Irene demanded.

"What Godfrey warned me you meddled in."

"Godfrey?"

"Norton. My employer."

"Oh." Irene was too agitated by the disturbing turn of recent events to consider past acquaintances from London, to even think of England.

"Perhaps we should go home, Irene. Mr. Dvořák is most concerned for you."

"I am singing 'Spectre Bride' next; I cannot go home. Besides, matters have not been settled with Willie."

"You mean . . . your relationship?"

"I mean this blatant disregard for the courts of justice." She took another puff upon the tiny cigar that had been feminized by the French suffix of *ette,* then crushed it out in a crystal tray. "I must talk to Willie first thing in the morning. Perhaps when his family is no longer present . . ."

"First thing," I agreed, rising. "And now let me play maid since yours has long since vanished—"

Irene cast me an alarmed look. "It would behoove us, Penelope, to wonder where our servitors go when their chores are done—a garret with bars upon the window?"

"I'm sure not. A servant's garret, certainly, but not so dreadful as that. And you say that *my* imagination has become baroque in Bohemia!"

"Perhaps mine has been blind, dear Nell; perhaps I have only seen what I cared to see, which is the first price of pretensions to royalty."

Chapter Twenty-two

A Scandal in Bohemia

❧❧❧

The King called upon Irene the next morning as she and I were indulging in hot chocolate and a surfeit of pastry in her sitting room.

"Good morning, dear ladies," he greeted us, in enormous good temper.

He looked like a man who had seen a great burden lifted from his shoulders, in great part thanks to Irene's investigation. The smart uniform he so often affected was brushed to its scarlet and black best, and his boots were as shiny as coal tar.

Irene brightened at the King's obvious good spirits. She had begun to think that her good deed in unmasking the late king's murderer had taken a very bad turn indeed.

He began on an intimate, teasing note: "Irene, you are a sight to make the angels sigh in envy. I must whisk you to Vienna to acquire more of those winsome little frivolities you ladies call combing gowns."

"Vienna! Oh, Willie, I feared I should have to kidnap *you* to get there again. As soon as 'Spectre Bride' is over."

"Tsk," said the King, sitting on the ottoman and putting his hands on his knees, fingers inward, elbows turned out. "We will go next week. We must wash the memories of past troubles from our minds. A jaunt to the capital will be like tonic water rinsing away impurities. Perhaps you could go now with Miss Huxleigh, and I could join you later."

"Willie, you are impossible! So set on one course and then, changing it, you rush in the opposite direction. I cannot quit Prague now; you know I am rehearsing 'Spectre Bride.' My investigative adventures must not distract you from my operatic efforts. I have never let them do that, I assure you."

"Your adventures, yes." The King sighed, a great bellows of a gesture from so heroic a chest. "It is best to forget these things. As for the opera, it is already attended to. You are free! You need never attend another rehearsal. The company will find another soprano to serve as *prima donna.*"

"What are you saying?" Irene stood, nearly overturning her cup of chocolate had I not rushed to steady it. "That can't be! Mr. Dvořák is depending upon me."

"Mr. Dvořák gives you his blessing. 'Go, go,' he says. 'I cannot stand in her way.'" The King demonstrated Mr. Dvořák's farewell with repeated flicks of his hand, as though shooing chicks from a hen-yard.

"Willie! Mr. Dvořák did not *dismiss* me?"

The King shrugged, looking for a moment like a guilty little boy. I glanced from Irene's white face to his robust, complacent one and was tempted to box his ears. Seated as he was on the ottoman, I could reach them nicely.

"Mr. Dvořák has no need of you, Irene. This . . . operatic delusion is simply a convenience, is it not? An excuse for your removal from Warsaw to Prague on my account. I appreciate your discretion, but—"

She clasped her hands until the knuckles went white. "Your presence here was not a deterrent, certainly, but always—always!—my primary purpose has been my career. Now you tell me that I am brushed away like a piece of lint—"

"No, no, nothing like that. Dvořák accommodates us, that is all."

"Us? Are you employing the royal 'we,' Willie?" Irene's voice was ominously level.

The King cleared his throat. "I speak for the future, and in the future it will not be necessary for you to sing. You will not need the money, for I will provide that. As for audiences, you will have no more loyal and exclusive admirer than myself."

Here he pressed his hand to the medals winking over the vicinity of his heart. I held my breath. Like most noblemen, he had learned to disregard persons of an inferior class like myself. Thus it was that I was witnessing the King of Bohemia proposing to my friend, Irene Adler. And she did not like it.

"An exclusive audience smacks of an empty opera house, Willie," she said.

"It smacks of a full palace, Irene, a beautiful palace in the verdant hills to the south. All yours, Irene. You may have your little English friend with you there . . . pets, if you so desire, all that you wish."

She listened to him, her head half turned away as if she tried to heed another voice, as if she could not quite believe what she was hearing.

"South? We will live farther into the . . . country?"

"Beautiful country, Irene. You will be mistress of your own palace, of all you survey."

"Mistress?"

"And Vienna, we will have trips to Vienna—Paris, even, on occasion. Yes, Paris is more discreet."

"Discreet? Has not Prague been discreet enough?"

He bit his full lower lip, making himself seem to pout instead of showing indecision. My governess instincts for brewing mischief were raising my hackles. Large Willie was up to something very naughty, something I itched to slap him for, did I dare, but I could no more see it than Irene.

"It is your father's murder," she said suddenly. "Your family wishes to hide the fact; you fear that I would not respect your desires in this matter. That is why you have had me dismissed from the National Theatre and talk of banishing me to the country— Willie, for God's sake, it is not necessary to silence me this way! It is, after all, your family's affair and I do not need the credit. I must respect your wishes even if I do not approve of the treatment of the criminal. And now, I must find Mr. Dvořák and reclaim my position—"

She glanced around the chamber, as if searching for her maid, her clothes. She no more saw me than he did, for a very different reason. Irene was utterly off balance; I saw it. She hardly knew where she was. Her astute mind, so used to building minute facts into inescapable conclusions, could not reduce the gross changes in the King's attitude into anything but . . . absurdity.

The King stood, his boot-heels thumping the floor as his weight returned to them. "You will not contact Dvořák. I forbid it."

"Forbid it!"

"I am King."

"Indeed, but I am not Bohemian."

"Irene, you must do as I say; I ask you, then, as a friend!"

"Why? Tell me why, Willie."

He looked away and down; perhaps he saw his reflection small and precise in the toes of his mirror-polish boots. "It is impossible that you stay in the castle."

"Very well, I will take rooms in the city. I always could have, it was you who insisted—"

"It is impossible that our association remain public."

"Public? You call a few drives along the avenue to Wenceslas Square public?"

"It cannot even be suspected."

"A bit late for that now, isn't it, Willie?"

"Irene, you are a sophisticated woman. We have had our little courtship dance and you know what comes after. I will not stint; you will enjoy every comfort and luxury. I will travel to the south as often as I can—"

"And here, in Prague? What will you do here in Prague? Will you attend the National Theatre and watch someone else sing 'Spectre Bride'? Will you drive out with some other woman?" Irene's voice took on sudden, if reluctant, certainty. "Will you live here at the castle . . . with some other woman?"

The King stiffened, as indeed would any man had tones so laced with contempt been aimed his way.

"Clotilde Lothman von Saxe-Meningen is not 'some other woman,'" he answered. "She is second daughter to the king of Scandinavia and my future bride."

"Ah . . ." Comprehension flooded Irene's face.

"With my father's death—however it occurred—my family and civil obligations have changed. I must consider the succession, the royal—"

"—pedigree? Is it your family who is so eager to see you wed just now?"

"Yes, but it was inevitable someday. I knew it since I was a child. It does not mean I love her, Irene—"

"No. Apparently not. So you have known, since—"

"I know this thing always, but I do not like to think about it. In my heart you will always be my queen, but I am King, and a man of state obligations. I cannot be expected to restrain myself in regard to you, to play the suitor forever. You must have known."

"I should have, yes. Will . . . your marriage . . . be soon?"

"Not for a year—a mourning period, you see—which will give you and me delightful times together, but we must be discreet, for Clotilde of Saxe-Meningen is of a delicate nature and would refuse the marriage should any hint of scandal taint me."

"Scandal," Irene repeated, in that same bewildered tone that so wrung my heart.

I watched them as the silence lengthened. Both their heads were lowered—the King's in shame, I hoped. Irene's head drooped like a flower's—in thought or sorrow or a blend of both. Her splayed fingertips touched the table linen, as if supporting her by this light contact with reality. She seemed very far away—from the King, from myself.

The King at least had the grace to sense her shock. He bowed slightly, in that stiff way favored by European gentlemen.

"I will withdraw and allow you to make plans to remove to the southern palace. It is a great change and must be accomplished swiftly. I expect that you will manage it with your usual flair."

Irene looked up again. Her lips lifted in a smile so small it required a magnifying glass. "Yes. My usual flair."

He nodded, pleased, and left without a last glance at myself.

Once his clicking boots had withdrawn across the marble hall floors, I could hear only the mantel clock ticking and the grind of the gears each time the minute hand was driven a centimeter forward.

Irene's fingers on the tablecloth twitched, then tapped, then began pantomiming the playing of a melody only she could hear. I poured some more hot chocolate and pushed the cup and saucer toward her. She ignored it. She stood there, head bent, as lost in contemplation as Tennyson's Lady of Shallot. I feared for her, feared that she, too, "had seen the mirror crack from side to side." That way lay madness and despair.

"Irene," I began, just as she looked up and said, "Nell . . ."

"What will you do?" I continued.

Her lips tightened. "Pack."

"Then you are leaving Prague?"

"Certainly."

"As the King wishes?"

"As he *demands*."

I stood, my throat very dry. "Irene, I will do all I can to assist you in your packing, but as for accompanying you to this palace, and remaining there with you in a compromised position, I am very sorry, but I cannot . . . cannot—" Here I almost choked on a rising tide of emotion.

Irene was staring at me as if I were mad. "Nell, you idiotic goose, you don't actually believe that I would agree to this revolting proposal?"

"Well . . ."

Irene began pacing so furiously that the train of her morning gown twisted into a thick tail.

"Though why you should think I had any sense left after the— lunacy!—I have displayed in regard to his Majesty, Wilhelm Gottsreich von Ormstein . . . 'G' says the fortune teller. 'Gottsreich,' say you. Do you know what that translates to—God's rule! Willie may be King of all bloody Bohemia, but he does not rule a centimeter of my soul, and I will go to the ends of the earth before I will submit my spirit or my body or my career to his royal convenience!"

The train lashed behind her as she continued raging. "Oh, I have been mistaken in him. He is a small boy to be wound around the finger of the family interest."

"My thought exactly," I slipped in. "A most immature attitude."

"But dangerous, Nell." She stopped and fixed me with an intense look. "Spoiled little boys do not like their toys taken from them. Especially royal little boys. We must leave, that much is clear, and 'discreetly.' So discreetly that Willie will not suspect that we are leaving for England instead of his hidey-hole palace in the country."

"Leave . . . when?"

"Now! As soon as possible. Our only advantage is that Willie is so smug, so . . . arrogant that he would never believe a woman would flee him as the plague. Oh, he will be furious when he realizes—Bohemia will tremble. Nell! You need not go with me. You could proceed home on your own, alone—that might be safest! Or wait until he finds I am gone—no, he might use you then to draw me back."

"Are you certain he is so set upon this course?"

"Nell, a man who would immure a free woman in a castle in the wilds of Bohemia because he is so convinced that his intermittent attentions would be that welcome . . . well, such a man is not liable to heed anything but his own colossal vanity. Mistake me not; Willie will be very dangerous foiled. He will stop at nothing to secure me if he can—I am caught like that poor little fool who poisoned his father because she believed political fairy tales. When do you think *she* will ever see the light of day again?"

"Oh, Irene, how have we snared ourselves in such a tangle?"

A rueful smile touched her lips. "Is that the royal 'we,' dear Nell? You are far more generous than the ruler of Bohemia. This mess is my doing and I will get both of us out of it, I swear."

"I trust you implicitly," said I, quelling a thousand uncertainties and a rather unpleasant flutter in my stomach.

She gathered my hands into her tight grasp. "How foolish I have been, and how wise I was to send for you. I thought you would arrive to witness my triumph, though I feared the machinations of his family. Now you can only testify to my utter ruin—"

"Ruin of what? Mr. Dvořák's regard? He wished you safely away from just such a snarl, I know he did. Your career? You still sing wonderfully and have served as diva at two opera houses of Europe. Your reputation? You have done nothing wrong; indeed, you flee the wrong."

"And my pride?" she asked.

I smiled. "Pride can always benefit from having a tuck or two taken in it, or so my father often said to me when he felt that my petticoat of self-regard was showing."

"Bless Parson Huxleigh! A tuck in time saves nine! Come, we must plan our campaign, for Willie—like the great grey wolves who prowl these ancient forests—will hunt us wherever we go."

Chapter Twenty-three

A Sudden Flight

—∿∿—

Within hours every hat in Irene's possession, every stocking and petticoat, every lace-festooned "combination" of corset cover and pantaloon was strewn about her rooms.

Open trunks lay in wait for unwary shinbones. An unlikely perfume of violet sachets and mothballs pervaded the suite. To this disordered atmosphere the von Ormsteins made pilgrimage in solemn turn to observe Irene's vanquishment. First came Hortense, smirking.

"I am so sorry to disturb you, Irene dear. When do you think you will be ready to leave?"

Irene combed a distracted hand through auburn curls, turning her impeccable coiffure into wild disarray. "Perhaps the day after tomorrow. I simply cannot manage to pack so many things any sooner."

"Surely your maid will do all that?"

"But first I must tell the maid what to do! It has all been so sudden." Here Irene sighed, carefully avoiding Hortense's gaze. Only I saw the Duchess's expression of cruel triumph, which further disfigured her unattractive features.

"I have some lovely mountain laurel sachets," the Duchess said with a sneer. "I will have my Angelica bring them to you as a parting gift."

"So generous," Irene murmured, adding as the King's sister-in-law left, "in her good-byes."

"Is that a quotation from something, Irene?" I wondered.

"Yes. My future memoirs. Hurry! The more insurmountable we make the packing look, the more time we buy."

So we delved into wardrobe drawers and hatboxes like maddened monkeys, flinging goods hither and mostly yon. I actually enjoyed the disinterring of Irene's vast wardrobe. I had never seen such a quantity and quality of wearing apparel and nearly swooned from the profuse luxury of it, despite my modest tastes.

"Luckily, I didn't spend it all on my wardrobe," Irene said, lifting a heavy chamois bag from the back of a drawer.

The coins within shifted with that satisfying rasp so dear to the ear and heart of a miser.

"Irene! You keep all this money here with you?"

"Is not the castle as safe as houses? For money, at least. Besides, I like my resources at hand. You see, I have saved various foreign coins collected in my journey—and plenty of good English pounds. This will be useful in our flight."

"I do wish you wouldn't call it that, Irene. He may . . . forget you."

"Hmm. I prefer to prepare for the worst."

"How deep should I pack these shawls? I am not sure which of them you are really taking."

"None of them."

"None? But they are exquisite!"

"So are all these things." She eyed the littered chamber. "Exquisite burdens we cannot afford. Here is our real baggage."

Irene bent to wrestle something from under her bedskirt flounces. "Carpetbags!"

"And shabby, modest, well-traveled carpetbags they are," she said with perverse pride.

"Wherever did you get them?"

"I bought them from the maids. 'Poor Miss Irene, you know, so distracted at being rushed out of the castle that she doesn't have the slightest wit left to pack efficiently.' There are two each; with that we shall have to make do. I've bribed the coachman to take some trunks away secretly, but he will have them sent to a friend in Paris—to put off our pursuit, if we have one."

I paused in folding a cotton petticoat of such fineness that it shone like silk. "When do we actually leave, then?"

"Tonight."

"Why such haste, Irene? Surely you can forestall the King for many days with your pretended disorganization!"

"I can, but I do not wish to. I will not spend one more night under this ancient roof than I must."

She spoke with such feeling that I was silent. Irene idly straightened the hair she had deliberately disarranged and regarded the carpetbags again. "I will carry the money in one. We will take a single change of clothing: escape before nicety. And . . ." Irene lifted the closed cabinet photograph from her bed table.

It blossomed open in her hands, lay upon them like a prayer book as she studied the photograph within.

"A sop, Nell, a sop to what Willie took for my greed, for all women's greed. It was not the crown jewels I cared about. They really are rather inferior; small ill-matched stones for an ill-matched couple. May the . . . delicate . . . Clotilde enjoy her reign in them. The late King was quite fat, Nell. Willie will get fat, too, like the Prince of Wales," she said with some satisfaction, "and *I* will not be here to see it."

Clapping her hands, she closed the case in a dramatic gesture, then weighed it in one hand. "I will take this photographic fable with me."

"As a reminder of your betrayal?"

"As a reminder of the King's folly in leaving such a trace of his indiscretion. And as a precaution." She slipped it into the gaudiest carpetbag just as the Queen Mother entered.

"I do not wish to interrupt you, my dear, but I did want to say that I am most grateful for your efforts to locate the person who poisoned the King. You must also know that I shall never think less of you for your . . . position with Willie.

"It is such a pity that this alliance could not be official. I shall miss your singing here in the castle, when you used to practice in the music room. I have urged Willie to have one of the pianos sent south as a surprise, so do not let him know that you are aware that I suggested it."

"No, I would not want to ruin his surprise." Irene spoke in a two-edged tone I recognized very well.

Yet she seemed pensive after the Queen Mother had left and sat sorting through the clothing in an abstracted way, her right hand pausing once to play those phantom notes on the coverlet.

"What piece do you practice?" I finally asked.

Irene glanced at me ironically. " 'Viennese Melody,' my pet. I can't seem to forget the tune."

We worked through dinner, asking that a meal be served us in Irene's sitting room. The truth was that neither of us could stomach taking food with the von Ormsteins any longer; I began to appreciate Irene's demand for instant action. Everything and everyone in the castle had become a reminder of a time now irrevocably past.

Willie visited us after dinner, when the candles had burned low and the fireplaces had been refreshed for the night. He seemed subdued, yet pleased.

"I admire your energy, Irene! How like a general you are, with your hatboxes and trunks and frivolities all lined up like obedient soldiers."

"Yes, I am a mistress of the frivolous, am I not?"

"I am delighted that you embrace my plans so swiftly. In truth, I feared a bit of a tantrum from you."

"A tantrum, really?" Irene inquired sweetly. "Why ever would you think that?"

"Oh, when women imagine some slight to their self-worth, they can raise quite a fuss. But in this, too, you are an exception, Irene. So pragmatic in your delightfully feminine way. I see I shall be escaping south often."

"Escape! What a clever way to put it. I shall regard my current . . . removal from Prague as an escape also."

I did not dare look up from my arranging of lacy handkerchiefs in fabric-covered boxes. The cutting edge of Irene's irony blunted on the King's impervious vanity.

He went to take her hands and pull her to her feet before him, like a ruler commanding a subject to rise from a profound bow. I quailed over my handkerchiefs, for I sensed Irene's underlying fury and feared his patronizing ways would push her past containing it. I needn't have worried.

She was a superb actress; never had she mimicked emotions so contrary to her real feelings. Not a false note was sounded, and the King never noticed that she no longer called him by his Christian name.

"I have brought you a gift, Irene."

"A gift? You amaze me, your Majesty."

"Do not thank me. I have never given you jewels—you refused all my attempts, saying that you would wear paste on stage, rather than seem as if your art were supported by admirers' bank accounts. Now that you are no longer in the public eye, you need not worry."

I had to see it. I glanced up, catching the green glint of the emerald gracing the King's signature ring in the shape of a snake. His left hand was extended, a box upon the palm. I could not view its contents from where I sat. How could I manage a change of pose that would not appear to be caused by curiosity? While I vacillated, Irene satisfied all my longings.

"Rubies!" She turned to lift a star-shaped brooch for my inspection. "How extravagant of your Majesty. But—"

"This strange stiff-necked notion of yours on gifts is incomprehensible. You must take it, Irene," he said anxiously, guilt tinging his expression. "There *is* no reason to refuse now."

"Not . . . now." Ice laced her voice. "It is lovely, and quite my color." She pranced to the mirror and poised it at the throat of her pale yellow shirtwaist. The starburst of rubies glittered like a wound. "I can hardly express my . . . amazement, my gratitude for your generous favor."

"Say nothing of it, Irene." The King had relaxed the moment she accepted the jewel, as if a contract he had worried about was now fully signed. "There will be more baubles. You shall not regret your current course, believe me."

"I do not, and I know I shall not," she returned, smiling. "Not ever."

"You will be ready to travel on the morrow?"

Irene glanced helplessly about the cluttered room. "Oh, I do hope so—"

"Never mind." He patted her hand. "I will not press you. The following day will suit as well. I want my dear friend to be well dressed when I visit her."

With that he clicked his heels in a farewell bow and left. Our maids came soon after. We set them to packing the trunks destined for Paris. I withdrew to my room and, once certain that the maids had retired at last, rose and claimed the two carpetbags I had hidden there earlier from under my bed. Into them fit most of the belongings that had accompanied me in my hasty departure from England.

Then I sat by the window and listened to the ormolu mantel clock tick. Below me moonlight polished the roof tiles to the color of cold steel. Everything seemed painted in shades of grey, like the foggy photographic features of Irene and the King. My room was unlit save by the fading fire. When the clock struck midnight, I lost track and counted thirteen o'clock.

A quarter of an hour later, as planned, the doorknob to my room turned. But an unexpected figure stepped over the threshold. I clenched my fists as the hall light shone between its trousered legs.

Chapter Twenty-four

Fox and Hounds

The train chugged deep into the prettiest valleys and high over the most picturesque hills in Germany. I often imagined the gigantic plume of smoke flung behind us as the engine cleaved the green landscape like a steel plough.

Every clack of the rails and puff of the smokestack seemed to be driving Bohemia, its King and our unhappy memories farther behind. I sighed and glanced at my traveling companion, who was—at the moment—absently fingering the amber dragon that topped his cane.

"You nearly precipitated my demise from sheer shock before we even left," I commented, "but it was a brilliant notion to travel in this guise."

A thin smile stretched my seat partner's rusty mustache. Even in the daylight streaming through the compartment windows, I could not detect the spirit gum that held it on.

"There is some awkwardness in the terminal comfort stations," Irene conceded, "but the benefits of traveling truly 'incognito' far outweigh the inconvenience."

Embarrassment prevented me from inquiring too deeply into the mechanics of her subterfuge. Irene would manage it, I told myself; it was not for me to know precisely how. As always, she made a most incredibly credible man. Her gait, posture and entire attitude altered when she donned male garb. The thought of that narcissistic tyrant immuring such acting talent in a forsaken pile in southern Bohemia quite made my blood boil anew.

But Willie was left far behind, I told myself, like the Devil and all his works. All had gone smoothly. Our stealthy exit from the castle and down the steep road to town led to the waiting coach Irene had hired to take "Rudolph and Hedwig Hoffman," brother and sister, to Dresden. (She did not trust to the Prague train terminal, the first place pursuers would look.) Since she spoke decent German because of her study of opera, this fiction was credible. In Dresden we stopped several streets away from the railway station, Irene wishing the driver to believe that we were visiting relations there.

She caught the four carpetbags that he slung down from the coach roof, allowing me only to carry one for greater authenticity. Male guise even seemed to increase her strength. Once aboard our train, which was composed of the new English-made, single-corridor carriages deployed throughout Germany and Belgium, she wrested our bags down the cramped passage into the compartment, thrust them atop the overhead racks with dispatch, then laughed off my amazement.

"No great trick to being the stronger sex, Nell! It's easy when not wearing a constricting whalebone fence and seams that split at any gesture larger than a drawing-room flutter." Irene sat beside me, crossed her legs and lit a self-congratulatory cigarette at our successful escape. I could hardly rebuke her for a habit that aided her disguise and our enterprise.

By evening the bucolic German landscape had evolved into a huddled urban mass—Nuremberg. After an interminable stop in the station there, we chugged through an utter darkness relieved only by the odd illuminated cottage window. Such cheery glimmers soon slipped from view, like falling stars.

Morning revealed countryside. So we traversed the thick neck of southern Germany, a vast farmland punctuated by the occasional city: Nuremberg, then Frankfort and at last, on the third day, the great Cathedral town of Cologne. Here we were to change trains, and I admit that my heart began beating rather recklessly.

Irene noticed my apprehension.

"You are quite right, Nell. The time between changing trains makes us most vulnerable. We are trapped in the conspicuous fish-bowl of a railway station, where any passerby could be a spy of the King's."

"But he cannot catch up with us!"

"My dear, he can telegraph ahead. He must have agents in all major German cities, any prudent king would. At the least his official friends here have unofficial henchmen they turn to in emergencies."

"I had not thought of him . . . telegraphing ahead."

"Your mind has been lulled by Bohemia's bucolic ways. You pictured a pursuit from Sir Walter Scott: the King, booted and spurred, harrying his exhausted charger over hill and dale, his cavalry thundering behind him. Our poor, placid train choo-chooing its way toward certain interception . . . No, these are modern times and the King will use modern methods to trace us. He will telegraph."

"I wish you would let me send a cablegram to Godfrey in London, as I did when I first arrived in Prague."

Irene winced as smoke curled around her bowler brim. "Already one too many times. If the King thinks to inquire at the Prague telegraph office, there will be a record of that message—and to whom it was sent."

"But we need someone in London to aid us—to find us rooms, for we dare not return to Saffron Hill."

"Unfortunately true."

"If I have been derelict in anticipating the King's actions, you have not foreseen the complications of our arrival, Irene. Unless we have discreet help, we shall have a hard time disguising our return to London, which is where the King will no doubt assume us to have gone."

"Not necessarily. He does not associate me with London, since he met me in Warsaw and I had come from Milan. And I am American by birth. Still, I would rather he not know where we had gone for as long as possible."

"Then let me telegraph Godfrey, I implore you!"

She looked at me askance from under her bowler. "You seem most attached to our erstwhile competitor."

"It is only that I know we can rely upon him, and if the King is as formidable a foe as you believe—"

"More so."

"Then I would feel ever so much better if Godfrey were involved."

Irene's eyebrows lifted with unmanly delicacy. "He is a barrister, I suppose. He must have some sense of honor toward a client, more than a King toward a woman, I would hope."

"You do not know him as I do, Irene. Godfrey has been like a brother to me. And—" I paused, for I had never told her this in my letters, feeling somehow disloyal. "And I have assisted him in . . . matters . . . like those you and I used to undertake. Godfrey is no fool. I would trust him with my life."

A smile activated her mustache. "You do," she said shortly. "And you may telegraph the admirable Mr. Norton, but not until we pass Brussels and are in the port of Ostend." Her expression tightened into worry. "Such a pity that there is but one route from Prague to London, and that riddled with changes of train!"

Irene pounded one leather gloved fist into the other, so much in character that I braced myself for profanity. None came. Instead she sat back against the upholstery, her eyes suddenly distant. I kept a respectful silence. Irene was thinking, and upon that process depended our successful escape.

At Cologne we were forced to pause; no connecting train to Brussels left till late the following morning. Nightfall abetted Irene's disguise as she managed the perilous interrogation of the ticketmaster, purchase of the tickets and inquiries after a hotel near the station. She left three of the carpetbags on being convinced that they would be locked up.

I confess I slept not a wink that night, though the lodgings were spotless and a featherbed as high as whipped cream promised sweet dreams. I knew that Irene chafed at every moment we hesitated along the way; *she* spent the night vigilant at the window.

Once I heard a sinister click as she took the small revolver from her pocket and examined it. I had forgotten the weapon she carried in London; somehow I'd assumed she had dispensed with such habits once her life had changed.

In the morning Irene drew me aside as we neared the station. "Nell, you must enter the station alone. Here are the baggage chit and some German coins."

"But I don't speak any German!"

"You will need none to reclaim the bags—and your coins will speak *for* you in convincing a porter to fetch them aboard. It is best to separate; they hunt for two. I have my ticket, here's yours. I will board just as the train leaves."

With that Irene vanished into the crowd pouring into the vast stone station building. I clutched the baggage claim and a fistful of foreign money, feeling quite as though I had been stranded by an ungentlemanly escort! At least she had undertaken to carry the heavy carpetbag, bearer of our money and the photograph and thus never out of her presence.

I entered the eddy of travelers and found myself harried along as a woodchip that is seized by a current. I was not used to managing such details as I had been assigned: Godfrey had kindly arranged my previous travel. I stuttered at the baggage man, but eventually was handed all three carpetbags. Then I scanned the bustling strangers for a capped porter.

Though I had seen dozens earlier, porters were scarce as dodos now. At last I attracted the eye of a slight fellow who looked as if he could carry a tea packet on a good day. He nevertheless managed to stagger the long way to our train and see me into a compartment, at which time I showered him with all the coins in my possession. He left clucking like a contented German hen; I settled by the window to scan the crowd for Irene's figure in its unfamiliar guise.

My heart was racing and my brow was veiled in an unladylike dampness. Steam from the stoking engine drifted past the window like an airy muffler. My lapel watch showed departure looming in less than two minutes, and German trains ran on punctuality as much as steam. Why had I ever allowed us to separate? I admonished myself, imagining an increasingly gruesome chain of possibilities.

The creak of the compartment door made me turn. A man's silhouette filled the stingy corridor; this time it was not Irene's.

"I fear this compartment is occupied," I told the intruder.

He grinned like an idiot and entered.

"No, no!" I waved toward the space. "I expect a traveling companion."

He stepped to the brass rack above me and—instead of adding his baggage to mine, for he had none—he reached for a carpetbag.

"Sir, that is mine!" I stood to defend my property, dismayed by what a burly fellow I contested. His thick-knuckled hairy hands already clutched the handles. I snatched a corner. My hat lurched onto my forehead, blinding me, as my shoulder seams sang of their imminent separation.

The bone-hard rap of a cane descending on knuckles came before my seams could scream their final dissolution. I pushed hat and hair from my eyes. The intruder's mouth was nursing a clenched fist. Irene stood in the doorway, her cane still raised.

She uttered a string of German as harsh as the Cockney she had used on the last person to lay hand upon a carpetbag of mine—the London guttersnipe of years ago.

The man kept sullen silence, eyeing not the cane but the metallic glint of the revolver Irene lifted from her pocket.

The train jerked into a shudder of departure.

"Perhaps he made a mistake," I said.

"He did," she responded tightly in English, so in character that even I almost feared her, but perhaps that was her intention.

More hiccoughs of motion signaled our immediate departure. I was jolted back into my seat, but Irene and our visitor kept upright on braced feet, his narrowed eyes alert for any weakening in her position.

Outside on the platform people's faces oozed past, blurring. The crowds thinned. We chugged through the shadow of the roofed station-yard, only tracks and distant trains accompanying us. I pictured Irene holding the man hostage all the way to Brussels. Instead she slung her carpetbag onto the seat opposite and stepped into the corridor, nodding for him to precede her to the carriage exit. "Wait here," she instructed me.

He regarded the fourth carpetbag as if it were a meal and he a starving Irishman, but moved along, his admonished knuckles still red. They disappeared. I rose to look, but saw only an empty passage.

Unsteady, I elected to sit again, eyeing my watchface. A minute ticked by, then two. An incoming train thundered past on a nearby track, doubling the sense of speed and my heartbeat at the same long instant. In another minute, the curtain of charging steel had vanished as quickly as it had appeared. No Irene.

Then she was back, sitting opposite me and slipping her cane through the compartment handles so no one could enter unwanted. Nothing was said as a lucifer struck the sole of her boot and the familiar haze of smoke veiled her pale features.

"Well?" I finally asked.

"He's off the train; that's what I wanted to ensure."

"How? We were already moving."

"So was he, when last I saw him. I wanted to make sure that the train was going fast enough that he couldn't leap back on again."

"He . . . could have been killed."

"So could have I." Irene shuddered for the first time in our acquaintance. "Not a pretty fellow, no court intriguer. Just a bully with an assignment. I was forced to hold him at revolver point by the car door: had the train's motion dislodged my balance, *I* would have gone out instead, I assure you. Besides, he landed with all the grace of a grizzly bear and shambled off. He'll merely have a long walk back to the station."

She finished her cigarette and lowered the window to dispose of it, angling her neck to see if our tormentor was still visible.

"Gone, I hope," she said, "as I hope something else is not gone." Irene pulled down the three carpetbags and began examining our things.

"Irene, you suspect our baggage . . . ?"

"Of being searched. Ah, one has been disarranged, but not the other two. Was there a delay when you claimed the bags?"

"Of course there was a delay! I do not speak German and the man was slow to understand me."

"Doubtless paid to be slower. So they had caught up with us just before our departure. Pursuit is always exponential, my dear Nell. In Brussels they will be waiting for us."

She sat again, drawing the fourth carpetbag against her hip like a child. "Our soon-to-be footsore friend had a good long look at this rather appalling and thus easily identifiable Hindustan print. I must reconsider."

I nodded, too worn to speak. The recent excitement and my sleepless night combined to induce an odd state of detachment. I watched the outlying residences of Cologne slip behind us as countryside again commanded the view. Limpid spring green swirled past in a mist of steam and fatigue. I slept.

Shadows were long and the setting sun was burnishing the horizon when I awoke. Irene still sat where she had, her face looking drawn in the light of the compartment oil lamps.

"Brussels?" said I with a start.

"Soon."

"What shall we do?"

"Change trains as quickly as possible. It would be good if we could change our guises, but we have no time for that." She gave me a quick smile. "I'm glad you slept, Nell; you will be fresher for the last leg of our flight. Be of good cheer; there is always a way out of a trap; observe the humble mouse."

"I have observed the humble mouse—decapitated!—many a time."

"Only the dull ones, Nell. Only the dull." Irene stiffened as the train slowed. Shadowy buildings slipped past us in the twilight. "All we do must be swiftly done. I will take this case; you the tapestry one. We must abandon the other two."

I nodded. In moments the train sat panting in the station. Irene and I darted off and through a maze of passages and stairs to the main station. At the ticketseller's window her German again sufficed. She turned well pleased from the bronze grating.

"Our boat-train leaves in forty-five minutes. We have only to keep out of plain sight and get aboard, which we will do just at the eleventh hour. Once our train reaches Ostend, it will go directly onto the pier where the passengers board the packet steamers. When our boat lands at Dover we shall be on English soil and better able to elude our pursuers."

English soil. Those two blessed words. I never wanted to leave my native island again. We ambled through the station, attaching ourselves to knots of strangers like a thin, trailing fringe stitched to the security of the greater shawl.

"A telegraph office, Irene! May I?" The notion of sending Godfrey a cablegram seemed like a line of sanity thrown to a sinking cause, as did the thought of those blessed modern submarine cable lines leading across the English Channel to aboveground telegraph wires stretching all the way to London and home. England and Godfrey—and, by all that's dear, that miserable, profane Casanova—seemed like visions of heaven at that moment.

Irene glanced from me to the telegraph office to the station interior. She nodded, her eyes urging speed. I rushed to the desk inside. The man there spoke English, thank God, for Brussels was near the Channel coast and Ostend, for generations a major embarcation point for Dover.

My pen paused over the message: "We arrive at Victoria at 10 a.m. tomorrow. Require discreet lodging, utter secrecy." I hesitated to sign my name, remembering Irene's caution that telegraphed messages leave trails. I thought, then smiled triumphantly, and signed, "Casanova."

The man plucked the proper Belgian coins from my multinational collection and I dashed to rejoin Irene. She was smiling tightly. "I wonder what Godfrey Norton will make of our adventures."

"I wonder if we will make it safely home to have the luxury of wondering what Godfrey will make of anything!"

"Quite right, Nell. At the moment we must loiter in a professional manner. We are supernumeraries now, who make fading into a background an art. We must neither notice our surroundings too sharply, nor ignore them for a moment. We must do that which is most difficult to simulate. We must appear normal; in short, we must render a performance worthy of the great Ellen Terry."

"Oh, dear."

"In other words, be yourself."

"You are not being yourself," I replied a bit testily as we strolled through the vast station.

Her tone grew pensive. "Apparently I have not been myself for some time."

By ten minutes before our scheduled departure, we had idled our way to the gate leading to the great, tracked expanse of the rail yard. Our train trembled beyond it. A *Daily Telegraph* was now folded under Irene's arm. She carried both carpetbags and the cane, balancing all these items by some prestidigitation I couldn't quite analyze. My fingers went often to my lapel watch but I forbore to check its fateful dial. I could almost feel it ticking atop the rapid beating of my heart.

Someone brushed into Irene, almost knocking her aside.

"I say, sir!" she protested in masculine indignity.

Another someone bumped, then steadied me with a firm hand. We were abruptly surrounded by someones, hemmed in at the wall.

Irene had no opportunity to drop her baggage and appeal to her revolver. Two men bracketed her, her arms in their firm custody. A third man had taken me by the elbow while a fourth confronted Irene with an expression of utter satisfaction.

German words exploded into her face. I frantically tried to translate, recognizing only the form of masculine address, "Mein Herr." Then an oft-repeated phrase began to come clear. They had recognized *me,* accepted her disguise and were asking Irene where Irene was!

She answered in rapid German, shaking her head. She seemed to be saying that she didn't know, for the surrounding faces grew grimmer and the men's color rose like a bloody tide. I felt fingers tighten cruelly on my arm, but said nothing, being mesmerized by Irene's awful predicament.

The men were large and needed shaving. I smelled damp woolens and stale beer. They were like a forest, those four, and we were lost within the circle of their force.

The fourth man kept asking, Irene kept denying. Without warning, his arm jerked back and he punched a fist into her mid-section. I would have screamed, but a salty, sardine-scented hand clamped my mouth. I bit a leathery finger and was rewarded with its withdrawal.

Irene had gasped and contracted at the blow, but was still standing. The attacker pulled back his fist with a respectful look at her slight masculine form. He shook his stinging fingers, crumpled them into a fist again and held it before her face.

I couldn't watch. He was going to strike her, not open-handed, as a villain strikes a woman in a melodrama, but with his fist, man to man. And I knew enough of how Irene submersed herself in her characters to know that she would endure it, like a man.

The German words flooded my ears, a brutal and ugly tongue threatening brutal and ugly things. I almost began to understand the refrain, "Where has she gone?"

I saw the brute's arm draw back. Irene braced for the blow.

"Paris, you fool!" I shouted in English. "She's gone to Paris with the trunks of all her best clothes. Do you think she would leave her wardrobe behind?"

The man lowered his arm, taking my desperation for truth torn from my weaker self. I recalled Irene's ironic acting advice: "You must appear normal, Nell; that is, be yourself." Certainly I could not have feigned my horror of what was occurring, my desire to stop it somehow.

The interrogator barked something at Irene. She slumped in her captors' arms, betrayed by my weakness. Her muttered German phrases apparently translated my words. I recognized "Paris."

Finally, the man nodded and the pincer around my arm released. The ruffians holding Irene freed her to take custody of the carpet-bags instead.

As fast as they had hemmed us in, the men streamed back into the flow of indifferent humanity that churned around us.

"Your watch, Penelope!"

I finally felt free to consult it openly. "Two minutes!"

"Let us hurry!" Irene strode for the gate, for the stairs. She had the tickets in hand and was seeking the track number even as we flew over the ground.

"There!" she said.

Through a cloud of steam the dark metal body of the train was sliding past, drawing into daylight. Leaving.

"Quickly!" Irene said, taking my arm.

We ran. Dear Lord, how we ran. Irene had the advantage on me with her low-heeled boots, but we were freed of all burdens save our-selves and ran and ran and ran, chasing the iron coattails of the van-ishing train.

Out of the huffing fog of departure I saw windows, incurious faces, a set of steps, Irene on them and I—I with my heart in my throat, my feet flying, my breath mingling with the steam and van-ishing.

"Nell! Jump for it! Come on!"

An amber dragon's head loomed from the steam. I clung to that slender lifeline of extended cane and was abruptly pulled forward. I leaped into the mist, struck a step with my foot and crouched against a throbbing wall of wood and metal . . .

⚜   ⚜   ⚜

"The smelling salts were in the atrociously patterned carpetbag we left to the King of Bohemia's henchmen," Irene said. "Sorry."

"I don't require smelling salts," I replied indignantly, sitting up in the compartment. The lumpy seat felt soft as home, the motion of a train at full thirty-miles-an-hour speed like rocking-cradle safety. I was unsure of how I had arrived here and didn't wish to know.

"We are . . . ?" I said.

"On our train, bound for the English Channel." Irene sounded most satisfied.

"But the carpetbags! The money! The photograph—your only defense!"

She smiled at my last word and touched her midriff. "So it was."

"Oh, Irene! I don't know how you survived that terrible blow. It quite . . . undid me. Surely you are not a secret pugilist? The brute acted as if you were stronger than he expected."

"As indeed I was, Nell. Righteousness shall arm thee in the camp of thine enemy."

"Irene, when you quote Scripture, even if it's pseudo-Scripture, I become suspicious."

" 'Oh, ye of little faith . . . ' " She patted her vest again. "I did have a secret defense, though. A nice leather-bound, padded defense, directly over my solar plexus, to put it delicately or at least medically."

"The cabinet photograph! You'd moved it from the carpetbag to your person."

"Indeed." She smirked.

I sat back to consider this. "Yet we've lost all the money you earned in Warsaw and Prague, money that is rightfully yours!"

"And so it still is." Here she removed her hat, not from any belated sense of courtesy, but to reveal the lumpish bag stuffed into the crown.

She chuckled. "If that fellow had struck me in the face a flood of gold coins and paper money would have inundated the station floor."

"That is all you worried about if he hit you? He was treating you like a man, Irene! There would be no mercy."

"But you were acting like a woman, Nell! I could not have done it better myself. It quite wrung my heart to see you capitulate and tell them all you knew. I admit I was surprised to hear you utter a falsehood, but it was effective. Here we are, bound for Dover. Safe, and not sorry. I . . . trust not sorry."

"Lying in the face of villainy is hardly that. You took nothing from Bohemia that was not yours, paid to you or given to you. Oh— what of the King's brooch?"

Her face deadened. She lifted a ruby glint from the pocket that held the revolver. "Some gifts are thorns, but perhaps they teach us something. I never wish to forget the lesson I learned in Bohemia."

"What is that?"

Her hands parted in a weary little gesture. "I do not know yet, only that it was a lesson."

⚜   ⚜   ⚜

Ostend was a blur, the steamer packet an abomination of motion that my constitution did not relish.

Victoria was merely another cavernous railway station—a palace for the aristocracy of travel—save that it was Home. I had not expected Godfrey to meet the train, and indeed quite started when a tall, dark man descended upon us from the crowd. I noticed that Irene's hand had automatically gone to her right pocket.

"My dear Miss Huxleigh, my dear Penelope! Nell . . ."

Godfrey took my gloved hands and shook them. Irene walked on as I hastened to catch up, knowing how weary she was and how much effort it took to continue her masquerade.

"I'd no idea what sort of accommodation you required," Godfrey said as we threaded through the maze of people, "but have found respectable rooms in a quiet neighborhood. Your baggage?"

"We have none," I admitted.

"Lost?"

Irene muttered in a convincing baritone, "Lost between trains in Brussels."

Godfrey regarded her in a puzzled manner. "There are indeed a good many changes of trains on your journey. You must be exhausted!" he said to me.

I nodded, beyond words. Sensing that, he asked no more questions, but saw us to the hired carriage. Irene waited while Godfrey helped me in. They eyed each other, then Irene entered and sat beside me. She gazed out the window while Godfrey sat and pounded his cane on the carriage ceiling to signal the driver to go.

"You seem to have left Bohemia in haste," he noted. "And secrecy. Your cablegram, Nell, was as curt as the letter that originally called you there. And the signature!"

"How is he?" I asked at once.

"Who?" Irene wondered gruffly.

"Casanova," Godfrey supplied with a smile at me.

Thoroughly confused, we all stared at each other and looked away.

"I don't understand," Godfrey finally told me, "I had assumed from your cable that your friend, Irene Adler, was to accompany you. You both seem exhausted and I'm sure there's a tale behind that, but I do believe that introductions are finally in order." He looked pointedly at Irene.

What could I say? The story was so long and convoluted and Irene's history and goings accomplished

She finally turned to him and lifted the bowler from her head, then the money bag. Last, she pulled the long tortoise shell pins from her hair and shook it onto her shoulders.

Godfrey Norton was not a barrister for nothing. Not a muscle of his face moved as Irene proceeded with her unveiling. During the following pause, Godfrey studied Irene from stem to stern. Then he said conversationally, "Miss Adler, I presume?"

In answer she pulled a cigarette from her breast pocket. Before she could withdraw a lucifer, Godfrey snapped a lighted one into his fingers. She inhaled long and shakily at its fire, then sat back.

"I could smoke one myself," Godfrey said.

Irene offered him her case. He managed to light a cigarette from the last of the lucifer before his fingers should scotch, then shook it out. Twin blue hazes drifted around the carriage and mingled sinuously.

I fluttered my hand for mercy. "I shall have to get out and walk soon, and, believe me, I do not wish to."

"Sorry." Godfrey cracked open a window so the smoke slithered into the glorious foggy haze of a London afternoon. "I confess myself at a loss."

Irene looked at me. I looked at her. We began laughing. She flicked her cigarette through the window slit. We began laughing harder. We laughed and laughed until we fell into each other's arms in relief and hilarity and hysteria.

Godfrey Norton watched us and wisely held his tongue.

At our new rooms on a still-shabby street of four-story rooming houses in Chelsea, Godfrey saw us into an adequate suite furnished with antimacassar—covered anonymity. "You apparently have funds," he began.

I nodded.

"Another day," Irene said from the window to which she had gone as a caged bird seeks the light.

The comparison reminded me of Casanova; I was startled to find my ears missing the parrot's *sotto voce* serenade of squawks, grumbles and ostentatious feather-preening, so like the subtle rustle of taffeta petticoats.

Godfrey eyed the stiff figure in masculine dress with the auburn hair cascading to its shoulders. His eyes sent mine a mute message of pleased greeting, then he bowed his way out.

Irene and I remained silent in our alien rooms, our only possessions the clothes on our backs, save for the money, the photograph and the ruby brooch from the King of Bohemia. She removed these items from her hat crown and her pockets and person, stringing them along the broad windowsill like offerings for the pigeons. I was startled to see that she had also saved the younger Tiffany's offensive octopod brooch. It lay entwined with the King's starfish of rubies, together the beginnings of a bizarre seascape.

"It was wise to telegraph Mr. Norton," Irene said from the window. "I could not have struggled on a moment longer."

I joined her there, once again viewing a carriage roof and a vanishing top hat. This time *I* knew its possessor and Irene was staring down in numb indifference.

She bent her forehead to the glass. "I am tired, Nell, so very, very tired."

Chapter Twenty-five

A Friend in Deed

꙰

True to his word, Godfrey did not intrude upon us.

This put me to some suspense. I found myself worrying when he did not even inquire at what point I might return to his employ—Irene's gold would not last forever, and, besides, I had my own living to earn—or when I would remove the unlovely Casanova from his custody. I felt redundant.

Irene, of course, was indifferent to Godfrey's absence. She occupied the first few days of our return with converting her foreign money into pounds.

Once she had funds to support herself, she set about restoring her lost clothing. Instead of haunting the used clothing markets with a hunter's passion as she had used to, or hieing to a dressmaker, she purchased excellent but unextraordinary items from the department stores (not Whiteley's) with as much enthusiasm as she would have bought dust cloths from the ragman.

All her actions those first days occurred in a methodical fog. After the enterprise of our headlong escape from Bohemia, it seemed a trifle tame.

One evening after dinner at a respectable restaurant, we sat reading in our forlorn rooms, both silent. I missed the familiar clutter of the Saffron Hill rooms, thinking it sad that much that once meant a great deal to Irene lay unused while we languished here.

She stirred and sighed. "I shall require an agent."

"For performance?" I chirped, cheered by the idea of Irene resuming her singing career.

She smiled wanly. "Performance seems a world away! No, we must find larger, more permanent quarters, and someone must inquire of my Paris acquaintance, without betraying my whereabouts, if my trunks arrived untrammeled. Do you think, Nell, that your barrister friend, Mr. Norton, would care to act for me in these—and more delicate—matters?"

I was astounded that Irene had accepted Godfrey as "my friend" rather than her long ago rival for the Zone of Diamonds or merely my (perhaps) former employer.

"I should be delighted to ask him," said I, relieved to have an excuse to visit Godfrey the very next day, as indeed I did.

What a glorious May day it was—crisp-aired, with budding leaves crimping every tree limb and bush. A faint porcelain blue bowl of sky yawned over London's everlasting grit and bustle.

"My dear Penelope!" Godfrey greeted me with genuine pleasure. "Come in; sit; have a dish of tea! I have been fretting over your welfare this past week, but did not wish to intrude uninvited."

I noticed an insipid-looking male clerk laboring in the outer office as Godfrey ushered me into his inner sanctum. There I felt that same cozy sense of belonging that I associated with my late father's study—the comfortable yet practical assemblage of furniture, the piled papers and open books, the air of quiet thought that suffused the chamber.

"Your 'intrusion' would never be that for me," I returned, "and as for being uninvited . . . I have come because Irene wonders if you would care to represent her in some matters both small and large, I think, though she has not confided her full intentions to me."

He leaned back in his chair, the tepid summer sunlight playing softly across his well-cut features. "Represent her! That is a change of tune."

"Her tune is not all that has changed, Godfrey." I rose at a familiar salutation and went to inspect Casanova in his cage. The old brute stuck out his black tongue at me, but I offered him a bit of biscuit from breakfast anyway. Then I faced Godfrey again. "I am worried. Irene is not one to sit back and let life buffet her, yet she has been most strangely . . . pensive . . . since our return."

"A rather harrowing return, I gather."

"That is not for me to say," I answered primly. "I can only state that she has been very badly used in Bohemia, and by one who had every obligation to defend rather than harm her. I can't say how much she will find it necessary to confide in you, but do not judge her harshly, I beg you. Irene has had no fault in this save failing to see perfidy behind the mask of friendship."

He toyed with the white horse-hair wig that lay askew atop a tower of law books. "You said Miss Adler sent for you because she needed help. Were you able to be of service?"

I smiled. "Yes, I think so; principally in providing a responsibility for her to meet in removing me safely from Bohemia. That is what I fear she lacks now—a focus for her energies and talents. She has come back with quite literally nothing, save money, and shows no sign of restoring what has been lost."

"You said 'safely.' Had things come to so dangerous a pass?"

"Irene thought so. Ask her yourself, Godfrey. I am not at liberty to speak for her."

"Very well. I'm trying a case in Fleet Street, but it should finish by mid-afternoon tomorrow. Bring her then."

He saw me out, murmuring "Adieu, 'Casanova' " in a most amused tone. Of the Italian libertine's colorful namesake he said not a word, which I found rather worrisome. Godfrey was becoming as sphinx-like as Irene!

I suggested to Irene that we lunch in Fleet Street and stop in at the Royal Courts of Justice to witness Godfrey's case. She agreed with uncustomary docility. I feared that her amiability reflected an indifference to everything around her, rather than any lifting of her mood.

I often had slipped into the visitors' gallery of the Royal Courts when Godfrey appeared before the bar. He was surely the youngest barrister pleading and looked ever so dashing in his fresh white wig and black gown—not like his elders, who resembled animated racks of overweight mutton in their yellowed wigs and whose several chins would barely allow the buttoning of their neck bands.

That day Irene wore a costume of pearl grey trimmed with violet embroidery. Her bonnet was violet velvet, with an upstanding red ostrich plume that showed far more starch than Irene did at the moment. She carried a sturdy black leather handbag that the old Irene would never have touched, much less purchased.

She watched Godfrey in court without comment, though I always enjoyed a glow of pride as I observed him make his "M'luds" and bows. To me, he was the only one who exhibited any style; I felt transported to the days when powdered wigs were everyday, when courtesy was an art and the art of argument was always attired in courtesy.

Irene leaned toward me during Godfrey's interrogation of a hostile witness. "May we leave? I find the air close."

We rustled softly out of the courtroom and crossed Fleet Street. I led Irene through the ancient archway to the Inner Temple, with the Crusaders' emblem of lamb and gold cross emblazoned high on the plaster.

"I thought Godfrey's interrogation adeptly handled," I noted.

"He has a flair for the dramatic," Irene responded noncommitally.

"From you that is a criticism?"

"It is a comment. I confess my mind was not much on Mr. Godfrey Norton, but on my own case."

We strolled through the Middle Temple yard toward the river, sparrows fluttering from gutter to gutter above us.

"I see why you love these ancient gardens." Irene stared at the

276 Carole Nelson Douglas

placid Thames rippling in the mild light. She sighed deeply. "This peaceful spot is somehow removed from the tawdry concerns of latter-day London."

"I love the Temple Church," I said, leading her next to that venerable building. She accompanied me like a child, obediently staring at the effigies of the land's first noblemen who had died in the days when knights knew the weight of shield and sword and holy crusade. The chancel was almost deserted. We were gazing up at the vast ceiling when a sudden skirl startled us.

The dissonant chords emitted from the massive freestanding organ soon resolved from bagpipe-rudeness to a mellow power. A lone soprano lifted over the softly growling organ's majestic bass. I saw a woman standing near the massive instrument, sheet music fanned open in her hands, her mouth an "O" of outpouring song.

Irene stiffened as if confronting a ghost. She brushed past me in her haste to leave. I found her outside staring bleakly across the yard.

"Godfrey must be through by now," I suggested.

"Yes, let us get this business over with."

He was indeed in, the wig and gown hanging from a coatrack crowded into a corner of his office. He offered no tea, sensing that Irene wished only to attend to business.

"Please be seated, Miss Adler." He gestured her into the leather wing chair facing his desk, leaving me to take a light side chair, which suited me perfectly. I had brought Irene to Godfrey, as she wished. I had no idea what she wished of him, or what she would reveal of herself and our unfortunate adventure.

"We left Bohemia in some secrecy, as you may gather," she began.

Godfrey nodded. Like most barristers, he had mastered the unintrusive nod and the noncommittal hmm.

"I need someone to contact a friend in Paris, to whom I have sent several trunks with my belongings. If they have arrived safely, I would like them discreetly transferred to my lodgings here."

"*If?*" Godfrey said.

Irene's lips almost twisted into a smile at his curiosity, but she did not answer his question. Instead she opened the handbag that she had lifted to her lap like a well-behaved little dog and brought out a slip of paper.

"My friend's name and address. Do you write French?"

"I do, and at times even read it."

"Ah." Irene was mildly surprised. "Balzac and Sand?"

"Dumas *père* and *fils* and Baudelaire," Godfrey said with a laugh.

Her eyebrows raised. "You have adventurous taste for a barrister."

"You have intriguing adventures for an opera singer."

Irene's smile faded. She sighed again, and Godfrey glanced sharply to me. He did not know Irene well, but he knew my tales of her well enough to realize that the woman who sat before him was oddly altered.

"I am uncertain how to proceed, Mr. Norton. Were any other recourse available, I assure you I should never rely upon the services of someone like yourself."

I cringed at Irene's disdainful tone; I knew it was directed at herself, not at Godfrey or his profession. He could not understand how galling it was for someone as independent as Irene to find herself asking another's aid.

Godfrey spoke without showing offense. "I assure you, Miss Adler, that you may depend upon me to respect your need for confidentiality."

She nodded, the flagrant red plume trembling in the filtered daylight. "The quandary is this: there are those in Bohemia who may feel it necessary to follow and find me."

"For what purpose?"

"I am not sure, Mr. Norton. One purpose might be so radical as to abstract me from England—it is unlikely, but possible."

"Another purpose?"

"Another motive might be to recover this." She wet her lips and lifted the cabinet photograph from her handbag. Now I understood the object's ungainly size.

"May I see it?"

"It is not necessary."

Godfrey immediately leaned back in his chair, as if to demonstrate no interest in the object.

"It is mine, a gift," Irene said ironically. "The giver has . . . reconsidered. He . . . wishes to become a taker. He would find my possession of this . . . item . . . threatening."

"Then return it to him."

"I cannot. By retaining it, I keep him from taking action against me. He has already had me dismissed from my position with the Prague opera."

"Dismissed?" Godfrey sat forward, his eyes flashing. "He interfered in your operatic career, your livelihood? Why?"

"It did not suit him that I should sing."

"Indeed! May I inquire the identity of this music hater?"

She smiled despite herself. "You may. I am not certain that I should answer."

"As you wish."

"Oh, Mr. Norton! You will forgive my sighs and indecision, but the matter is complicated. Perhaps you have a right to know your opponent and the range of his power, if you undertake to aid me in avoiding him. He is no one less than the King of Bohemia."

"The King! Why should he be taken with such great antagonism toward you?"

"Because he was first taken with great affection toward me. Is that not always the way of the world; time turns what is good to bad?"

"Not always." Godfrey frowned handsomely. "That is a sober philosophy, Miss Adler. Perhaps your outlook is curdled at the moment." He glanced at the closed photograph case. "As to securing that, I could consign it to some bank safe—"

"No! I must have instant access to it."

"—I was about to say that a safe would be unsatisfactory. For now, you keep it with you?"

"Always."

"Let me think upon it. What are your other needs?"

"I am undecided as to how I may proceed now that I am in London. I would like more permanent lodgings."

"And you feel that you cannot go back to Saffron Hill without betraying yourself?"

"Yes."

"New lodgings would not necessarily attract attention if they were discreetly procured. You have means?"

Irene nodded. "A great plenty, for now."

"Essentially, then, you need to resettle in London, regain your lost clothing and your possessions still kept at the Saffron Hill address and secure your valuable . . . charge."

"Precisely."

"Then leave it all to me, save the photograph." He stood to see us out.

Irene stopped as if struck. "Photograph? It could be a jewel case."

"Elementary, my dear Miss Adler—the size and style of case, the fact that the item could discomfit a friend turned enemy. It must be irrefutable evidence of something the King of Bohemia would wish forgotten. Monsieur Daguerre unleashed a mighty weapon when he invented the photographic plate."

She nodded and clutched her homely handbag close as we left. I looked back at Godfrey. He was smiling, his barrister's eyes alight with speculation and his aquiline nose almost visibly twitching at the alluring scent of a mystery.

It struck me that Irene was in no state to notice that Godfrey Norton was as formidable in his way as the King of Bohemia.

Chapter Twenty-six

A Barrister Bearing Gifts

Within a week Godfrey called at our Chelsea rooms.

Irene had been lounging on the chaise when he arrived. She did not rise to greet him but remained reclining, rather like a queen who awaits a favored subject.

Godfrey was all brusque energy and information. He ignored Irene's languor and paced, rubbing his hands together, as he brought us up to date.

"I have inquired into the matter of your trunks, Miss Adler, by writing to a Paris associate who will contact your friend discreetly. I have no reply as yet, trusting as I am to the post rather than the more efficient cable. Cable would be speedier, but would, of course, leave a trail. I expect a return letter within the week."

Irene nodded regally.

"In the meantime, I have made progress in London. I have leased a house—a two-story villa in St. John's Wood with a charming garden at the back. The rooms are commodious and well furnished. There is a carriage house. I have taken the liberty of engaging a cook-housekeeper, a maid and a driver, given the place's rural locale."

"St. John's Wood?" Irene said, frowning.

"North of Regent's Park," Godfrey explained. "Off the Edgware Road. An area a bit Bohemian, if you will pardon the expression, but well-to-do. It is rural enough to escape the attention of anyone bent on scouring London for your whereabouts. In fact, I should like to show you both the property tonight, if you have no objection."

"Such efficiency," Irene commented languidly, extending a hand so that he could help her rise. "You quite wear me out, Mr. Norton."

Godfrey smiled and bowed to kiss her wrist, a gallantry that surprised me. But as we gathered our coats to leave, he favored me with a wink.

Our new coachman, John Jewett, drove the party. He was a hearty man of middle years with a nicely protective air toward his female passengers. I confess myself excited beyond the stimulation of a change of permanent address, my first in six years. I sensed a tension in the air, more in Irene's aspect than Godfrey's. She was quiet, her normally incisive eyes heavy-lidded as she expressed a dangerous spiritual *ennui* alien to the Irene I knew. She reminded me of certain photographs of Sarah Bernhardt, resembling a gorgeous, coiled lazy serpent waiting for the right moment to slough off inactivity and strike.

The villa in St. John's Wood looked promising by night. Lights warmed the long, ground-floor windows that reached the floor in the Italian style. The coachman waited while we disembarked to view the property.

"It is called Briony Lodge," Godfrey said.

"What a lovely name!" said I at once.

Irene remained silent as Godfrey escorted us within. The place was as advertised: spacious and well appointed. As we examined the rooms both up and down, I saw that Godfrey had already imported our furnishings from Saffron Hill. I gasped to see the "Jersey Lily" standing guard in the upper hall. To all this care, Irene responded with the barrister's noncommittal "hmm."

The kitchen below-stairs was clean and well-equipped. The cook had retired for the night, but we were assured that she was adept. Godfrey at last brought us 'round again to the handsome sitting room. He went to the tall windows from which we had seen the gaslight pouring, drawing the blinds in turn with a dramatic flourish.

"And lastly, ladies, I present a feature that most recommends this particular property." He moved to the fireplace wall, where a tapestry bell-pull hung.

"I have seen a bell-pull before, Mr. Norton," Irene noted sardonically, "although I have never before personally possessed such a luxury."

He said nothing, but pressed the painted paneling just beside it. A recessed panel sprang back with a snap. Beyond it lay a dark compartment large enough to accommodate the cabinet photograph.

I clapped my hands in delight.

"Bravo, Mr. Norton," Irene murmured, moving to inspect the space. "The villa came with this hidey-hole?"

"Indeed not. I had it put in myself."

"Oh?"

Godfrey regarded her expressionless face with amusement. "The carpenters were brought here blindfolded, by carriage, and so returned. They saw only this room and were driven from Greenwich to Battersea both coming and going to confuse their sense of direction. This nook is our secret, we three."

"What of the coachman who drove them?" Irene demanded.

Godfrey assumed a look I could only describe as belonging on a choir boy at Westminster.

"There was no coachman. I drove them myself."

Irene lowered her eyes. Otherwise she moved not a muscle. I realized that the entire situation rested on her approval.

At last she lifted her head, and her hand, as in one motion. She was mistress of exquisite gestures. The limpid flex of her wrist reminded me of the languid power of the Diety's hand reaching toward Adam on the Sistine Chapel ceiling. Irene held this artistically presented hand at shoulder level, as a queen extending a favor. Her lips lifted like the Mona Lisa's.

Godfrey hesitated a moment; he respected women, but tribute

was not his coinage. Then he took Irene's hand, swiftly turned it and
brushed his lips across the inside of her wrist.

I couldn't help wondering how she avoided giggling at the tickle of
his mustache, but Irene looked quite sober and more than a bit taken
aback. She turned to regard the hidden compartment, giving us both
her back.

"Well done, Mr. Norton," Irene murmured as she gazed into the
empty space. "Very well done indeed."

"Everything?" he inquired.

She half-turned to face him, her profile tilted up to his. "Everything." Neither moved nor spoke for a long moment.

I stood frozen like the audience at the climax of a play. Then the
moment was gone and Godfrey and Irene were turning to me. It was
all I could do to resist applauding.

"My dear Nell," Godfrey said, as if noticing me again. A broad
smile stretched his dark mustache into a thinner black line. "I have
quite forgotten a special surprise for you."

"Oh, really! Indeed, I do not require any special surprises," I said
modestly, thrilled nevertheless.

He led me into the dining room, Irene following. In a dark corner of the chamber he paused and, whisking a garishly figured cloth
aside, revealed the brass cage of Casanova.

"Ex Why-Zed," the parrot caroled.

I glanced to Godfrey, who was grinning and tilting his dark head
at the same angle as Casanova's scarlet and yellow poll. "You had
started him on his A-B-Cs when you left, my fine Nell. Casanova is a
reprobate and difficult to teach, so I brought him directly from J-K-L
to X-Y-Z. At least he goes from A to Z now."

"Cut the cackle!" Casanova screeched.

Someone was laughing. It was Irene and it ill became her.

"Really, Godfrey," said I, "you need not have relinquished the bird
so soon. No doubt he would have learned much under your tutelage."

"Fleurs du mal, fleurs du mal," the feathered fiend hooted.

"Baudelaire! Mr. Norton, you didn't!" Irene was openly shriek-
ing in laughter behind me. "Not Nell's bird! Baudelaire!"

"It's not my bird," I asserted. "And I barely speak French, so your hilarity is lost upon me." They were both laughing uproariously, Godfrey collapsing against the wall, Irene covering her mouth with both hands, tears streaming from her eyes. "Furthermore, Irene, I wonder how you shall welcome this beast's vocalizations when you must overhear them daily."

"Are you finished, Mr. Norton?" she inquired at last.

"Not quite. If I may be excused?"

She nodded curiously as he left the room and then the house.

"Casanova aside," I confided, "I like the situation."

"Yes." Irene moved to the cage. "What a vulgar creature; he is dyed all the colors of the rainbow."

"I believe that Godfrey has done well," I persisted.

"Oh, Godfrey has done excellently, though he takes a great deal upon himself. Such perfection quite chills my blood."

"Perhaps you are not accustomed to it, save in yourself," said I.

Godfrey's hasty steps sounded in the hall. We rushed out. Godfrey carried some burden in his arms like a baby.

"There's a small parlor to the right," he said, dashing into this last unseen room.

Irene and I followed to see him deposit his burden on a table with a thump. It was his father's chest.

Irene was drawn to it, running her hands over the wood as if to shape its contents as well as its exterior.

"Another of your erstwhile belongings," Godfrey said.

"I ceded it to you," she reminded him.

"I ceded it back, as I do Nell's blasted parrot. I have not been able to make head nor tail of its contents. Perhaps you would care to try again . . . ?"

Irene spun away from the chest, from his persuasive voice. Only one kerosene lamp lit the room, casting more shadow than light. She moved toward the ill-lit bay window, pausing beside a huge, crouching silhouette of furniture. The flickering lamplight picked out the cabbage-rose pattern of a shawl.

Irene's hand suddenly swept away the shawl, the fringe shivering in light and shadow, to unveil another surprise. A grand piano squatted in the bay.

"This came with the furnishings?" she asked stiffly.

I remembered the throat-soothing potions she had left behind in Bohemia and considered that no elixir could smooth the emotion that roughened her question.

"It goes with the house," Godfrey said, quite firmly.

"I see." Irene was silent for a long while. "Lock up the place, then, and take us home. I am tired."

So we returned to Chelsea, both of us eager to quit our impersonal rooms there, yet each dreading to confront the special gifts that Godfrey had brought to our new quarters.

"We can keep the cover over the parrot," Irene said that evening, brushing her radiant hair.

"And can we keep the piano shawl over the keys, as well?" I asked.

"You and Godfrey Norton! You rush in where angels fear to tread."

"Then we will be at home in heaven," said I, and doused the light.

"More logically and likely in hell," she predicted from the dark.

Chapter Twenty-seven

A Familiar Form of Address

❧

I cannot say which of the three objects in our new quarters was the more ignored in the week that followed: the Norton chest, the grand piano or the bird, Casanova.

The parrot required food and water (our housekeeper, Mrs. Seaton, cleaned the cage). It greeted me as rudely as ever, but in the course of my tending I found that plying it with peeled grapes (a great favorite of Irene's) encouraged a gentler diction. We even were making progress on "Cassie want a crumpet?"

Irene sometimes paused beside the cage to coo French at it in hopes of stimulating some *risqué* phrases. I wouldn't have recognized a naughty French phrase if I heard it, which is no doubt why a foreign language is always favored for such things. I quite suspect that the French couch their most licentious thoughts in English or German.

Save for a daily drive at five o'clock through Regents Park, our lives were models of domestic tedium. I had never before appreciated how much the struggle to earn one's daily bread gave life structure and even excitement.

Godfrey called on us once or twice a week, not pleased by our lethargy. He frowned at the closed chest and the covered piano and whispered little French nothings, of a salacious nature, I fear, to Casanova.

His third visit was quite different, however. On being admitted that evening by Mrs. Seaton, he burst into the sitting room, where I sat sewing and Irene reading.

"News!" Godfrey flourished the *Daily Telegraph*.

Irene sat forward. "Of the King? He is in England!?"

"No, of your former employer, Tiffany. He is in France. He is in Paris, in fact, for the auction of the French crown jewels."

"Oh, is that all?" Irene reluctantly set aside her book.

"It is the auction of the century. Diamonds dating back to Cardinal Mazarin will be sold, as well as those inadvertently left behind by the fleeing Empress Eugenie."

"What is it to me?" Irene said. "I have funds, but not so many that I may bid against Mr. Tiffany."

"Miss Adler, this is the collection of jewels from which the Zone of Diamonds disappeared. They are its sister stones, so to speak. I propose that we go to Paris to observe the auction. We both speak French. Perhaps we can uncover some clue to the Zone's whereabouts."

"Go to Paris?" Irene took the folded newspaper Godfrey had been waving under her nose and studied it. "The auction occurs in only three days."

"We can be in Paris in one."

"The best clue to the Zone lies buried in that box of your father's."

"I know, but if we are stalled in the present, then we should inquire into the Zone's past."

"This is mad!" Irene laughed despite herself. "One can't simply pick up and go on a wild goose chase to Paris—"

"Why not? My time is my own, as is yours; no cases pend. We could reclaim your trunks in person. Besides, Paris in May is most delightful."

Irene worried the braid on her skirt as she considered. I had never seen her so indecisive. Suddenly she glanced up at Godfrey. "Very well. If you are game, I am. But I still think the scheme is mad."

"As do I!" I put in. "Irene, it would be most improper for you to travel with Godfrey unchaperoned, and I have no intentions of going to such a sinful city as Paris!"

"A pity," Godfrey said, "for if you went you would see that Paris is not so much sinful as seductive, therefore the guilt, as with beauty, lies in the eye of the beholder. Yet it is best that you remain to tend my office in my absence; I've dismissed your replacement."

Delighted as I was to contemplate the daily discipline of work, the notion that Godfrey could so blithely forego my company on an adventure stunned me. I glanced at Irene, who was regarding Godfrey's determined face with equally keen surprise.

"Irene?"

She shook herself at my voice as if escaping a reverie. "Mr. Norton is quite correct. This will be a whirlwind trip, will it not?" He nodded. "Dear Nell, I cannot in good conscience drag you from pillar to post so soon after our thrilling escape from Bohemia. And we . . . might uncover news of the Zone."

"You will go, then?" Godfrey said hopefully.

Irene nodded. "Despite one serious drawback to your proposal." She glanced sternly at me. "And that drawback is not propriety, Nell; I refuse to abide by conventions that hamper my freedom. No, the great pity is that our flight has left me with no suitable gowns for my first visit to Paris."

"My dear Miss Adler, you would take Paris by storm in rags, like a good Republican; in what you wear tonight, the city will fall at your feet."

"An exaggeration, Mr. Norton," Irene said drily, "most out of character for a barrister. We would leave . . . ?"

He shrugged happily. "The day after tomorrow, and return in three days. I will make the arrangements first thing in the morning."

Godfrey left soon after, leaving me speechless, but not for long.

"I suppose it will do me as much good as Casanova to croak about your plans," I said. "I must express myself, however distasteful you find my opinion. Irene, this jaunt with Godfrey is most improper."

She had returned to her book, so all I saw was the top of her hair where lamplight kindled auburn flames among its wood-brown luster. Her glance flashed its former fire.

"My dear Nell, if the outing were not half-mad and totally improper, it would not be any fun! Your friend Godfrey is well aware of that. He feels that I waste away here and wanted to provide me with an irresistible lure to action."

"Apparently he has," I huffed.

Irene smiled. "Apparently, but I think he has misjudged the lure."

"You are not going because of the diamond auction?"

"No more than he is."

"But why, then?"

She simply smiled again and shrugged. Later, I heard her humming *"Frère Jacques"* to Casanova.

✦ ✦ ✦

Even the Temple's almost celestial air of peace did little to quiet my conscience while I worked at the pile of manuscript in Godfrey's Temple offices. The temporary typists employed during my absence had misplaced everything, lagging pitifully behind in their work.

I rapped the keys at my usual brisk pace, finding the activity a good method of dissipating my distemper. Pages flew through my platen, entering pristine and white to emerge soiled with type.

So I viewed the state of Irene's reputation, until I finally considered that her liaison with the King of Bohemia, no matter how innocent, had likely ruined that reputation forever. And then, I could think of no man on this earth by whom I would prefer her to be improperly escorted than Godfrey Norton. In this case, he was the least of all possible evils.

Yet I also felt a sense of abandonment, as I had on Irene's first removal to Europe. This time the pang was doubled; the two people most dear to me appeared perfectly able to dispense with my presence. So sometimes I typed through tears of self-pity, for which I berated myself, and then I made a stupid mistake and had to rip out the sheet of paper and start all over again . . .

Someone entered the office at a moment when I least felt like dealing with the public. I kept typing to the end of the sentence, then turned, about to exercise my frustration on whoever had been unwise enough to enter.

The visitor was a tall slender man with sharp features. His plush velvet top hat was properly in his hand, but he looked at me so intently that I felt certain he could see the tears ebbing in my eyes.

"Mr. Norton, I perceive, is away from chambers for a few days," he said swiftly.

I glanced through the open door to Godfrey's sanctum. His wig and gown hung on their proper hooks and the cluttered desk retained an air of occupancy, perhaps because of his hasty departure.

"He is on the Continent," I announced importantly. "But how . . . ?"

The visitor smiled wearily, as if the question were all too familiar. "An empty envelope bearing the name of a Fleet Street ticket agent has fallen on the floor by the door. Obviously Mr. Norton discarded it just as he left."

"With all this paper hither and yon you noticed that?"

"Observation is my profession."

"Indeed. Many could say that. If I did not observe these handwritten documents properly, I should not be able to typewrite them accurately. I have a great deal of that very thing to do, so I suggest that you call again—"

"Perhaps you can settle my business now. Can you tell me whether Mr. Norton is a son of the late John Chapple Norton?"

The query doused my composure like a bucket of ice water. "How in the world should I know that?"

"You have worked with Mr. Norton for some time, although not in recent months. And you are observant, Miss—"

"Huxleigh!" I barked. "And it is true that I have . . . been away, but—" I would not, I would *not* ask this odiously prescient man how he had determined the length and interrupted nature of my employment.

He smiled briefly. It was not an expression that softened his angular features.

"You are reordering the documents on the shelf above you. Half the files are kept horizontally, half vertically, but the fattest— therefore the oldest—are vertical. Obviously, a substitute who is too lazy to reach a bit higher has interrupted your admirable system, Miss Huxleigh."

"I had already concluded that the recent temporary was lazy, for the work is sadly behind. Any fool could see that. *He* apparently could not keep up."

The gentleman smiled again. "But you have not answered my question."

"I . . ." What to do? I couldn't lie, yet I didn't want to betray information Godfrey wanted to keep to himself. "It is not for me to say. Is it a matter of . . . inheritance?" I knew, of course, that Black Jack Norton had died penniless, but wished to ask the expected question.

"It is not for me to say," the gentleman returned, "but I have been trying to trace relations of the late Norton for some time."

I shook my head. "You must ask Mr. Norton when he returns."

"And that will be?"

"Thursday."

The gentleman nodded and replaced his hat as he stepped to the door.

"Sir! Whom may I tell Mr. Norton to expect?"

"Oh, I doubt he knows of me. But the name is Holmes, Sherlock Holmes. I will leave my card."

I took it wordlessly and watched the tall figure move through the clutter with catlike precision. My eyes didn't leave the door until long after he had closed it. When they did, they settled on the card, which contained not only the name of Irene's rival for the Zone of Diamonds, but also an address that was hauntingly familiar, even from the day when Irene and I had first met, and then together met the late Mr. Jefferson Hope.

"Two-twenty-one-B Baker Street," I whispered, perhaps hoping that saying the address aloud would banish it. The print remained quite unaltered.

Chapter Twenty-eight

The Return of Sherlock Holmes

~~◆~~

"Sherlock Holmes!" Irene exclaimed.

I was too bursting with the news of my recent encounter to withhold it a moment after my friend's return to the door of Briony Lodge.

Now she stood in mid-threshold, her face blank with shock.

"Who," Godfrey asked from behind her frozen figure, "is Sherlock Holmes?"

"*Sherlock Holmes* was making inquiries about Godfrey's father?" Irene repeated in disbelief.

"More about Godfrey, actually," I said.

Irene glided like a sleepwalker into the hall, reaching to unpin her bonnet—a smart new one with "Paris" written all over it. Godfrey hovered behind her as she lifted her veil before the mirror. Despite her shock, Irene's face radiated well-being. Three days in Paris had erased weeks of heartbreak in Bohemia, as if that clever Parisian milliner had put stars in her eyes and roses on her cheeks along with the fashionable bonnet atop her head. I developed new respect for millinery then and there.

"Irene." Godfrey spoke low, his gloved hands pausing urgently

on her shoulders, "what is so sinister about this Holmes fellow inquiring about my father? I no more like having my family history
unearthed now than when you did it, but surely the matter is not so
serious as you seem to think."

She gave him a vague, reassuring smile. "No, it is not, Godfrey. It
is simply that the paths of myself and this Mr. Holmes have nearly
crossed at times in the past. The first occasion was when Mr. Tiffany
employed us both to trace the Zone of Diamonds."

Godfrey set hat, cane and gloves on the hall console. "So the trail
warms again. I wonder why?"

"Likely for the same reason that you wish me to concentrate on
finding the Zone—the sale of crown jewels we have just attended in
Paris. Perhaps Mr. Tiffany has engaged Mr. Holmes to renew the investigation."

"Or this Holmes fellow has stumbled on a new clue," Godfrey
said. "I suppose I shall have to see him; better I be forewarned."

"I regret greeting you with such disturbing news," I put in, feeling utterly forgotten and more than somewhat aggrieved since my
dramatic news had precipitated the conversation, "but when the gentleman gave his name, I thought my poor heart would stop."

But my past cardiac condition was not as pressing to them as the
present matter of Sherlock Holmes.

"What is this man's interest anyway?" Godfrey sounded a trifle
annoyed—perhaps not only by this revived interest in his unhappy
family but also by Irene's fascination with the man Holmes. I had
never observed a possessive streak in him before.

"All mysteries are his interest," Irene said, warming to her subject
and growing even more radiant. "Sherlock Holmes is a consulting detective and a splendid one. From what I've read—or inferred—in the
papers, his fine investigative hand has touched every criminal sensation of the past decade."

"I have never heard of the man!" Godfrey objected.

"Of course not. The police are quick to claim all credit for themselves. Subtlety was never their chief virtue."

"Apparently subtlety is not this man Holmes's virtue, either,"

Godfrey grumbled, "or he would not have come openly to my chambers."

"How could he know that your type-writer girl has an astute nose for intrigue and a very long memory?" Irene, amused by Godfrey's discomfiture for some odd reason, smiled fondly at me. "We must consider this latest development that Nell presents us, but first I will change."

I accompanied her upstairs while Godfrey cooled his heels in the sitting room. I privately pitied him, for the news of Sherlock Holmes had eclipsed his inspired trip to Paris as a thunderclap outshouts a firecracker.

"How was Paris?" I asked, helping Irene to remove her traveling things.

"Divine! We saw the Tuileries from which the Zone was looted in 1848—the flower beds were breaking into fragrant bloom and the stone goddesses posed as if alive among the greenery. We took tea at an open café in Montmartre. The air was fresh, everything so delicate and clean, the city afloat in an amber wash of sunlight. It was superb!"

"And the jewels? From the illustration in the papers they seemed rather . . . large."

"Large, oh, yes, and more than superb." Irene sat on the dressing chair, her eyes glittering. "Such jewels will never be seen again in their present form, for Mr. Tiffany, whom I saw there, plans to sell the stones separately. You should have seen, Nell! The Empress Eugenie's favorite comb had nine flexible diamond streamers cascading to the shoulders, a waterfall of sheer white fire! Mr. Tiffany bought six of the comb's eighteen lots for two hundred-eighteen-thousand francs. I told him that the piece was meant to be whole."

"Irene, you didn't! What did he say?"

"He laughed and said, 'Yes, and on your head, Miss Adler, no doubt.' He said that the diamond corsage he lent me for the Milan opera is finally finished and is to be displayed at the Paris Exhibition next year. He was *most* pleased, however, that I wore his son's brooch the day of the auction."

"The agonized octopus? Why, I'd forgotten about it . . ."

"I had not, nor had Mr. Tiffany. His son, he said, is doing rather well with craft work, stained glass and the like. Perhaps this will be worth something someday," Irene mused, removing the disgusting Tiffany brooch from her reticule.

"Did Mr. Tiffany mention the Zone?"

"Indeed. He said it was a pity that I hadn't been able to trace it. I responded," Irene said firmly, "that the greater pity was that it would have been sundered if I had. He reminded me that good business is never a pity. At least I know to whom to sell the Zone if I find it."

"You . . . will look again?"

"I will, Nell. I have caught diamond fever in Paris; Godfrey's jaunt was successful in that. And I do have one small souvenir of that delicious malady."

She pulled a tiny leather case from her reticule and lifted the lid to show the "Tiffany and Co." stamped into the velvet lining. On the crimson cloth lay a diamond brooch—a crossed key and musical note design with pavé diamonds sparkling like ice flakes.

"Goodness, Irene, Mr. Tiffany has given you another brooch! Whatever for? You did not promise him the Zone!?"

Irene's smile was unreadable. "It was acquired at Tiffany's on the rue Richelieu but the gift is not his."

"Not his? Whose then?"

"Godfrey's," said Irene. "He was struck by the design, which he said merged my interests of mystery and music. He was convinced it had been made for me."

"Godfrey's! Godfrey cannot afford to give you jewels."

"Likely not," Irene said, still smiling, "but this bauble is not so precious as those many-carat-sized stones illustrated in the *London News*."

I would not have known it, however, from the delicate way she returned the brooch to its case.

"I will keep it in the secret compartment with the photograph of the King of Bohemia's crown paste," Irene decided. "It is far more worthy of care for having been given freely."

"Speaking of things given freely," I put in, "I noticed that you and Godfrey address each other by first names since your trip."

"How quick you are! No wonder the estimable Mr. Holmes pried only sour little nothings from you. Yes, we do." Irene smiled mysteriously. "You could say that over-much familiarity breeds . . . familiarity."

Irene donned a ravishing emerald velvet wrap and a pretty pair of beaded house slippers before going downstairs again. Godfrey had not been idle in our absence; a tray of piping hot chocolate and the assorted teacakes for which Irene had such a passion awaited us. He must have roused Mrs. Seaton to prepare this bounty while we gossiped above.

We three settled before a dancing fire that spat warmth into the interior chill, a sudden odd reticence in the air. Before we supped, Irene deposited the Tiffany box in the secret compartment. She settled on the sofa beside me, at a right angle to Godfrey, whose eyes never left her profile. I felt we were all forced into places assigned us in a play, yet despite the stiff propriety among us, we sipped chocolate in contented silence, the others weary from the exhilaration of their journey, I pleased to have them safely home again.

Evidently we all mused on the same unspoken subject, for when Irene suddenly announced, "I have made a decision," both Godfrey and I sat bolt upright.

She smiled at our eagerness. "Hounds on the trail, both of you! I agree, Godfrey, that we must find the Zone before another party snaps it up. When Sherlock Holmes calls again, you must give him only the snatches of your family history that he could cull from other sources. But to me . . . you must tell all."

"I don't understand—" he began.

"Your memory is the key to the puzzle, to the objects jumbled into the chest. I must know every particular that you recall of your father and your childhood."

"For almost thirty years, I have striven to forget that unhappy time."

"I know," Irene said, "yet often the past rests easier once it has been fully examined. You wish me to find the jewels; I must first de-cipher the nature of the man who had them."

Godfrey gazed into the hearth for a long moment. I could see the flames reflected small in his mirror-pale eyes. At last he faced Irene. "How must we begin?"

"With the box and its contents. They must stir some associations for you, however unfortunate."

They rose and went into the small front room. I remained to finish a George Eliot novel I had begun in their absence, certain that any revelations would be told first to me. Yet I could not con-centrate upon the page; Irene and Godfrey both acted so bemused, so distracted. Could more than Sherlock Holmes and the Zone of Diamonds be responsible for their odd behavior? For Irene's radi-ance and Godfrey's air of . . . well, I could only call it . . . extreme satisfaction . . .

The house was quiet, save for the ticking clock and an occasional squawk from Casanova. I heard Godfrey's and Irene's rising and falling voices as a dappled murmur in which some phrases came clear and others muddy. When I glanced through the open doors, they looked like children playing a parlor game, their brunette heads bent close together—his the darker—the lamplight burnishing their pale faces and hands with the innocence of harmony.

My uneasy speculations were surely only the maunderings of an old maid! I rejected my suspicions as I returned to the sitting room and my novel, permitting myself to feel only the sublime satisfaction of a governess who knows that her innocent charges are safely occu-pied and can do themselves no harm.

"You have lost all contact with your brothers?" I heard Irene's voice lift incredulously. That question had intrigued me as well, so I allowed my ears to attend to what they were saying.

"They sided with my father," Godfrey answered, "feeling our mother was an embarrassment. As the eldest, I had witnessed my fa-ther's cruel behavior toward her. My brothers saw only that we lived apart from him and that society looked askance. Later, when my fa-ther sued for my mother's writing income, they chose to live with him. Not that he cared for their company that much; it was more a matter of asserting his 'authority.'"

"Yet you kept him in his old age."

"My brothers were nowhere to be found by then. Life with father was not so gentle that they stayed a moment past necessity. I believe that they have left England."

"That may be why Mr. Holmes was unable to trace you sooner. Many Nortons call this small isle home, but only one could lead him to 'Black Jack.'"

"You pronounce that epithet with relish."

"And why not? If you were denied a noble sire, be pleased at least to have a notorious one. There is some distinction in that."

"You sound as if you speak from experience."

"You sound as if *you* interrogate *me* now."

"I am a barrister."

"I am not a witness."

"No, but you are most reluctant to speak of some things."

"Such as?"

"Your . . . family origins—yes, I know I am cautious there, too— and the nature of your association with the King, other than that you fled him. I understand, Irene, that these small eastern dukedoms are ruled by autocrats. I can even understand that the ruler of such a backward place might think he could command your love—"

"It was worse, Godfrey, although what you say is very close to what happened, but it does not name my fault in the business."

"What you *imagine* to be your fault—"

"No! My fault. My . . . overestimation of him, and of myself. It was not that the King thought he could command my love, but that I thought that I could win his."

"You did, else why would you have had to flee him?"

"That is not love," Irene said disdainfully. "That is possession. You of all men should know that, Godfrey, for your mother fled that kind of trap herself. The King never bothered to disguise his power with the cloak of marriage; even your father did that."

"The King was a fool, and a deceptive fool!"

"And quite right: a woman in my position need not be married. Oh, I do not crave the state; indeed, I doubt I shall ever marry. It was insanity on my part to imagine for a moment that a man mired in such traditions as the King of Bohemia was could be as unconventional as myself. You see, for him to have married me would have been the height of *un*respectibility. I could never respect a man who cannot dispense with respectibility."

Godfrey laughed heartily. "Your logic is impeccably skewed; it reminds me of the contradictory wit of this young Oscar Wilde: 'Life is much too important a thing ever to talk seriously about it.' The poor King must have lumbered to follow your quicker mind like an elephant after a gnat. What you mean to say is that he was not king enough, nor man enough, to risk anything for you."

"Or for himself. But how did we proceed from your lost brothers to my ignoble King? You are a circuitous examiner, sir. Now tell me what this ring of keys recalls to you?"

"It reminds me of returning to my quarters for rest. Perhaps your questions will bring me answers in a dream. Let us attack the matter fresh tomorrow."

There was a silence. I heard a sudden rude metallic rattle and started, guiltily lifting the Eliot within range of my pince-nez.

"Poor Nell," I heard Irene whisper shortly after from the passage, "she has read herself half-blind and almost asleep while we toyed with the residue of your father's past. Go out quietly and I'll get her to bed."

It was most annoying to have to feign a sleepy state, but better than admitting that I had heard Irene discussing the King in such plain and personal terms.

I slept well despite my small sin of eavesdropping, but received ultimate punishment. I awoke to the throb of piano chords from below. My bedside clock revealed a dreadfully late hour, so I quickly dressed and went downstairs. The remains of Irene's breakfast lay crumbled in the dining room. I went directly to the little music room, from which swelling chords of Liszt were ringing.

"Good morning, Nell!" Irene greeted me over a ripple of melody.

"This piano is in fine tune for a rented furnishing. I must ask Godfrey about that."

"You have been asking Godfrey a good deal lately," I noted.

"And he, me." For a finishing flourish, her hands lifted off the keys like a conductor's before settling decorously in her lap. "I have found a dreary, diligent task for him."

"Just what he needs after a trip to Paris."

"Oh, you have not had breakfast! I can tell it by your temper. Have Mrs. Seaton whip up whatever is your favorite. If you cannot go to Paris at least you can eat well."

"And what will you do while I play glutton?"

"Play," Irene said, executing a rather extravagant glissando with the back of her nails.

Indeed she did play, until I began to wonder if a singing Irene was as evil an addition to our residence as a speaking Casanova. The bird was mute during my meal, its yellow-and-red head cocked while Irene trilled through her exercises in the other room.

I considered what misery I would suffer if Casanova learned to imitate the exaggerated vowels affected by opera singers: "ah-ah-ah-AH-ah-ah-ah, oh-oh-oh-OH-oh-oh-oh, ee-ee-ee-EE-ee-ee-ee and eu-eu-EU-eu-eu-eu-eu," repeated in relentless sets of seven.

Yet I confess myself most happy to hear it.

Godfrey arrived late that afternoon. He admitted that the piano had been freshly tuned at his orders.

"Then I must play you something," Irene insisted, whirling down onto the stool and performing the Liszt with far more panache than I had heard that morning.

"But you cannot sing to 'Liebestraum,' " Godfrey protested when the final lush chords had faded.

"I am not ready to sing," Irene said, folding her hands in her lap like a child who has been admonished. She looked up mischievously a moment later. "But perhaps *you* are ready to work."

She went to the table to fish the ring of ill-matched keys from the chest and toss them to him. "You must, as heir, apply to every bank active in London the past—oh, thirty-some years—to inquire if your father had a safe-deposit box with one of them. Several of these keys are of such a type. I believe that they are the true clue in the chest; the rest is . . . clutter."

"Every bank in London!?"

"You wish to find the Zone, do you not? Then you must look for it."

"And you? What will you do in the meantime?"

Irene flounced down at the piano. "I? I shall practice. Is that not why you brought the box and had the piano tuned—so that I could solve and practice? Investigation is tedious, methodical business, Godfrey. I would be happy, of course, to visit the banks, but, as your father's only available heir, you alone can claim the contents of any safe-deposit box you find. As I said, you are the key, quite literally."

"There is no guarantee that I will find anything."

"There is never any guarantee of anything. Do let us know how you progress."

He took the ring of keys in reluctant custody and bid us good day.

"Irene!" I sat in the chair Godfrey had vacated. "It is cruel of you to set Godfrey such a massive task."

"Cruel but necessary. Oh, Nell . . ." Her hands struck a dissonant chord on the keys. "I know not what else to try, save the keys. I would rather have him think that I was being high-handed than that I should have an obvious treasure trove of clues before me and not be able to solve a single one."

" 'Pride goeth before a fall,' " I quoted. "But I do not believe that is the reason that you set Godfrey on such a chase."

"What other reason would I have, pray?"

"This quest will occupy him greatly over the next weeks. You are anxious to limit your association with him."

"Why on earth should I wish to do that?" Irene was the picture of cavalier disinterest: her right elbow lying atop the piano, her studiedly innocent face propped by a gracefully posed right hand. Her left hand idled up the steps of an octave. "Godfrey has been most helpful to us since our return."

I recalled the truism of the right hand not knowing what the left is doing, but stated only the obvious. "He has been nigh indispensible and has single-handedly prodded you from a malaise over the Bohemian affair. You do not wish to be reminded that you are obliged to any man."

"How far-fetched, my dear Nell! You should consider becoming a writer of melodramas. I am only doing what Godfrey wishes: reviving my twin interests—mystery and music."

Godfrey had his revenge: he stayed away for an entire fortnight, calling one evening to report that Sherlock Holmes had indeed returned—a full week before.

"He called at your chambers a week ago and you did not tell me?" Irene demanded.

"I was most busy with the banks," Godfrey said with an air of false martydom. "Nothing of import transpired. We spoke for only five minutes. He went away apparently satisfied."

"How can you know with a man like that? You may have handed him the vital clue to the entire matter and never have known it."

"I doubt it," Godfrey said. "I am used to guarding my thoughts in court." He offered Irene a cigarette, which she took rather gracelessly.

"Oh, why am I cooped up here hiding from a phantom pursuit!" she cried, pacing our rented Turkish carpet. "What was he like?"

"Who? Holmes?" Godfrey smiled and leaned back in his chair to choose his words while Irene fretted with impatience.

She had already extracted my impression of the man, but he intrigued her like a legendary chimera: nothing would suit but that he be known to her in some ultimately personal manner.

Godfrey began his summation. "He was quick and to the point— a tall, almost cadaverous man in appearance, hawk-nosed and sharp as a hypodermic needle, with an astuteness that implies a man far beyond his years. I should not like to plead against him in court.

"He evinces a touch of the dramatic common only to slightly vain men, yet his hands and fingernails were blotted with what I first took for ink and later concluded was an assortment of chemicals, like those of a boy who has been toying with a magic set. The cold-blooded inquiry of the scientist resides in his eyes, yet he has the makings of a fine judge—mercilessly fair but unfailingly decisive. Not a man to kowtow to convention, I think, or to be intimidated by rank. There is a . . . certain machine-like acuity to his manner; he would be cold company to a woman, or a cat. I should rather earn his admiration than his enmity."

"Quite a thorough character sketch from five minutes' conversation," Irene mocked. "But you may not be the best judge of what a woman would find cold company."

"And *you* may not be the best judge of me," Godfrey returned, unruffled.

Chapter Twenty-nine

Music Lessons

⚜

St. John's Wood rang with music as that summer of 1887 fluttered into autumn. Irene soon engaged an instructor: even a few weeks away from her art had caused a diminution in range. She had a photograph of herself wearing Mr. Tiffany's dazzling corsage of diamonds reproduced, making it known through an agent that she was available for select concerts.

Her Continental experience had enhanced her reputation beyond tarnishing. Offers drifted in like falling leaves; Irene chose only the most prestigious. She avoided the operatic stage as too likely to be publicized abroad, instead evolving a program of Schumann songs, *"Frauenliebe und leben,"* which were well received.

Despite my joy at seeing Irene take up the notes and staff of her career again, both Godfrey and I harbored doubts. Once he called when Irene was at the dressmaker's, for her concert engagements required new gowns. He lifted the illustrated circular from the side table and studied Irene in her queenly evening dress, only a tiara missing to complete the picture.

"It is a bit more spectacular than Lillie Langtry's famous 'little black dress,' is it not?" I said.

"Irene could sell more than soap with this," he agreed. "It is right for her to sing again, but must she advertise herself so successfully?"

"You think it brazen?"

"Of course it's brazen—and brilliant!" Godfrey smiled. "I should expect nothing less of her. But the King of Bohemia will not have forgotten her. Such publicity may attract pursuit, may even kindle his jealousy and rage."

"He is to be married next spring. I have read it in the papers."

"A civil marriage will not distract him from losing Irene. She has outwitted him. Only the rare man will accept that from a woman."

"Would you?"

"I? I do not attempt to outwit her, therefore can never be outwitted by her. It is, as we say in law, moot. Do you think that I do not discern the real purpose of the nigh-hopeless task she has set me among the banks?"

I blushed but could not defend her.

"She is like my mother," he said abruptly, "mortally wounded by the way the world would limit her. To think that I am following her purpose will make her feel less constricted. Performing again will help also. I only wish that I were more certain the King of Bohemia will not strike at her as she becomes visible again."

"Do you not think that Irene has considered that fact?"

"Of course. She misses nothing. But I do not know whether she is ready to face it. And there is a difference."

Autumn came, and with the turning leaves even more concerts for Irene. I assisted Godfrey at chambers, even, on occasion, relieving him of the effort of contacting yet another bank. Our inquiries met only polite denials. No institution in London guarded a safe-deposit box engaged by the late Mr. John Norton.

"Then we shall have to widen our search to the surrounding cities," Godfrey said calmly.

I sometimes believed that he continued this systematic search in the perverse hope of proving to Irene that the Zone was within reach.

I was reminded of fairy tales where the princess sets her suitor an impossible quest to prove his worth, though surely Godfrey was no suitor and Irene certainly not a princess, much less a queen.

Yet Irene was evading something, as Godfrey had implied. Whether it was her past—or the future—I could not say. It was sad to think that Godfrey might be paying the price owed by the King of Bohemia.

We heard no more of Mr. Holmes, although Mr. Tiffany was often in the newspapers as the grande dames of American commerce— the Mmes. Pulitzer, Vanderbilt, Astor and Stanford—proceeded to snap up the best of the French crown jewels.

Still, none of them had ever worn the spectacular diamond corsage that glittered from shoulder to hip like a royal sash of office on Irene's concert bills. That November a Tiffany case arrived by messenger. The leather box enfolded a single row of diamonds set on a velvet collar and banded by pearls; a note from Mr. Tiffany thanked Irene for stirring global interest in the soon-to-be offered corsage. The necklace suited her for concerts, as the supple velvet would not impede her singing.

Irene felt secure enough to begin taking solitary drives in the landau with John Jewett at the reins each afternoon at five, returning for dinner at seven. This salutory combination of freedom and fresh air emphasized the pinked cheeks and sparkling eyes I had not seen since my first days in Bohemia.

So matters settled into a well-worn rut, as carriage wheels carve tracks into fresh snow. Yet snow melts. I had a sense of terrible anticipation, as if all our lives were hanging fire before some unforeseen, climactic event. I blamed my overimaginative tendencies and applied myself more industriously to typewriting, as Irene concentrated on her singing and Godfrey contacted outlying banks when he had time.

The brightest spots during those dark, London winter days were the enthusiastic receptions of Irene's recitals.

"I cannot account for it!" she complained in the landau on our way home from her latest performance. "When I poured my energies into a career in London, I was ignored. Now that I am forced to abandon my operatic ambitions and give only the occasional discreet concert, Success falls upon her knees to me!"

"Not every apple on a tree sours at the same time," I said, unearthing an ancient Shropshire proverb.

"Enjoy Dame Success's fulsome bows," Godfrey urged. "She dispenses blows soon enough."

The horse's hooves padded through the light snow coating the cobblestones. Passing gaslights bloomed at the carriage windows, striking fire from the thin line of diamonds at Irene's throat, painting Godfrey's formal shirtfront an almost phosphorescent white.

It was a warm and comfortable moment. Godfrey always attended Irene's concerts, as did I, and invariably escorted us home afterward. Like myself, he realized that Irene needed conversation following a performance, that her artistic nature did not taper off with the last note, but required a period of activity before facing sleep.

Nevertheless, there was peace in our very vivacity. We three seemed suspended in a scene from a Christmas globe that shakes slow-falling snow upon its little world. In the snug carriage interior, our feet upon hot bricks, it seemed that hardship and unhappiness could never touch any of us again.

We descended before Briony Lodge while Jewett took the equipage around to the mews. Caps of snow crowned the gateposts; falling snowflakes carpeted the walk and sifted against the lighted windowpanes.

Godfrey took our elbows and we minced over the cold white carpet nature had provided. Our footsteps ruffled its smoothness as our skirts etched odd swirling patterns in the snow. The entire scene glimmered under a midnight blend of gaslight and moonlight.

Irene paused on the doorstep with a sigh. "It is good to be home. This is the first place I—what is it, Godfrey?"

He had taken the key from her and unlocked the door, but it did not open, despite the click of the chamber. From within the house, where presumably Mrs. Seaton slept, came a muffled thump.

"She'll just have to leave her bed and let us in if the key's caught," Irene said.

Godfrey's head lifted as another bump sounded within. In a moment he had overleaped the steps and was ploughing into the snow-shrouded hedges before the sitting room windows.

He rattled a window frame, forcing the flimsy lock and jumping through it as if it were a door. A sound of scrabbling within the house magnified, accompanied now by grunts and inarticulate curses.

Irene turned as if to follow Godfrey's eccentric entrance route, but I clutched her arm, just in time.

Behind us the front door cracked open. We spun to confront two unfamiliar male faces as startled as our own. The men pushed roughly past us, running down the narrow aisle of snow and through the gate before vanishing into the foggy white corridor of the street beyond.

Another man loomed in the doorway. I lifted my reticule in defense, but Godfrey's voice deflected my blow.

"Are you both all right? Come in, though I can't recommend the sight."

He led us into the hallway, where a side chair lay askew by the wall, and locked the door behind us.

"The photograph?" Irene's voice was chiller than the night.

"Haven't looked," Godfrey said, winded. "Better to secure the house first."

We lit what lamps we could to cast light into the villa's darkened corners. Godfrey refastened the sitting-room window against the riffling snow, drawing the blinds. The upheld lamps cast our distorted shadows upon a landscape of disordered furniture. Cushions were scattered, drawers sagged and rugs lay rumpled, as if moles had tunneled under them.

Godfrey proceeded to search the premises. Below-stairs we found Mrs. Seaton bound and gagged in the pantry. Casanova, ungagged as usual in the dining room, shrilly whistled "Hsst! hsst!," a new saying owed to the burglars. I tended Mrs. Seaton while Godfrey and Irene explored the upstairs, floors creaking with their steps. I finally rejoined them in the first floor hall, where we all stared at the disarray of Irene's bedroom. Her wardrobe shrouded the furnishings, as if some clumsy maid had resorted to covering the furniture with clothing instead of dustcloths.

I was not certain that it was proper for Godfrey to observe the storm of Irene's most personal items of apparel, but forgot my reservations when I saw the state of my own room as well.

"What have they gained from this upheaval?" Godfrey asked.

"Nothing that I can see." Irene moved stiffly through the chaos. "Is it safe yet to inspect the compartment?"

"We are alone, I believe," he said.

"I sent Mrs. Seaton to bed with a soothing tisane," said I. "She is more indignant at the invasion of her realm than injured."

In the sitting room, Irene quickly approached the fireplace wall and pressed the secret panel. The mechanism tripped obligingly open. She withdrew the two Tiffany jewel boxes and, lastly, the photograph.

She sat with a sigh on the cushionless chaise longue, pausing for the first time to turn back her veil and draw off her gloves.

"Housebreakers?" I suggested hopefully.

"Curious housebreakers," Godfrey said with a grim smile, "who brace the front door against early interruption—and easy escape— then flee past the lady of the house without pausing to tear the diamonds from her neck."

I stiffened to realize how vulnerable Irene and I had been as we faced those desperate men on the threshold.

"Godfrey, have you been engaging in fisticuffs?" Irene asked suddenly.

By the lamplight I saw a dark smudge angling across his cheekbone. "Ruffians!" I said.

"Nothing so elegant as fisticuffs, Irene." Godfrey smiled ruefully. "More in the nature of a blind scuffle in the dark. And those men were nothing so rude as 'ruffians,' my dear Nell. They said not a word when I challenged them; simply ran. I suspect they speak Bohemian."

"The disarray?" Irene wondered.

"These are not professional burglars, who know how to search without advertising their presence. They were in haste, hence the destruction."

"But the photograph is safe." Irene studied the broken room. "How . . . pathetic of Willie to have sent men to do this and still come away empty-handed." She glanced at Godfrey. "I suppose you will chide me for my resurgent singing career, for having brought this distasteful attack down on our heads."

"No, I congratulate you upon it. Apparently your new fame has reached all the way to Bohemia. Do you still think he might wish to abduct you?"

Irene shook her head until the melted snowflakes on her veiling shone like diamonds and trembled free like dew. "No. He is concerned only for himself now, for his . . . security. How it must frighten him to know that I am free, with the photograph, and have no reason to protect him because I feel obliged to protect my own reputation. Such hypocrisy he practices!"

"Frightened men are dangerous," Godfrey warned.

"So are free women," Irene replied.

"Must we move now?" I wondered.

"No." Irene stood. "We are safer where they think there is nothing to be found. Besides, the compartment remains secret. No one will find it."

⚜   ⚜   ⚜

Shortly after Christmas we were burgled again. The signs were slight but telling.

"Professionals this time," Irene said, her voice hard.

"Godfrey will not like it."

"Godfrey need not know."

"But he has been so kind—" I protested.

"Precisely why I do not wish to worry him, dear Nell. He is occupied quite enough. Now drink your tea and fret no more about the King of Bohemia's little games. He who has lost his Queen always pushes the pawns about."

"I don't play chess."

"Perhaps I exaggerated my figure of speech. This King is about to gain a Queen, after all. Have you seen the afternoon edition of the *Telegraph*?"

"Is your portrait in it?"

"No, but hers is."

"Hers?"

"Clotilde Loatheman von Saxon-mine-again, or whatever she is called. Would you like to see her?"

"Certainly not. She cannot be half so handsome as you!"

"Handsome is as handsome does, and Clotilde does very well in the blue-blood department. Have a look!"

There was nothing to do but take the rustling pages Irene forced upon me. My eye fell on the offending likeness instantly—a portrait of one of those broad-browed, thin-skinned, pale-haired Nordic women whose noses could well serve as a ski slope. So I told Irene, at any rate.

She beamed. "Sometimes, Nell, your descriptive powers verge on the poetic! No wonder Mr. Wilde was so enamored. But have you read her pedigree?"

"It is almost as long as that of Mrs. Chandeley-Monningham's pekinese in Shropshire," I commented. "But of course, *his* ancestors' nobility traces back to ancient China. I suspect the King of Scandinavia's daughter has a pedigree that only extends back to the Dark Ages; before that, enter the Huns."

"Really, Nell, had you not been so tenderly reared in the parsonage, I believe we could have made a first-class society cat of you! I had no idea you ever knew anyone named Mrs. Chandeley-Monningham!"

"Even Shropshire has its country bumpkins," I retorted.

Irene began giggling in a way that I could only describe as girlish, and so Godfrey found us when he arrived.

We had by then descended to speculation on the size of the unfortunate Clotilde's feet, which Irene likened to a form of American savage transport she called "snowshoes." She was in the process of describing this fanciful footwear when Mrs. Seaton showed Godfrey into the sitting room.

"Is it charades?" he asked eagerly, "because if it is, I have a mime to offer as well."

"Indeed." Irene sat back to give Godfrey the floor.

This he took full advantage of, pacing the carpet, harried and hat in hand, knocking at many doors to make a pantomimed request.

"A beggar!" Irene guessed.

He quelled her with a look. "Only an agent of the merciless Irene Adler."

Next Godfrey trudged down some mythical steps, lower and lower. He seemed to dodge hanging spider webs. He knelt before something he regarded with awe.

"A minister!" I offered.

"Sir Galahad and the Holy Grail," said Irene.

"Only a worshiper at the feet of Mammon, I fear," Godfrey admitted.

His hands drew something toward him. He turned on one knee and presented the vacancy on his palms to Irene.

"I give up," she sputtered through her laughter. "You are too outrageously obscure."

"The Worthington Bank of Islington went bankrupt eighteen years ago," he told her. "Its unclaimed resources are stored in a warehouse in the Brixton Road. Among them is—"

"A safe-deposit box in the name of John Norton!" Irene stood, her eyes blazing with unexpected triumph. "I am brilliant! And you, dear Godfrey, are"—she gazed into his eyes as he knelt before her "—ridiculously diligent. Now get up and let us go to the Brixton Road!"

"First I require the keys to your heart."

"What keys?" she demanded, growing restless at their mock-courtship pose, at Godfrey's wicked smile.

"What heart?" I murmured under my breath.

"The keys are in the music room—" Irene began, moving to get them.

Godfrey captured her hand with melodramatic finesse. "Fetch them, Nell," he ordered.

"I'll get them; stay!" Irene said.

Torn between two masters, I naturally obeyed the one least likely to take offense and fled the room. I found the keys and returned them to Irene, hoping to assuage both my household gods at once.

"The keys, fair queen!" Godfrey importuned.

She slapped the ring ungraciously in his upheld hand. "Oh, very well. You must have your applause, I suppose. Fairly done. Rise, I dub you Sir Persistence."

He rose just enough to seat himself on the sofa and turn the keyring in his hands. Irene stood for a moment, then sank reluctantly beside him.

A strange, awkward silence settled over us, broken only by the jingle of keys in Godfrey's restless hands.

"There are many keys in my father's ringdom," he quipped at last. Suddenly we all laughed in shared delight. "Which one shall open it?"

"We shall try all if we have to," Irene said.

Her eye fell on the newspaper pages, which had dropped to the carpet in the excitement. The likeness of Clotilde Lothman von Saxe-Meningen stared up at us.

Godfrey took Irene's clasped hands in one of his and, as they unfolded, filled them with the ring of tarnished keys.

"Mystery and music, Irene," he reminded her. "They are your proper kingdom."

She regarded the many-shaped keys spilling like brazen jewels from her palms.

"Both pursuits require keys," she said, "but I did not expect such a choice. These . . . possibilities"—she shook her hands until the keys and rings chimed like little bells—"result from my wit and Godfrey's work, not any pedigree. I will follow them wherever they lead. I think that this is the lesson I learned in Bohemia."

Chapter Thirty

The Good Book

~~❦~~

A new object lay on the music room table along with the odd-
ments from Black Jack Norton's treasure chest—a book in an
elderly tobacco-brown binding.

This small rectangular object, plain save for the title and author's
name gold-stamped on the spine and front cover, was the sole fruit
of plundering the safe-deposit box.

"Why would he hide away this, of all things?" Godfrey demanded
in utter mystification.

"He had no attachment to your mother's novels as the source of
his brief good fortune?" Irene wondered.

"Good heavens, no! He abominated her fiction works. I can't believe that he ever had one in his possession, much less that he read
one."

"Did you?" Irene said.

Godfrey looked startled. "I? Well . . . no. I—I was not of the age
to read these genteel romances and then, she had stopped publishing
and it . . . never occurred to me."

"But you possess some?"

"I suppose so, somewhere among my bookshelves."

Irene cast her eyes heavenward, although the only illumination they found was the glow of the ceiling-hung gasolier. "So passes all artistic glory. Her own son."

"Her books were considered suitable for a female audience," Godfrey said stiffly. "For all that I resented my father commandeering the income from them, it never occurred to me to actually read one. And once she was dead, the exercise would have been sad as well as pointless."

Irene weighed the little book on her palm. "Where best to hide the key to a treasure but in an out-of-print book by a deceased author, one that the author's own sons—and one's own sole heirs—can be counted upon to overlook?"

"I don't follow you, Irene," I put in. Godfrey, properly chastened for filial delinquency if not literary snobbery, remained silent.

"If Black Jack Norton loathed his wife's novels," she said, "why hide even one, with the key buried in a mass of keys? I tried twenty keys before finding one that turned that rusted old lock. This is the true clue to the Zone's whereabouts. It must have pleased your father's perverse sense of humor to know that if he died with the secret to the Zone forgotten, it would be because his wife's work was forgotten by all, even his sons. Especially his sons."

"You are not being fair to Godfrey, Irene. He has been an exemplary son to both his parents. Certainly he supported his mother when no one else would."

"Hear, hear," she said in good humor. "But his time would have been better spent reading his mother's tomes, for then we might know why"—Irene peered at the spine's glinting gold—"*Cloris of the Crossroads* was so particularly important to the late Black Jack Norton."

"A message might be pricked out beneath certain letters," Godfrey suggested.

"Wonderful! I shall set Nell and her pince-nez to reading this devilishly small type looking for pricks that are not merely the tracks of bookworms!"

Irene set the volume down, slightly open, on its spine, then did it again. And again.

"It opens to variant pages, Irene," Godfrey said. "I already attempted that trick; it is not the clue."

"Invisible ink!" said I with sudden inspiration.

"And how do we make it visible?" Irene said.

"Hold it over a fire, like in the melodramas!"

"These brittle old pages would flash into flames. Besides, Black Jack could have written in invisible ink on anything. He did not need one of his wife's books."

"Except that he thought no one would look into it," Godfrey reminded Irene, reviving her own argument.

"There is only one thing to do," Irene declared.

"What?" we begged, glad of any action.

"I will have to read the book myself."

Irene marched to the sitting room, sat and began reading. So she remained that entire afternoon, hardly stirring even when I rustled into the room at twilight to light the lamp at her elbow.

Godfrey and I toyed with the chess pieces in the music room.

"Do you play?" he asked me once, glancing at the piano.

"I was taught to execute a few pieces—and execute them I did. I dare not touch the keys with Irene nearby; I would not benefit by comparison. Were you—are you—musical?"

He laughed. "As musical as a hedgehog! I am of a more literal bent, I fear, as are you. The mathematics of music—and the puzzling aspects of mystery, go hand in hand."

"Yet we unmusical creatures attend Irene's performances."

"They also serve who only sit and clap," Godfrey observed, paraphrasing Milton.

I drew the keys across the tablecloth, watching them spin randomly on the ring. It was the chance aspect of mystery that annoyed me, the unpredictable combination of the tedious and the inspired.

The chiming keys recalled the tinkling chimes in the Prague orchestra pit. "The King of Bohemia must have been most musical," I mused. "He wept to see Irene sing."

Godfrey was quiet for a moment. "Then we differ, he and I. If I would weep, it would be to see her *not* sing."

"Perhaps that is not a matter of music at all, Godfrey. For all his easy feeling, the King had little faith in Irene. And you can take credit for rousing her from her malaise."

"I have done nothing. Work has, in both arenas."

We heard a single clap from the sitting room. Irene found us moments later, the finished novel held prayerfully between her hands.

"Well?" Godfrey rose.

"I have learned much. Cloris of the Crossroads was the only daughter of a harsh Scottish laird, an innocent driven onto the moors for daring to love a crofter's son. After much travail she had a hand in rescuing Bonnie Prince Charlie, fomenting an uprising of the Scots peasantry and engaging in a secret mission to the Court of France."

Godfrey sat beside me again. "And you would have had me read this folderol? Then the book is a *cul-de-sac*."

"Not necessarily, but I shall have to think it over. It would make a grand opera—tragedy both political and personal with room for tender arias among the heather . . . Do you remember, Godfrey, where your mother was living when she wrote it?"

"How can I forget? In Chelsea, down the street from that impecunious Leigh Hunt and half the other poor but artistic denizens of Chelsea in that period. It's hard to credit that the same neighborhood is so fashionable three decades later. Tite Street, I believe."

"The number?"

"Sixteen. But the neighborhood has changed utterly since."

"Hmm," Irene said, and would say no more.

I put my hand out for the book. "May I read it now that you have finished?"

Irene playfully withdrew it. "I do not know, Nell, it is full of toil and trouble of a most sordid nature, not to mention certain ardent although unsanctified unions."

"Oh, Irene, don't be such a prig! It's Godfrey's mother's book and he is the one to say whether I shall read it or not."

"Then you shall," Godfrey obliged, "for two heads may bring more light to bear on the puzzle. And after you are finished, *I* will read it."

"This literary unanimity is admirable," Irene said, "but I think it will get us nowhere."

My opportunity to consume *Cloris of the Crossroads* was short-lived, however. Irene commandeered me at eleven the next morning.

"Hurry, Nell. The landau is coming around shortly and you must dress better than that when calling upon your dear former admirer, Mr. Oscar Wilde."

"We have not seen that popinjay in years; he is not my admirer. And you claim that we are going to *call* upon the creature?"

"Indeed."

"Where?"

"At his home, of course. Number sixteen, Tite Street."

This effectively silenced me. After adding a grander jacket and hat, gloves and reticule to my attire, I was ready to join Irene in her mysterious journey.

Mr. Wilde had married in the years since we had seen him, Irene informed me in the carriage.

"You must be careful to remain discreet before his wife, Constance," she twitted me, as if I were the Siren of Warsaw.

"I shall have no difficulty in regarding Mr. Wilde with the same propriety as before," said I.

Tite Street was a short avenue off the Royal Hospital Road a bit east of the Stokers' residence on Cheyne Walk, if they indeed still resided there. Irene thought not. The row of eighteenth-century, four-story red brick dwellings peered through a lacework of bare tree limbs. Number sixteen was indistinguishable from its fellows, though I had expected a design of lilies, or at least sunflowers, to decorate the door, which was painted a bilious yellow.

The interior was not as outré as I had anticipated—strange floral borders of gold leaf painted on dark walls, perhaps, Oriental fabrics and a profusion of Japanese blue ceramic ware so popular among the set, with peacock feathers as profuse as parlor palms.

Instead, I was favorably impressed by the cool sitting room shades of dull gold and cream played against the chaste white carved mantelpiece and a frieze of framed etchings along two walls.

I was relieved to hear from Mrs. Wilde's lips that her husband was at the "office," having accepted the editorship of *The Woman's World* magazine the previous summer.

"And you yourself contribute, do you not?" Irene asked as we seated ourselves at Mrs. Wilde's invitation. "Are you not the author of those charming articles on muffs? I must confess a certain partiality to muffs myself."

"Why thank you, Miss Adler. My husband has noted your return to the London concert scene. He mentioned that he had been an admirer of your vocal talent years ago."

Mrs. Wilde was a slim, grave little woman with lovely eyes. The folds of loose aesthetic dress she favored—or her famous husband imposed—overwhelmed her delicate figure, but I was not offended by this unconventional attire, for if any one attribute shone from the visage of Constance Wilde, it was a sober sweetness.

"We have heard so much of your home, it is quite the marvel of Chelsea," Irene went on. "May we see it?"

I readied myself to blush at my friend's forward request, but Constance Wilde leaped up as if delighted to have been given a mission. She led us into the dining room with its white enameled dado and chairs. Charming accent pieces of blue and yellow heralded the forthcoming spring year-round. We exclaimed quite sincere praises of the decor.

"No wonder Mr. Wilde now edits a magazine of fashion and society," Irene noted, "his sense of style and simplicity bounds ahead of the most radical among us."

"If only I could persuade him to exercise that simplicity in his own lair," Mrs. Wilde said, leading us upstairs to the poet's study.

A burst of buttercup yellow walls erased the grey day outside. Curios and books littered the chamber, reminding me of the male clutter in Godfrey's chambers. Mrs. Wilde paused at a chair set before what was obviously the owner's writing table. Her fingers stroked the wood.

"It was Carlyle's. So many of his things were sold after his death."

I stared at the surface upon which Carlyle scribbled his

masterworks of history, wondering if any more immortal writings would be scribed across that sere wooden expanse.

"Mr. Wilde is not the first writer to dwell here," Irene said suddenly, "in this very house."

"Indeed?" Constance Wilde was not surprised. "Writers and artists have called Tite Street home for decades. Jimmie Whistler lived down the road until recently. A foolish suit on his part has reduced his means. Oscar tried to warn him . . ."

"I am thinking of an earlier resident, the mother of an acquaintance of mine," Irene went on. "Caroline Norton, the versifier and novelist."

Mrs. Wilde offered a puzzled smile; clearly she had heard nothing of the woman.

"You did not find souvenirs of another writer in the house?"

"Anything we found is gone now. The rooms were completely redecorated on our marriage, under the guidance of Mr. Whistler—when Oscar would deign to take it," she added. "They are rather cross with each other now, I fear."

"Two artists, like dueling peacocks both fanning their glorious tails, no doubt," Irene said.

"Exactly. Two outraged peacocks, more likely. Have you ever heard a peacock scream, Miss Adler? The sound is unearthly. Mr. Carlyle, disturbed in his work by such while he lived, called them 'demon fowls.' I know how they shriek because Mr. Rossetti kept peacocks; since his death some have wandered wild into the neighborhood."

"What a charming neighborhood it is." We began wending our way downstairs again, Irene pausing to glance out of the landing window. "Gracious, what a delightful garden you have as well."

"The winter still holds sway. It will charm more when the vines green."

"And that most picturesque stone cross—is is it something precious from your husband's Irish youth?"

"The cross . . . ?"

Mrs. Wilde leaned into the light to remind herself of the object of Irene's inquiry, a small stone monument of the kind that dots graveyards and landmarks in Ireland, a cross with a circle uniting its four diverging arms. In the dull daylight her pallor emphasized the lines that two swiftly successive childbirths had etched in her countenance. No doubt I shall soon look as worn as a token of my custody of Casanova.

"Nothing to do with Oscar, save that it is Irish," she said of the cross. "A garden ruin we inherited that has leaned forever at that disreputable angle. I wanted to straighten it, but Oscar insisted that aesthetics favor any veer from the upright. 'A ruinous lean has its own allure,' he said, 'greater than the perfectly upright pillars of rectitude.' Oftentimes I can hardly keep up with his charming perversity."

"I should not wonder," Irene murmured sympathetically. "No doubt your children shall be rising from their naps soon; we must say good-day."

"I will tell Oscar of your call, Miss Adler—and you, Miss—" She glanced at Irene's card to no avail, since my name was not on it.

"Huxleigh."

With polite smiles we went down the several steps and paced our way back to the carriage, which Irene had left by the Royal Hospital gates.

"A pointless visit, with Mr. Wilde out," I mentioned as we strolled under the skeletal branches. "A pity he no longer works at home."

"On the contrary, a most fruitful exploration. Now I must determine what to do about it. Perhaps the most courteous thing would be to consult Godfrey, since his mother is concerned, if not his Zone of Diamonds."

"Irene! You know where the Zone of Diamonds is?"

"Of course. Oscar Wilde has it."

"Oh, but—" I stopped walking, but Irene caught my wrist and urged me on.

"He doesn't *know* he has it, silly. Now the problem remains how to repossess it without him knowing that we do so."

"Is that not . . . larcenous? He is not a rich man, despite his fame."

Irene, stiffening, looked at me as if I had suddenly turned into a Medusa of moral turpitude.

"Nonsense. He never paid me for the return of his cross of gold. Now he will, in kind, and he will not even be troubled by knowing about it. What could be more simple? Next you will be telling me that the bauble is rightfully Godfrey's."

"You do not mean to abscond with it, leave Godfrey without any fruits of his labor after all he has done for us, and for you?"

"He has made himself useful, as a good barrister should. Besides, I have paid for his professional services."

"Irene! All men are not the King of Bohemia. You must not be callous. Surely Godfrey is of more consequence to you than, than . . . a luggage porter!"

"You confuse matters of the heart with those of head. Good business is never a pity, as Mr. Tiffany quite rightfully corrected me not a year ago. I would I had heard his advice before engaging on my charade in Bohemia. If I had thought more of myself and my career then, I should never have been lulled into such a weak position. It will not happen again."

"Love and admiration are not weaknesses!"

"But to wish to *be* loved and admired is, my dear Nell—an addictive emotion that we of the artistic bent often undergo, as Mr. Wilde could tell you in iambic pentameter. I've no doubt that poor woman behind us 'loves and admires' her aesthetic husband, for all the good it will do her, for all the good it did Caroline Norton when she was a bride. She must have married Black Jack for some reason, though why an intelligent woman who prizes her independence would ever marry is quite beyond me."

"Irene, I feared you had lost your capacity to shock me, but I see that I was grievously wrong."

"Good." Irene smiled as we neared our carriage. "Mr. Wilde is indubitably right about one thing: the capacity to shock is pure sweetness in a sour world."

At that we entered the landau and returned to St. John's Wood. I held my tongue during that long ride, having learned from my association with Irene Adler that the only antidote to her desire to shock was my ability to keep still.

Chapter Thirty-one

Twilight Zone

❦

Dusk came to Chelsea as the sun sank into the grey, wavy mirror of the river Thames and wraiths of fog twined through the wrought-iron fences of Tite Street and Swan Walk and Cheyne Row. Figured curtains cast ghostly glows against the streetside windows as the lamplight streamed through their diaphanous folds. The river's stale perfume mingled with the homely odors of coal fires piping from a dozen surrounding chimneys, invisible in the lowering dark.

I clasped my jacket collar closer against the cold and fog, wondering how I came to be roaming picturesque Chelsea by twilight.

From the adjacent Royal Hospital grounds came hoarse whispers of mischief, while the Physic Garden across the way echoed with sounds of attempted illegal entry.

I myself was skulking about Oscar Wilde's garden in the dusk, trying desperately not to sneeze.

"Irene," I croaked, "we shall catch our deaths—or at least bring the police down upon us."

"Nonsense. We are invited guests, hardly trespassers."

"Under false pretenses!"

"Only we know that."

"Why did you send Godfrey off to Carlyle's former house?"

"Because that is how he is most useful: leading the bulk of the party as far as possible afield."

"Surely this racket shall attract undesirable interest—won't Mrs. Wilde notice us poking about her garden?"

"Certainly we shall attract attention if you continue questioning me in such ringing tones. Your whisper reeks more of the stage than of the confessional."

"I cannot help it! I am contracting the influenza already, I am sure. Oh! We shall be apprehended, and such a scandal will result."

"Nonsense," Irene repeated. "After all, the festivities are in my honor, are they not? One does not arrest the guest of honor."

"You call this noxious stumble through the damp and dark of a Chelsea evening a festivity?"

"We may have much to celebrate if things go as I planned. Here, I have stubbed my boot-toe on something. Is it that Celtic cross?"

"Perhaps. It is rough and wet and in our way—why can we not carry a torch, as the other parties do? Now that the sun is gone it is nearly pitch dark."

"Because we wish to attract no unnecessary attention—and we need our hands free to dig."

"Dig? Not again? The rules were that only the chief prize should require digging for; surely it is not concealed at the host's very house? You set the rules yourself."

"The rules are for the rest of the hunters and the ordinary objects of the hunt. We are after special game, Nell. Ah, it is loose! Help me lay it back upon the ground."

"Overturning crosses, even Celtic ones, is not something my father would have endorsed."

"This is a garden ornament only, nothing sacred. Lean into it, Penelope. It will take both of our full weights to dislodge."

I did as commanded, resting my back against the cross and pushing my booted feet deep into the dead leaves and wet turf surrounding it.

Suddenly and silently, it toppled, I collapsing atop it.

"Quickly! We must dig." Irene thrust a wooden stake into my hand.

My hand followed the handle down to a spade-shaped end, garnering several splinters in my woolen gloves. "This spade is tiny!"

"What else would fit into my petticoat pockets? These are toy spades, for children."

"Really, Irene. This is your greatest madness yet, an expedition out of Gilbert and Sullivan. I know not whether to laugh or to cry."

"Do neither," she advised tersely from the dark. "Dig."

At least I was already upon the ground. I got to my knees in the soggy leaves and joined Irene in clawing at the lumpen earth with my petite implement.

The sky was overcast, though a pallid moon shone through the lime trees as the winds swept its face free of clouds. That milky glow was our only illumination. Irene's face looked dead white; the fallen cross had attained the color of long-dead bone. Fortunately, I could not see myself.

"Why could you not have enlisted Godfrey for this mission?" I grumbled as the scent of overturned earth and wet wool gloves assailed my nostrils. I quailed to think what creatures of the clay our frantic and half-blind digging was disinterring . . .

"He is not aware of it," she replied, digging as madly as I.

My child's shovel struck something rock-hard, conveying a shudder all the way to my shoulders. Irene, hearing the dull chime of metal on sterner stuff than clay, applied her own implement to the spot until our shovel blades clashed like tangled knitting needles.

"I'll dig and you draw the dirt aside," Irene suggested hoarsely.

"The damp is bad for your voice, I knew it!"

"Hush. I will happily stay mute for a week if we find what I suspect we will. There—a nice squarish sort of rock we have found. Buried treasure."

"Likely only some deceased bird or kitten a child buried near the cross."

"We have neither the light nor privacy to investigate now. I will slip our prize into the commodious pocket I have sewn into my pet-ticoat, then we will lay our little shovels to rest in Mother Earth and give them a decent burial. Poor things, they have served in their time and now 'tis done."

Irene stood and began kicking clods of dirt into the hole we had made. Raising the cross was four times more difficult than overturning it, but eventually it stood in place—properly askew. We began tamp-ing down the surrounding earth, Irene pounding her feet upon the site like a frenzied Spanish dancer, her skirts caught in her hand so her pre-cious box should not be rattled.

"Now may we leave?" I said.

"Of course. We must repair to the Physic Garden to collect our legitimate quarry."

I sneezed my displeasure, but Irene was already tripping toward the house, which was fortunately still empty except for the maid, and out to the street.

We returned an hour later to the Wilde residence to find the mel-low sitting and dining rooms afire with lamps and a merry company of red nosed denizens of Chelsea gathered there, surrounded by an arcane collection of trivia.

In removing my wraps before the mirror I saw my nose was as cherry-bright as the others'—though Irene maintained a dignified pal-lor despite her exertions. When she spoke, however, her voice rumbled like a foghorn.

"Punch?" Godfrey joined us, bearing cups of a steaming libation. We downed it ravenously, like twin Oliver Twists in hopes of more.

"How went your hunt?" Godfrey asked, but before Irene could an-swer, our towering host approached, a feather duster rakishly sprouting from his breast pocket.

"My dear Miss Adler and the classical Miss Huxleigh! You are the last to return. What an inspired idea it was to suggest a scavenger hunt instead of the usual Sunday tea. It has all been too, too utterly delicious fun. Shall we compare lists and see who has carried off the prize?"

"By all means." Irene joined the ladies by sitting demurely on the sofa arm, the only vacant perch. The gentlemen lounged against the dado with their punch cups tilted.

Godfrey drew a straight-backed chair from the dining room into the circle for me, and the evening's ceremony began. Each participant flaunted the fruits of their night's hunting: several had dead grape clusters from the late Mr. Carlyle's garden. Irene produced a peacock feather she claimed had been dropped by one of the late Dante Gabriel Rossetti's feral flock, which still wandered the vicinity.

Perfectly respectable actors, writers and painters (if any of those can be deemed perfectly respectable or even imperfectly so) flourished common objects and sprigs of pirated vegetation as though they were pearls of great price. Mr. Wilde had obtained the required feather duster from the cook three doors down, for instance, and you would have thought he had talked an angel out of its wings, such was the pride he took in its acquisition.

There were herbal trophies from the Physic Garden, that relic of the seventeenth-century botanical garden which provided America with the cotton seed that resulted in Civil War. I could not approve of this venerable site's plundering. The room fairly reeked of dessicated eucalyptus, scents overcome only by the punch, which Godfrey later told me was rum. Had I known, I never would have touched it, no matter how warming. As it was, I had three cups before I learned its composition.

Perhaps that is why we women were able to laugh at the sorry state of our skirts; Irene and I were not the only ones to have dampened ourselves—several gentleman wore wet and baggy knees.

The prize of the entire hunt was to be one of Oscar Wilde's yellow silk neckcloths with a mother-of-pearl cravat pin, which had been buried earlier that day and which no one had found.

The company deliberated at some length before declaring Bram Stoker the winner for having collected the most items from his list. He smiled with touching pleasure, this red-bearded giant, and gazed upon his tawdry array as if they were jewels.

"You see, Irene." I leaned close to whisper into her ear. "*You* likely have unearthed the major prize, but foolishly refuse to examine it."

"Yes . . . and no," she said.

"Poor Irene!" Mrs. Wilde said suddenly. "The hunt was in your honor and you have won nothing! That hardly seems fair."

"I have seen my friends enjoy themselves; that is reward enough," Irene answered, with a salute of her punch cup to the company.

Everyone toasted her sentiments. Our carriage arrived soon after, for St. John's Wood was a long drive. At Briony Lodge Irene showed a strange disinclination to examine her buried treasure. I was too weary and influenced by the rum to care. We parted to our separate chambers, but I could not resist making a prediction.

"You have unearthed no more than a tumbled array of bird bones and I am glad I shall not be present to see you discover it. Or, if you were lucky, you have recovered Mr. Wilde's saffron silk square and pearl cravat pin," I added thickly, longing for the sheets where Mrs. Seaton had installed flannel-wrapped warming pans for our feet. "You have carried off the prize of the scavenger hunt without even claiming it."

"Perhaps," Irene conceded hoarsely from the doorway of her bedchamber, "we could consider that poetic justice."

Chapter Thirty-two

Diamonds are Forever

❧

The morrow was chill. Irene's voice had faded to a croak and I fought the sniffles. Rain rapped its fingers on our windows all day long, while Irene played bits and pieces of a half-dozen composers and I refused to inquire after the boxy rock she had unearthed in Oscar Wilde's garden.

Godfrey arrived unannounced that afternoon, unimpaired by the previous night's labors but oddly strained. He joined us in the music room.

"We are most mawkish today," Irene warned him in a contralto rumble.

His eyebrows raised at her unlovely speaking voice, then he studied my reddened features. "I fear you will feel more mawkish when you hear my news."

We cocked our heads in tandem, neither wishing to waste our energies in speaking.

Godfrey spread his hands helplessly. "I discreetly induced a man in the foreign office to apprise me of any unusual movements by London-bound Bohemians."

Irene pressed a dramatic, trembling chord on the piano keys, as

if underlining the dialogue at a melodrama. Godfrey ignored her ir-
reverent response.

"I have learned only this morning that a . . . personage from
Prague has reached London."

Irene's fingers left the keys. The little color remaining left her
face. "A personage? What does that mean?"

"It means that the traveler is identified as 'Count von Kramm, a
Bohemian nobleman.'"

"That is ridiculous." She paused to gather some timbre for her
shattered voice. "No such nobleman resided in Prague when I was
there. You think this man is an agent of the King?"

Godfrey frowned. "My dear Irene, I think he *is* the King."

"Even more ridiculous! The King is to marry this spring. Why
rush to London when his agents have been unable to procure the photograph after two attempts?"

"Two? You have not been frank with me."

Godfrey looked quite angry. I really wished myself out of the
room, but Godfrey had paused near the doorway and there was no
gracious exit for me. I cleared my throat but neither one heeded me.

Irene stood slowly, her fingers fanned at her throat as though to
press the voice from her abused larynx. "You truly believe the King is
in London?"

"What is worse, this Count von Kramm's secretary has made inquiries at the foreign office after the services of a specialist."

"Specialist?"

"He was directed to Mr. Sherlock Holmes of Two-twenty-one-B
Baker Street."

Irene sat even more slowly, as if uncertain that the bench—or indeed the floor—remained beneath her. "Sherlock Holmes. Oh, I
would give a great deal to meet, to match wits with that gentleman,
but not now! And not both of them together, the King and the detective. How unfair life is sometimes, Godfrey!" Her fist hit the keys.

"Always, Irene. What do you wish to do?"

She stared for some time at her hands. I found it hard to believe
that these pale, delicate fingers with the nails clipped short for the piano

had joined mine in clawing at Mr. Wilde's garden turf only the night before.

Irene seemed so diminished at the moment—her voice, both her glory and her weapon in meeting the world, blunted; all the promise of her past having become a threat in the present. She lifted her head then as if having heard my worry made audible.

"What do I wish to do? I wish to go into the sitting room."

Godfrey and I exchanged a worried glance. Yet Irene still possessed that commanding calm of hers. We followed her across the hall and watched as she paused before the bookshelves.

"You promised to read your mother's novel," she said to Godfrey. "Take it."

Some unspoken strain was thickening her voice, though Godfrey was deaf to it, as most men are to the nuances of women's emotion.

"Irene, we have no time for novels now; it is possible that you have been written into the climax of a rather sorry story yourself."

"Please, forget this . . . rumor. I want you to take your mother's book."

Both Godfrey and I stared at the humble brown spine on the shelf.

Godfrey was beginning to sense her fevered emotional pitch. "Irene, this is ridiculous. We must make plans for your defense, perhaps for your swift removal from London."

Irene closed her eyes. "Godfrey, please!" she pleaded, her magnificent voice in shreds. "It is vital to me. I wish you to take your mother's novel. Do it!"

He stepped forward like a duelist, in one long stride, and sharply pulled the book from the shelf. There came a rapid patter, like raindrops or running mice feet. Splashes of random light spilled from the space the book had occupied. A papist rosary seemed to dangle there, crystal beads strung in neat decades—perhaps my clerical background was deceiving my short-sighted eyes . . .

Godfrey lifted a slow hand to the object as though dislodging a cobweb in a dream. He pulled the strand of light. There came more clicking, more tumbling of bright white beads to bookshelf, length after length until the beads were pooling like hailstones on the shelf below . . .

I came over, a dream walker myself. They were not beads of crystal, but diamonds, an entire Zone of Diamonds.

Tears were glittering on the sickle of Irene's lower lashes, tears of suppressed triumph.

"I wished to surprise you, Godfrey, but you would not cooperate! Your mother's book *was* the one true clue, if you had only read it. Cloris of the *Crossroads,* don't you see? It was at the crossroads on the moor that poor benighted Cloris first lost her true love, there that she rallied the prince and the peasants, there that her heartless father died at novel's end—clutching the Celtic cross that marked the roads even as he expired and *there that the family jewels were found buried* beneath the stone cross.

"Your mother penned that novel in the very house we visited last night. Nell and I found this Zone buried beneath the same Celtic cross that inspired your mother and your father in two very different ways, possibly the only thing besides their children that they truly shared."

She paused, exhausted, while Godfrey numbly drew the lengths of white fire through his hands.

"It *is* glorious, Irene, beautiful. Nell?" He held the glittering skein out to me and I drew closer, as one mesmerized.

The piece was antique, the stones cut in the old French style, but the fiery length of it was stupendous. We truly regarded the last vestige of the *Ancien Regime,* something that belonged more to the past than to any present claimant.

Godfrey finally looked from the Zone to Irene, bemused.

"I thought you had failed to find it when you were so subdued last night."

Now she was surprised. "You . . . expected me to find the Zone? Surely you did not suspect when I proposed a scavenger hunt to the Wildes?"

"But I did. I knew precisely why you manipulated that particular entertainment for the evening in that particular neighborhood."

334 Carole Nelson Douglas

"Godfrey! You are not prescient. You are not Sherlock Holmes. How did you know?"

"Irene," I put in, "you musn't strain your voice."

"Oh, be quiet, Nell!" she snapped, turning once again on Godfrey like an angry lioness. "How *could* you know, Godfrey Norton?"

"I simply took some good advice; I skimmed my mother's novel days ago. When you proposed this expedition through Chelsea, I deduced that you knew the site of a local Celtic cross."

"Why did you not tell me? Why did you not ask last night?"

He shrugged rather sheepishly. "I wanted you to have the fun of finding it."

"Fun?!" I squeaked, remembering the dark and the damp and digging.

Irene drew back. "But . . . I could have concealed the fact that I had it. Even Nell did not know. I could have fled London, as you are about to advise me, and have kept the Zone to myself. You would not have even so much as seen it."

Godfrey smiled. "One does not miss losing what one has never had. That is why the King of Bohemia is so tenacious. He knows that he can never reclaim you; the photograph is more than a threat to him, it is the sole momento of what he has lost."

Godfrey lifted the Zone like a tangle of dew in his hands and held it out to Irene. "This is a sorry memento of my father's wrongheaded pursuit of pleasure instead of honor. Now that I have seen it, I do not need it. Nor, I think, do you, now that you have found it."

Irene stared bemused at the diamonds girdling her hands. "I cannot believe that the dazzle of so fabulous an artifact can fade so quickly. I had wanted you to discover the Zone for yourself because I wanted to give you something that you felt entitled to. Now I find I have failed at that, that the Zone was never as important to you as it was to me. I have not given you something that you wanted at all."

"Perhaps you can give me something other that I want even more," Godfrey said.

Irene looked up from the Zone of Diamonds, puzzled.

"I think, my dear Irene," he said, "that first you should spare your voice."

For once in our association, I saw it before she did.

I clasped my hands at my breast, bit my tongue, paused, and fled the room.

Neither of them appeared to observe, but I glimpsed the Zone of Diamonds clattering unnoticed to the thick Turkish carpet and Godfrey stepping to Irene as I drew the doors shut.

I found and instructed Mrs. Seaton on no account to go in the sitting room and retired to my room, where I applied a cool cloth to my temples, in the accepted treatment for incipient hysteria.

Chapter Thirty-three

Smoke Screens

֍

I crept down to breakfast the following morning with a raging headache. It was only to intensify. My appetite was strangely delicate so I took only a cup of tea and wandered into the music room, where I found Irene staring fondly at the piano she had once refused to touch.

She looked up as I entered, a strange expression in her eyes.

"Poor Nell," she said in greeting.

"To what indignity am I to be subjected next? Must I take a teaspoon and go tunneling through the Chelsea Physic Garden by moonlight?"

Irene smiled wanly and ran her palms over the shawl draping the grand piano. "I shall regret leaving this pretty instrument."

I kept silent, knowing Irene would soon explain her odd comment, as indeed she did. First she shook herself, as though shaking off happy emotions that nevertheless saddened her.

"I am afraid, my dear friend, that another hasty flight is in order, this time *to* the Continent instead of from it. With the King here in London and Sherlock Holmes on my trail—and the Zone of

Diamonds as well as the photograph now jeopardized—Godfrey and I have decided that there is nothing else for it."

" 'Godfrey and I?' "

She paced the room slowly, with none of the fevered fury she had shown in Bohemia.

"As you may imagine, dear Nell, Godfrey and I have reached an . . . understanding." She stopped to stare out the window as if her thoughts were drawn elsewhere, a hand to her bemused face. She turned to me with sad concern. "We must be ready to leave London at a moment's notice."

"You and Godfrey," I clarified.

"Yes." Irene stepped toward me, then paused. "Oh, I am being ridiculous! After all you and I have shared, I should not be so tongue-tied." She sat abruptly at the piano, taking courage from the smooth ivory keys beneath her absently caressing fingers.

"Nell . . . I have come to share your good opinion of Godfrey Norton. Indeed, I have exceeded it rather . . . excessively. Despite my initial distrust of him, of all men since the King of Bohemia, and despite my railings against the restrictions that matrimony imposes on women—I have completely lost my head and am about to enter that state myself. Godfrey and I have decided to marry as soon as possible so that we can escape at a moment's notice with no social awkwardness troubling us."

"Ah. A marriage of convenience, like the King of Bohemia's," I put in with some acerbity.

Irene blushed for the first and only time in our association. As blushes went it was a royal one, a becoming rosy tide that swept her cheeks and forehead.

"No, Nell, I fear there is nothing convenient about it. Godfrey's devotion to me since our return has been obvious; what has not been obvious—even to myself—was how deeply I returned his regard. He is worth six kings of Bohemia!" Her eyes shone. "I cannot now even regret that miserable episode, for it has shown me by contrast how a man of true worth may behave."

"Godfrey is uniquely sympathetic to a woman's position," I murmured. "I have always found him most considerate. I do not see why you are so apologetic, Irene; after all, I have thought highly of him even longer than you have."

"Perhaps that is why I am chagrined. I—the worldly and self-sufficient actress snared by the most predictable of emotions. Then, I cannot ask you to share my danger again, Nell, yet am desolate to leave you behind. We shall . . . worry about you."

"I can typewrite," I said a trifle sharply. "You must not fear for me. I enjoy a certain entree at the Temple, you know, thanks to you and Godfrey."

"Of course you shall survive without me—us. But shall we survive without you? It is a great change in my life I contemplate. In a way it frightens me."

"You? Frightened? Come, Irene, you have faced vast anonymous audiences and armed bullies and an imperious king. Marriage and Godfrey cannot be so frightening." A squawk from the dining room punctuated my assertion. "No, what is truly dreadful is the prospect of my being left alone to the tender vocal mercies of Casanova."

"You—and Casanova, of course—could join us abroad once we are settled," Irene suggested with a trial glance from under her brows.

I considered it. "Yes, I suppose we could. For a holiday, at least. After all, you and Godfrey will be respectably married—"

Irene's rich arpeggio of laughter interrupted me. "I cannot guarantee respectability even if married. Be warned! Godfrey and I intend to be very scandalous spouses, I assure you. Our first business abroad will be to sell the Zone of Diamonds."

"Sell it! But you have hardly had it in your possession."

"We will need a source of funds, although I can give the occasional concert as I do here. As for Godfrey . . ." A frown edged into her features, vanishing as the knocker rapped briskly.

The maid had opened the door and Godfrey was rushing in, hat and gloves already in hand. He threw them down upon the hall console, nodded a greeting to me and took Irene's hands to draw her into the sitting room. I followed with a cat's shameless but soft-footed curiosity.

"It is as we suspected," Godfrey announced, pacing the carpet. "I have made inquiries in Baker Street of the usual loungers: a handsome brougham and pair was observed drawing up to two-twenty-one-B last night even as we left the Wilde residence. The man who stepped out was described as 'a bloomin' giant' with knee-high boots, enough 'furrin fur on his coat to 'ide a 'orse' and wearing 'a sweet little 'alf-mask, like a 'ouse-breaker.'"

"The King, and no doubt! Then there is virtually no time!" Irene exclaimed.

"I have made arrangements at the Church of St. Monica. We must wed by noon if it is to be legal."

"Noon? By noon?" Irene looked as she seldom did, dazed and indecisive.

"It is the law." Godfrey's frantic pacing stopped. "I thought we had settled matters last night."

"Yes, but—such a sudden series of changes: finding the Zone, the King, Sherlock Holmes, marriage . . ."

"Irene. You are not a woman of hesitation."

"Not ordinarily, but Godfrey, I can sing anywhere. What of the law? You cannot practice in Europe—"

He scissored his arms in front of him like a conductor commanding silence. "The law is everywhere, as are the English. I will find some occupation."

"But to give up all you have attained at such personal cost here in London—the Bar, the Temple, everything!"

"You mean that I shall be giving up my respectability."

"I suppose that I do."

"Then away with it! I have earned my entree to the bar. Now I can master some other challenge. Did you not abandon all you had in Bohemia—opera, illusions, even your clothing? Can I do less?"

"This is *my* battle."

"Exactly. What you battle, I do as well. And it is mutual. Do you suppose I am ready to let you slip away to Europe with the sole proceeds of the Zone of Diamonds? I have a certain familial claim."

He did not mean it, of course, but his argument of self-interest helped soothe Irene's contrary conscience. She glanced quickly at me. "I've told Nell what must happen in the next day or two."

Godfrey drew his gold pocket watch. "We have scant time. I will meet you at the Church of St. Monica's in twenty minutes. First I have an errand in Regent Street."

"Godfrey—twenty minutes! You will need wings."

"I already have them, my angel!" He caught Irene in a hasty embrace, then dashed into the hall. We heard the front door bang shut, then Godfrey's muffled instructions to his waiting cabman. "Drive like the Devil! First to Gross and Hankey's in Regent Street, then St. Monica's in the Edgware Road. Half a guinea if you can make it in twenty minutes!"

The cab's wheels rumbled as its horse's hooves beat out an increasingly swift pace. Inside the house, Irene and I stared at one another, then rushed for the stairs as one.

"It is like Paris again," she said, laughing, when we had reached her bedchamber. "The event of a lifetime and not a thing to wear!"

"Well, you are certainly not dressed as grandly as in your portrait as Cinderella," I admitted, though she wore a charming house dress of striped wool chamois trimmed on bodice, sleeves and skirt with stripes and bows of bright green velvet ribbon. "No diamond corsage," I added slyly.

Irene began bundling up her draped overskirt complete with demi-pannier while I wondered what she had tucked away in her amazing petticoat pockets now.

"Quickly, Nell, help me."

I played lady's maid and lifted her outer skirts as she swiftly buckled the Zone of Diamonds around her waist. It sparkled and clicked like silver rain against the flounces of her taffeta petticoats.

"No one will see it," I complained as I settled her dress over the petticoats again.

"I will know it. A bride should wear *something* old and this certainly qualifies. Now for the proper bonnet."

While she puzzled over her headgear I slipped into my room and found my father's Book of Common Prayer, into which I thrust a blue velvet ribbon as a marker.

I returned to Irene's room to find her donning a green velvet toque surmounted by a poll of iridescent black cockfeathers. She looked splendid.

I placed the prayerbook in her hand and picked up her reticule. "Something borrowed and something blue. Now you must hasten."

At the front door she paused. "Penelope, your bonnet!"

"I am not going, though I would wish to. I can better serve by packing your things here. You shall not leave all behind you again if I can help it. Now—go!"

She embraced me, then ran through the door, pulling on her gloves, her husky voice calling to the coachman, who had brought the landau around. "The Church of St. Monica, John, and half a sovereign if you make it in twenty minutes!"

I smiled to myself and then ran to consult the mantel clock. Twenty-five minutes to twelve. The horse would require wings, too. I breathed a quick prayer and retreated upstairs to begin sorting Irene's things into packable piles.

An hour had passed before I had separated the shirtwaists from the corsets. I heard the faint clop of returning horse's hooves and flew down to the door, arriving with our maid. Irene was coming up the walk alone.

"Godfrey?" I said.

"The Temple." Irene paused by the hall mirror to remove her hat and gloves.

"Let me see it!" My eye had caught a new glitter on her left hand.

We slipped into the sitting room, where she fanned her fingers for my inspection. The ring was a lengthways lozenge of pierced gold that covered one knuckle, containing a center-set emerald flanked by two opals.

"It is . . . most striking," said I.

"Most modern, you mean. Godfrey did well in five minutes' choosing. He said we will save diamonds for Paris."

"Speaking of which, does he know the nature of your girdle?"

"Penelope," she rebuked, "a woman must have some secrets from her husband."

"If he is that, why is he not here?"

"He will return, at his usual hour. For now we are discreet—and we were almost not married."

"Not! What happened?"

Irene loosened the Zone and let it slither down her petticoats to the floor. She retrieved and coiled it into the secret compartment like a diamond serpent. Then she perched on the chaise and patted the cushion beside her.

"It was the most amazing comedy of errors, Nell. Poor Godfrey was white with worry. I need never wonder if he truly wished to wed me; the man moved heaven and earth to accomplish it. The 'heaven' was our clergyman, who demanded a witness since our license was so fresh and no banns had been announced. Not a witness was to be found. People usually devote their noon hour to food for the flesh instead of the soul."

"Indeed, so my father often lamented."

"It was five minutes to twelve before Godfrey spotted some threadbare lounger in a side aisle, who represents the 'earth' in our equation. He pounced upon this unlettered unfortunate like Little Jack Horner on a plum pudding.

" 'Come, man!' he whispered loudly enough to wake the dead. 'Only three minutes. You'll do.'

" 'Do what?' asked the honored worshiper, looking as if he has been invited to witness a hanging instead of a holy matrimony.

"Godfrey dragged the fellow before the clergyman, hands him the ring and tells him to do as he's told. Such blinking and stuttering, but the man performed adequately, with the result that Godfrey and I were maritally linked just as the church bell began to bellow twelve o'clock."

"I cannot believe it, Irene. Can you not even marry in a conventional fashion? And now you come home husbandless."

"Godfrey had matters to attend to at the Temple, and no Nell there to help him decamp."

I put my hands to my cheeks. "Goodness, he will make an utter mess of the papers if he tries to deal with them himself."

"He is assigning the lot to a fellow barrister. Let the new man deal with it."

"And what do you do now?"

"Rest. Pack. Drive out at five and dine at seven as is my custom. If I am being hunted it is best to cleave to my usual routine so as not to alert the hounds that the fox is digging an escape tunnel."

"You are a marvel, Irene. Your life is turning upside down, yet you remain cucumber-cool."

"What am I to do?" She spread her hands helplessly, the new ring winking. "The next move is up to our opponents."

⚜   ⚜   ⚜

So the excitement of the forenoon became the routine of a quiet afternoon at home. John brought the landau around at five p.m. when Irene, more finely dressed by then than she had been for her impromptu wedding, went out for her drive in Regent's Park. I suspected that Godfrey would take a cab to meet her there, as he no doubt had been doing for some time. It was my affair even less now than before.

At seven I was established in the middle of Irene's bedchamber floor, arranging gloves, trimmings and handkerchiefs into piles by color. I was nothing if not thorough.

I heard our front door bang and a bustle below and rounded the stair to see our door agape. John and a stranger were carting an unconscious man into the front hall. A murmur of voices from the street beyond gave a sense of confusion and hubbub.

"Here," Irene was directing the men with their burden, "the sitting room." She spied me on the stair. "Oh, Nell, this poor kind-hearted clergyman has been grievously struck down, and in my defense."

I clattered downstairs in time to see the man laid upon the chaise longue. He looked so much like my own late father that I quite froze in the threshold . . . a dear, frail old fellow with snowy hair, baggy black coat—and a horrid red gash upon his venerable forehead.

"Irene, what has happened?"

She was busy laying the clergyman's broad-brimmed hat upon the table and loosening the white tie at his throat.

"Serpentine Avenue has attracted a convention tonight. Not only guardsman courting nursemaids and young idlers but a pair of rude characters who thought to earn a copper by opening my carriage door; instead they fought each other for the privilege and little else.

"They had trapped me between the landau and their own wind-milling arms, despite John's best efforts to reach me. Had this passing clergyman not undertaken to defend me, I should have been pinned like a butterfly to velvet. One of the ruffians struck the old fellow senseless—hence he is here. Ah, thank you," she said as Mrs. Seaton imported a wet cloth from below-stairs.

I watched Irene daub the wound. The fallen man groaned as his eyes fluttered open behind the thick spectacles that perched askew on his aquiline nose. He struggled half upright, then fanned one hand weakly before his face.

"The window!" Irene directed the maid. "He requires air."

The woman flung the long French window open to the night. The clergyman gave one last, sharp hand gesture, then fell back. We stared at him, awaiting some further sign of revival.

"Smelling salts!" Irene ordered, turning away to direct Mrs. Seaton to fetch this essential item.

At that moment the knot of spectators in the road beyond raised their dull murmur to sudden alarm.

"Fire!" someone shouted, then several took up the call. "Fire!"

We turned as one to the window, shocked to see smoky plumes coughing into the sitting room. Smoke curled along the floor like fog and spumed up toward the ceiling. In a few instants the room was choked with grey clouds.

Beside me I heard Irene gasp, then she was gone. Fire? The pho-

tograph! The Zone! I turned to see a dim figure stumbling against
the bell pull, and heard the snick of the secret compartment as it slid
open.

I looked back at the window, thinking to escape that way. The
cleric was sitting upright like an animated corpse, his wavery voice
raised.

"Not fire, ladies. False alarm. Surely not fire. Be calm and the
smoke will disperse."

The quick dispersal he predicted revealed a strange cylindrical
object on the floor. John had joined us and retrieved it with a grunt.

"Plumber's rocket," he said, frowning at the clergyman. "Some-
body's played a nasty trick."

"Amazing, most amazing evening," that worthy stammered. "Well,
I feel quite recovered now." He peered about to thank his hostess, but
Irene had vanished, with the smoke.

I felt some embarrassment at this rude dereliction of her charge
and escorted his slow steps to the door. "Are you sure you are fit to
leave?"

"Indeed, yes. I must trouble your household no longer. So
pleased to have been of service to such a fine, kind lady."

The old fellow tipped his broad hat brim and toddled down the
walk. The previous crowd had thinned like smoke. I was surprised to
note that John had slipped out to drive the carriage around to the
mews. When I retreated inside again, Irene was not downstairs—nor
was she below-stairs or upstairs.

In her bedchamber, filled with neat stacks of her clothes, the
wardrobe doors gaped, her evening's attire piled before them. I suppressed a superstitious shiver, remembering the magician's curtain of
smoke in our sitting room and Irene's shadow by the fireplace and
then seeing her no more.

I wandered the ground floor, puzzled. Mrs. Seaton and the maid
were setting things to rights and had no idea that she had gone, much
less any notion of where. I paused by Casanova's cage and offered him
a biscuit from the sideboard.

"I shall be glad when Godfrey is solely responsible for her comings and goings," I confided to the bird, who sidled close to the bars to hear me.

"Godfrey, Godfrey!" he crowed with a cocked head. "Ex-why-zed, jay-kay-el, ay-bee-cee."

What could one do with a bird that got even the alphabet backwards? I retired to the sitting room and read *Cloris of the Crossroads* until half past ten, when hooves clattered up our quiet street once again.

There in the house Irene found me, for I refused to give her the satisfaction of leaping up to greet her.

"Still up?" she inquired. She sounded breathlessly pleased about something and oddly alert. "We shall be up longer, I fear. I have sent John and the landau for Godfrey."

I dropped the book and turned.

Irene, a bowler pulled low over her brow and a muffler pulled high over her chin, stood behind me in gentleman's garb.

"Irene . . . what on earth?"

She moved briskly to the compartment to withdraw all its hidden booty. "We are discovered. Our self-sacrificing clergyman keeps his rectory in Baker Street."

"He was a spy?"

"He was a spy and a pseudo-arsonist and something of a theatrical director. If I am not mistaken, he hired and directed that entire cast of supernumeraries outside the house tonight, and arranged for the special effects of the smoke."

"But why? Why would a man of the cloth . . . ?"

"He changes his cloth like an actor. I followed his cab to two-twenty-one-B Baker Street, where he paused on the threshold with his companion—the rocket hurler, I suspect—to extract the key. I could not help myself—ah, vanity, thy name is indeed woman. I passed behind the pair and taunted him with my knowledge."

"What did you say!?"

"Why, nothing but 'Good night, Mr. Sherlock Holmes.' I moved quickly on, and John picked me up around the corner. But Godfrey and I must leave immediately. You and I must finish packing so I may flee as soon as Godfrey arrives."

"Irene . . ." There was no time for sad farewells. Irene was already bolting up the stairs, bowler and muffler in one hand and the compartment's treasures in the other.

"I must travel in my proper sex, I fear," she said in her bedchamber. "The whole point of marrying Godfrey was to stifle comment."

She was stripping off her male attire while I tumbled her most essential clothing into a single trunk, my color-sorted piles all come to naught.

She paused in her shirt sleeves and came to take my shoulders in her hands. I looked into her face, too desolate to truly feel our imminent separation. She smiled at me, smiled her old wicked, speculative smile that used to fill me with dread and a certain, quite uncalled-for anticipation.

"I would give anything, my darling Nell, to see Mr. Sherlock Holmes arrive at this house to find the den empty and the fox fled. Anything!"

Her smile deepened as her voice became a thick, cajoling honey.

"Who else can I rely upon for an accurate and thorough account of that delicious moment? Could I prevail upon you, dear friend, to don a slight alteration of feature, to play the left-behind maid and admit the hunting party to the empty house, hmm?

"Just a dusting of white powder over your hair, a dozen minor wrinkles . . ." She had propelled me before the pier glass and was sprinkling face powder over my nutmeg brown hair. A pale cloud of smoke seemed to have obscured my youth, my familiar features.

"Not any deep deception, simply something superficial that would disguise you from future harrassment. After all, you stay to face the music we flee. If you would deign to play a role for the briefest of times. Just this once, this one first and last time, I swear . . ."

Chapter Thirty-four

A Superior Woman

❧

"That was odd," I remarked to Holmes when he had removed the clergyman guise and was smoking a victory pipe in his own semblance.

"True, I would not expect anyone to address me by name when I am disguised, but my back was to the street. Perhaps the fellow didn't even look at whom he spoke to."

"I must confess, Holmes, that I feel rather ashamed about deceiving that humanitarian lady I watched ministering to your so-called 'wound' tonight. Have you no compunction about tricking one who has offered you only sympathy?"

"The race is to the swift, Watson, not to the sympathetic. Irene Adler may be lovely in more than appearance, but I have engaged to save the King from his folly . . . though I find that his story of their liaison and her supposed intention to harm him does not tally with what I have thus far observed of the lady."

"Really, Holmes, perhaps you have undertaken to help the wrong party in the affair."

Holmes laughed heartily. "You would have been utterly demoralized, Watson, had you been in my rather tattered shoes at the Church of St. Monica earlier today. When Miss Irene—or I should say Madam Irene—gave me the sovereign for my witness duty, she did it with the air of an angel offering a sample of heavenly grace. I will have the coin put on my watch chain as a memento . . . there they were, the wedded couple, one on either side of my disreputable self, thanking me as if I were St. Peter himself and had admitted them to their particular paradise."

"Again you reward civility with deception! Still, she's not a respectable woman, I suppose, despite her marriage."

"To use less than my full wit in my client's behalf would insult the woman's own intelligence, Watson. No, Madam Irene is not one to sue for consideration. I hope this Norton is worthy of her."

"A fine-looking fellow apparently, from your report."

"Looks," Holmes said a trifle sharply, "are no guarantee of either wit or character. Witness the King of Bohemia. However, I must admit to a certain glee at having succeeded where all the King's men have not with Madam Irene." He briskly rubbed his hands together and spoke again.

"We must retire soon and rise early. I wish to surprise our quarry at home tomorrow before the fact of her marriage changes her life and habits. That is why I have asked you to wire the King on your way home tonight. One cannot expect royalty to rise at six o'clock without cause, but in this case I imagine the King will be all too happy to lose some sleep if he regains the photograph."

"And then, tomorrow morning?"

"Then we will call en masse, as it were. You, I and the King. We will be shown into the sitting room and may decide to decamp even before Madam Irene can arrange a suitable toilet to come down to greet us. The King may enjoy retrieving the photograph with his own hands. I do owe him some small satisfaction for all his money."

"You would leave without seeing her face-to-face in your own stead? That seems a bit ungentlemanly, Holmes."

He shrugged in that fine careless way he had in all matters to do with women. "Is it me you wish to meet her face-to-face—or yourself?"

"I am soon to be a married man, Holmes!"

He smiled tightly. "But not blind, Watson, decidedly not blind. As I am not. You had not seen the object of our hunt until tonight. There, too, I had the jump on you; I had met her before noon. I detect in your questions an unspoken wish for more than this case affords. Madam Irene is a married woman now also, I remind you, and I am not a marrying man. Please do me the courtesy of burying any fond hopes you may have cherished in the matchmaking way. We are natural opponents, she and I, and so it shall remain."

Holmes had let his pipe die and set it aside. He was silent a moment, then made one last comment on the matter I was some future day to title "A Scandal in Bohemia."

When Holmes spoke again, it was with the abstraction that signaled his retreat to the Elysian Fields of his intellect.

"Obviously, Irene Adler—and that is how I shall always think of her—is a superior woman, but she shares with most of her sex a certain emotional short-sightedness that handicaps them in matters of a purely intellectual nature."

"Holmes, I cannot sit here and permit you to libel the intelligence of women again. What of Miss Violet Hunter, that plucky young governess! You yourself called her 'a brave and sensible girl, a quite exceptional woman.'"

Holmes smiled around the stem of his pipe. "I see by your accurate recall that you are scouring your notes and preparing a narrative for another of my cases. What do you plan to do with these tales?"

I bristled a bit. "It is possible that they may someday find their way to print, if you have no objection."

"If they are accurate I will have no objection. Yes, I recall Miss Violet Hunter, and a clever, brave female she was, but not on the level of Irene Adler, who likely harbors unsuspected depths. However, at bottom she remains a woman and prone to the sex's reliance on intuition and sentiment. That will be her downfall."

"Perhaps I should make a note of this," I said with a modicum of sarcasm.

"You will at least concede, Watson, that the emotional exhilaration of Madam Irene's recent marriage will have blinded her to the vulnerability of her situation—but, come, cheer up! No harm is to be done. It is not as if we were wresting some valuable prize from her grasp, is it? Although that would be a sweet end to the business, if we were to unearth some treasure beyond a mere photograph from her secure hiding place. Do not stare, Watson, it is possible."

Holmes's face shone with a self-mocking glee I could not inter-pret. He was often terse until ready to unveil all aspects of a case; now I sensed some greater constraint against speaking freely, as if he cherished hopes even he dare not voice prematurely. He seemed to be dropping clues before my very nose, knowing that I should never show his acuity in finding them, much less following them to their conclusion.

Holmes clapped his hands together. "So. Madam Irene will lose only a photograph that cannot mean much to her anymore, and she has gained a husband. Splendid, for any vindictive feelings she might have harbored toward the King—perhaps with good reason—are now moot. I trust that she shall not feel too vindictively toward myself; I am told that true love consoles for a variety of losses. I shall not lose, how-ever. Triumph awaits us on the morrow, Watson, when I shall at least justify the princely payment the King has given me and recover the scandalous photograph."

"Perhaps I should write the case up now and not bother to wait until tomorrow, since the outcome is so certain."

"You could, no doubt," Holmes responded with a twinkling eye. "But wait a day; there will be many details so dear to the writer's heart, I assure you, Watson. Many nuances of expression, perhaps even some surprises. Oh yes, I entertain hopes of a surprise. And think how Madam Irene will be shocked to find her nest empty—you are quite right, Watson. I should remain to witness her chagrin. It is the only gentlemanly thing to do."

At this he leaned back in the easy chair, narrowed his eyes and chuckled at the contemplation of some intensely private pleasure.

Chapter Thirty-five

Closing Curtain

~ev~

It was the happiest of days—and the saddest.
It was the loneliest of tasks—and the most selfless.

It was the wickedest thing that I have ever done—and the most delicious.

But I must save the best for last. (In truth, I need not do so, but I have acquired *some* sense of drama from my years with Irene Adler.)

After John had conveyed Irene's baggage to the landau, we sat up all night—Irene and Godfrey and I. We picnicked before the sitting room fire on all the teacakes Mrs. Seaton could provide. Godfrey had brought a magnum of champagne and I fear I drank my share. At one point in the evening I actually went to the dining room and imported Casanova's cage to the party so he could hear Godfrey's telling of the Mutterworth will and its discovery, in which the parrot had played such a key but inadvertent part.

"Topiary *parrots!*" Irene cried in mirthful disbelief often enough that Casanova soon joined her in the chorus. He had an ever-ready ear for the irrelevant.

We laughed, we reminisced, we looked forward to the foiling of the King through his peerless agent, Sherlock Holmes, on the morrow. We discussed Irene and Godfrey's plans, which were appallingly sketchy.

They would return to Paris. "A proper honeymoon," Godfrey declared. Glass brims chimed. The new ring glittered on Irene's hand. For a moment the emerald glow reminded me of the snake ring the King had worn.

I shivered as the clock struck three. Irene put a steadying hand on my shoulder. "You will be magnificent, Nell. It is time for your transformation."

Upstairs I sat before her dressing table mirror watching my likeness fade under her expert hands. Another visage clarified in the looking glass—older, paler. For a moment I saw the face of my future. Still, there was some resolution to the features no matter how enfeebled.

"Men are much easier to disguise," Irene mused, "they wear so many styles of facial hair; that is how Mr. Holmes's snowy locks and holy demeanor last evening took me in. We women must always go bare-faced—unless we mimic men, as I have on occasion, or paint our features, and even artifice is no disguise."

"You are certain Mr. Holmes does not suspect your rash greeting?"

"He would have been here by now if he did. I did not dare look back, but he must have wondered who had recognized him in his clerical guise. Of course it was dark and his own doorway; he undoubtedly decided that a passerby had recognized Dr. Watson, assuming the other figure to be himself. How he will berate himself when he reads my note!"

"What note?"

"The one I have left in the secret compartment in place of the photograph he expects. Remember to show no surprise at anything that occurs tomorrow."

"Tomorrow! Today."

"Indeed," Irene said, fluffing my powder-greyed hair.

She brought her vibrant face to mine, so we were paired in the mirror like Siamese twins. "Oh, my dear Nell, I shall miss you! We

354   Carole Nelson Douglas

are veterans, you and I, of so much. Godfrey and I are newly conscripted into alliance, and I confess some small apprehension. I am old to embark on wedlock."

"Then it is about time," I said stoutly. "You would not want to be an old maid like myself."

She shook me in mock admonishment, giving my image a palsy to match its aged appearance. "I am thirty and you but thirty-two. Much yet awaits us both in life, if we are willing to meet it open-eyed and with courage. You, after all, are about to make your theatrical debut."

"I am sure that Ellen Terry is quavering in her buskins. Now do not disarrange my wrinkles, for I have spent a whole hour acquiring them."

I rose from the table to confront my altered image no more. Yet the ghost of it hung over me like a veil. It slowed my step and my speech and invested me with a mantle of dignity that served me well for the remainder of that long night.

At four I heard the lonely clatter of John bringing the landau around; the horse had undergone a busy time of it, too.

"Our train leaves at five-fifteen," Irene explained. "I expect Mr. Holmes to arrive shockingly early, the better to catch me napping."

"I look forward to encountering this legendary creature while he is in full pursuit of his quarry. I suppose you will want a detailed description?"

"But of course! Oh, I do wish I could see his face when he—ah, but he is too dangerous to trifle with."

"The description need not be too detailed," Godfrey put in.

"It will be thorough," said I, accompanying them to the door. My backbone had stiffened by then, as with the iron of age. I remained remarkably calm, quite in character.

Irene embraced me suddenly at the threshold. Godfrey held my hands so tightly that I feared my arthritic old bones should snap.

We said nothing. In the gaslight's dull glow I could see pre-dawn damp glistening on the street and the horse bowing its weary head.

"Good-bye," we three whispered in concert, as if the world were eavesdropping; then we were all at once abruptly silent.

They turned and walked to the carriage. I stood at the open door while the landau drew slowly down the avenue. Irene's pale face in the carriage window moved away, seeming as remote as a museum portrait that one recognizes and then passes by.

I stood there a long time, the chill night air cloaking me, hearing the hooves dim into the distance, feeling the peace of night settle again over Briony Lodge.

Returning to the house, I cleared the dishes from the sitting room and dusted the table. With every movement, the role of a maid, an emotionless employee, burned deeper into my bones. I began to understand the fascination impersonation held for both Irene and her rival, Sherlock Holmes.

It was while I haunted the familiar rooms, awaiting my brief moment on stage, that I understood something else as well, and stood stock still to contemplate it. The role Irene had assigned me also removed me from the immediate pain of parting. She had given me a task beyond watching her and Godfrey go. I quite approved. Work is always the best antidote to sorrow.

At a quarter to eight, a most uncivil hour to call, I heard hoofbeats in the avenue. John had returned at seven, when I had instructed Mrs. Seaton and the maid to remain below-stairs. I approached on the door and opened it.

A brougham as shiny as the pair of chestnuts that pulled it stood before the gate. A tall, thin man stepped out, followed by a shorter, stouter one. At last the King himself appeared; I drew in a deep breath as I recognized his larger-than-life form.

The trio advanced on me.

"Mr. Sherlock Holmes, I presume?" said I, pleased that the quaver in my voice sounded more indicative of old age than of fear.

It was splendid to evoke such surprise on that self-contained face. He was not a handsome man, but intensely alert in an engaging way. His expression as he answered was pleasingly nonplussed.

"I am Mr. Holmes."

"Excellent. My . . . mistress instructed me that you would call. She left by the five-fifteen train from Charing Cross this morning for the Continent, with her husband, Godfrey Norton."

My news almost staggered the detective. "You mean that she has already left England?"

"Never to return," I put in rather untruthfully for the greater shock. I confess I took indecent pleasure in wielding the whip-hand in front of his Majesty, King Willie.

"She cannot love him," that nobleman murmured in the background, as if he had recited this chorus before to convince himself. He showed little shock at the news of Irene's marriage, instead pushing past the two men to demand, "But the . . . photograph. All is lost!"

I nearly answered *Yes!* with insufferable complacency.

"We shall see." Mr. Holmes brushed past me and into the sitting room as if he knew the house, as indeed he did.

I followed unnoticed, beginning to appreciate how easily servants fade into the woodwork.

The three men stared about the room, which I had taken the liberty of disrupting so that drawers gaped open and books lay askew. I felt that some stage dressing would enhance the scene of hasty departure.

Mr. Holmes bolted to the bell pull and pressed the secret panel, exposing the compartment. He stuck in his thumb and pulled out a plum—a photograph in its case, and an envelope.

First he opened the photograph case—and his face fell. He ripped the envelope open, quite properly, for I had seen it addressed in Irene's dashing green ink: "Sherlock Holmes—To be left until called for."

He read the letter within aloud—quite well, I must add, with the proper emphasis, so I could almost hear Irene's amused voice speaking along with him.

"It is dated midnight, yesterday."

The King groaned and brought his big fist to his mouth. What a spoiled little boy he looked, for all his title and bristling blond whiskers.

"My Dear Mr. Sherlock Holmes:

"You really did it very well. You took me in completely. Until after the alarm of fire, I had not a suspicion. But when I found how I had betrayed myself, I began to think. I had been warned against you, yet with all this, you made me reveal what you wanted to know. Bravo! Even after I became suspicious, I found it hard to think evil of such a dear, kind old clergyman. But, you know, I have been trained as an actress myself. Male costume is nothing new to me. I often take advantage of the freedom it gives. I sent John, the coachman, to watch you, ran upstairs, got into my walking clothes, as I call them, and came down just as you departed.

"Well, I followed you to your door, and so made sure that I was really an object of interest to the celebrated Mr. Sherlock Holmes. Then I, rather imprudently, wished you good night, and started for the Temple to see my husband.

"We both thought the best resource was flight, when pursued by so formidable an antagonist; so you will find the nest empty when you call tomorrow. As to the photograph, your client may marry in peace. I love and am loved by a better man than he. The King may do what he will without hindrance from one whom he has cruelly wronged. I keep it only to safeguard myself, and to preserve a weapon that will always secure me from any steps which he might take in the future. I leave a photograph which he might care to possess, and I remain, dear Mr. Sherlock Holmes, very truly yours,

"Irene Norton, née Adler."

A silence inhabited the room.

The King broke it. "What a woman—oh, what a woman! Did I not tell you that she has a soul of steel?" He took the photograph and studied it. It was of Irene wearing Mr. Tiffany's diamond corsage, Irene as Cinderella, a role that in real life had offered her only a craven Prince. "She has the face of the most beautiful of women, and the mind of the most resolute of men. Would she have not made an admirable queen? Is it not a pity that she was not on my level?"

⚜   ⚜   ⚜

Mr. Holmes glanced from the photograph in the King's hand to his prideful face. "From what I have seen of the lady, she seems, indeed, to be on a very different level to your Majesty," he said icily. "I am sorry that I have not been able to bring your Majesty's business to a more successful conclusion."

"No, no!" the King cried. "Nothing could be more successful. Her word is inviolate. The photograph is now as safe as if it were in the fire. I am immensely indebted to you. Tell, me, how can I reward you? This ring—"

I stiffened as the King pulled the emerald snake ring from his finger and offered it to the detective on the palm of his hand.

Mr. Holmes regarded the jewel as if it were . . . well, a snake. "Your Majesty has something that I should value even more highly."

"Name it!"

Mr. Holmes pointed delicately to the photograph. "That."

The King's face showed shock yet again. "Irene's photograph, but—certainly, you may have it."

"I thank your Majesty," the detective said suavely, claiming his prize. "I have the honor to wish you a very good morning." He bowed and turned away without taking the hand the King had extended to him.

His companion, who looked as stunned as the King at this turn of events, bowed and withdrew as well. I trailed them out, leaving Willie, King of Bohemia, staring around the room as if hunting traces of his lost quarry.

"I was wrong and am not ashamed to admit it," Mr. Holmes was murmuring as I slid by them in the hall to open the door. "*The* woman is incomparable, Watson. From his Majesty's unguarded opinion just now, she apparently combines Petrarch's rare blend of beauty *and* virtue. In addition, she has anticipated me, which is an even greater achievement. Brava, Madam Irene!" he whispered under his breath, as if partaking in a standing ovation at some concert hall.

I do not know what possessed me next. Some imp of improvisation, perhaps, some theatrical taint I had donned with greasepaint and powder.

As the pair moved through the door, I couldn't help saying,

"And a very good morning to you, Mr. Sherlock Holmes." Perhaps the tiniest bit of superiority imbued my tone.

The detective spun on me like a striking cobra. He fixed me in his cold, piercing eyes while I froze in horror at my hubris.

He seemed to see through me to the very soles of my shoes; indeed, to my very soul. The intensity of his inspection invited not a blush, but a quiver. My disguise seemed to peel away under the eye of a master of disguise. I had failed Irene, failed myself . . . oh what a blunder, what a prideful, foolish, wrong-headed gesture!

Suddenly Mr. Holmes raised his hand to his hatbrim and bowed. His grey eyes, so like Godfrey's, were alight with suppressed merriment.

"And a very good morning to your mistress, wherever she is, and to her husband, Mr. Godfrey Norton. I can certainly . . . bear witness to the fact that they make a most handsome couple, and don't doubt that they shall remain healthy, wealthy and wise."

He began laughing then—a delighted somehow secret bark of glee that followed him and his companion all the way down the avenue. They did not wait to take the King's brougham but walked toward the thoroughfare where cabs could be found.

As for the King, he left later, walking stiffly. His blondness seemed to have faded to the grey of ashes. He paused midway down the walk to look again at Briony Lodge. I rather suspect that a man would so look at the box that had contained some treasure now lost to him.

"She cannot love him," he muttered as if I were not there, and indeed, so had he always treated me. For certain now, Irene was not there, either. He vanished, as had she, into the interior of a carriage.

The King's brougham left with a tossing of the horses' chestnut manes. I went upstairs to wash off my false face, thinking how much time and heartache it would save if we could do as much so easily with others.

Epilogue

Well-Gotten Gains

≈≈≈

"Well, Penelope, what do you think of Paris?"

"Very nice," I said demurely. "It certainly seems to agree with both of you."

Irene and Godfrey looked in the bloom of well-being—healthy, wealthy and wise. My friend reclined on a Louis XV chaise longue in their cottage in Neuilly near Paris; Godfrey leaned on the chaise's back. I had not realized how wan Irene's Bohemian adventure had left her until I saw her here, blooming like a rose at the end of the long French summer.

"We have a surprise for you," Irene said.

"For me? Really, I cannot accept any more of your generosity— this trip, my keep. I must return to my own two feet—and London— soon."

"But Casanova is so at home here," Godfrey protested mischievously. "It would be a pity to return him to the London fog; I think it harshens his voice."

I glanced at the vile bird in his cage by the open garden doors, gargling his lexicon of phrases at the wrens outside, where the setting sun tinged the poplars the color of a wounded rose. Godfrey knew quite well that Casanova's vocal well-being was hardly a prime concern of mine.

"Besides," Irene put in, "you must not think of our generosity as wholly ours. You were as much engaged in the quest for the Zone of Diamonds as we. A third share is yours, and even your late father could not claim the proceeds were ill-gotten, as the Zone had gone beyond the clear title of any one person."

"Perhaps," I conceded. "What did Mr. Tiffany say when you offered it to him?"

"He said that he was delighted that I had persisted in finding the gems but that my timing was pitiably unfortunate: he would have had more profit in it if I had found it when employed by him. I reminded him of his own motto: that good business is never a pity."

"How good was business?"

"Nell, you have become quite plain-spoken," Irene said in a teasing tone. She leaned elaborately forward and whispered a sum in my ear.

"That good?"

"And a third is yours; you need never typewrite again."

"But I *like* to typewrite! I am quite good at it."

"Exactly why Godfrey now acts as an agent for certain important persons in various delicate matters. He, for instance, handled the sale of the Zone and is quite a fierce negotiator, I assure you!"

Irene raised her right hand to her husband behind her. A blinding flash of greeting winked from the sole stone from the Zone of Diamonds still in her possession—set in a magnificent ring that converted to a pendant, designed by Tiffany and Company of Paris.

Godfrey returned his wife's compliment by kissing her hand. They both regarded me with the blissful idiocy that one expects from those new-wed, even if they are clever and usually clear-headed.

"What of the business of the news reports?" I wondered, for a recent disastrous train wreck in the Alps had listed Mr. and Mrs. Godfrey Norton among its fatalities. "It was most disturbing to read this on the train to Paris; I was quite distraught. And then when you met my train . . . !" I shivered expressively.

"That is the only drawback to the incident," Irene said with great sympathy, "that it has distressed you and may distress others who know us."

"Otherwise," Godfrey went on cheerfully, "it could not have been better. We had cancelled our trip to Italy when we heard that you at last would honor us with a visit. Apparently, our names remained on the passenger list. Irene need not worry about the King pursuing her now."

"Or Mr. Sherlock Holmes," I added.

"Or Mr. Sherlock Holmes," Irene said.

"Or Mr. Sherlock Holmes," Casanova parroted.

We laughed in a chorus.

Irene settled into her chair like a child preparing for a favourite bedtime story. "Tell me again, dear Nell," she purred, "what they said when they found us fled and the house empty?"

"You know it all backwards and forwards."

"Willie actually said that my word was inviolate?"

"Yes."

"Mr. Holmes really refused the King's emerald ring and would take only my photograph as payment?"

"There is nothing 'only' about your photograph," Godfrey put in.

"Have I ever lied?" said I.

"Almost never." Irene frowned. "And Mr. Holmes said that he could *testify* that we made a handsome couple?"

I nodded wearily.

Irene stared toward Casanova happily gnawing a corncob in his cage. "And he also said that he was certain that Godfrey and I would *remain* healthy, wealthy and wise?"

"Yes! Do you wish me to consult my diaries for the exact phrasing?"

"No, Nell, no . . . it is just that Mr. Holmes's final remarks are most intriguing—almost as if he knew more than he really ought to by rights . . . but that is the past, and the future lies before us like one great, plump teacake. We must not dwell on old puzzles."

It was I who injected a graver note. "But Irene, you will not be able to perform publicly if you tolerate this notion that you are dead."

Her face sobered. "No, but it seems the wisest course. We can always resurrect ourselves, can we not, Godfrey? I have always wanted to come back from the dead; it is so dramatic."

"Then indeed you shall," Godfrey promised, leaning close to pat her hand. "Whenever you wish."

"What a sense of power; it almost surpasses performing! Don't worry, Nell, I sing for myself—and my friends. And perhaps some . . . curiosities will come my way. Paris, is fully as rife with sin and crime as London, I assure you."

"But the weather is better," Godfrey put in, "and would be even more so if you would join us in enjoying it, Nell."

"That brings us to your present." Irene rose and left the room. I admit that I did cherish the hope of another loose stone from the now-separated Zone . . . something discreetly large that would look well in a modest brooch. . . .

Irene returned with her hands full. Dangling from them was a zone of fur—the limp form of the largest, fattest, furriest black Persian cat I had ever seen.

"Meet Lucifer," Irene said. "He is 'Parisian,' if you will. We felt, Godfrey and I, that you needed something to remind Casanova of his p's and q's."

"Not more of the alphabet, Irene, you haven't really! You haven't increased his vocabulary while Casanova and I have been visiting you?"

"But of course she has," Godfrey said, watching as Irene laid the feline beast across my lap. "Up to P-Q-R."

"He reminds me of your old muff," I observed, mollified.

"Hmm. There are probably as many teacakes in him as there ever were in the secret pockets in my muff."

"He has a sweet tooth?"

"Indeed; he should find Casanova particularly toothsome."

"I am not sure that my current landlady would accept a cat," I began.

"Then replace the landlady, my dear Nell," Godfrey put in as he lit one of Irene's revolting little cigarettes for her. "We come highly recommended."

"You are not serious!"

"Indeed we are," Irene said. "We have grown used to your assistance."

"And your good sense," said Godfrey.

"We really cannot do without you, dear Nell."

"But," I mumbled, "your . . . wedded bliss surely would not welcome a witness."

Irene laughed until Godfrey joined her . . . and I and Casanova . . . and, I swear, the cat.

"We have had several months of ease and idleness," she said. "Now, it is time to *work*."

"Yes," said I, setting Lucifer aside. He revealed a rosebud tongue and began lashing his silver ruff into a halo of angelic beauty. "What is the first order of business?"

"A toast to our success," Irene said, lifting her wine glass.

"At what?" I wondered.

"At whatever we elect to do," Godfrey said.

I should have known better than to expect logic from them.

I hoisted my Vichy water as Casanova began cawing, "Cut the cackle" by the window. Lucifer turned his head and tumbled soundlessly to the floor. Then a low black shadow was sidling along the carpet toward Casanova.

Irene paused for attention, looking as pleased as Lucifer.

"And," she said, theatrically lifting her voice as well as her wineglass, "I do believe we owe the past one last bow. A toast, my dears: Good night, Mr. Sherlock Holmes—wherever you are."

Coda

~っ⦿⦿~

The foregoing collation integrates the diaries of Penelope Huxleigh, recently (and ironically) found in an abandoned safe-deposit box at a Shropshire bank, with fragments of previously unknown writings attributed to John H. Watson, M.D.

Alert readers will notice discrepancies between this work and the story "A Scandal in Bohemia," first published in the July 1891 issue of the *Strand Magazine* of London. That purported "fiction" was written by the same Dr. Watson who chronicled other exploits of Sherlock Holmes, the consulting detective.

These Holmes tales—a century after their creation—stand as sacred cows to many, who regard them as not only literal truth but unbiased reportage. To such enthusiasts, any objective re-evaluation of such sanctified bovine conventions raises a red flag: it is viewed as an attack on the "Canon."

True Holmes fanatics occupy two equally ridiculous camps: one holds that the tales as written by a historical Dr. Watson comprise authentic Victoriana and therefore cannot be challenged as to full candor or veracity; the other, even more extreme camp avers that a

Scottish medical man of Irish antecedents, Sir Arthur Conan Doyle, authored these pieces as pure fiction. This is patently ludicrous.

More sensible students conducting postmortems on the Sherlock Holmes literary corpus agree that Doyle merely acted as literary agent for the actual, retiring—if not completely anonymous—Dr. Watson.

Now new evidence offers an opportunity to put the Holmes As Literary Invention theory on its ear, where it rightfully belongs. The Huxleigh diaries prove that Irene Adler, at least, was no fiction and thus lend credence to the actual existence of Holmes, Watson et al. The foregoing collation also supports a new and startling revelation: that, whatever its origin, *some* authentic Holmes material was *suppressed*.

These new-found fragments, integrated with the Huxleigh accounts, make superior chronological and narrative sense of many discrepancies in the so-called Canon, the very inconsistencies that fuel the arguments of those who would debunk Holmes, his cases and his contemporaries as mere fictional creations.

Literary suppression—particularly of memoirs—was all too common in nineteenth-century England. Consider Richard Burton (the *other* one, an explorer and translator of "The Arabian Nights"), whose unpublished writings were burned on his death by his prudish (Victorians would have said *prudent*) widow.

Similarly, witness the long loss to history of the Huxleigh account with its frank and surprising depiction of a liberated American woman in Victorian England. It differs significantly from the then-dominant male view, evident even in the Holmes stories, in which women swooned with "brain fever" at the first sign of crisis.

As Watson observes in a rediscovered Holmes text, "Irene Adler did not swoon." Exactly! And exactly why her un-expurgated adventures were suppressed—certainly through the modesty of her chronicler and later by other "judges" of their suitability for publication.

We will never know the diaries' full history; the principals are long since dead, though Holmes fanatics persist in granting their hero immortality, as if actuality were not enough. No such claque avers the same for Irene Adler, another symptom of surviving male chauvinism in the worlds of history and letters, if not fiction.

Understandably, Irene Adler's strong sense of personal liberty would have been scandalous in her day—the men's "walking clothes" and cigarettes, her theatrical profession and excursions into problem solving if not crime solving—but the Huxleigh diaries contradict Watson's assertion in "A Scandal in Bohemia" that Adler was sexually promiscuous (an "adventuress . . . of dubious and questionable memory").

The Huxleigh accounts testify that Irene Adler was *not* one of the socially ambitious, sexually pragmatic women then labeled adventuresses. Though Penelope Huxleigh remains reticent on the issue of Adler's past, the opera singer—during her years with the parson's daughter, through her liaison with the King of Bohemia and up to her marriage to Godfrey Norton—avoided compromise in fact if not in appearance.

Cynics might argue that Irene Adler was unchaperoned in Bohemia, but Adler herself tells Penelope that the King has been "patient." Indeed, his fury at her defection smacks more of a forever-frustrated suitor than of a man losing a mistress.

Another discrepancy exists: the Huxleigh account shows Holmes visiting Godfrey Norton's chambers twice, yet the detective appears to know nothing of Norton (and the Zone of Diamonds) in "A Scandal in Bohemia."

Two possibilities occur: Holmes kept his fruitless pursuit of the Zone from Watson, not wishing to appear fallible in his chronicler's eyes, or . . . *Watson himself* suppressed the Master's significant failure in that regard, especially since Holmes failed to acquire the photograph that was his immediate object in the story as it stands. Losing *two* elusive objects would have been more than even Holmes's reputation could have survived.

The new material only clouds the matter of Watson's marriage—to whom, how many times and when. Here he clearly was wed by March of 1888. Citations in the Doyle/Watson material confirm this, although they also have Watson not meeting Mary Morstan until *July* of that year. This leads some foolish apologists to assign Watson *two* wives during his association with Holmes. The truth remains elusive, as does much involving this controversial figure and his biographer.

Another minor inconsistency persists, even in the face of the Huxleigh revelations.

In "A Scandal in Bohemia" the King claims that he met Irene Adler in Warsaw five years earlier. The Huxleigh papers show Adler meeting the King in 1886 and fleeing Bohemia in 1887, only a year prior to March 1888, when Watson dates "A Scandal in Bohemia" as occurring.

Two possibilities explain the time discrepancy. Could not the Doyle / Watson stories, though true, have been partially "fictionalized" to protect famous persons of the day? Thus dates may have been manipulated. Before the discovery of the Huxleigh diaries, some so-called Holmes scholars insisted that "Irene Adler" was a fictionalized version of the day's notorious mistress/actress, Lillie Langtry, known as the "Jersey Lily" for her birth on the Channel island of Jersey. (Hence, these deluded analysts would have it, Adler's American birth in "New Jersey.")

These self-appointed "experts" even question the King of Bohemia's identity, suggesting that the elderly Franz Josef, then ruler of the vast Austro-Hungarian Empire of which Bohemia was a province, was officially "King of Bohemia." They fail to mention that he never used the title.

No. The King of Bohemia was Wilhelm Gottsreich Sigismond von Ormstein, Grand Duke of Cassel-Felstein. The notion that he was anyone other—a notion aided and abetted by the chaotic dissolution of these Slavic-Germanic ruling families in the upheavals of the late nineteenth and early twentieth century that eventually occasioned World War I—only demonstrates how overeager Holmes addicts can stretch skimpy evidence into full-blown assertion.

Yet the chronological question remains: When did Irene Adler meet the King? Facts favor the Huxleigh timetable's biographical consistency and meticulous revelation of character.

For Irene Adler to have loved and lost the King of Bohemia some *five* years before his forthcoming marriage, to have kept the incriminating photograph for so long and then threatened to produce it to ruin his nuptials (and an innocent woman's happiness) doesn't fit the admirable woman depicted in both "Scandal" and the Huxleigh diaries. (In the diaries she *never* threatens to release the photograph; the King's own guilt causes his insecurity.)

Why should Irene Adler have waited until the royal marriage loomed when she could have damaged the King's marriageability earlier—when their association and her indignation was fresher? And why fear his acting against her unless their liaison had ended recently enough for the King to attempt to regain her—or the photograph?

"It won't wash, Watson!" Holmes would have said, and so says logic.

The most reasonable conclusion is that the King of Bohemia misrepresented to Holmes the date of his first meeting Adler, in order to excuse his behavior as a youthful indiscretion and to represent his "cruelly wronged" opponent as vengeful and thus win Holmes's sympathy. (Otherwise his Majesty would have looked like a disgruntled suitor and a bully toward women, as he certainly appears to unflattering effect in the Huxleigh account.)

Given Adler's parallel activities to the Great Detective and her own documented puzzle-solving proclivities, a greater question teases all Holmes adherents, whether they subscribe to the silly "fiction" notion or accept the historicity of these individuals. Did Irene Adler and Sherlock Holmes ever meet again?

This question stands apart from the obvious fantasies indulged in by such noted Holmes experts of times past as William S. Baring-Gould, who fabricated not only a future meeting between Adler and Holmes, but a love affair resulting in a son! To accomplish this miracle of self-delusion, Baring-Gould had to defame Godfrey Norton as a worthless wife-beater, a characterization that the Huxleigh diaries hardly support nor does it do Irene Adler justice.

Yet it is not impossible that these two inventive individuals' paths should have crossed again. Further volumes of the parson's daughter's diaries remain to be collated with the Holmes Canon and its lost fragments—and presented, if research confirms their veracity, to a waiting world.

Fiona Witherspoon, Ph.D., F. I. A.*
November 5, 1989

*Friends of Irene Adler.

Good Night,
Mr. Holmes

Reader's Guide

"Perhaps it has taken until the end of this century for an author like Douglas to be able to imagine a female protagonist who could be called 'the' woman by Sherlock Holmes."

—GROUNDS FOR MURDER, 1991

To encourage the reading and discussion of Carole Nelson Douglas's acclaimed novels examining the Victorian world from the viewpoint of one of the most mysterious women in literature, the following descriptions and discussion topics are offered. The author interview, biography, and bibliography will aid discussion as well.

Set in 1880–1890 London, Paris, Prague, Monaco, and New York City, the Irene Adler novels reinvent the only woman to have outwitted Sherlock Holmes as the complex and compelling protagonist of her own stories. Douglas's portrayal of "this remarkable heroine and her keen perspective on the male society in which she must make her independent way," noted the *New York Times,* recasts her "not as a loose-living adventuress but a woman ahead of her time." In Douglas's hands, the fascinating but sketchy American prima donna from "A Scandal in Bohemia" becomes an aspiring opera singer moonlighting as a private inquiry agent. When events force her from the stage into the art of detection, Adler's exploits rival those of Sherlock Holmes himself as she crosses paths and swords with the day's leading creative and political figures while sleuthing among the Bad and the Beautiful of Belle Epoque Europe.

Critics praise the novels' rich period detail, numerous historical characters, original perspective, wit, and "welcome window on things Victorian."

"The private and public escapades of Irene Adler Norton [are] as erratic and unexpected and brilliant as the character herself," noted *Mystery Scene* of *Another Scandal in Bohemia* (formerly *Irene's Last Waltz*), "a long and complex jeu d'esprit, simultaneously modeling itself on and critiquing Doylesque novels of ratiocination coupled with emotional distancing. Here is Sherlock Holmes in skirts, but as a detective with an artistic temperament and the passion to match, with the intellect to penetrate to the heart of a crime and the heart to show compassion for the intellect behind it."

⊰ ABOUT THIS BOOK ⊱

Good Night, Mr. Holmes, the first Irene Adler novel, opens in London with Sherlock Holmes and Watson discussing the events of "A Scandal in Bohemia" and especially the woman at the center of that first Sherlock Holmes short story, the American diva Irene Adler.

Often rated the favorite Sherlock Holmes story, "A Scandal in Bohemia" is recommended reading, or rereading for a discussion of *Good Night, Mr. Holmes,* which retells the Doyle story from Irene's point of view, not Watson's. The novel also embellishes on the events in the story and presents the characters in a different light, especially Irene Adler, who has been revived and reinvented as a fully fleshed-out leading lady in her own right.

⊰ FOR DISCUSSION ⊱
Related to Good Night, Mr. Holmes

1. Did you know the Conan Doyle story that this novel expands upon before reading this book? Or after? How are the two pieces similar, and where do they differ?

    If you've only read the novel, are you interested now in reading the Conan Doyle story? Why do you think the author plucked the particular character of Irene Adler from this particular series of stories for revival a hundred years after the story involving her was published? If you know the Holmes stories well, are there any other women characters who'd lend themselves to their own novels? Whom would you pick?

2. Sir Arthur Conan Doyle "killed" Irene Adler in the same story that introduced her. Yet many readers are intrigued by this

woman who was the only one to fascinate the monkish Holmes, as well as outwit him. Why would he have done that?

Conan Doyle gave Irene both beauty and brains, but he didn't make Holmes both handsome and brilliant. Does this make such a "perfect" woman character less believable? Less likeable? Does she show any failings in this novel?

3. *The Drood Review of Mystery* observed of *Chapel Noir:* "This dark tour de force proves by its verbal play and literary allusiveness that Douglas wants neither Irene nor herself underestimated in fiction. More important, she wants women fully informed about and capable of action on the mean streets of their world."

Why do you think the author chose to give Irene her own "Watson" to narrate the novel? How does Nell Huxleigh echo or contrast Dr. Watson? Does using a traditionally restricted Victorian woman as the narrator make you more aware of any Victorian remnants in the upbringing and lives of contemporary women?

Religion and morality are underlying issues in the novels. This element is absent from the Holmes stories. How is this issue brought out and how do Nell's strictly conventional views affect those around her? Why does she take on a moral watchdog role yet remain both disapproving and fascinated by Irene's pragmatic philosophy? Why are Irene and most readers so fond of her despite her limited and self-limiting opinions? Is there a bit of her in all modern women still? Are women still expected to monitor matters of morality in contemporary families and lives? Are younger women breaking out of the sexual double standard, and is there a price?

4. What do you think of the major men characters in this novel: Sherlock Holmes, the King of Bohemia, and Godfrey Norton? What attitudes to women do they each embody? Why did Conan Doyle make Holmes so "allergic" to women? Is he saying that intellectualism is purely masculine? He made Watson something of a ladies' man, who has consorted with the women of "three continents" and has two or possibly three wives over the breadth of the stories. Why are modern readers, and some writers, always trying

to give Holmes a romantic interest? Do they see him as incomplete? Or do they want to see this somewhat misogynistic man succumb to female power? What does he have in common with Mr. Spock from the *Star Trek* universe? Can you think of other "Holmes-like" characters in modern storytelling on the page and on-screen? What is their mythic appeal?

For Discussion of the Irene Adler Series

1. Douglas mentions other authors, many of them women, who have reinvented major female characters or minor characters from classic literary or genre novels to reevaluate culture then and now. Can you think of such works in the field of fantasy or historical novels? General literature? What about the copyright contest over *The Wind Done Gone,* Alice Randall's reimagining of *Gone with the Wind* events and characters from the African-American slaves' viewpoints? Could the novel's important social points have been made as effectively without referencing the classic work generally familiar to most people? What other works have attained the mythic status that might make possible such socially conscious reinventions? What works would you revisit or rewrite?

2. Douglas has said she likes to work on the "large canvas" of series fiction. What kind of character development does that approach permit? Do you like it? Has television recommitted viewers/readers to the kind of multivolume storytelling common in the nineteenth century, or is the attention span of the twenty-first century too short? Is long-term, committed reading becoming a lost art?

3. Douglas chose to blend humor with adventurous plots. Do comic characters and situations satirize the times, or soften them? Is humor a more effective form of social criticism than rhetoric? What other writers and novelists use this technique, besides George Bernard Shaw and Mark Twain?

4. The novels also present a continuing tension between New World and Old World, America and England and the Continent, artist-

tradesman and aristocrat, as well as woman and man. Which characters reflect which camps? How does the tension show itself?

5. *Chapel Noir* makes several references to *Dracula* through the presence of Bram Stoker some six years before the novel actually was published. Stoker is also a continuing character in other Adler novels. Various literary figures appear in the Adler novels, including Oscar Wilde, and most of these historical characters knew one another. Why was this period so rich in writers who founded much modern genre fiction, like Doyle and Stoker? The late nineteenth century produced not only *Dracula* and Doyle's Holmes stories and the surviving dinosaurs of *The Lost World,* but Trilby and Svengali, *The Phantom of the Opera, The Prisoner of Zenda,* Dr. Jekyll and Mr. Hyde, among the earliest and most lasting works of science fiction, political intrigue, mystery, and horror. How does Douglas pay homage to this tradition in the plots, characters, and details of the Adler novels?

) An Interview with
Carole Nelson Douglas (

Q: You were the first woman to write about the Sherlock Holmes world from the viewpoint of one of Arthur Conan Doyle's woman characters, and only the second woman to write a Holmes related novel at all. Why?

A: Most of my fiction ideas stem from my role as cultural observer in my first career, journalism. One day I looked at the mystery field and realized that all post-Doyle Sherlockian novels were written by men. I had loved the stories as a child and thought it was high time for a woman to examine the subject from a female point of view.

Q: So there was "the woman," Irene Adler, the only woman to outwit Holmes, waiting for you.

A: She seems the most obvious candidate, but I bypassed her for that very reason to look at other women in what is called the

Holmes Canon. Eventually I came back to "A Scandal in Bohemia." Rereading it, I realized that male writers had all taken Irene Adler at face value as the King of Bohemia's jilted mistress, but the story doesn't support that. As the only woman in the Canon who stirred a hint of romantic interest in the aloof Holmes, Irene Adler had to be more than this beautiful but amoral "Victorian vamp." Once I saw that I could validly interpret her as a gifted and serious performing artist, I had my protagonist.

Q: It was that simple?

A: It was that complex. I felt that any deeper psychological exploration of this character still had to adhere to Doyle's story, both literally and in regard to the author's own feeling toward the character. That's how I ended up having to explain that operatic impossibility, a contralto prima donna. It's been great fun justifying Doyle's error by finding operatic roles Irene could conceivably sing. My Irene Adler is as intelligent, self-sufficient, and serious about her professional and personal integrity as Sherlock Holmes, and far too independent to be anyone's mistress but her own. She also moonlights as an inquiry agent while building her performing career. In many ways they are flip sides of the same coin: her profession, music, is his hobby. His profession, detection, is her secondary career. Her adventures intertwine with Holmes's, but she is definitely her own woman in these novels.

Q: How did Doyle feel toward the character of Irene Adler?

A: I believe that Holmes and Watson expressed two sides of Dr. Doyle: Watson, the medical and scientific man, also the staunch upholder of British convention; Holmes, the creative and bohemian writer, fascinated by the criminal and the bizarre. Doyle wrote classic stories of horror and science fiction as well as hefty historical novels set in the age of chivalry. His mixed feelings of attraction to and fear of a liberated, artistic woman like Irene Adler led him to "kill" her as soon as he created her. Watson states she is dead at the beginning of the story that introduces her. Irene was literally too hot for Doyle as well as Holmes to handle. She also debuted (and exited) in the first Holmes-Watson story Doyle ever wrote. Perhaps Doyle wanted to establish an unattainable woman to excuse Holmes remaining a bachelor and aloof from matters of the heart. What he did was to create a fascinatingly unrealized character for generations of readers.

Q: Do your protagonists represent a split personality as well?

A: Yes, one even more sociologically interesting than the Holmes-Watson split because it embodies the evolving roles of women in the late nineteenth century. As a larger-than-life heroine, Irene is "up to anything." Her biographer, Penelope "Nell" Huxleigh, however, is the very model of traditional Victorian womanhood. Together they provide a seriocomic point-counterpoint on women's restricted roles then and now. Narrator Nell is the character who "grows" most during the series as the unconventional Irene forces her to see herself and her times in a broader perspective. This is something women writers have been doing in the past two decades: revisiting classic literary terrains and bringing the sketchy women characters into full-bodied prominence.

Q: What of "the husband," Godfrey Norton?

A: In my novels, Irene's husband, Godfrey Norton, is more than the "tall, dark, and dashing barrister" Doyle gave her. I made him the son of a woman wronged by England's then female-punitive divorce law, so he is a "supporting" character in every sense of the word. These novels are that rare bird in literature: female "buddy" books. Godfrey fulfills the useful, decorative, and faithful role so often played by women and wives in fiction and real life. Sherlockians anxious to unite Adler and Holmes have tried to oust Godfrey. William S. Baring-Gould even depicted him as a wife beater in order to promote a later assignation with Holmes that produced Nero Wolfe! That is such an unbelievable violation of a strong female character's psychology. That scenario would make Irene Adler a two-time loser in her choice of men and a masochist to boot. My protagonist is a world away from that notion and a wonderful vehicle for subtle but sharp feminist comment.

Q: Did you give her any attributes not found in the Doyle story?

A: I gave her one of Holmes's bad habits. She smokes "little cigars." Smoking was an act of rebellion for women then. And because Doyle shows her sometimes donning male dress to go unhampered into public places, I gave her "a wicked little revolver" to carry.

Q: Essentially, you have changed Irene Adler from an ornamental woman to a working woman.

A: My Irene is more a rival than a romantic interest for Holmes, yes. She is not a logical detective in the same mold as he, but is as gifted in her intuitive way. Nor is her opera singing a convenient profession for a beauty of the day, but a passionate vocation that was taken from her by the King of Bohemia's autocratic attitude toward women, forcing her to occupy herself with detection. Although Doyle's Irene is beautiful, well dressed, and clever, my Irene demands that she be taken seriously despite these feminine attributes. Now we call it "Grrrrl power."

I like to write "against" conventions that are no longer true, or were never true. This is the thread that runs through all my fiction: my dissatisfaction with the portrayal of women in literary and popular fiction—then and even now. This begins with Amberleigh—my postfeminist mainstream version of the Gothic-revival popular novels of the 1960s and 1970s—and continues with Irene Adler today. I'm interested in women as survivors. Men also interest me of necessity, men strong enough to escape cultural blinders to become equal partners to strong women.

Q: How do you research these books?

A: From a theatrical background that educated me on the clothing, culture, customs, and speech of various historical periods. I was reading Oscar Wilde plays when I was eight years old. My mother's book club meant that I cut my teeth on Eliot, Balzac, Kipling, Poe, poetry, Greek mythology, Hawthorne, the Brontës, Dumas, and Dickens.

In doing research, I have a fortunate facility of using every nugget I find, or of finding that every little fascinating nugget works itself into the story. Perhaps that's because journalists must be ingenious in using every fact available to make a story as complete and accurate as possible under deadline conditions. Often the smallest mustard seed of research swells into an entire tree of plot. The corpse on the dining-room table of Bram Stoker, author of *Dracula,* was too macabre to resist and spurred the entire plot of the second Adler novel, *The Adventuress* (formerly *Good Morning, Irene*). Stoker rescued a drowning man from the Thames and carried him home for revival efforts, but it was too late.

Besides using my own extensive library on this period, I've borrowed from my local library all sorts of arcane books they don't even know they have because no one ever checks them out. The Internet aids greatly with the specific fact.

Q: You've written fantasy and science fiction novels, why did you turn to mystery?

A: All novels are fantasy and all novels are mystery in the largest sense. Although mystery was often an element in my early novels, when I evolved the Irene Adler idea, I considered it simply a novel. *Good Night, Mr. Holmes* was almost on the shelves before I realized it would be "categorized" as a mystery. So Irene is utterly a product of my mind and times, not of the marketplace, though I always believed that the concept was timely and necessary.

Selected Bibliography

Belford, Barbara. *Bram Stoker.* New York, NY: Alfred A. Knopf, 1996.

Bunson, Matthew E. *Encyclopedia Sherlockiana.* New York, NY: Macmillan, 1994.

Coleman, Elizabeth Ann. *The Opulent Era.* New York, NY: The Brooklyn Museum, 1989.

Crow, Duncan. *The Victorian Woman.* London UK: Cox & Wyman, Ltd, 1971.

Doyle, Arthur Conan. The Complete Works of Sherlock Holmes. Various editions.

Mackay, James. *Allan Pinkerton: The Eye Who Never Slept.* Edinburgh, Scotland: Mainstream Publishing Co., Ltd., 1996.